THE VOICE OF ELYON

A.L. BOWKER

Scripture verses are taken from English Standard Version 2016 and New International Version 1984

This novel's story, characters, places, and events are based off the author's imagination. The lessons learned in it, however, are entirely real.

ISBN: 979-8-9871816-1-4

Copyright © 2022 A. L. Bowker

Edited by Mrs. Paula Callahan

Cover Art by germancreative

Map Concept by Calvin Callahan

Final Map by Aaron Rakuu

To Dad
You will always be my Knight in Shining Armor
And to Doug
You encourage me more than you will ever know

Name Pronunciation

Marta ——- Mar-dah

Camilla —— Kah-mill-ah

Geralt —— Gerr-ahlt

Amaryll —— Am-a-rill

Arailt —— Air-alt

Seamus —— Shame-us

Ewan —— Yew-anne

Jeannie —— Jeen-ee

Place Pronunciation

Ropheka—— Ro-fee-kah

Ildaile —— Ill-d-aisle

Elroith —— Elle-roy-th

Hylen —— Hi-lenn

Kakorio —— Kahk-oh-reeoh

Rodenheim —— Raw-den-hi-uhm

Rhonwyn—— Ron-when

Laochailan —— Law-oh-k-aye-lan

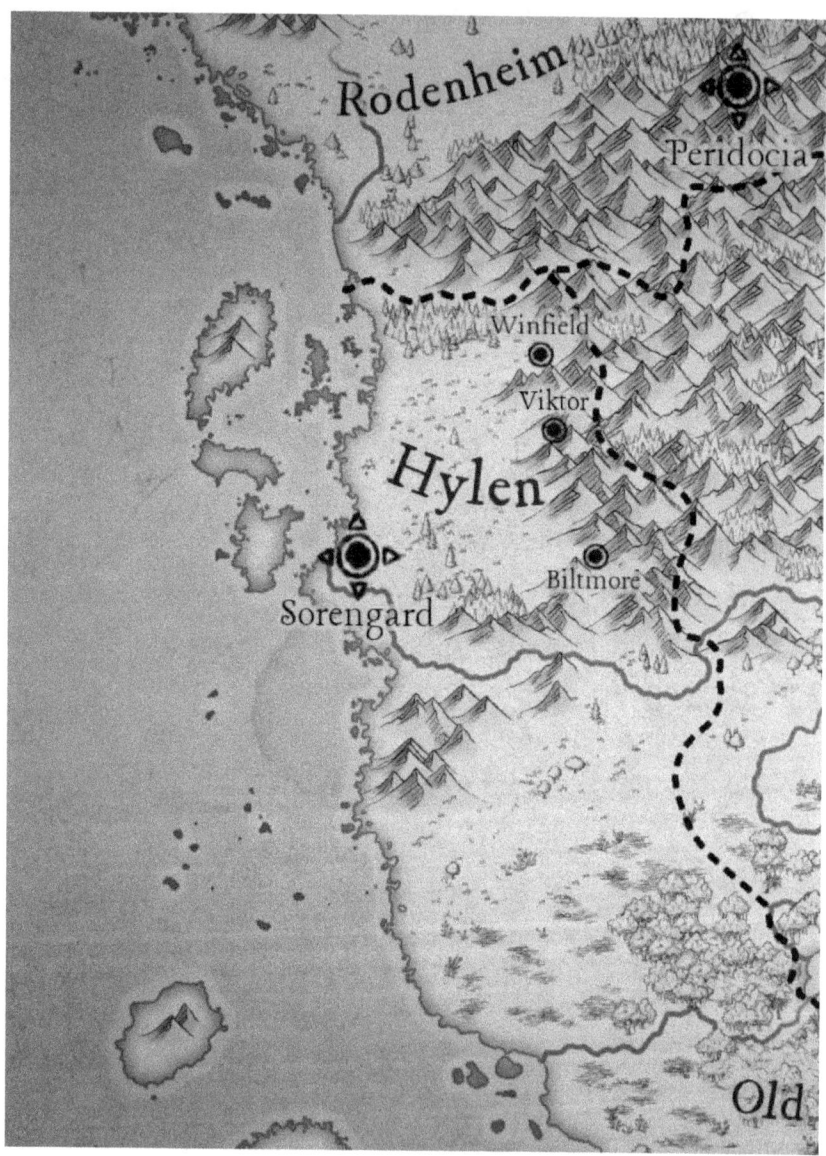

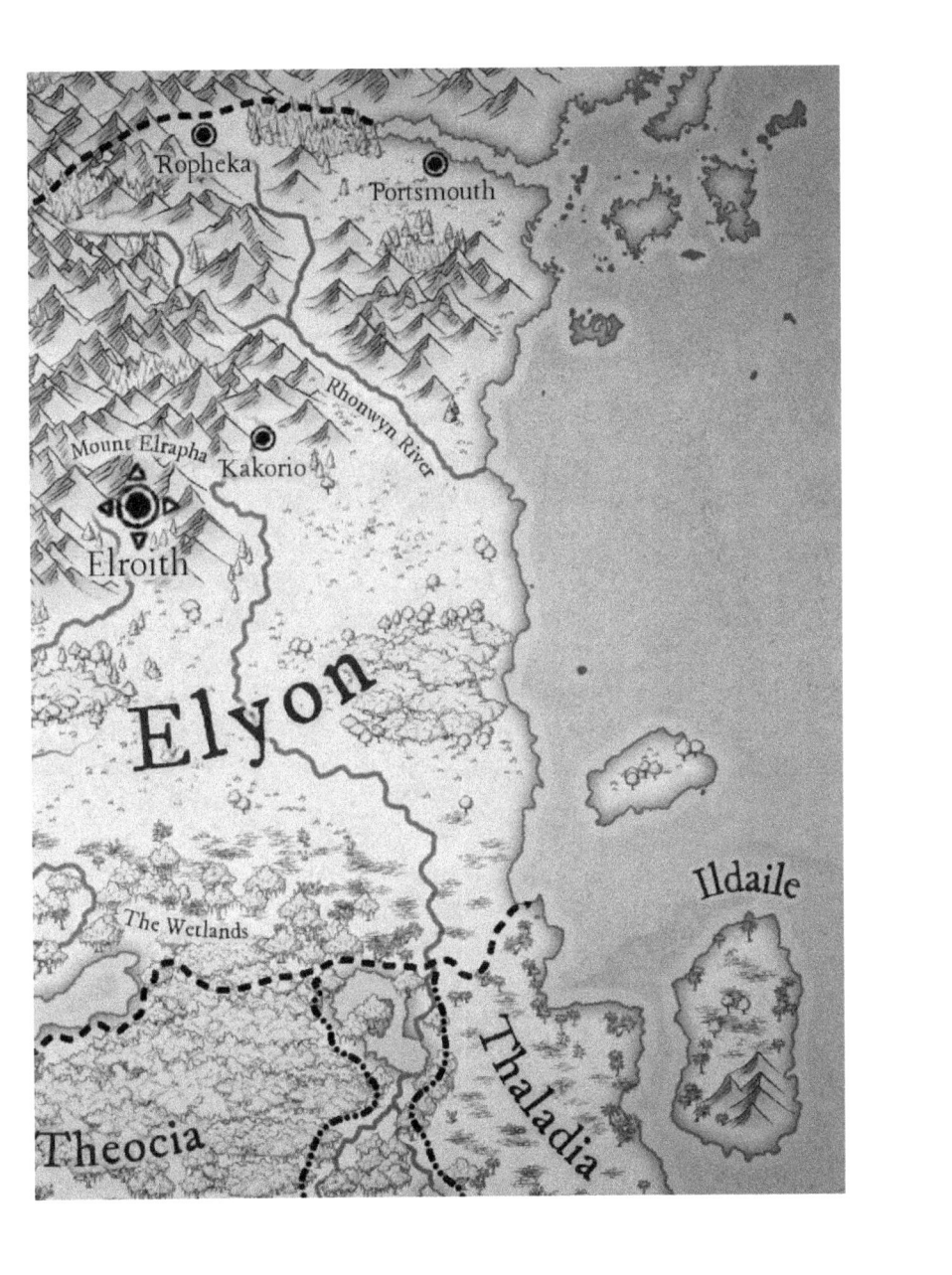

Contents

Prologue

Scents of blood and metal stung the air around them, the groans of the dying echoing through the valley. The dirt was soaked with the blood of hundreds of innocents and warriors alike.

King Thomas examined the battlefield from where he knelt, sword deep in the ground. It had been an excruciating battle, and the few lives they had been able to save were now being escorted across the river into safety.

Safety. He laughed curtly, the taste of the thought almost nauseating. *Will there truly be safety for them?*

The sound of boots crunching on the gravel drew his attention to his brother, Peter, striding towards him. He stopped to salute.

"Your Majesty."

"You may approach," Thomas sighed as he stood.

Peter took several steps forward. The young brothers were strikingly similar, Thomas' brown hair the only difference between them. Peter's blond locks fell from behind his head as the twenty-four-year old bowed.

"My Lord, the enemy has escaped."

"How many of them were there?"

"About fifty or so. Half of them were wounded."

Thomas examined the field around them once more. His soldiers were dead or dying, and they had a limited amount of those Gifted with Healing there with them. It would take a long time before any more Gifted Ones showed up to help.

"Let them go," Thomas nearly groaned. Peter blinked in surprise.

"My Lord?"

Thomas yanked his sword out of the dirt and handed it to a soldier to clean for him.

"You heard me. Let them go. We don't have the strength left to fight them. We need to recover before we go chasing them down."

The soldier handed Thomas his sword and excused himself as a messenger came running up the hill.

"Your Majesty! Your Majesty!" The young man huffed as he tried to kneel, but Thomas waved him to stand. Peter made a sound of disapproval and looked away.

"Your Majesty, I have a very important letter for you from the captain of the Tenth Regiment!"

Thomas reached over and took the letter from him. He broke the seal and pulled out a yellowed parchment. Peter glanced over and noticed his brother's face pale.

"Thomas?" he asked nervously. Already the army was starting to crumble, their trust in the twenty-seven-year-old king waning. When their father died just a few months prior, both men had been forced into the forefront of a bloody, brutal war. As if things couldn't get bad enough—

"They're planning another attack," Thomas sighed, folding up the letter and setting it alight in his palm. The men watched the paper disintegrate into ashes in the air, the weight of its contents never releasing despite its absence. "They're moving to Ropheka and are planning on destroying the Tower there. They're hellbent on getting to it before we do." Thomas turned as Peter nodded and left to give instructions to his soldiers. Thomas looked out at the small camp of the wounded and weary and felt the desperate weight of duty on his shoulders.

I know that You have put me in this position, God, but why didn't You prepare me for it? I am too ill-equipped. Anyone else would have been a much better king than I. He turned and noticed a bloodied doll on the ground. *I've failed miserably. And now Ropheka might be lost as well.*

God help us.

CHAPTER ONE

Murmurs In Ropheka

Marta's hand glowed a faint golden color as it hovered above the young boys' arm. Markus winced and watched, eyes wide, as the broken bone seemingly pieced itself back together.

"Whoah!" he exclaimed as he held up his arm and wiggled it. Marta chuckled and reached over to the drawer sitting next to the infirmary bed.

"Here, Markus," she handed him a small piece of candy. He took it happily and popped it into his mouth as his mother shook her head and laughed.

"The abilities of a Life Gift never cease to amaze me. Thank the Lord He's put you here in our town."

Marta grinned as she sat up and smoothed out her blue dress. "You know it's my pleasure, Deena."

"Momma?" Markus gurgled with the candy in his mouth. "Wha—what is a—"

"Finish chewing, son," Deena warned with a smile. Markus crunched into his candy and swallowed.

"What is a Life Gift?"

Deena sighed wearily before Marta spoke up. "You see, Markus, God has given everyone a Gift. These Gifts are to help others. When we say '"Life" Gifted One', it means that person is gifted with special abilities to heal others, as well as grow plants." She held out her hand and a sunflower grew from her palm.

"My friend said you can talk to different animals!" Markus beamed and clapped his hands. "Can you show me?"

Marta chuckled as Deena rolled her eyes. "Maybe later, Markus. She's used a lot of energy on healing you."

"Energy...?" he asked curiously. Marta laughed and patted his shoulder.

"Perhaps if you discover you have these types of gifts or have the ability to become a Chosen Knight, you'll find out more how this works one day. You don't have to be a Gifted One or a Knight to have special abilities, though, God gives all His believers different kinds of gifts. For now, don't go jumping off hay bales!" She held up a finger and gave him a look of warning, her green eyes twinkling. Markus nodded and held up his arms.

"Yes ma'am! I want to be a big strong Knight one day!"

Deena laughed. "Of course you do. Now, let's get going." She stood and helped her son to the ground before turning to Marta as she stood. She nodded and quietly asked, "How much do I owe you?"

Marta smiled and shook her head. "Nothing, my friend. You know the Tower pays us."

Deena nodded solemnly, then sighed. "I truly am thankful to have a Tower here. It makes me feel better knowing we aren't completely by ourselves this far north."

Marta waved as they left before cleaning up. Other Gifteds in the room were talking quietly, busying themselves with their own patients. She reached down and grabbed her little box of salves. When not on duty in the Tower's infirmary, she would sell medicines and tinctures to her fellow townspeople. While it was fairly easy to heal almost anyone they came across, she was the only Life Gifted in Ropheka, and expending energy on small wounds and ailments was exhausting.

Her shift over, Marta stood and gathered her small bag and headed to the dining hall. The Tower was an academy for Gifted Ones and Chosen Knights alike and were spread all across the continent. They also served as churches, community centers, hospitals, and more.

The usual cacophony of students making their way between classes was unusually hushed as most seasoned Gifteds were on the battlefield. Some professors and several young students who lived in Ropheka still milled about, greeting Marta as she passed. She could smell the history of the building as she walked down stone corridors, the light shining through ancient amber stained windows. Memories of the classes she had taken in the different rooms would surface occasionally, some bringing laughter and some bringing a grimace. She nodded to one of the professors she knew and rounded the corner to the eating area.

The dining hall was an elaborate room with large windows on either side revealing the expansive glacier lake outside, the sunlight glinting off its still surface. The academy had once been a castle, its many rooms converted to classrooms or dormitories. Tables were sprawled out across the room, most seats empty except for the few Gifteds and Knights eating dinner. She turned toward a table as her friends Brianna and Isaac glanced up and waved her over.

"Look at you, all dressed up in your Tower uniform!" Brianna smiled as Marta sat across from them. Marta adjusted her white cloak as she sat, wiping off her blue skirt.

"You know we have to look professional when we're on infirmary duty," she smiled lightly. Brianna chuckled.

"It's better than the dress whites they make you wear, Marta," Brianna mused as Isaac nodded. As a Knight, Isaac wore the Tower armor they gave him, with a dark green tunic and brown pants. With an Earth Gift, Brianna wore the same blue dress Martha wore, except she had a green cloak pinned to her shoulders.

"Blood actually comes out of white rather easily, if you know how to clean it," Isaac pointed out as he stuck his nose in the air and took a whiff. Marta could smell it, too, a meal made fresh that day. The warm scent of garlic, onion, carrots, and delicious beef in a dark broth made her stomach grumble. She turned and spotted the waiter with a brass cart wheeling towards them. He greeted them with a smile, adjusting his black waistcoat as he set out three bowls. Steam wafted from the beautiful copper tureen he dipped his ladle into as he served them each a hearty portion. The group thanked him and he smiled before continuing on his way.

"How long will you two be here on rotation?" Marta asked after a moment. Brianna and Isaac exchanged glances before sighing.

"It seems not much longer. We're being transferred to Portsmouth within a few weeks." Isaac rubbed his temple. "It seems the unrest there has grown stronger, and the Tower needs more people who can fight."

Marta nodded slowly. "I can understand that. I'll be praying for both of you," she smiled softly. The thought of her two dear friends leaving made her heart hurt, but she knew God had a plan for them. *If only He would tell me mine…* With a Life Gift, she was classified as one of the more powerful workers of the kingdom, yet she had little to no defensive abilities. Since she had not yet found —or been given —a Knight to protect her, she was kept on the home front to help with the wounded army brought back to safety.

"I'm going to miss you," Brianna reached over and held Marta's hand gingerly. "The three of us haven't really been separated like this before, have we?"

Marta shook her head slowly. Even after they got married, Brianna and Isaac made sure to maintain contact with her and to invite her to meals.

"We'll be back," Isaac smiled reassuringly. Somehow, that didn't put Marta's mind at ease. She noticed Caleb and Camilla, two of the Tower's Shepherds, walk through the door.

"Well, we'd better get going. I have a training I need to get to." Isaac sighed as he stood. They exchanged their goodbyes and Marta watched her friends disappear through the door.

I really hope they will be okay....Lord, please protect them. She sighed inwardly as she stood. Caleb and Camilla noticed her and walked over with smiles.

The two both wore Tower uniforms but around their shoulders was a thick tartan fabric colored light blue and white. Caleb, a larger man with a thick reddish brown and gray-dappled beard, swallowed Marta in a hug.

"Marta! 'Tis good to see you!" He bellowed as he laughed, his accent thicker than her own. Marta couldn't help but smile in the older man's embrace. Camilla, his sister, tugged on his arm.

"Ye'll squish the poor lass!" She laughed. Her voice was smooth and silky, and her thin frame was much smaller compared to her brothers'. They both had white speckled brown hair and dancing hazel eyes. Marta caught a whiff of the rugged woods, a hint of vanilla on his sash.

Caleb released Marta with a laugh. "Ah'm sorry, m'dear, Ah jus' cain't help myself when Ah see a friend! Now—" he sat down on the bench, shifting to get comfortable— "tell me. Why the long face?"

Marta sighed, knowing these Gifteds could see right through her. She sat down heavily.

"I just... Bri and Isaac."

Camilla nodded and sat next to her, wrapping her arm around her shoulders. "It's hard to see your friends go."

Marta nodded and glanced away, a far-off look in her eyes. *I wish that God would show me where I'm supposed to go... Isaac is supposed to be by Bri's side, and Bri by his, and they have their purpose together. I know I can heal and all that, but no one lets me out of the Tower...*

Caleb sighed. "Correct me if Ah'm wrong, but y'look weary wit' life again, m'friend."

Marta slowly turned and nodded at her mentor, her eyes full of tears. "I am. I am thankful to do my best here in Ropheka, especially since this is where I grew up, but sometimes I want to do other things. Go to other Towers, help in more meaningful ways."

Camilla reached forward and held her hand. "Marta, no matter where yeh go, every life yeh touch is important."

Marta made a face. "I know that, Camilla. Believe me, I do. But I feel like… I feel like I'm not where I'm meant to be. I don't know…"

Caleb chuckled slightly. "Ah, the age old question. 'Wha' 'tis my purpose in life?' Forgive me if Ah sound too much like a Shepherd," he grinned, "but one thing Ah've learned is that God reveals things t'us in His time. Now, it may not be of much comfort to yeh now because it's not *yer* timing, but Ah promise t'will all make sense. Who knows? Maybe you'll lead an army against Arailt!" his laugh boomed. Marta shook her head with wide eyes.

"You know I don't have any offensive gifts!"

"Exactly m'point! Yeh never know what adventure He has planned for yeh." Caleb grinned. Camilla chuckled and shook her head.

"While seemingly a wee bit crazy, he does have a point. One thing Ah had t'learn was that God's timing is always, always better. Even," she smiled as she squeezed Marta's hand, "if it doesn't line up with our timing."

Marta sighed. "I just don't understand why there aren't any doors opening. I've applied to transfer to other Towers, to even be on the battlefield where I can help more, but everything has been denied." Caleb and Camilla exchanged a glance as Marta threw up her hands. "I am not content with where I am, yet I can't move anywhere."

"Marta…" Camilla whispered quietly. Caleb shook his head and stood.

"Marta, Camilla, please come with me. Ah think 'tis time we told 'er."

Marta blinked as Camilla nodded solemnly before standing. She followed behind the siblings as they walked to one of the empty classrooms in the main hall. Caleb shut the door and motioned for Marta to sit at one of the wooden desks. Camilla sat next to her as Caleb leaned against the wall with a sigh.

"There is nothing wrong with yer performance, first of all, Marta," Caleb began. "We just cain't let yeh leave here fer yer own safety."

"I don't mind not having a Knight!" Marta protested. "I trust the other Knights to protect me should it—"

Caleb held up a hand, gently quieting her. "Marta... ye're one of the last Life Gifteds left."

Marta blinked in surprise. "What... what do you mean, last Life Gifteds left?"

"Exactly what he said," Camilla sighed sadly. She turned to her friend with tears in her eyes. "Arailt has launched an assault on all Life Gifteds, we think because they tend t'be the backbone of our forces. While almost every Tower is in need of a Life Gifted, there aren't enough t'spare. Until we kin find a suitable Knight t'pair y'with, Ropheka is honestly the safest place t'be."

Marta swallowed hard. "You mean... they're dead?" The thoughts of those friends she had made in her trainings, those who had gone off to war and would never return, settled deeply in her soul. Tears welled up in her eyes. "I can't... I can't even imagine the pain their families are..."

Caleb sighed heavily. "Arailt has even interrupted the mirror transports. Have yeh noticed no one has been in'r'out a' the mirror room lately?"

She nodded solemnly.

"Or why we haven't been using mirrors t'communicate? Arailt has overtaken them too. Caused a lot of chaos on the battlefield it has, an' King Thomas's suffering because of 't."

Marta peeked up at that. "He's not going to lose, is he?"

"Ah know ye trust our King, jus' like the rest o' us in Ropheka. Ah doubt he would let Arailt take over Elyon so easily." Caleb smiled comfortingly. "But... 'tis been difficult for him after King Martin passed away. 'Twas all so sudden..." Caleb shook his head. "Ah woodn' be surprised if Arailt had a hand in— ah, there Ah go again. Nevermind that, Ah jus' wanted to let y'know. Please do not spread this information, lest it induce a panic. For now, perhaps there will be new Life Gifted Ones found an' brought here for yeh to train."

Camilla nodded enthusiastically. "Whatever yer journey may be, Marta, God goes before yeh, behind yeh, and beside yeh. He will guide yeh through 't."

Marta smiled weakly at her two friends. The thought of being hunted did not sit well with her, but it was indeed a relief to be here in Ropheka. The town was too far north and out of the way for any sane ruler to try and attack. Besides, if they did, the Rophekans had the upper hand as they were nestled in a mountain valley that required a journey through the pass to reach. Any enemy would be a sitting duck.

"Oh dear." Caleb mused as he put his pocket watch away. "Ah'll be late fer my message tonight!"

"Le's go together." Camilla smiled as she reached out her hand. Marta took it gratefully as they stood to leave. They walked towards the Tower Chapel, a beautiful room with a large stained glass window on one end. It depicted numerous Biblical stories, but in the very center was a lion and a lamb curled up next to each other. Gentle colorful streams of sunlight rested on the pews, flecks of dust illuminated in the air.

Some of the younger students were already in the room, none of them more than fifteen years old. These particular students were in training to become Shepherds themselves once they were of age. A few girls laughed and caught Marta's attention.

"Remember when we sat in these benches at that age?" Camilla mused wistfully. Marta nodded and smiled.

"I've had many a conversation with Jesus in this room."

"As have I." Camilla agreed, chuckling slightly. Her expression suddenly turned to that of slight panic. "Oh, Marta! Ah forgot!" she turned and motioned for her to follow. Caleb began his lesson at the front as the two women left to go to Camilla's quarters. Once there, she began rustling through her things.

"Ah forgot t'give Geralt back his book. He let me borrow it a week ago, and Ah've already read the whole thing. Ah doon know when Ah will be back in town, but would yeh be willing to give 't t'him on yer way home?"

Marta nodded and took the thick leather-bound tome, holding it tight. It looked like a fantasy book, and her interest was piqued. Camilla caught her glance and blushed slightly.

"'Tis a novel from another continent. It talks about elves and a king and queen, Ah really enjoyed it."

Marta grinned. "I'll make sure it gets back in one piece. I might have to ask Geralt if I can borrow it, myself!"

Camilla laughed. "Ah'm sure ye'd love it!"

The two women hugged in parting and she waved as Camilla went back to the chapel. Marta turned and walked out the large wooden door and into the courtyard.

Cool mountain air greeted her as she stepped into the waning light. The courtyard was not very large, with a simple cobblestone pathway leading through some shrubs and trees planted along the carriage path. She waved at the Knights guarding the aging iron gate as she passed through. The glacier valley was surrounded on all sides by steep cliffs and mountains. Behind her, a waterfall cascaded into the lake behind the stone castle the Tower took up residence in. The town of Ropheka lay before her, smoke gently wafting from numerous chimneys. She inhaled deeply, smelling fires being lit for the evening and dinner bubbling over the stoves. The town was small but very well-built, the roads lined with cobblestone and alleys in dirt. Townsfolk bustled back and forth finishing up their duties for the day. Summer would be over soon, giving way to the explosive colors and smells of fall. Familiar gray peaks, some already topped with snow, loomed over the valley as she continued into the town.

Several people stopped her to chat, thanking her for her help or requesting more supplies. Gladly she sold them what they needed and provided advice on different ailments. Her snug cottage was on the other side of town, barely a thirty minute walk from the Tower. The tavern, fondly named *The Dazed Knight*, was strategically placed in the middle of town and required only a slight detour to get there.

Marta pushed open the door and glanced around. Numerous men were here, some looked haggard, some regular patrons. She waved back at a few of her friends who were over at a table. The tavern was noisy with clinking glasses, scraping plates, and boisterous conversations. Geralt, the tavern owner, stepped out from the back with a cloth in his hand. As he opened the door she could smell his famous stew simmering on the stove, her stomach growling for a bowl. She could taste the softened potatoes, the juicy onions and well-done carrots. Geralt paused as she walked over, then produced a bowl of stew for her. She took it happily and had to refrain from licking her lips.

"Marta! Good t'see you. Not too much business, Ah pray?"

Marta smiled at her good friend. To most, Geralt was large and imposing, but he was actually a gentle soul. The scar on his neck attested to his time in service as a Knight, but his wide smile drew people's attention first. She set down her bowl as he gave her a big bear hug and released her with a laugh.

"You know, the usual. Mostly the adventurous children of town falling off of things. I have a few tinctures to make here and there, but nothing too serious."

"Ah, as long as there are wee bairns in our town, ye will always have a steady flow of business." He laughed heartily. Marta grinned and turned as one of the older gentlemen in the corner raised his glass.

"I, for one, appreciate having one of the Life Gifted in our small neck of the woods!"

A few patrons around the tavern lifted their glasses and yelled "Hear, hear!" bringing red to Marta's cheeks. Geralt patted her back and laughed again before quieting suddenly.

"What did ye say?" he asked pointedly, staring at one of the patrons. Marta followed his gaze and saw a middle-aged man swaddled in his cloak staring back.

"I said, where were the Life Gifteds when *we* needed them?"

Marta blinked in confusion. Geralt stepped up to the man and folded his arms. "She's right here, d'you need—"

The man threw off his cloak, revealing a heavy, fresh scar running across his face and down into his tunic. Marta gasped as the four other men at the table took off their own cloaks, revealing similar wounds.

"Where was the precious Gifted army of Elyon when Mulligen needed them most?! Nowhere! Nowhere to be found! Y'all spout about how peaceful it is here, how ye don't have a care in the world. We spoke of such things too, yet here we are!"

"What is it yer goon on aboot?" Geralt asked in a low growl. "'Tis not Marta's fault, nor is it—"

"No, it's not *her* fault." The man doused his anger with another swig of his drink, "It's that worthless King Thomas' fault."

The other men at his table nodded in agreement, making similar statements. The tavern's atmosphere shifted uncomfortably, and Marta stepped back as Geralt's eyes grew cold.

"Ye want t'slander our king, ye kin get out of me tavern."

"Ye're a fool to believe in a king who has turned his back on his own people!" the man spat angrily as he stood to meet Geralt's gaze. "I survived the attack in Mulligen, but only because the enemy was lazy! King Thomas—" his voice was laced with venom, "—was nowhere to be found."

"He's been trying to push back the attack on Gardiel, how were they supposed to know Mulligen would be attacked?" Robert, an older man, grumbled from the back. The stranger started to turn, but didn't quite turn his back to Geralt.

"It's his job to rally his armies, no?"

"Cut the man some slack. He's only human, he's trying his best after his father died—"

"—to his own hand!"

The room erupted in a roar, men starting to fight with one another.

Marta knew she should leave, but she was transfixed on Geralt's calm behavior. He held out his hands and grabbed the man by the back of his collar, separating him from another man. "Shut it!"

His bellowing voice shook the timbers of the room, and it stilled almost immediately.

"Tha's better. 'Tis not polite to fight with a lady present."

Marta was suddenly aware of the eyes turning to her, and she stepped behind Geralt.

"Don't be afraid, Marta." Geralt laughed. "I won't let one of 'em put a hand on ya. An' I won't send any of 'em to ya either," he said in an obvious warning to those around. He looked at the table of wounded men and sighed. "I can understand feeling abandoned, but King Thomas is doin' his best. We all here in Ropheka know that. We have to do our best to help all of Elyon, not just ourselves. Most of our Knights and Gifteds *are* on the battlefront. Ye came to the wrong place if ye think ye can spout yer nonsense here."

The man's face was red with heat. "I'm not here to spout nonsense." He said, chillingly calm. Marta felt it immediately, shuddering under the weight of his words.

"I'm here to warn yeh."

"Warn us? From what?" came a voice in the back. The man opened his eyes, resting his gaze on Marta for a moment before slowly turning to everyone else in the room.

"The armies of Arailt are moving through the western mountains. Ropheka is their next target."

The tavern erupted again, and this time, nothing would stop it. Geralt whisked Marta through the tavern and out to the door.

"Doona' pay any attention to him, Marta, he's got somethin' loose in his head. Poor guy. He did survive a pretty brutal attack, but tha's still no reason to cause panic." Geralt patted her head and winked. "Ah'll take care of it, an' like Ah said, Ah won't send anyone t'yer clinic tonight either. Have a good night Marta. Git home safe."

Marta nodded and was about to leave, before she remembered the book in her hands. Geralt took it, smiled slightly, and patted her hand. "Be safe, Marta. I can feel a storm brewing." He rolled his eyes and went back into the noisy fray. Crickets called through the bushes as she stepped down the stairs and paused on the road. *I never finished my stew,* she lamented as she made her way home in the twilight. She reached her snug abode just as darkness enveloped the small valley, and she looked towards the western mountain, illuminated by the rising moon.

Will they really come here? A chill ran through her spine. She got the comforting feeling she would be safe, but the thought still stuck with her. *Are we really their next target?*

CHAPTER TWO

Nightmares

Marta felt herself falling, sinking ever deeper into the icy water. An ocean swept over her, and she struggled for air. She flailed desperately, trying to do anything she could to get out of the mire. She could feel something emerging from the muck and wrapping its dark tendrils around her neck, pressing on her chest, slowly wrenching the life out of her. She woke up suddenly, covered in sweat and tears. She sat up and wiped off her face. It was dark outside, and a gentle fog was softly illuminated by the moonlight; except, based on the time she thought it was, the moon would have set hours ago. She could feel a presence in the room, but she didn't know what or who it was.

Get up.

Marta recognized the Voice, her whole body erupting in chills. She blinked and wondered if her nightmares had made her hear Him wrong. She glanced around and began slowly taking off the covers.

Now.

Marta flew out of bed, grabbing her cloak and quickly putting on her boots. Her mother's ring flashed through her mind, and she grabbed it before a horrible foreboding surrounded her.

Get out of the house!

Marta had no sooner opened the door than a giant ball of fire came crashing onto her roof. She tumbled forward with a grunt as her house splintered and collapsed, timbers alight. Stunned, she shook her head and looked behind her to see a dark army standing on the mountain ridge. Scores of shadows were there, most running down the mountain with thunderous cries. Fear began to suffocate her.

Get to the Tower!

Scrambling to her feet she rushed towards the village, wailing beginning to pierce the air. Adrenaline coursed through her as the yells of throngs of soldiers echoed through the valley. She stumbled up short as she entered the town. The enemy was already there.

It was a slaughter.

Houses and businesses lay in shambles around her, and bodies of townsfolk littered the streets. The overwhelming smell of death weakened her, and she staggered several times as she ran onward. One thought spurred her on; *get to the Tower!*

A young boy ran out of a house, chased by a dark soldier with a twisted grin. He raised his sword for the kill, but Marta grabbed the boy and tumbled to the side.

"Ha! You die together," the man growled menacingly. Marta froze in fear and closed her eyes in prayer as the man swung. Instead of pain, she heard a sickly *thud*. Opening her eyes revealed Isaac, standing between her and the man. The soldier's body slumped to the ground as Isaac turned, blood splattered on his face.

"Get to the Tower!" he ordered, and Marta nodded. Brianna ran up to them, out of breath, brown light dancing around her fingertips.

"We are getting everyone evacuated. Get to the Tower, as fast as you can! They're taking the wounded there." Bri reached out and rock erupted from the earth, swallowing another round of soldiers. Marta nodded, understanding her assignment, and ran with the boy in her arms.

"Mama!" the boy screamed through tears, squirming in Marta's grasp. Her eyes welled with tears as she rounded a corner; she didn't know if this boy would ever see his mother again.

A soldier stepped in front of her and wasted no time in his swing. Marta's hands glowed and branches and vines sprang from the ground, pulling the man back. He caught her arm with his sword, and she yelped but kept running. Golden light began to glow from her wound as it stitched itself back together.

The last thing the man thought was the unusual golden light emanating from Marta's arm; Isaac relieved him of any other thought with one swing. Isaac watched Marta rush toward the Tower and prayed she would get there safely.

Marta trudged up to the Tower gate and several Knights stepped forward to help shield her back. Once she made it inside the courtyard, she heard a cry and saw a frantic woman being held back by two Knights.

"Johnny! Johnny!"

They released her and she stumbled forward. The wide-eyed boy turned and started sobbing again. Marta relinquished the boy as his mother clutched him to her chest and wailed.

"My son, my son! You're alive!"

Marta trembled as adrenaline continued to course through her. One of the Knights helped her get the woman to her feet so they could get inside to safety. Caleb and Camilla met her at the door, eyes wide.

"Praise God, you're alive!" Camilla quickly hugged her before letting go. Her soft hazel eyes were alight with concern, yet she remained surprisingly calm. "Come with me, the wounded are over here. I've been healing as I can but you're much better at it than I am."

Marta nodded and rolled up her sleeves, trying to ignore the sounds of the war outside. Caleb stood and stretched out his arms, a similar golden light radiating from his palms. He prayed for protection and the Tower was surrounded in an ethereal barrier, allowing the townspeople in but keeping the Enemy out.

She knelt down next to a Knight, his eyes closed and blood seeping through his tunic. He had been caught by surprise and was nearly dead.

"God, give me strength!" Marta whispered as she held out her hands. Golden light erupted from her as the man's wounds began to stitch themselves together rather rapidly. Once his wounds were manageable and his breathing was normalized, she left him with a Water Healer and moved onto the next person.

A few more people spewed into the Tower's main hall, but it became strangely quiet outside. Marta glanced up at Caleb, who stood with arms outstretched. Sweat poured down his face, and she could tell he was weakening. The barrier wouldn't hold forever. Agonizing hours passed as the remaining survivors sought refuge in the small Tower hall.

Marta heard a cry and watched as Isaac carried Bri into the hall, her face caked with blood. He set her down and promptly collapsed himself, although he wasn't badly injured. She healed her friends the best she could and moved onto the next injury. Her strength was being sapped and as dawn's light filtered through the windows, she collapsed against the side wall.

Geralt strode up to her, his arm in a sling. He knelt in front of her and handed her a flask of water.

"Drink up, me gal, there's still a fight left 'ootside." She took a deep sip and sighed. Geralt's steely eyes were noticeably different. For the first time, Marta saw fear in them.

There was a horrible cracking noise as air pushed through the room. Caleb faltered and fell to one knee, the barrier sucking inward. Marta lunged to her feet to catch him and Camilla ran to him, bracing her brother. Geralt took up from behind although his strength was failing as well. Caleb's breathing was labored, but he fought hard. The barrier still held but now it only protected the hall. The front doors burst open, and a burly man with a jagged scar across his face stepped inside and up to the barrier.

He lazily held his battle axe on his shoulder, examining the room. His gaze fell on Caleb, who met his glare with a warrior's demeanor.

"Ah. Of course there would be a Shepherd here," the man growled low, his lips parting in a vicious grin as a crack resounded through the hall, the barrier faltering for but a second. Marta heard the sound before she saw it; a black arrow shot just above the man's shoulder which found its mark square in Caleb's chest. He reeled back and the barrier broke. Geralt caught him and Camilla wrenched out the arrow with glowing blue fingers.

As the stranger started to step forward, Marta launched to her feet and threw out her hands. A thick hedge grew around the destroyed wall, separating the army from the hall of wounded villagers. All was quiet for but a moment before the man's billowing laughter filled the room.

"You really think you can protect these people, do you? Fine. I'll make a deal with you." The sound of boots scraping across the stone floor filled the room and they knew they were surrounded. In a moment of panic, Marta moved her hands and used the hedge to shove most of the army out the door.

"I admire your tenacity, girl, but you test my patience. Since you seem so desperate to save their puny lives, send out your strongest Gifted One to beat me. Should they win, I will let you all live. I don't need to say what will happen should they fail." He laughed again, the sneering sound shaking their very souls. "I will give you ten minutes to decide. Time is ticking."

The enemy moved away from the hedge, the hall filling with silence. Marta panted heavily before turning to look at Caleb. His eyes were wide, his hand clutching his chest. Sparks moved across his skin as his life force seeped out through the wound. It was a gentle golden light, dripping down his chest and oozing around his hand. She lurched forward to begin healing him. It was excruciating since the arrow's dark poison had drained most of his strength.

"Caleb…" Camilla breathed, worry etched in her features. She and Marta stepped back as Geralt helped him stagger to his feet.

"I must protect my flock." He fell to one knee again, coughing violently as blood splattered onto the floor. It was evident he was in no position to fight. Marta looked desperately around the room, but all of their capable warriors and Gifteds were either wounded or too young to stand up to this threat. Geralt was in bad shape too, although she could tell he was on the verge of rushing outside to try and take on the captain.

Who will fight for us? she groaned inwardly.

You will.

Marta began trembling violently, frozen in place. *What?! Me?! Do You know how useless I am—*

Trust me. Go before My enemy and stand tall. I will protect you.

She shuddered in a breath and closed her eyes.

Caleb tried to stand again. "I—"

"I'll do it."

Everyone gasped as Marta slowly opened her eyes. Her stomach lurched as she stepped forward towards the hedge.

"I'll go."

"Marta—!" Camilla and Geralt started, but Caleb held up his hand and wheezed.

"He told you to, didn't He?"

Marta nodded slowly. Caleb smiled ruefully and collapsed to the ground. He reached up and placed a bloodied hand on her head as she knelt next to him.

"May He protect you as He did King David against the giant," his eyes fluttered closed as he wheezed. Camilla reached over and continued healing him with her Water Gift, nodding to her friend.

"God can take care of him from here. Godspeed, Marta."

Marta nodded and turned to Geralt, who sighed heavily. "Ah recognize tha' look in yer eyes. Wha Caleb said tis true, idn't it? Well, if ye were told to go, Ah've no doubt He will keep His promise." He patted her shoulder, a strange trusting look on his face. Marta took a deep breath, stepped back, and walked through a gap she made in the hedge. Each time her foot stepped on a stone she could feel herself practically sinking into the ground. The entire army began howling with laughter as she strode forward. The commander turned around and swung his axe into the ground.

"What?! The girl?!" his expression changed from that of surprise to hatred. "This is a joke. Let's end this quickly."

He moved like lightning, and Marta barely had time to react before his hand was clutched around her throat. She croaked loudly as she grasped at his hands.

Not like this! was all she could think as her whole body started thrashing, desperate for air. Her nightmares flooded her in full force, fear coursing through her body. *I don't want to go like this!*

I will protect you.

The roar of an army reverberated through the valley, giving everyone pause. Marta immediately felt a comforting tingle down her spine, and she started smiling as her vision faded. The commander released his grip on her neck and she tumbled to the ground. He yanked her up by the hair and whirled her around to hold her against his chest, a dagger at her throat.

Help had come.

*****

Thomas rubbed his face, scratching his reddish-brown beard in frustration. They still had a full day's ride ahead of them, but the attack could happen any moment.

He leaned back in his chair and sighed heavily, crossing his arms. His commanders and his brother glanced at each other nervously. The small tent was stifling, the lamplight smoking and dim. A map laid out on the small table before them showed Elyon's mountains and valleys with the rivers and towns in between. A dark chess piece was set on one of the towns in the northernmost part of the continent, Ropheka. The royal coat-of-arms, a golden lion atop a red field, was inscribed on another chess piece. Ropheka lay on the other side of the mountain, and the passage to the town was dangerous.

"I still don't understand how they were able to get there so quickly! We had them running the other way, when did a regiment break loose to go up there?" Jerome, one of Thomas' older commanders, grumbled through his beard.

"Probably had it planned from the beginning." Peter sighed, nibbling on his finger. "Your Excellency, I don't see what we can do. We can try to send a message via the mirror to evacuate them—"

"The connection has been blocked," Amaryll, a woman in her mid 40's, interjected. As the commander of the Gifted force under Thomas, she was adept in Fire Gifts. Her raven hair was tied back behind her head in a taut bun. "Arailt is very good at taking down lines of communication wherever he goes. It's been down for weeks…" she shook her head at Peter.

"So our only option is t'ride overnight," Finlay, another commander, sighed thickly. He stroked his red beard in thought. "Ropheka may be very well protected, but 'tis one of the best Towers in our country. If it falls, it will severely damage the infrastructure of our—"

Thomas tuned out the voices of those in the room, rubbing the bridge of his nose. If they rode overnight, their horses would be exhausted by the next day, and they wouldn't be able to escape a dangerous situation if they needed to retreat. On the other hand, it was as the commander said, Ropheka was a critical hub for the Gifted and Knight academies the Tower hosted. The future of the Towers in the kingdom could very well be at stake here. He slowly glanced up and met his brother's gaze.

Peter had a characteristic smirk on his face, unnoticed by anyone except for Thomas. Peter returned his attention to the commanders, but that smirk was burned in Thomas' mind.

As if I need another reminder that even my family believes me to be incapable of leading this country.

Thomas stood slowly and examined the map. The others in the room quieted and focused on their leader for his command. It would be nay on impossible to make it in time…

Go.

Thomas blinked slowly. *I… I recognize that Voice. Did I hear correctly…?* He shook his head, but a strange tingling sensation pressed into his chest. He *needed* to get to Ropheka. But why? He warred with himself and could feel the voices of those around him pleading for him to call off a pursuit. It would be negligent, they could lose men in the process of maybe making it to the town in time. He glanced around the map one more time and stiffened his back.

"Prepare the troops and Gifteds. We ride overnight."

He turned and strode out the door, the gasps of his commanders the only thing he left behind.

"Thomas!"

Thomas rolled his eyes as he halted, the tents of soldiers and Gifteds around him shuddering in the wind. He turned as Peter ran up to him, wide-eyed.

"Thomas, you can't be serious! Carrick is already there, there's no way anyone will survive! Most of the Gifteds and Knights are gone already, what is a few casualties when—"

"No. I will not abandon my people. We will ride overnight, and we *will* make it!" His ferocity startled even himself. What was it that was nagging him forward, urging, pressing him towards Ropheka? The tiny glacier town was mostly unpopulated, but it was what Carrick was looking for there that made Thomas shudder.

"Besides, Peter, if Carrick is there, there's a very good reason for him to be there. I shouldn't need to explain myself to you," his voice took a dark turn as he narrowed his eyes. Peter bowed.

"I apologize, Milord. I meant no offense," he murmured, his voice laced with venom and as annoying as only a sibling knows how to be.

When did we become such bitter enemies? Thomas lamented as he watched his brother stiffen and walk away with a scowl. *He was my best friend and confidant. And now...* Thomas shook his head and returned to his personal tent. A knight was waiting there with his armor and sword.

"Your Majesty," he bowed, "Your sword and armor are ready for you."

Thomas nodded and thanked him as he was helped into his armor. *Ever since Sarah came along, Peter has gotten very... no, has it been longer than that? Father's death just aggravated already open wounds.* He winced as he strapped on his sabadons, the memory of his father still raw.

I need to believe it was murder, father. I do. I need to find the person responsible and do to them what they did to you. But the evidence is piling up, and I'm not sure I can... I can justify that it wasn't your own doing. He sighed heavily and adjusted his gauntlets before attaching his sword to his hip. *I can't afford to dwell on this now. Either way, this war has continued on too long, and we must defend our people. Carrick must have found a Life Gifted. But the last report we received stated no Life Gifteds in that area...* He ruminated as the tents were taken down swiftly and weary soldiers, Knights, and Gifteds all gathered their belongings onto horses and wagons.

This particular section of the army had nearly 1,000 men and women, but only about one quarter would make it to Ropheka by the next morning. Foot soldiers would take a couple of days to arrive. Based on their reports, the Gifteds and Knights they had gathered should be able to stave off the attacks. Even better, their chances were high of actually defeating the opposing regiment.

If only we make it in time. I won't let you slip from my grasp again,

Carrick.

The night was long and brutal, and the horses were pushed past their limits. They foamed at the mouth and panted as they crested a hill. Smoke billowed from the flames in the dark distance and he knew the attack had already begun.

"My Lord, we should make it by daybreak," Amaryll reported as she rode up next to him. Thomas nodded slowly.

"Let's be on it, then."

They rode down the hill and through another valley. This would be the hard part, as soldiers were stationed by the pass. Elyon's armies were swift, however, and the battle lasted but a few moments. Arrows rained down on the attacking army, effectively crushing the enemy. Thomas examined the field and turned back to Amaryll and Peter.

"How is our army faring?"

"The soldiers are exhausted," Peter complained. Amaryll cast him a sideways glance and looked back at Thomas.

"The Knights and Gifteds are few, but they are ready."

"Then we will take them and leave the soldiers behind."

"What!" Peter exclaimed, catching his brothers arm. "You can't be serious!"

"If they're exhausted, they can stay here. We will go onward."

"That's a death blow to their morale!"

"We have a duty to our people. If our soldiers are tired, we will return for them. I don't need more deaths on my hands." Thomas' eyes flickered with light, and Peter snapped his mouth shut.

"Leave one of my captains here with the wounded or weary, and I will head up the battalion."

Thomas nodded the command, and they began riding on a dirt road through the pass. It turned into cobblestone just as the light began to break and they made it into Ropheka.

The Tower was nearly decimated, and they could see Arailt's army surrounding the castle. Thomas glanced to the side and saw a house completely caved in by a large boulder, embers still alight. Gifteds and Knights of Elyon's army who had been here, who lived here, gave out a cry when they saw their homes nearly destroyed. Thomas utilized that energy and encouraged their war cry, rushing the castle. He needed the people inside to know help had come at last.

CHAPTER THREE

The Call

Thomas dismounted his horse, sword at the ready. Arailt's forces were certainly haggard and Elyon greatly outnumbered them for once. Many soldiers stood between them and a strange hedge, the morning light casting shadows through the fog. Peter counted the enemy army and began whispering orders to the soldiers around. Thomas' focus, however, was on the young woman in Carrick's grasp.

"Ah, Thomas!" Carrick held out his other hand, lazily swinging around a dagger. "What a surprise! I didn't expect you to come after us so—"

Thomas held out his sword, his jaw set. "I think we both know how this will end, Carrick."

Carrick glanced down at the woman, then smiled. "You're a man of your word. Just the two of us, and I'll let the girl go."

"Fine."

The kings' response surprised everyone, even himself. It was as if the words just spewed out of him. But looking at the woman, something moved inside of him. It was a feeling he hadn't felt in a long time, yet it was all too familiar.

"Deal, then?" Carrick threw the girl forward and Thomas had to swipe his sword out of the way before he impaled her. He barely missed, nicking her arm and drawing blood.

*****

Marta shuddered, her breath caught in her throat. Here she was, in the arms of the *king* no less, with an army of malicious soldiers around her. Thomas held her carefully and looked at her with dazzling blue eyes. They almost flickered with light when she met his gaze.

"Are you alright?"

"Y-yes sir. Your-your Majesty." She blinked several times, simultaneously embarrassed and relieved she was alive. Pinpricks of golden light began bursting from her wounds, sealing her skin back together. She felt a sting of pain and glanced down, the king following her gaze.

"You're a—!"

"Life Gifted!" Carrick exclaimed, his expression turning from glee to panic. He grabbed his battle-axe in a flash and lunged towards Thomas and Marta. She closed her eyes as Thomas jerked and met Carrick's blow with his own sword, using his other hand to hold the flat side of his blade. Carrick's force pushed Thomas back, but he threw off the battle-axe and used the momentum to drive it into the ground. The armies of Elyon roared as they sprang forward, decimating the enemy army. Marta watched with wide eyes from Thomas's grip as the king ran Carrick through. The commander reeled backwards and fell to his knees, panting heavily. He glanced between her and Thomas, never flinching as the king's sword touched his neck.

"You've been looking for Life Gifteds and decimating their numbers. Why?" he asked in a tone that made Marta shudder. Carrick raised his gaze and gave Thomas an indecipherably dark look.

"I have failed my Master."

Marta screamed as Carrick jerked his head, slicing his neck on Thomas' sword. Thomas turned Marta away as the enemy commander spasmed, his life-blood spurting to the ground. Marta covered her face and steadied her breathing as the world started spinning. Thomas picked her up as the battle around them began to still, the enemy defeated. Had the townspeople not been taken by surprise they actually would have stood a chance against the invaders. The Tower was in shambles but the small hall remained intact. He carried her over to the hedge, which dissipated as he entered it.

The townspeople all gazed in shock as the king brought Marta inside, slowly setting her down against a wall. Camilla glanced between Caleb and Marta, but Caleb gently took her hand.

"Watch," he whispered, his eyes sparkling. Camilla looked over and gasped.

Marta looked up at the king in pain and weariness. He blinked several times as light crossed through his pupils.

*****

She is the partner I have picked for you.

What. Thomas blinked. After months of silence from the God he so desperately cried out to, *this* is what He had to say?!

Of all the things, this is what You have to tell me?? How do I even know it's You?! He shuddered slightly as familiar warmth poured over his head. His soul was starved for this warmth and soaked up every second. The young woman who sat before him also blinked, and a golden light gently filtered through her green eyes. Thomas nearly groaned aloud.

A… Life Gifted? Truly? A strange thought flitted through his mind as he stood and glanced around. *Did Arailt know this? Is that why he's been trying to—*

My enemy knows I have a great destiny in store for you. He will do everything he can to stop it, to stop you.

Now that he thought about it, he did remember his father telling him something about a Life Gifted long, long ago. The memory was too blurry to remember, but he recalled his father's mournful voice. He blinked and realized the people in the room were kneeling in respect.

"Ah, you all may stand."

Peter rushed over to him as the villagers hobbled to their feet, his face sweaty. He bowed and glanced down at the young woman behind him. She had a look of confusion on her face.

"Your Majesty, the enemy is dead. We had no casualties."

Thomas nodded and moved towards Caleb. He reached down to help him stand, and Caleb took his hand gratefully.

"Your Majesty, it is an honor to meet you. Thank you for saving our people!" he wheezed, grinning wearily, leaning on Camilla for support. Thomas couldn't help but feel depressed as he looked around at the townspeople— *his* people —and the sorry state they were in.

"Words cannot express my regret at not being here in time. I take full responsibility for—"

"Your Excellency, if I may?" Caleb interrupted gently with a thoughtful look on his face. Thomas smiled slightly, not minding the interruption, but instead curious to hear what the old Shepherd had to say.

"You may, Shepherd."

"God used ye t'save us. God has His timing, an' we have no control over't. Those who went home t'Him today are not lost forever, 'though we will miss them greatly. Ye came, y'obeyed Him, and that s'what matters."

Thomas felt strength and forgiveness stir ever so slowly in his soul and he sighed heavily. "Thank you for your words of encouragement, Shepherd. They are greatly appreciated. I still must take responsibility."

Caleb nodded. "I do understand, Sire. I take responsibility as well."

Thomas nodded absentmindedly, then turned to look back at the woman. Peter was having a conversation with her. Her expression was mournful, and for some reason he wanted to know why.

"What can you tell me about her?" he asked quietly. Caleb smiled softly.

"I believe you should ask her that question, my Lord. But her name is Marta."

*****

Marta blinked in confusion. *Did… did I hear You right? I must be hearing things!*

You are his help-meet, Marta. I have chosen you both to be together before you were even born. This is no accident.

Marta blinked again and watched as Thomas walked over to Caleb, then she noticed a young man staring at her. Based on his looks and demeanor, he was the prince of Elyon, Peter. He knelt next to her with a strange look.

"You should be dead."

She shook her head in surprise. "I-I mean—"

"Carrick had you in a grip that has ripped people in two. You should be dead!" Stunned, he shook his head. "I'm… surprised to see a Life Gifted here." He glanced around for a moment, wary of having his back turned to a group. "So many of them have been hunted down and killed, I believed there were no more left."

Marta furrowed her brow. "I… had heard that just recently, as well…" she glanced at the room as the truth settled in her chest. Already there was so much death, but having someone else confirm what Caleb had told her earlier set it in stone. Thinking about her friends losing their lives in the grip of the man she had just encountered, who Thomas had bargained with, sent a shudder of horror down her spine. *Why did I get to live when they didn't…?* And now, she was supposed to be with the king?? How was she supposed to convince him—

Thomas and Caleb both turned in unison to look at her. Caleb had that understanding look on his face, and Thomas had one she couldn't decipher. In one moment, she knew Thomas had been told the same thing.

I am... way out of my depth here.

Camilla rushed over to her and knelt by her side, nodding politely at Peter. Peter turned away with a humph and folded his arms.

"Marta, thank the Lord you're alright. I was so scared when you stood up to volunteer yourself, but at the same time—"

"You *voluntarily* faced Carrick?!" Peter exclaimed, returning his attention to the two women. Camilla nodded as Marta sighed wearily.

"She did, your Highness! After that arrow of darkness struck my brother, we all thought we were done for. But Marta stood up and despite her exhaustion, she pushed them—"

"Are you insane?!" Peter retorted angrily, turning towards Marta. She winced as his raised voice echoed in the cavernous room. "You *knew* that Life Gifteds were being hunted and yet you tried to foolishly sacrifice yourself in order to—?!" he clamped his mouth shut as he felt a hand on his shoulder. Caleb stood there with a grave look on his face.

"I know you think what Marta did was foolish, your Highness, and in an earthly way it was. But I assure you, she was following much Higher orders. God knew she would buy us enough time for all of you to arrive." He smiled fondly at Marta, who sat with unfocused eyes.

He... he's really standing up to the prince for me?! I don't understand what I did wrong, but prince Peter is so angry!

There was a deep sigh and the group turned as Thomas stepped forward. It was then she could get a really good look at the man they all called sovereign. He wore brilliant silver armor, the crest of Elyon emblazoned on the front. His sword was strapped firmly to his side, and she recognized the Ela metal on the hilt. Ela was an energetically sensitive ore that, once refined, could augment a Gifted's specific abilities. It was used in the mirrors the Tower used to communicate or travel with. *I heard rumors the king had a Light Gift, but never realized he was trained in it...!*

He combed his fingers through his dark brown hair and nodded to Caleb. "Marta, is it?"

She nodded slowly and tried to bow from her spot on the floor. Caleb and Camilla grinned as Thomas shook his head.

"No need for formalities right now, Gifted One. I wanted to thank you for your bravery. In battle every second counts, and you did truly buy everyone here time," he commented blandly. Marta blinked and shook her head.

"I appreciate the compliment, your Majesty, but it was God and *you* who saved us in the end. I was merely a stopgap, in a way," she smiled slightly. Thomas was taken aback.

She seems humble, yet...

Peter scoffed slightly. "You have no idea what we had to go through in order to—"

Thomas shot him a glare and he snapped his mouth shut.

"Forgive me, your Excellency. I will go see to the rest of the army." He stiffened as he walked away. Marta noticed the sadness in Thomas' eyes as his brother stormed off. *He cares for his brother a lot... I wonder what happened between them?*

Thomas sighed again and turned back to Marta. He held out his hand and she took it gently. He helped raise her to her feet slowly.

"Thank you, your Majesty!" Marta blushed deeply and bowed. Caleb laughed heartily as Thomas shook his head.

"I told you, no need for—" her genuine smile caught him off guard, and he stopped. "...Formalities," he stammered. Marta's blush deepened and immediately she began glancing around the room.

"Does anyone else need any help? How is Bri doing? Anyone—" she faltered in her step and Caleb and Thomas both caught her.

"Whoah there, lass. Ye're not in good enough shape to be worrying about everyone else," Caleb shook his head with a smile. "Everyone is stable. For now, just go get some rest. The Gifteds who arrived have enough Healers among them to help."

Marta nodded, realizing in that moment how exhausted she really was. Camilla took her arm and smiled calmly.

"Let's go, we've set up a room for people to rest. I'll take you there."

Thomas watched as the Gifted and Shepherd left, Marta staggering and faltering a few times. He had to admit, he was intrigued by the slight blonde haired woman who had come crashing into his life. Although, whether he had heard God right was yet to be seen.

"She is a wonderful woman," Caleb replied, as if reading Thomas' thoughts. "Ever since she was born, her parents knew she would do great things."

"Where are her parents?" Thomas asked absentmindedly, glancing around the room. Caleb sighed mournfully.

"They went t'be with our Heavenly Father several years ago. Her mother Kylah was also a Life Gifted, her father Alistaire Kylah's Chosen Knight. They left on a campaign wit' King Martin."

At the mention of his father, Thomas straightened his back. *This entire war really began so long ago, didn't it… at least, the very beginning did, back when we had no idea what was to befall our country…You had the upper hand, father. I don't know where we lost it.*

"T'was on that campaign," Caleb continued as he glanced towards Marta woefully, "that her parents were killed. Poor Marta was only sixteen. Ah'll never forget goin' t'her house in the middle of th'night to tell her…" he shook his head. "Ah know that being thrust into power at a time like this has been hard, yer Majesty, but—"

"You don't know anything about me," Thomas scowled. Caleb paused, startled, before nodding solemnly.

"You're right, Ah don't know much about you. Forgive me for misspeaking. Ah simply meant to say, it must be very hard for you to be going through this right now. Yet," he smiled softly, "Ah want t'remind you that you are not alone." He motioned to the people in the room. Despite their brokenness and their losses, the people looked to Thomas for guidance and hope. Thomas swallowed hard.

"Your Majesty!"

Thomas and Caleb turned as Amaryll rushed forward. She spotted Caleb and smiled wide. "Shepherd!"

"Ah, my dear Amaryll!" he enveloped her in a hug, and Amaryll laughed. Thomas' eyes widened; he had never seen her act this way before. She stepped back with a grin, composed herself, and turned to Thomas seriously.

"Your Majesty, we were able to find the orders on Carrick's body. Arailt sent them here knowing they would die."

"Then why—?" Thomas shook his head incredulously.

"His orders were to find and kill the Life Gifted One here." Caleb groaned at that.

"Ah believed it may have had somethin' t'do with Marta. Before the mirrors went down, Ah had a meeting with the council of elders via mirror. That's when we discovered Arailt was deliberately hunting down the Life Gifted." He rubbed his face angrily. "Ah mentioned all of our Life Gifteds had been dispatched… except for one."

"You had no way of knowing he was intercepting the mirror transmissions, Caleb," Amaryll replied softly. "I'm just glad she's safe."

"Can someone please remind me what is so critical about Arailt killing the Life Gifteds specifically?" Thomas burst out angrily. "I don't want any of my people targeted, but why them?"

Caleb and Amaryll exchanged glances.

"Your Majesty..." Amaryll began trepidatiously, "do you not remember the prophecy your mother gave?"

A memory flashed in the back of his mind, tattered edges he couldn't quite place. He shook his head.

"Your mother, who you know had a Light Gift, had a prophetic ability," she continued. "She had a vision that you would... well, that you would one day marry a woman with a Life Gift." She glanced curiously towards the room Camilla and Marta had entered.

His heart plummeted into his stomach. "And you're saying this is why Arailt has been exterminating them?"

"They are also crucial members of our forces," Caleb interjected. "They possess the most powerful healing ability. Even though Water Gifteds can sometimes heal, it's certainly not to the same caliber as a Life Gifted. Imagine the heir of a Light and Life Gifted union?"

Thomas rubbed the bridge of his nose. *This explains a lot. But why wouldn't I remember something that important, especially if it had to do with me?* The sensation of Carrick willingly piercing himself on Thomas' sword rather than face his master sent a shiver down his spine. "No matter. The fact that any are still remaining is a miracle in and of itself. For now, Shepherd, what can we do to help? The remainder of our forces will be here shortly. I will need to confer with my generals, but we have not heard word of any more attacks... yet."

Amaryll nodded. "It seems Arailt has retreated to regroup, though who knows for how long."

"If only we had enough strength to remove him once and for all..." Thomas grumbled aloud. Caleb cleared his throat and motioned to the room.

"For now, your Majesty, get some rest. We can go from there."

CHAPTER FOUR

Dwelling in the Past

Marta woke up to Camilla gently shaking her shoulder. Her Shepherd friend smiled wearily and sat down next to her.

"You've been asleep for quite awhile. Though ye've needed it after the day we've had."

Marta sat up and rubbed her eyes, examining the room. Afternoon sunlight shone through the decimated doorway with rubble lying about it. A few people sat here and there, some were on cots brought from the infirmary. Several soldiers walked around helping the wounded, bringing them water or blankets, but otherwise the room was relatively quiet. Caleb and Thomas were nowhere to be found. Camilla handed her a small cup of water and she drank deeply.

"Is Caleb alright?" she wheezed. Camilla nodded.

"He is. He's still weak, but thank God you helped him out. Ah'm surprised y'didn't pass out sooner with the rounds you were making, but you always have been natural at healing. And Ah'm incredibly thankful!" Camilla smiled faintly as Geralt walked past, nodding at the ladies on his way around the room. Marta winced and took another sip.

The past days' events hit her again in yet another fresh wave, and the words spoken to her heart earlier in the day settled on her chest. She stared into the water inside her cup and sighed.

"What is it?" Camilla asked in concern. Marta looked up at her friend slowly.

"I... I know what I'm supposed to do."

"Oh?"

Marta glanced back into her cup. *A... queen? Really? Me? I'm not special enough for that! It's too much of a fairy tale... Besides, I don't know how any of that works, how to help him! He's so much more mature and responsible than I am. I'd really just get in his way...*

Camilla turned her head insightfully to the side and frowned slightly. "Whose voice are you listening to right now, Marta?"

She shook her head trying to dispel her thoughts. "I don't know," she groaned. "I want to trust that what I heard is correct, but at the same time, I wonder if it's just the emotions of the moment that I was listening to."

Camilla nodded. "Ah can understand that. If it really is from God, He will affirm it to you. Here," she held out her hand, "come with me. We are trying to gather supplies for everyone. The soldiers are gathering those who went home and we will have a funeral later."

"How many...?" she was afraid to finish the sentence. Camilla helped her stand and sighed.

"About thirty of us. The Aikmans' lost their pa and two sons, all of the Balderstons, the Haddows' lost Lucy and Gail, the Linseys..." Marta's head began reeling with each family lost and grief welled up in her chest. Camilla continued, "Mr. Haddock as well, Deena and Markus McKay—" Marta had to stop and lean against the wall as sobs blurred her vision. Memories of the sweet little boy with a toothy smile wrenched her heart open. Her whole body ached and her mind and emotions were spent. She clasped a hand over her mouth as a sob escaped her throat, Camilla sadly holding her friend as she cried.

"On second thought, let's get you to a room. The Earth Gifteds that came have already rebuilt parts of the Tower, so let's get you to a bed."

Marta nodded slowly and wiped her face on her sleeve. Camilla guided her through broken hallways to the dormitory. She glanced outside and noticed the burnt remains of the homes and businesses she once frequented. She felt numb, like an empty hole had replaced her stomach. Her chest was heavy and her throat on fire. Something caught her eye as she turned away; it was some of the people she had healed the day prior, working along with the soldiers to find food for everyone else. Watching them go back and forth, she hesitated.

"Marta?"

She turned and met Camilla's concerned gaze.

"I want to go help. Crying and lying in bed won't help. I want to help."

"Marta, you did help—"

"But I can help *more*," she strengthened her resolve. Camilla glanced around nervously, then conceded with a sigh.

"Don't push yourself, Marta. You're our only Life Gifted left. Promise me you won't overdo it?"

"I promise."

Camilla and Marta walked back to the main hall and out the door. The afternoon sun felt warm and somewhat comforting as they walked down to the destroyed town. A cool alpine breeze broke the scent of burnt wood and melted metal wafting through the air. Soldiers and townspeople were scattered around, some of the Gifted helping to begin rebuilding homes and others recovering items. Marta took one firm look around and rolled up her sleeves.

"I think I'll start by recovering some of the fields."

Camilla nodded. "Ah'll join you."

The pair walked out to the outskirts of town where the farmers were working with some Earth Gifteds to restore their charred crops. Marta reached out her hands and walked along the fields of decimated grain, her hand glowing as the burnt wheat twisted and regrew. She slowly exhausted herself; after just a few hours the farmers sent her back to the town center. Camilla walked beside her in silence.

"'Tis… strange."

Marta glanced over at her friend. "What is?"

Camilla put a hand on her chest. "This deep grief, but also this peace. Ah know everything will be okay, even though it looks so disastrous now."

Marta turned her gaze back to the road in front of them. "I suppose you're right. I hadn't thought of it before, but everyone does seem relatively calm. Although, it could just be trauma," she grinned ruefully.

Camilla chuckled. "Sometimes when everything is dark, the light shines all the brighter. Oh! It's almost sunset! The funeral is going to start soon, Ah need t'help prepare!"

Marta nodded. "Go on ahead of me. I'll make it in time."

Camilla winced. "Are y'sure? Ah don't want to leave you alone."

She pointed towards some houses barely peeking out from the crest of the hill. "I can see the outskirts from here. I should be fine."

"Alright. Be safe!" Camilla hiked up her skirts and rushed forward up the lane. Marta watched her friend go with a soft smile. She rounded the bend and saw her own house down the road.

The home she had grown up in was completely destroyed, a large tarred boulder smashed through the center of the roof, resting in her living room. Burnt wood and furniture was splintered around, some pieces still smoking. She stopped in what used to be her doorway and sighed.

In her mind's eye she saw a younger version of herself running through that door, laughingly chased by her mother and father. All of them were giggling as they tumbled together in the yard. Her father picked both her and her mother up and carried them back inside. Another memory of Camilla coming to babysit her young self wandered through her imagination, until it was replaced by the memory of Caleb coming to tell her that her parents were dead. This home held numerous memories, but the ashes reminded her that all things in this world would end eventually.

She turned and plodded up the path to the town as the sun began streaming down behind the mountain. She joined a few quiet villagers as they struggled to the Tower for the funeral.

*****

Thomas sighed and rubbed his face. The funeral service was one of the best he had ever seen, with Caleb the Shepherd giving a heartfelt sermon. From his spot in the front row, Thomas watched as each of the 30 hastily-cobbled caskets were carried out by townspeople and Knights to be buried in the quiet cemetery just up the hill from the Tower. Each box was a reminder of his failure to be there for his people. The smallest casket went by last, only big enough for a tiny soul. He had to look away lest his emotions explode.

The chapel grew quiet as he took in a deep breath. *I won't let this happen again. I will protect my people!*

"Your Majesty?"

Thomas turned and blinked at Marta, who leaned over the end of the pew with a concerned look.

A dark thought slipped into his mind. *She's only pitying you because you're the king.*

"Are you alright?" she asked quietly. She stood a polite distance away with her hands clasped in front of her. Thomas noticed her disheveled blonde hair was braided loosely to her hip, and it looked like she hadn't brushed her hair in days.

"Maybe I should ask you that question?" he replied dryly. Marta glanced towards the door them towards him in confusion.

What, how could I be so insulting?

He sighed heavily and closed his eyes, folding his arms. "I am doing alright, if that's what you want to know." *Not really alright, considering the deaths of so many under my care and the state of this village—*

"Well, I'm glad you're alright then." She smiled slightly in an effort to be comforting. Thomas turned away with a scowl. *Why do I feel so guarded with her?*

"I wanted to say thank you, your Majesty. Thank you for saving us. And..." she fidgeted, "thank you for... for saving me."

Thomas glanced back at her. *So that's what this is about?* He nodded slightly. "I only wish I could have been here to save *them*." He motioned to the empty space where all the caskets had been not fifteen minutes prior. Marta followed his mournful gaze and nodded.

"I wish I was strong enough to have kept them alive..." she murmured as her expression shifted and a distant look invaded her eyes. Thomas noticed immediately. *She's upset about something she didn't have any control over? Doesn't she realize there was nothing more she could do?*

Don't you?

Thomas paused as warmth dripped over his head. He shook off the feeling of comfort and stood slowly.

"Perhaps there was nothing more to be done. As your Shepherd said, God has His ways and we have ours. They don't always line up the way we'd like." The taste of his own words was nauseating. Yet, it was what so many had told him, so it must be true, right?

Marta met his gaze and nodded slowly, then smiled, much to Thomas' surprise.

"I also wanted to thank you for helping us rebuild our village. It is very kind of you. I know... I know you probably have a lot on your mind and a lot of things to do, but it means so much to us. I've... we've always believed in you, your Majesty." Her face flooded with color and she turned as the other Shepherd, Camilla, stepped towards them.

"Oh! Marta! I—I'm sorry, I didn't mean to interrupt—"

"No no it's okay Camilla, I was just about to—" Marta turned and curtsied clumsily before rushing over to Camilla. Thomas couldn't help but chuckle ruefully.

This is supposed to be my wife? Our queen?

The warmth spread over his head again as Martha glanced back at him, nodded slightly, then turned and walked with Camilla out the door. He groaned and shook his head.

"You certainly seem intrigued by the Life Gifted One."

Thomas glanced up as Peter stepped beside him, one hand on his sword, his expression terse. Thomas looked away grumpily.

"There are only a few Gifteds in this town, Peter. I am bound to run into them a few times."

Peter tipped his head to the side. "Yet you keep finding yourself bumping into *her*."

Thomas shrugged at that. "Who are you to tell me what I should or should not do?"

Peter's eyes took on a sharp darkness that startled Thomas. "This is about the prophecy mother had, isn't it?"

"And what if it is?"

Peter shook his head and laughed mirthlessly in disbelief. "You really expect a so called vision from a dying woman would result in this?! In a commoner, no less!"

Thomas stood abruptly and grabbed Peter by the shirt. "Don't you dare disrespect our mother that way!" He shoved him backwards as Peter scowled.

"You don't even remember our mother—"

"Enough!" Thomas bellowed. The hall echoed with his outburst as both men stood fuming. Thomas fought to regain control of the situation, much to Peter's amusement. "This is not the place to discuss the past, Peter," he growled low.

"You certainly dwell in it enough," he retorted.

Thomas turned away and stalked off. Peter watched him go with a sneer.

"Fine, turn the kingdom over to an inexperienced peasant! See how far that takes you!" he goaded as Thomas left the room. His grin dissolved immediately into the vicious whisper, "You're a fool, Thomas." He left quickly, his sword clanging against his leg. Behind him, Caleb and Camilla stood in the darkened doorway exchanging a glance.

*****

The Next Day

Marta sighed as she sat back and wiped her brow. The Knight in front of her smiled.

"Thank you so much, Marta. I really appreciate it," the woman grinned as she waved her arm back and forth. Marta frowned slightly as she heard Markus' laughter ring in her ears, the memory of how he wiggled his arm very much the same way still raw. She nodded listlessly.

"You're welcome."

The knight stood and began to walk out but suddenly halted as she snapped to attention. Marta glanced up as Thomas entered the infirmary, nodding to the Knights.

"Thank you, at ease."

The Knights stepped apart and continued on their way. Marta began to stand to curtsy but Thomas waved at her to remain seated. He glanced around for a moment before taking a seat in the chair in front of her.

"Are you hurt, your Majesty?!" she inquired in alarm. Thomas chuckled and shook his head.

"No, not physically. I came to talk to you."

She hesitated at that. *Have I done something wrong?* "Is... is there anything I can help you with?"

He scoffed. "Why do you always insist on helping everyone? No, I don't need your help. At least, not in the way you think," he winced. She shrank in confusion then sat up straight. What if he was here to talk about what she had heard God tell her?! He leaned back and sighed.

"Marta, I wanted to know a little bit more about you. After all, I haven't had the pleasure of meeting very many Life Gifted Ones before." He settled deeper in his chair and examined her. She could feel her cheeks and ears heating to a deep red.

"Well, your Majesty, I—"

"Thomas," he smiled forcefully. "You can just call me Thomas."

Her eyes widened in disbelief. *I don't think he realizes the idea of me speaking to him so informally...* "Well, I appreciate the gesture. I am not very interesting, though... I've just been here," she motioned around the room. The memories and the laughter and the pain she had experienced in this room came at her full force, and her throat tightened up. The longing to escape her village was replaced by guilt. "All my life," she whispered quietly, a far-off look in her eyes. Thomas folded his arms.

"You mean you've never left Ropheka?"

"I've traveled via mirror once or twice to attend specialized trainings at other Towers. I wouldn't leave the campus, however, and we only had one Gifted capable of maintaining the transports." She sighed. "Even with the mirrors lined with Ela, it still takes a considerable amount of one's energy to be able to transport people through them. Communicating is so much easier," she pulled out her pocket watch and showed it to him. The back opened up to reveal a small mirror lined with Ela, a blueish metal. "It just relies on the energy of the one establishing the connection."

He nodded slowly. "I have to admit, I saw my father using these quite frequently. But recently, I haven't been able to use one."

"It's probably because Arailt has severed the connections," she heaved a sigh. He raised a brow.

"No one has been able to fully explain to me what that actually means."

"Mirrors form a powerful connection. With enough energy, one can intercept that connection with their own. Numerous council meetings have been infiltrated and information leaked. That's why no one really uses them right now. From what I heard Caleb saying, Arailt has numerous Dark wizards specifically tasked with intercepting mirror communications of any form."

"You seem to know a lot for someone uninteresting, as you say."

She glanced up at him and caught a glint of a smile on his lips. "I, well, a lot of people come to talk to me about things. I hear a lot of things from Caleb and Camilla, actually. And at the *Dazed Knight*—"

"The tavern?" he raised a brow again, leaning forward. "You didn't strike me as the type to frequent there."

"I-I don't *frequent* there, per se. It's really the place where everyone goes to talk about things. That's actually where—" she paused and glanced up. Thomas followed her gaze, but no one stood out.

"What are—?"

"Oh, I hope he's alright." She jumped up out of her seat and rushed up to a burly looking knight. Thomas recognized him as the man he had met the night before, Geralt, was it? The man shook his head and pointed to another part of the infirmary. The simple cloth of the dividers set up to maintain privacy gently billowed as a rush of wind blew through the broken windows. Marta turned but Geralt grabbed her arm gently.

"Don't go over there alone." Geralt warned. "He's incredibly unstable and—"

"I'll go with her." Thomas interjected as he stepped forward, a hand on his sword. *What could possibly have this burly knight on edge like this?*

Geralt sighed. "Yer Majesty, that may no' be such a good idea…"

Marta had already started moving towards the room. Geralt lunged forward for a moment and then stopped and grumbled under his breath, "Lass has no thought in 'er— Marta!"

Thomas turned and casually walked over to the curtain behind Geralt. Marta was already inside the makeshift room, and he immediately noticed a badly injured man laying on a cot. He had bandages over his left eye, his arm was in a cast, and it looked like he had sustained a blow to the chest. A Water Healer was slowly working on him, his hands glowing a gentle blue, but he glanced up as the group came in. The Gifted's eyes widened when he saw Thomas.

"I, ah—!"

Marta knelt beside him and smiled reassuringly. "You're doing great, Leo. How is he?" She reached over and her hands started glowing with a beautiful golden sparkle. Thomas watched incredulously as the man's wounds slowly stitched themselves together with the golden light. The stranger's eyelids fluttered slightly as he groaned. Marta moved her hand and Thomas winced as she began to falter backwards. He reached forward and held her shoulders, his own hands glowing yellow for a moment. Marta gasped slightly as color returned to her face. She glanced up at the king with a bewildered expression.

"I, ah… learned that the Light Gifteds can sometimes impart energy to help when someone else's strength is running low," Thomas coughed slightly. Marta exchanged glances with Geralt, who shrugged, before beaming widely.

"Thank you, your Majesty."

She turned and continued her focus on healing the man. He coughed wretchedly and his eyelids flew open.

"Damned king!" he bellowed as he thrashed under the blankets. Geralt moved quickly to pin him down to the cot. "Let go a' me, we warned ye didn't we?! He told ye Mulligen was gone and ye were next but no, no one listened!" he thrashed and knocked Marta backwards. Thomas caught her quickly, a calm demeanor in his features. "Now Duncan's dead, me brother's dead! Damn the king—"

Geralt held the man down with a growl. "Shut up, y' fool! The king saved our lives, don't make me knock yuh back asleep just to shut y'up!"

The man struggled more before collapsing exhausted onto the bed with a cry. "My family, my Bennie… she's gone, she's gone… let me go be wit' her…" he covered his face and sobbed. Geralt breathed heavily and sat back, letting the broken man wail. Marta's eyes welled up with tears and Thomas stepped back, hand on his sword. His expression was grim.

Marta glanced back as Thomas excused himself from the room. She looked at Leo then Geralt, who nodded at her, and she stepped out after him. Thomas was quick and she had to run to catch him in the hallway outside the infirmary.

"Your Majesty!"

He didn't turn. She caught up to him breathlessly, grabbing the back of his shirt. "Thomas!"

He whirled around with a disgusted look. She took a shocked step back but knew in an instant he wasn't disgusted with her; he was disgusted with himself.

He looked out the amber stained glass window, his lips pressed together. "Surely you must see me for the worthless king I am."

"What?" she stepped back in shock. "You can't save everyone. How were we to know this would happen?"

"*I* knew," he growled, not looking at her. "And yet everyone told me it was a foolish mission to try to come here. It's because of my own hesitation we got here too late." He gripped his sword angrily. *I don't deserve to be king. I wasn't ready, I am ill-suited for this role!*

"You got here when God wanted you to be—"

"*God* gets a lot of things wrong, doesn't He?" he cursed, turning to face her. "All my life, that's all I've heard. 'God put you here for a reason', 'God will qualify you for your call', 'it's God's timing'—where was God in *this*?!" he motioned to the town outside the window, still smoldering. Martha followed his gaze mournfully. "Where was God in Mulligen, in Gardiel, in my father's death?! Forgive me if I fail to see the 'great goodness of God' in death and mindless destruction. All this, this carnage to find my future mate and wipe Elyon off the—" he clamped his mouth shut and rubbed the bridge of his nose in frustration. Marta's eyes were soft, yet filled with pain. She looked up at him slowly.

"When my parents died, I felt very much the same way. Why would God let my family be slaughtered so mercilessly?" Thomas wiped his face and looked down at her. Tears were streaming down her cheeks yet her voice remained steady. "Why would a God who is supposed to be good let so many bad things happen? I learned from a very wise friend that this world we fight against, in and of itself is not good. The Light came into the darkness, but the darkness did not understand it." She turned and faced the window, leaning against the windowsill.

"Whether we will follow Him or go our own way is the choice we each must make. And because of that choice, because of that sin, there will always be repercussions." She shook her head. "Arailt has chosen his path and he will do whatever he can to accomplish his goals."

"Then why," Thomas asked, his voice just above a whisper, "would a God who is all-powerful not stop this carnage?"

"In His way, He does." Marta shook her head. "Everyone living today is a testament to that. And what the Lord has planned for us will grow us and shape us into the people He wants us to be."

Thomas motioned towards the infirmary. "Then why would God allow any man's wife to be taken from him? What about his children, his family? Wouldn't that make Him weak?"

"I don't know all the answers, Thomas!" she replied in exasperation. She hesitated and glanced away. "Your Majesty. I've learned long ago that I may never get the specific answers to what I seek." She exhaled slowly. "Not on this earth, anyway. But I do know that God will answer them in His time, and although I don't like His timing, He has always shown me that it is far better than my own. What His plan is, what good will come out of this, I don't know. But I know that in the end, it will be good," she paused. "That's what having faith is all about."

"You sound like a Shepherd," Thomas sneered. Marta chuckled ruefully.

"Aren't any of those chosen by God Shepherds to some extent?" she asked quietly as footsteps came rushing down the hall.

"Your Majesty!"

They turned to see Jerome and Peter rushing along the corridor. Peter cast Marta an indecipherable glance before turning his attention to Thomas.

"We just received word from General Adrian. The southern forces have defeated Hylen's army. Arailt has retreated."

Thomas sagged heavily in relief. "How are the other battalions faring?"

"Similar situations, my Lord." Jerome nodded. "We still don't know what Arailt is planning, but for now, we have the upper hand."

Thomas nodded. "Bring the wounded soldiers back to Elroith. I don't want any mirror travel right now, we don't have enough strength of resources for that. Once we have finished rebuilding Ropheka we will travel home."

"Yes, Sir." The two commanders saluted and walked off. She was taken aback as Peter sneered at her covertly behind Jerome's back.

What's his problem?

Always disrespectful. Thomas groaned inwardly before turning back to Marta. She stepped back and took a breath before bowing.

"Thank you for allowing me to talk to you so freely, your Majesty." She stood up straighter and smiled. *That cursed smile,* Thomas grumbled. *How can she smile at a time like this?* His head shook slightly as he stepped backwards, a thought intruding his facade; *Gorgeous...*

"And thank you for sharing a little bit about yourself, too. Although I would like to know what things you *do* like," she chuckled slightly. "But... maybe that's for another time."

Thomas examined her slowly. Sure, she was beautiful, with long blonde hair and bright green eyes. She wasn't so thin as to question her health, but it was evident she had had several sleepless nights and a lack of appetite. Her smile, however, was nearly ever-present. What was it that made her so content? A sly thought eased its way into his mind, swelling his anger.

"...your Shepherd told you, didn't he," he rumbled low. Marta's smile faded, replaced by confusion.

"Told me... what?"

"Don't play with me," he scoffed. "You know about the prophecy don't you."

Her brow furrowed further. "Prophecy...?"

The familiar dark voice spoke to him again. *Her stupidity is insufferable.* "Forget it. Be in the main room tonight by six," he motioned to her pocket watch. "Make sure it is correct, royalty is very strict when it comes to timeliness."

He turned and stormed off, leaving Marta blinking in bewilderment.

CHAPTER FIVE

The World Ahead

Camilla's fingers moved purposefully as she meticulously punctured the white fabric in her hands with her sewing needle. The siblings' study was quaintly furnished, with comfortable chairs and rows of filled bookshelves. This section of the Tower had blessedly been spared during the attack, although she spent most of the morning cleaning up the debris elsewhere. She had dedicated a lot of time decorating this room with calming blues and neutral grays to lend a peaceful atmosphere whenever someone sought them out for advice. She winced as Caleb's incessant tapping wrenched her from her thoughts, causing her to prick herself with her needle. She quickly stuck her finger in her mouth and glanced up at her brother.

Caleb had a blank look in his eyes as he tapped his quill on his desk. A small black puddle had formed on the paper as ink gushed across the page. Camilla could smell the metallic liquid seeping through the paper and soaking the oak desk. She processed what was happening in an instant and set down her sewing to stand.

His tapping slowed and she paused as light flickered through his eyes. He blinked and his eyes cleared, focusing on her as she gingerly approached the desk.

"Oh, Camilla…. How long, this time?"

"Only a few minutes," she smiled painfully. Her hand glowed faintly and the ink collected itself back into the pen. She lifted a palm to Caleb's head as water pulled from the air around them to cool off his feverish skin.

"Thank you," he groaned heavily as he leaned back in his chair, staring intently at the desk. She stood there patiently, and after a few minutes he met her gaze.

"Ah need to speak to the king."

Camilla nodded knowingly. "Ah figured as much."

He rubbed his face and slapped his hands on his knees. Leaning up out of his chair, he grumbled and steadied himself with one hand. His chest ached and his muscles pulled, his breathing labored. It was a stark reminder of God's saving grace. He nodded to his sister and adjusted his wool cloak before stepping out into the hallway.

It didn't take long for him to find Thomas standing in the main doorway, speaking with Amaryll and Jerome. Amaryll nodded enthusiastically, bowed, and rushed out the door, her red cloak billowing behind. Jerome nodded as Caleb approached quietly.

"Good morning, your Excellency. General Jerome." Caleb inclined his head respectfully. Thomas turned, one hand on his sword, and nodded in acknowledgement.

"Shepherd, good morning. Has something occurred?"

"Not yet."

Thomas inclined his head in curiosity as Caleb chuckled ruefully. "Actually, your Majesty, may Ah speak with ye privately?"

Jerome glanced between the two men suspiciously, one hand on his sword. Thomas held up a hand to Jerome and nodded.

"Peace, General. Yes, Caleb, you may. Lead the way."

Caleb nodded and led him back to his study. Camilla was setting down a tray of tea things as they came in. She smiled, bowed politely towards Thomas, and quickly excused herself.

If this was simply a request for aid, he would have mentioned it outside. Thomas' mind reeled. *No, this is about me.* Alarm swelled in his chest and he sat in one of the chairs uncomfortably. *Did Marta tell him about my outburst earlier? I shouldn't have let my emotions get in the way, I have to be more careful—*

"Tea?" Caleb motioned as he sat with a grimace. Thomas could smell strong black tea with notes of berries wafting from the teapot. It looked like Camilla had brought cream and sugar to go along with it.

"Please." He shifted awkwardly and glanced about the tidy room as Caleb poured him a cup and handed it over. He took it gratefully and sipped. It was very strong and bitter, a very earthy tasting tea but it woke him up. He set the cup down as Caleb leaned forward and laced his fingers together on his desk.

"May Ah speak frankly, from one Light Gifted t'another?"

Thomas nodded slowly. "I appreciate any and all advice." *He seems sincere. I'm not sure I want to know what he has to tell me, though... I already know I'm a failure, I don't need to be reminded of it.*

"Ah can see that there is… turmoil amidst those closest to you."

The king paused and tipped his head to the side. "What do you mean?"

"What Ah mean is, Ah see a house divided. There are those who wish you well and will do what they are called to do to help you. Then there are those with…." he motioned as he struggled to grasp the right word, "…less than noble intentions."

Thomas set his cup on the table and shrugged nonchalantly. "It is only natural for a king to play politics, even within his own realm."

Caleb sighed wearily. "Not to this degree."

"Have you asked me here to tell me how I'm running the kingdom wrong, how I've committed some egregious sin that God is punishing me for?" he retorted blandly, although the anger rising in him told a different story. Caleb simply gazed at his king woefully, taking Thomas aback.

"My Lord, a house divided against itself cannot stand long. Ah can only imagine," he held his hands open, "that you keep those around who can benefit the kingdom, despite their intentions. Ah'm not here t' tell ye who or how, but it has been concerning to me." Caleb's eyes flickered with golden light. "After you spoke with me regarding Queen Rosa's prophecy, as well as what you heard God tell you, Ah've been seeking our Creator's wisdom. He revealed something to me and Ah wanted to encourage you."

Thomas's eye twitched as he settled back into the chair, folding his arms in exasperation. *I grow weary of prophecies. I will humor him but I don't want to get tangled up in something I don't—*

Caleb's eyes were steel, his normally bright hazel irises almost dull. He was so serious Thomas had to make a double take to be sure it really was the fun-loving Shepherd in front of him. Warmth poured over his head and he could immediately feel a presence in the room.

"You are both walking into a battle," Caleb began, "and depending on your choices, you will either walk out together or you alone, Lord Thomas, will walk away alive. Our Enemy has always held a special enmity towards Eve's daughters, but especially those with the Life Gift. After all, it was through the woman that our Savior was born and defeated Death. One of your duties as husband— and Knight— is to protect your wife, to guard her from our Enemy. With your decisions to embark upon this journey together, your enemies will become hers and her enemies *should* become yours." He leaned back in his chair and motioned towards the door. "Already there are those who oppose you who are opposing her as well."

Thomas flinched as he recalled Peter's boorish behavior towards Marta earlier. Caleb nodded slowly as if seeing his thoughts.

"He will not be the only one, Ah know you are all too familiar with those types of followers. Ah wanted to encourage you and," he held up his hand, "give you a word of warning. You *must* defend Marta. You are very much a part of her destiny as she is a part of yours. Arailt has already tried several times to eradicate her. You must be her bulwark."

Thomas eased into the back of the chair as he felt that familiar soul-satisfying warmth weeping onto his head and neck. He shook his head incredulously. *How can I protect her if I can't even protect my own people?* Realization settled deeply in his soul, darkness enveloping his heart as the despair he tried so feebly to hold at bay threatened at his door. Caleb's eyes immediately flashed with light and he lunged forward to put his hand on Thomas' shoulder.

"Holy Spirit, protect this man from the darkness threatening to envelop him. In Jesus' name let there be revelation and protection from the heavenly realm. Ah come against the forces of darkness looming over him and in Jesus' name command them to leave."

Thomas balked as the warmth he had observed earlier grew hot. It was like searing oil had started pouring over his head. Caleb prayed breathlessly, and Thomas couldn't quite make it out because of the roaring sounds in his ears and head. It sounded like he was speaking in a completely different language.

All at once, a weight on his shoulders shifted and slid off. His eyes widened and he had to steady himself. It felt like an old wound, festering and oozing, had been released. As Caleb's eyes opened he prayed, "let there be peace."

Thomas exhaled slowly as the very air around them shifted. He could abruptly smell the fresh crisp alpine wind from the open window, the sickly sweet smell of burnt wood from the homes in the street embedded in the breeze. The darkness that swirled around him constantly had dissipated, and for once he felt like he could stand tall.

Caleb leaned back and absentmindedly rubbed his chest where the arrow had pierced through the day before. Thomas haltingly shook his head.

"What...?"

Caleb wheezed faintly, yet his characteristic smile was plastered all over his face. "You certainly carry a battle around with you, my Lord."

Thomas opened and closed his hands distractedly. *I haven't felt this since before Father—* he clenched his fists. *After years of silence, I've felt You more in the last two days than I think I have my entire lifetime. Why did you abandon me??*

Why did *you* abandon *me*?

Conviction settled on Thomas' chest and he shook his head. Caleb chuckled ruefully as he took a sip of tea.

"Ah, Father, You have perplexing ways of handling things."

"Tell me, Shepherd," Thomas murmured low, his heart threatening to seep out of the box he kept it suffocated in, "after what you have seen, do you still think she should marry someone like me?"

His brutally honest question jolted Caleb. "Your Majesty… God doesn't call the qualified. He qualifies the called. While you both have a whole lifetime to learn what He has in store for you," he smiled warmly, "He will guide you both through it. You just need to trust and obey Him."

Thomas laughed derisively. "Trust. Just trust. I have trusted Him, Shepherd," his tone climbed higher as anger tugged at him. "What was I rewarded with? Death. Destruction," he motioned around, "Brokenness." Bitterness began to creep back in, locking its claws around his guarded heart. He could feel his throat closing up. "It sounds foolish to me to have a woman with no experience marry someone like me."

"Why, because she is not of royalty?"

"Because I am unbefitting of my role already and if I am not enough for my kingdom how can I expect to be enough for—?!" he clamped his mouth shut and lunged to his feet. He rubbed his face angrily and skulked to the bookshelf. Caleb sat there in bewilderment, yet his face twisted in pain for the broken man before him.

Oh, God, what horrors has he seen? What has broken him so? I pray You bring those alongside him to guide him through this turmoil! Protect him from the Enemy of his soul! Caleb beseeched inwardly.

Thomas rubbed the bridge of his nose, his face and neck hot with embarrassment. *That's the second time today I have said too much. I am only affirming what I fear.* He inhaled sharply and in so doing locked yet another layer around his heart. The torment sitting just under the surface was numbed yet again and he fought to regain his composure.

"Caleb, forgive me. I spoke out of turn. Should Marta make her choice, either way, I don't care." Even as the words left his mouth he struggled with whether he actually believed them or not. "We will present this to her tonight. I will hold no enmity towards her should she choose to stay here." He turned and indignantly walked to the door.

"Your Majesty-!"

Thomas opened the door and hesitated.

"Shepherd, did you or anyone else tell Marta about my mothers prophecy?"

Caleb stood behind his desk, concern etched in his features. He shook his head. "Nay, Milord."

He nodded absentmindedly and hastily closed the door behind him.

*****

Marta stood before the door to the main hall, her pocket watch in her hand. It was just a minute before six. She pocketed her watch, adjusted the white cloak on her shoulders, and took a deep breath. *I don't know why he was so severe with me... He must have a lot on his mind. Did something I say offend him? Was I wrong, God? If so, please correct me!*

The door opened and she stepped back in surprise as Peter nearly ran her over. He paused and looked her up and down.

"Ah. You."

Marta tried to smile politely. "Good evening, your Highness. How are—"

"Hmph." Peter turned and walked away, blatantly ignoring her. She sighed wearily. *Are you sure this is such a good idea, God?* She remembered her words from earlier as she pushed open the door, conviction settling on her chest. *Yes... I know. Your timing, not mine.*

Thomas sat at a table that had been set up after the room was repaired, with plenty of food set out. From smell alone she could tell the cooks had prepared a feast of vegetables, warm fresh bread, and a delicious stew with chicken and onion. Her stomach growled and she stifled a nervous giggle. Caleb and Camilla were there as well as Thomas' commander, Amaryll, and his general, Jerome. They glanced up as Marta shuffled forward.

"Ah, Marta!" Caleb grinned as he stood and enveloped her in a hug. He smelled like the woods, a familiar faint vanilla on his blue and white sash. She stepped back and smiled warmly.

"What's going on?" she asked quietly as Thomas spoke with Amaryll and Jerome. Caleb winked.

"Just a conversation. The king asked to meet with us to discuss some things."

"Some... things?" she murmured quietly as Caleb escorted her over. She sat next to Camilla and across from Thomas, who nodded at her solemnly before resuming his conversation.

I feel like I am back in my Tower interview. Everyone is so on-edge and official...

Thomas motioned to the rest of the table. "Please, start eating. Everyone who needs to be here is here."

Marta noticed Amaryll and Jerome glance at each other. It was obvious Peter had been removed from the dinner table. From his reaction, there had been a bit of an altercation before Peter left. Thomas nodded at Caleb and he led a prayer to bless the food.

"Father, thank You for the opportunity for us to gather here. Thank You for those who served and those who sacrificed everything to keep us safe. Please bless our leaders, give them wisdom and strength, and bless the hands that prepared this meal. In Jesus' name we pray, amen."

"Amen," everyone murmured. Dishes clanked and silverware scraped together as they passed plates around. It was strange, Marta was expecting Thomas to be served. She wasn't complaining, though; this was how she would normally have meals. She glanced up at Thomas, a pensive look on his face. He caught her gaze and looked away pointedly.

I definitely did something wrong...

"So, Marta," Amaryll broke the tense silence. "I hear that you enjoy sewing."

She nodded as she passed a bowl to Camilla. "Yes, ma'am. I don't sew very often anymore, but my mother taught me a lot of things when I was young. It's something to do when I want to work with my hands."

Amaryll and Camilla nodded understandingly. Jerome looked like something was bothering him greatly, so when the conversation changed, Marta leaned in to Camilla.

"Is everything okay? That general looks like he is going to be sick. Does he need anything?"

Camilla's gaze rested on Jerome for a brief moment before she smiled at Marta reassuringly. "They've been talking about a lot, lately, so I'm sure it's just the stress." She leaned back and feigned a smile. Marta frowned at her friend, knowing something was behind those words.

"Camilla, what's going on—"

Thomas tossed his silverware on the table and sighed heavily. Everyone jumped and glanced at him.

"This is insufferable. Marta, I brought you here for a reason, so let me get right to it." His blue eyes shone in the candlelight as he looked up. She glanced between the gazes turning her way.

"I apologize if I've done anything wrong…!" she replied worriedly. Caleb laughed heartily at that. Amaryll smiled fondly and Jerome looked like he had swallowed a frog.

"Ah, Marta. Y'didn't do anything wrong, my dear. He's talking about Queen Rosa's prophecy," Caleb grinned.

She blinked in surprise and turned to Thomas, who sighed in relief.

"Her Majesty's… prophecy?"

"Queen Rosa had a Light Gift," Camilla replied. "She was renowned specifically for her prophetic gift. God spoke to many through her."

"She gave one final prophecy as she lay on her deathbed," Thomas sighed as he pushed his food around the plate with his fork. "I can't say I remember it, unfortunately, but I do know it is true."

Marta's brow furrowed in confusion. Amaryll sighed.

"His Majesty lost some of his memory after the attack that took our queen from us. Before she passed, she said she had a vision of Thomas and his wife," she paused for a moment. "She said Thomas' bride would bear the Life Gift."

Marta's breath caught in her throat. Her face flushed but her ears turned red as she nodded. "Alright…"

"And," Jerome cleared his throat, "she said that it would be Thomas and his queen who would finally put an end to Arailt's reign."

Marta froze as realization dawned on her. "Wait… is that why Arailt has been hunting Life Gifteds?"

The group nodded solemnly. She glanced at her friends with a look of despair, feeling like she had been left out. Thomas rubbed the bridge of his nose.

"I am not just picking any Life Gifted I find," he warned, "but I… I heard God tell me that you were meant to be my wife." He finally looked directly at her, and she caught the red ever so slightly tinging his cheeks. Her eyes widened in surprise.

"So—so it wasn't just an exhausted delusion!" she gasped. Thomas raised a brow as Caleb and Camilla turned to her.

"What do you mean?" Camilla asked. Marta turned to her, her green eyes sparkling.

"After his Majesty brought me in here after the attack, I heard God tell me that I was—" she blushed profusely and glanced sheepishly at the other people around the table, "that I was... supposed to be his help-meet."

Caleb laughed and patted Thomas on the back. The young king had a bewildered look on his face.

"I—I didn't know if I had heard Him right, because it sounded so ridiculous that—"

"Marta, you of all people should know that the Lord works in very mysterious ways," Caleb grinned, turning to Thomas gleefully. "How's that for confirmation, yer Majesty? Not only did yer mother confirm it, but now you and Marta have heard Him as well."

Marta held her burning cheeks in embarrassment. *Is this really happening? I don't know if I can be a good queen... what about Peter? And the others? Would the kingdom be happy if he returned with me as his bride?*

Thomas sighed and stood as he leaned over onto the table.

"I know the amount of pressure this puts on you. If you are not comfortable with this, I understand."

Marta searched his eyes for a moment. In them, she could see his weariness and his confusion at the whole situation; yet as light crossed his pupils she saw a resolve she had not seen before. She felt a familiar comforting warmth flood her body and her hair stood up on end.

"If you will have me, your Majesty, I will do my best to serve you in whatever way I can."

Thomas blinked in surprise. He turned as Amaryll stood with a smile, followed by Caleb.

"That sounds like a resounding yes." Caleb smiled and winked at Marta, who nodded sheepishly. Thomas gazed at the young woman only three years younger than him and wondered what he was getting into. For a wife, she seemed eager to help and caught on quickly to things. Perhaps training her wouldn't be so difficult. However, there was the problem of her having a Life Gift in regards to his succession...

"Your Majesty?" Amaryll shook him out of his thoughts. He stood up straight and nodded.

"If you are sure, then I would like to be married here." Thomas replied.

"So soon?" Jerome croaked. Marta blushed profusely as Thomas nodded.

"I don't know what Arailt has planned knowing we destroyed his army here. Maybe he thinks the Life Gifted died, or he realized he failed and is planning something else. I don't know, and I would rather have *this* matter set in stone before we arrive home. As some have already reacted..." he glanced towards the door where Peter had stormed out, "I don't want there to be any discussion or disagreement. It won't be easy, Marta." He turned to her with a steely glance. "There is a lot of trouble with the war. There are assassins, Death Wizards, Seekers, Pseudonyms... other royals," he spat in disgust. She nodded solemnly.

"While I don't know what lies ahead, I am willing to weather it together."

He sighed and rubbed the bridge of his nose. *She has no idea how the castle works or about the risks, like being attacked in the middle of the night. The politics, the endless mind games, the danger of being queen--She is oblivious about the world she is willingly going into and yet—* He opened his eyes and saw her resolve burning in her bright green eyes, and he chuckled despite himself.

"So be it." He turned to Caleb and started making plans. "The army needs to return shortly, so we will have our ceremony tomorrow morning. I would prefer it to be a private affair to keep it as unnoticed for the time being as possible."

"May I please have Camilla there with me?" Marta asked softly, holding her friend's hands in hers.

"Fine, so be it." Thomas acquiesced and the group disbanded. Camilla giggled happily as they stood.

"I'm so excited for you! You're going to be a Queen!"

Marta paled but smiled in disbelief. *I only pray I can be a good one!* She turned as Amaryll took Marta's hands and smiled warmly.

"It will be so nice to have another Gifted One in the castle. I will teach you whatever you need to know about how the castle works, and I'm sure Nicodemus will help as well."

At her look, Thomas stepped over. "Nick is my advisor and the castle's Shepherd. He is currently running the country in my absence. Although, how well of a job he is doing has yet to be seen..."

"Ah, Nick!" Caleb chuckled. "I remember teaching him to be a Shepherd years ago."

Thomas nodded and glanced down at Marta. She had slight blue smudges under her eyes and he could see that a weight had settled on her shoulders. Yet, as she met his gaze, she smiled the same as she always had. It stirred something in him and he shifted uncomfortably as he held out his arm.

"I'd like to talk with you about a few things if I may. I'd like to see your home as well, if possible."

She bashfully took his arm and glanced away. "My home was destroyed in the attack."

He winced and sighed as he began walking. "Well, then, where is your favorite place to go that wasn't…?"

She nodded. "Go that way."

The odd couple strolled through the halls of the Tower, only a couple of Gifted Ones and Chosen Knights out and about. A few gave them curious glances, a few others smiled wide. Marta guided Thomas outside and behind the castle to the edge of the glacier lake. It was still light outside as they sat on a rock near the water. The pine trees shifted in the wind and the faint smell of vanilla drifted through the alpine air. It was woefully interspersed with the sickeningly sweet scent of burnt wood. Snow had settled on the gray peak above the lake, lending a chill to the evening.

"I used to come here a lot when I wasn't doing well in classes, or when I lost a patient," she fiddled with her fingers. "My mother would also bring me here sometimes, too."

Thomas nodded and gazed out over the small lake. The gray stone broke at the bottom of the falls, hundreds of years of erosion working their way into the cliff face. He looked back at her and a flash of light filtered through his eyes.

"I'm…sorry for how upset I got earlier. The stress has gotten to me and what happened yesterday was the last straw. I apologize you had to witness such a pathetic outburst."

Marta shook her head. "Thank *you* for trusting me enough to share that with me."

He cast her a sideways glance. *She's thanking* me?! He wrestled with that for but a moment before locking down again. *…she probably doesn't want to offend me by telling me the truth.* "On that note, I don't expect you to trust me right away," he swallowed hard as Caleb's warning suddenly rang in his ears, "but I will do everything I can to keep you safe."

Marta grinned. "You're saying you'll be my Chosen Knight!"

Her enthusiasm made him chuckle endearingly. "In a way, yes. I did receive some Knight training, though with a Light Gift it makes things a little… strange."

"I understand. Oh! Thank you for the apology."

He fidgeted uncomfortably, leaning forward and twiddling his thumbs. She chuckled inwardly at this very un-kingly display.

"Marta, I wanted to make a few things clear. I don't expect you to like me right away." He scratched his brownish-red beard awkwardly. Marta nodded slowly.

"Alright..."

"As such, I don't expect you to... be around me. A lot. Right away." She held her breath. "Oh...?"

He shook his head and rubbed the bridge of his nose. *Good, she's naive, I can just let it be. Perfect.*

Does he not want to be around me? She pondered, alarm rising in her chest.

"On the journey back to Elroith, it will be hard, of course, not to interact." *Why am I struggling so much? I'm a king!*

She laughed at that, her head tipping back slightly. Her laugh filled him with a strange sensation of warmth, yet he still felt wary around this strange —albeit strangely beautiful— woman. Her green eyes seemed to reflect the setting sun, mixing with gorgeous amber hues. An unsettling thought struck him now that he saw her in the waning light, *Do I really already fancy her that much?*

"I do appreciate the thought, but that's just another thing I expected. After all, we will be married starting tomorrow!" Thomas smiled lightly as Marta laughed in embarrassment. His smile dissolved into a frown.

"Your... Shepherd told me about your parents. If you don't mind me asking... why don't you have any more siblings if your mother was Life Gifted, as well? Everyone knows Life Gifteds are worse than rabbits."

Marta chuckled ruefully as she leaned forward, swishing her hand in the cool water. For some reason, this place always helped her open up about the things she kept locked away in her heart. She peered up at the frigid peak with a solemn expression. *It's only natural he wants to know more about me, and I don't really have anything to hide.* "My mother... had a severe injury shortly after I was born. There are some things even Life Gift abilities can't heal," she sighed heavily. "And sometimes, it's just not in God's plan."

Thomas gazed at her with a mixture of sadness and regret. Had he made her talk about too much too soon? Without thinking, he slowly reached out and took her hand. She let him, smiling fondly before returning her attention to the water.

They sat there for a few minutes listening to the birds calling to each other over the lake, the ripples lapping at the shore before them. Thomas released her hand and stood slowly, hoping he hadn't struck a nerve with her. "If you need to collect anything, I would recommend you do it now. We will leave tomorrow and make it to the outpost camp by tomorrow evening. From there, it is a several week journey by horseback to Elroith."

Marta nodded. "I just need my uniforms and a few changes of clothes. The only thing I have left is this," she held up her right hand, a golden ring sitting on her ring finger. It struck him that he hadn't noticed it before. "This was my mother's ring."

He gently took her hand and examined it. "It's certainly beautiful." An idea struck him but he hesitated as she looked up at him quizzically. A quiet, small voice in the back of his mind whispered to him and for once, he heeded it. "Marta, may I borrow this for a little bit? I promise I will give it right back."

She nodded and took it off, handing it over to him. He took it graciously and put it into his pocket with a smile.

"Let's get you back inside."

*****

The Next Morning

Marta stood at the door to the chapel in her white dress uniform. It was the only white dress she owned to constitute a wedding dress, with beautiful gold straps across the front and her dress cloak flowing behind. Overnight, Camilla and a few of the other women had taken the time to sew on a purple trim to the bottom of her cloak, denoting her new status as a royal. The door opened and Thomas stood up straight. Caleb took her arm, wearing his own white dress uniform, and walked her down the aisle. His snowy cloak was adorned with a gold trim, labeling him as an elder. As per usual, his blue and white tartan was sashed across his shoulder and chest. He also wore a kilt that matched with all the tartan of the Tower. He handed Marta over to Thomas, who stood there with a serious look on his face. He was adorned in freshly polished armor and a red tunic underneath. The golden crest of Elyon glittered on his chest plate, and his red cloak draped off his left shoulder. Caleb stepped around them and smiled.

"Ah never thought Ah would be performing a royal wedding, as quick as it will be," he winked. Marta and Camilla chuckled as Thomas sighed with a smile. Amaryll and Jerome sat behind them, whilst Peter leaned up against the wall in the back with a scowl and crossed arms.

"In the Scriptures, marriage can be described as a cord of three strands. A strand for husband," he motioned to Thomas, "for wife," he motioned to Marta, "and one for Christ. Independently, we alone are easily undone, but a cord of three is nearly impossible to break. No matter what life hurls at you, where He takes you or what happens, remember that He is always with you. Keep Him at the center of your marriage, and He will guide you through any storm or gale." Caleb smiled softly. "Together, you are not only partners but you are warriors fighting this fight together. Remember to lean on each other and learn to trust each other." He gently patted Marta's arm and she smiled. "Standing here before these witnesses, you are embarking on a new adventure. This adventure will last your entire lives; hopefully a very long time, God willing. This covenant is not to be broken. It is a serious commitment that both of you must work on together to cultivate. If you choose to accept these vows before Father, Son, and Holy Spirit, you may exchange rings."

Marta leaned back and took a ring from Camilla. Thomas blinked in surprise.

"How did you...?"

Marta smiled softly. "I was able to get one from the goldsmith. It may not fit, and may not be the best quality, but..."

Thomas chuckled. "That is fine. Here," he reached into his pocket and pulled out her mother's ring, freshly polished. Her eyes widened as he gently put it on her finger. She grinned and put the gold band on his finger as well. Caleb beamed.

"Before our Lord and these witnesses, Ah proclaim yeh husband and wife."

Thomas wrapped his hand behind Marta's neck and kissed her gently. To his surprise, she met his embrace. They stepped back to a smattering of applause. Out of the corner of his eye Thomas saw Peter leave the room, shutting the door behind him. Caleb patted him on the back with a full smile.

"May God bless you with a quiver full of children!" He laughed heartily at Marta's embarrassed look. He held her shoulders and smiled at his young friend. "Now, then, you have a journey to embark on."

Marta hugged her friend and mentor with tears in her eyes.

"Ah, blessed one, ye'll see me again. Whether here or in Paradise, you'll see me again." He kissed the top of her head and then stepped back. She nodded, trying to smile as tears rolled down her cheeks, wiping them away discreetly. She turned to Camilla, who stepped forward and hugged her close.

"Be blessed, my friend," she whispered, tears in her own eyes. Marta laughed.

"Go visit Geralt more often." Marta winked as Camilla's cheeks turned red.

"Oh, dear!"

Caleb's laugh bellowed through the room. "Let me know if you need anything, my dear." They walked towards the door as his expression turned a little more serious. "Godspeed, my Lady."

With that, Thomas guided Marta out the door. Bri and Isaac met them, dressed in their own Tower uniforms. It seemed someone had let the news slip and the entire force of soldiers, Gifteds, and Knights had assembled outside the Tower.

What struck Marta first was that everyone was bowing in respect. She paused with a blink, then looked up at Thomas, who nodded. "You'll have to get used to it," he murmured as everyone stood up straight. Bri rushed forward and gave her a hug.

"How exciting, your *Majesty*," she grinned. "I can't wait for you to experience what a bond feels like."

"A bond?" Thomas asked curiously as they stepped forward. Marta nodded.

"The bond formed between a Gifted and their Chosen Knight. The stronger the relationship, the stronger the bond. You can communicate without speaking, you can feel the other's pain, and you can locate them easier. From… what I have been told." She hesitated sheepishly.

"Interesting…" Thomas mused as he glanced away. A few captains saluted and crowded forward to give him information. Marta stepped back in surprise as Amaryll brought forward a beautiful brown mare. Thomas motioned to Marta.

"This is Maggie, and she is now yours."

"Maggie…" Marta leaned forward as she gently held out her hand to the mare. She sniffed Marta's hand before moving up her arm.

A Life Gifted One… Marta sensed Maggie thinking. She nodded with a soft smile.

"Yes, I am. I am pleased to meet you, Maggie. I know we will work well together."

It is my pleasure, your Majesty. Maggie shook her mane. Thomas glanced between the two before Camilla chuckled.

"It is a Life Gift ability to be able to speak to animals. Marta is not very fluent as some… were, but she knows enough to get by."

Thomas nodded and watched as Marta flicked her wrist. A carrot materialized with golden sparks in her hand and she fed it to Maggie, who took it gleefully.

"Are you ready?" he asked as the army began preparations to leave.

Marta glanced up at her husband— *husband!*—and nodded. He gently grasped her hips and lifted her into the saddle, making sure she got situated. He blinked in surprise. *I didn't realize women could be so… dainty.* He glanced over as Amaryll hefted herself onto her own saddle with ease. He stifled a laugh. *I guess it depends on the woman.*

Thomas took Maggie's reigns and helped guide her from astride his own steed. Marta turned around and waved, her friends standing on the hill in front of the Tower waving back. The horses hooves clopped against the familiar cobblestone streets, the stench of burnt wood and metal stinging her nostrils. Townspeople from all walks of life lined the road as the enterage slowly plodded through. She reached down and touched the hands of her friends, those she had spent her whole life with. Many waved and called out to her as they rode through, and it finally sunk in that she was leaving. She looked back again to see Caleb and Camilla still standing before the courtyard with Bri, Isaac, and other Gifteds and Knights. Homesick tears sprang to her eyes and she struggled to gain control of her grief.

"Oy, Marta!"

She turned to see Geralt standing on the porch of the *Dazed Knight* waving slowly. His smile was comforting, but the tears began streaming down her face when she saw him. A lump gathered in her throat and her chest squeezed tight. When he noticed and rushed over, he stopped next to the paused Maggie and held her hand.

"Now, Marta, chin up! We'll see ye again. Maybe next time ye'll have a wee bairn wit' yeh, eh?"

She sniffled through a laugh, wiping away her tears with her palms. He smiled warmly and patted her knee.

"Ye always had yer father's rashness to ye. T'wasn't *always* a bad thing!" he laughed. "Godspeed, m'dear. M'Lady!" he corrected and bowed. She wiped her face again, feeling her eyes and cheeks growing red and puffy from tears. Geralt handed her a clean handkerchief. As she blew into it, it had the familiar smells of vanilla, her favorite stew Geralt made with the potatoes, carrots and onions, and a hint of mead. She handed it back and he simply folded her hand over it.

"Keep it as a pitiful gift t'a dear friend."

She sniffled and held it to her chest. "Thank you."

He kissed her hand and patted Maggie's side. "A'right then, off y'go."

She waved as Maggie clopped forward, Geralt's sad smile never fading. She continued to wave until the last house—her house—disappeared from view. A quiet loneliness settled on her chest as she turned to face the road before her. Home, as she had known it, was behind, and a large strange world ahead, with its many paths and trails to tread. Amaryll smiled knowingly as Marta sobbed quietly, her heart mourning what had been. Thomas kept himself busy by conferring with Jerome regarding the troops, lending her some privacy.

God…You know the plans for my life, You have set out my story long before I was born. You saw this moment and knew it had to happen. I pray that You go before me, meet me in the places I need You most, stay close to me in the hills and the valleys. Protect my friends, Lord, and if it is Your will please let me see them again! She shuddered in a breath and blew her nose, dabbing at her soaked cheeks. A gentle warmth, almost unnoticeable, surrounded her and held her close.

They were soon past the farthest point she had ever been outside the village on foot. It was strange, the trees and rocks around her seemed familiar and yet she had never seen any of them before. They stopped for lunch halfway up the pass, and she could see the whole glacier valley and Ropheka in the distance. The sheer magnitude of the world she had lived in struck her. *And Elroith is more than ten times bigger than Ropheka! I can't even imagine!* She bit into a sandwich the townspeople had made for the army's journey and sighed. She never imagined a simple sandwich would be her wedding luncheon. She had dreamed about Camilla's tiny iced cakes stacked tall on a table. The familiar tastes of home wouldn't follow her, she would discover new things, yes, but maybe she could talk to the castle cook about Ropheka's recipes? Was that something she could even do as Queen, or would that be too selfish?

The gray peaks disappeared after they summited the pass and began their descent into another valley. Unfamiliar mountains loomed before them, trees stretching out as far as the eye could see. The ride was mostly silent as Thomas continued planning in hushed tones with his generals. Marta didn't mind since she had the opportunity to enjoy the new area, praying quietly about their future. By evening, they saw the lights from a camp up ahead on the road.

CHAPTER SIX

Cuppa?

Thomas slid off his horse and walked up to Maggie, holding out his hand. Marta took it gingerly and disembarked, her face turning red from the close contact with her new husband. The soldiers at the camp stood at attention as Thomas stepped forward.

He motioned downwards and they all shifted. Marta watched in awe as several captains came forward to talk to him.

It's so strange to see how everyone respects him. They're all in sync and waiting on his command. It must be a lot of pressure to have so many eyes on you... She pondered as she stood carefully by the horses. She twirled the gold ring on her finger and blushed again, the days' events catching up to her. *I can't believe just days ago I was wondering what I was supposed to do with my life, and now I'm married to the king!* She glanced around at the soldiers continuing with their duties. Some of them gave her curious looks but most just ignored her. She turned as Peter walked up to her.

"My... Lady," he hissed, venom laced in his voice, "the Knights are preparing a tent for you."

She watched as Thomas turned around, his gaze flickering between her and Peter. He held out his hand to her, and she nodded at Peter.

"Thank you, your Highness," she smiled genuinely and walked to Thomas. She could feel the hundreds of eyes watching them as he took her hand solemnly. He caught the glances of a few soldiers and cleared his throat.

"I... need to find you a captain."

"A captain?" Marta tipped her head to the side. Thomas laughed suddenly at her raised eyebrows and genuine confusion.

"Yes, a captain. For your Guard. Queens don't always spend their time in the castle, they have duties too. And I won't always be able to be around you to protect you. I may be your Chosen Knight, but I still have my own duties to care for. That's where the Queen's Guard comes in. They'll be able to protect you when I can't."

For some reason, that thought bothered Thomas. *What's the big deal? Sure, Caleb told me to protect her, and I will! Once we get her combat trained, I'm sure she can fend more for—*

Marta squeaked slightly as she tripped over a rock. Thomas didn't even budge as he caught her and helped her stand. *Or... maybe not.* A few soldiers nearby laughed under their breath, and he could feel her face flood with heat.

"Soldiers." They stood at attention at his fluid but stern voice. Thomas stared ahead. "Five laps around the camp. *Now.*"

"Yes your Excellency!" they sprang up and began their run. The couple walked to the command tent in silence. He pulled back the flap and escorted Marta in.

Finlay glanced up from the table and stood. His gaze rested on Marta for a moment before he looked back at Thomas.

"Yer...Majesty?"

Thomas shook his head as if reading Finlay's thoughts, tugging Marta around to stand next to him. She tried to stand tall but Thomas could tell she was afraid.

"Finlay, this is Marta... the Queen of Elyon."

Finlay's eyes widened as a scoff escaped his throat. Thomas narrowed his gaze as he shook his head.

"Y'... yer *queen*?" he asked in disbelief. Thomas nodded and looked down at Marta.

"Marta, I believe Amaryll will be joining you for dinner."

Amaryll blessedly appeared through the flap on the other side of the tent. She saluted and stepped forward with a smile, holding out her hands to Marta.

"Your Majesty, I'll escort you to my tent."

Marta nodded slowly and released her grip on Thomas' arm. She took Amaryll's outstretched hand and was whisked away by her new friend.

Finlay and Thomas stood in terse silence.

"Are yuh out of yer damn mind?!"

Thomas rolled his eyes and rubbed his face. "Yes, probably."

"Yer queen. *Queen.* Her?! Jus' what happened in Ropheka to make you—?" he reached up and put the back of his hand to Thomas' forehead. "Yer temperature's fine—"

Thomas smacked his hand away and walked around to the other side of the table. "I—I can't quite explain it to you right now, Finlay, but one thing I can tell you is that she's Life Gifted," he retorted, flustered. "Maybe the last one…" For some reason, "God told me to" felt too awkward to say outside of the Tower.

"S'what, because of one thing yer mum — God rest her soul — said years ago yer gonna marry anyone with a Life Gift that comes yer way?!"

"It's more than just that, Finlay. Would you trust me?! Amaryll and Jerome were there, it is legitimate, no I'm not bewitched, I just—" he threw up his hands and sat hard. He rubbed his face angrily. "I'm still reeling from it myself. I married her just this morning—"

"This *morning?!*" Finlay exclaimed. Thomas held up a hand and he rolled his eyes in response. "Oh, God help me."

"Look, Finlay. You can talk to Jerome and Amaryll about this. I don't have time to waste trying to explain this to you," Thomas grumbled. Finlay turned and held a hand to his head.

"What about his highness Peter? How does he—"

"Enough." Thomas stood and shook his head. "I told you, if you want to talk about this, speak with Jerome or Amaryll. If you will excuse me." He turned and stepped out of the tent. Finlay sat down hard, his eyes wide.

"What has gotten into him…?"

*****

Marta thanked Amaryll as the older Gifted One handed her a hot cup of tea. She took it and inhaled deeply.

"Wow, there's a lot of cinnamon in this." Marta grinned and carefully took a small sip. "Mmm, and lots of spice, too." It tingled as she breathed in, then sighed.

Amaryll smiled as she sat on the cushion across from her. "It is a special blend to help relieve stress. It's a calming tea."

"I can see why!" Marta chuckled as she sat the cup down on the table and sighed again. "Lady Amaryll, do you think… do you think I can be as good of a queen as Thomas needs?" she asked with a wince. Amaryll took a sip of her own tea and looked up reassuringly.

"I think that who *you* are is what his Majesty needs. He needs someone who is compassionate, yet not easily won over. Someone who is wise and willing to stay with him despite the circumstances."

Marta nodded slowly and looked down at her amber colored tea. She noticed the ring on her finger and stared at it solemnly.

"I feel like I'm in way over my head," she chuckled ruefully. "I don't know how to react around people, or how to interact either."

"That's what I am for, at least for the time being," Amaryll smiled. "Let's go ahead and start here. Do you know how a formal tea works?"

Amaryll stepped through the phases of a high tea, showing her how the different plates are sent out, in which order to eat the appetizers, how to pour tea without a drip, and so forth. As night fell and dinner was served, Marta was exhausted from all of it.

"And this is just *tea!*" Marta mourned as she held up a spoonful of stew. It tasted like the cook didn't know what to put into it, so they threw in whatever they could find. She could spend time identifying the various plants and things they had found but she *really* didn't want to think about it. "I can't imagine what else will be in store..."

"It is a lot," Amaryll agreed, "but you're already learning quickly. While on the road I can teach you formalities and other sorts of etiquette. I'm sure his Excellency can teach you history and defense."

"Defense?" Marta tipped her head to the side, her eyebrows raised. Amaryll laughed.

"Yes, of course! Despite his Majesty being your Chosen Knight and whoever you pick to be your captain, you still need to learn how to defend yourself. Many noblewomen have met their demise simply because they didn't know how to move out of the way!" She shook her head in disdain.

Marta grew quiet as she watched lanterns move past the tent. "Amaryll..." she lowered her voice just above a whisper, "can you tell me what happened with Queen Rosa? I have been told she died because of a Dark Wizard, but no one really knew what happened. Or they didn't want to tell me..."

Amaryll hesitated before setting down her cup. "Well... it was almost eight years ago now. Queen Rosa and King Martin had been on the battlefield against Garchuk, an old kingdom that had attacked the dwarves."

"Dwarves?!" Marta blinked in surprise. "I thought they didn't like humans!"

"Some don't," Amaryll paused thoughtfully, "but most do, actually. King Garchuk was a horrid king who had been given a Light Gift. When he turned to Darkness, his whole kingdom fell. He commanded a legion of dark soldiers and tried to force the dwarves into slavery to mine Ela ore for him to use in weaponry."

Marta shook her head. "I had heard dwarves had an uncanny ability to sense and locate Ela."

Amaryll nodded. "That is correct. And where there is Ela, there are usually several Mordiern crystals, as well." She chuckled at Marta's expression. "I'm not surprised you haven't heard of it. Mordiern feeds off of energy, thus its close proximity to Ela. It is outlawed in almost every kingdom since it is mostly used to negate the abilities of a Gifted One. It is incredibly rare, though, thankfully. And of course, since we get our gifts from God and He has already won the battle, Mordiern can be overcome. Just... not by our own power. We have confiscated metal cuffs inlaid with Mordiern that Arailt used to capture Gifteds and interrogate them."

"That... is terrifying," Marta exhaled slowly.

"It certainly can be, and you can understand the risk of failure. King Martin and Queen Rosa, who were allied with the dwarvish kingdom, went to battle over it. It was there that Queen Rosa sustained a horrific injury laced with such powerful dark venom even she could not overcome it." She glanced at her hands sadly. "She was brought home but perished merely a week later. The king was beside himself. Life, Water, even other Light Gifteds all tried to heal our Lady, but to no avail."

"You mentioned that Thomas had sustained memory loss during the attack?"

Amaryll nodded slowly. "Thomas was fourteen and therefore at the battle with them. The king wanted Thomas to experience war firsthand as a deterrent so he would know how costly and dangerous it could be. He was not anticipating the death of his wife nor a near fatal blow to his son. As Garchuk lay dying he loosed one final blow and it caught Thomas on the side of his head. They brought him home thinking he would be alright, but after Rosa passed away he collapsed. He was in a coma for weeks but blessedly, he came through. He has no memory of that battle nor what occurred afterwards."

Marta rubbed her arm with a mournful look on her face. "I never saw my parents die, but just knowing they were gone took such a huge toll on me. I can't even imagine watching your mother die like that... and having your father die too!" Her eyes welled up with tears. *He has so much on his shoulders, how has he not been crushed by its' weight?!* The thought struck her and she had to pause to fully realize the implications… *I must help relieve him of at least some of that burden.*

Amaryll nodded again and glanced around. She motioned Marta closer and whispered in her ear. "I believe it is Arailt who murdered King Martin, although there is an ongoing investigation regarding that. King Martin was found in his room and the soldiers who were with him report watching him slit his own throat."

Martha swallowed hard, feeling queasy. Amaryll shook her head and leaned back.

"I know our king. Too many unknowns surround his death, but one thing's for sure, it was foul play," she groaned. "But that is just my theory." She opened her mouth to speak but hesitated. "I… apologize. I have said too much."

Martha nodded slowly. "I wonder… if metal cuffs can be made to feed off someone's strength, wouldn't a combination of the Ela and the Mordiern create some sort of effect?"

Amaryll blinked in shock. "Marta… I had never thought of that. I always assumed that Mordiern canceled out the effects of Ela, and we didn't find anything like that on King Martin's body…"

"But if they can hone it a certain way and refine the Ela, it would be possible, wouldn't it? We use Ela to communicate or transport with; what if, in this case, the Mordiern affected the Ela and that, in turn, affected King Martin somehow?"

Amaryll's jaw dropped. "The dwarves use Ela in weaponsmithing. Numerous factions have been enslaved by Arailt, perhaps he forced them to discover—" She turned and frantically went through her bags. She snapped and several candles around them lit, providing more light. She pulled out a leather notebook and a pen and began writing.

"You use those new fountain pens?" Marta asked after several moments. Amaryll glanced up at her and nodded before continuing to write.

"I'm not so old-fashioned that I don't keep up with the times. His Majesty and Nick prefer to use quills, they say it's much more fluid. I prefer the ease and containment of a pen." She finished writing and smiled. "Marta, I think you just made a breakthrough in this investigation. I will give this information to Nick as soon as I can." She wrapped up her notebook and grinned. "Oh, your tent should be ready! Let me take you there."

Marta stood and followed Amaryll out the door. The camp was still bustling with activity; she could hear the clanking of armor as soldiers patrolled around and the voices of men and women alike. It smelled musky and sweaty, but the cool air brought with it the faint sickness of the destruction in Ropheka. Amaryll nodded to a few soldiers sitting around a fire as they passed, embers popping in the air.

It's actually getting chilly… Marta mused as she pulled her thick cloak around her. Amaryll paused when they got to an empty spot.

"That's strange, it was supposed to be right—"

"Ah, Lady Amaryll!"

The pair turned as a young woman dressed in the blue Tower uniform stepped forward. In the dim light, Marta could make out the red trim at the bottom of the woman's skirt, denoting her with a Fire Gift.

"I was just sent to come find you. His Majesty requests that you bring the Queen to his tent." The young woman gazed at Marta for a moment, who nodded in reply. She smiled warmly and turned her attention back to Amaryll. A Knight stepped forward from the darkness and Marta realized he had been standing there the whole time. *He must be her Chosen Knight, I barely saw him!*

"Alright. I will take you to him." Amaryll turned and started walking towards the northernmost part of camp. Marta spotted a slightly larger tent than all the rest, but not so grand as to dominate everything around it. Two soldiers wearing slightly different armor stood on either side of the tent's door.

"Your Majesty, I have brought my Lady." Amaryll spoke as she grinned at Marta.

"Thank you, Amaryll. You may come in, Marta."

She nodded at Amaryll in parting before the soldiers opened the flaps of the tent for her. Both stared straight ahead, and she felt a little timid going in.

The tent was dimly lit with candles and a desk had been set up on the left hand side. Thomas sat there scribbling away with his quill. He finished and glanced up.

"Ah, Marta. I apologize for the surprise. I wasn't comfortable with how far away they were putting you, so I had a bed made in here." He turned back to his papers. She glanced down and saw two bedrolls stuffed with hay, one on one side of the tent, one in the middle. She rubbed the back of her neck and chuckled slightly. A privacy screen had been set up on the far side of the tent to change behind, and several trunks sat around the edge. She spotted hers at the end of the bedroll by the side of the tent farthest away from Thomas' desk and walked over. She took off her cloak and set it down gently before retrieving her nightgown from the chest.

"Did you have enough to eat?" Thomas asked absentmindedly as he continued writing. Marta glanced over at him and smiled.

"Yes, I did. Thank you my Lord."

She stepped back behind the screen and shrugged out of her uniform. She gently laid the white jacket on a chair, folded the cape, and took off her skirt. The petticoat came off next, followed by the corset. She shrugged into her nightgown with a shiver. *It's actually really cold, but I don't want to ask him for a blanket.* She gathered her clothes and stepped out. Thomas was still at his desk, dutifully writing whatever it was he was focused on. She snuck over to her bed and knelt down to put her clothes away.

She heard his scribbling slow down for but a moment before picking up again. She turned and saw Thomas leaning on his hand, facing away from her. She put her things away as quickly as possible and spread her cloak over the bedroll before climbing in. She fell asleep surprisingly quickly, exhausted and sore from riding all day.

Thomas glanced over at his wife, the blankets rising and falling gently with each breath she took.

I can't believe I looked. He groaned slightly and put the quill in its stand and rubbed his face, unknowingly smearing ink across his cheeks. *I barely know her. Yes, she's my wife, but I don't know her that well! Why are my thoughts immediately going to—* He blinked as he heard blankets rustling. He glanced over and noticed she was curled up into a ball, shivering. *You should've said something if you were cold.* He quietly stood and grabbed a blanket from one of the chests, bringing it over and gently draping it over her. Her shivering slowly stopped and he could hear her breathing still.

Ask me next time. He shook his head and returned to his desk.

*****

Marta knew she was dreaming when she glanced around the fuzzy scene, yet the roars in her ears felt anything but a dream. A dark figure stood before her, his face unseen, but she was frozen in terror. Death exuded from his very being, tendrils of darkness wrapping themselves around her every time she looked at him. She felt them crawling up her leg, crossing her belly, creeping up to snag her throat. She couldn't move as the figure laughed. She gasped for air as her throat suddenly released as the scene changed. She recognized Thomas standing in front of her. She watched in horror as a blade crossed his shoulders, and he fell to the side. The terrifying figure from before stood there with a malicious grin as Thomas' head rolled. She opened her mouth to scream, but nothing could come out. The figure reached for her and she jerked backwards and fell.

A blurry, rainy Ropheka greeted her. At her feet were Caleb and Camilla, their lifeless hazel eyes staring at a bleak sky. She looked up to see the bodies of her friends, of Geralt, Bri, Isaac, Amaryll, and others, all stacked in a bloody heap.

She woke up with a start, the tan tent wall greeting her. Blinking slowly, she reached up and touched her puffy cheek, wet with tears. Her chest felt hollow and her stomach lurched. She groaned slightly and rubbed her face. Her head was fuzzy and she felt groggy. She sat up slowly, painfully glancing around.

The tent was still quite dark, she could just make out her breath condensing in front of her. She heard something shift and glanced over as Thomas stared from his bedroll, eyes wide.

"Are you okay?" he whispered quietly, his voice deep. She hesitated before nodding.

"I didn't mean to wake you up," she whispered back as he sat up and rubbed his face, scratching his beard. He shook his head and yawned.

"It's alright. I was awake anyway." He sat there for a moment as if willing himself to get up.

Even kings have bad mornings, hmm? She chuckled inwardly as he started to take off the covers, then paused.

"Marta, would you mind turning the other way?"

She blinked and turned slowly when the realization dawned on her. She covered her face as it burst into color. *And I just walked in front of him in my nightgown last night without a thought! Oh my goodness...*

He stepped out shortly thereafter from behind the screen, tucking in his shirt. He didn't look her way as he walked over to the desk.

"Ah, if you'd like to, you can..." he motioned to the screen without sparing her a glance. She rushed over and eventually stepped out in her Tower uniform. To her surprise, Camilla had also added the purple trim just above the white trim on her skirt. She shook her head fondly.

You're too good to me, Camilla. Homesickness tugged at her, and she made the effort to shake off her nightmare.

After donning her cloak Thomas guided her outside the tent. The early morning light was barely creeping in to the faded gray sky.

Everything was covered in mist, the tall pine trees disappearing into the low clouds. The air smelled wet and crisp with ice. Several guards walked by on patrol and two soldiers, different from the previous night, stood beside the tent. They nodded in respect as Thomas guided Marta out.

She glanced around. "It's so quiet…"

"The soldiers prefer to stay up late than wake up early," Thomas groaned quietly as they started walking. Barely anyone was awake, but she noticed several Knights on patrol. They nodded politely and continued on their way.

It's actually quite peaceful.

Thomas opened the door to the command tent and she stepped inside. Jerome was already there, a hand on his dark gray-flecked beard. He glanced up as the pair came in and nodded.

"Your Majesties. Good morning."

"Good morning, Sir Jerome," Marta smiled quietly. For once, Jerome smiled back.

"What's the news?" Thomas asked firmly, his demeanor changing immediately. Jerome nodded and gestured to a few of the pieces on the map. Marta's eyes grew wide. Elyon was a huge country, encompassing most of the northern mountains. It had a few ports that provided access to the ocean through the fjords on the eastern side, but otherwise, Elyon was rugged and wild mountain country. To the west lay the kingdom of Hylen where Arailt ruled. It was surprising to her how close the kingdoms were to each other, yet it also made sense. Elyon was teeming with produce farmed in the fertile calderas and soil between the mountains. Fauna was plenty here and Elyon was known for its Ela mines. To the far north, Marta could see another kingdom, Rodenheim. Her eyes widened further when she realized it was a dwarven kingdom.

"Arailt has retreated. We caught a great number of his army at the border, yet there are still several passes and mine shafts we have yet to uncover," Jerome pointed. "He's gone quiet since the attack on Ropheka."

"What of the status of his armies?"

Jerome shook his head. "We never did get a solid count on the full strength since he kept several regiments within his own borders. We do know, however, that with the battle at Gardiel we dealt a significant blow. We have been unable to locate any outposts within our borders."

"Is that because there are none left, or because we have so few of our own left?" Thomas grumbled. Marta stood awkwardly as she listened in.

He's taking it so hard. I would, too, though, to be fair. Those men and women have families. And since he's seen war firsthand for so long…

"I believe, then, the best course of action is to return home. I want to make sure Marta is safe. She must begin her studies."

Marta glanced up at Thomas, who had a pensive look on his face. He smiled distractedly and turned back to the map. Anyone else would have thought he was dismissing her, but for some reason, she sensed he was being genuine.

"I agree," Jerome nodded, turning to Marta. "My Lady, we will be coming up on a town in three days' time. I will gladly accompany you to the weaponsmith to pick out a suitable piece for you to train with. I would also suggest you watch the Knights and soldiers practicing, you may be able to find a suitable captain for your Guard there. I have a few recommendations, if you would allow."

"Thank you, commander," Thomas remarked absentmindedly. Marta simply nodded appreciatively, not sure what to say.

CHAPTER SEVEN

The Pseudonym

Marta flinched as a Knight fell back into the mud, the victor walking over and helping him stand with a pat on the back. The warm air was permeated with sweat and musk, the lush mountain meadow covered in mud from the afternoon rains.Thomas chuckled from his spot next to her.

"They know we are looking for a captain for you. Anyone who isn't chosen as captain may get the opportunity to be a part of the Guard, so either way, they're trying to do their best." He shook his head and laughed derisively. "If only they'd try this hard during battle practice…"

Marta fidgeted under the hot sun, adjusting her stays discreetly. She could already smell herself, although, she wasn't nearly as potent as some of the men around them. *I've been watching them for three days, just like Jerome said. But I don't even know what to look for!*

"Your Majesty," she turned to see Jerome bowing behind her. "If you are ready, I will accompany you to the blacksmith."

She glanced up at Thomas, who nodded and frowned. "You don't need my permission to do everything, Marta. You're Queen now."

"I know, but…" she fidgeted awkwardly.

"My Lord, she is new to royalty and how things work. She also probably doesn't understand what she can or cannot do now that she is your wife. Forgive me if I'm wrong, my Lady." He bowed again. Marta shook her head emphatically.

"No, you're exactly right."

Thomas scratched his beard in thought. "Very well. For now, don't let them know you are my Queen. This blade you purchase will just be used for practice, I will have one made specifically for you once we get home. But," he glanced lazily at Jerome, "do make sure it is of good quality so it doesn't break easily."

"Yes, Milord."

Marta took Jerome's arm and he led her to Maggie. They were soon off, riding with a group of Knights and Gifteds to town. Thomas watched her go and sighed.

It's only been a few days and I still don't know much more about her. Although, I have been busy... He rubbed his face, thankful for the mental distractions from his wife. Movement in the corner of his eye caught his attention, and he watched a dark figure move between two tents.

Oh? His eyes flickered with light as a suffocatingly malevolent presence exuded from where the figure had disappeared. *How did I not notice...* He stepped forward and unsheathed his sword.

*****

Marta stood, mouth agape, at the numerous blades and weapons lining the walls. Some of them had sinister curves whilst others looked like a long metal toothpick. Jerome stood at the counter examining different one-handed swords.

These blades... they are all so different! Marta glanced down at a dagger sitting next to its' jeweled sheath. It was small and dainty but looked incredibly sharp. The jewels inlaid on the hilt sparkled, the base color a gentle blue. When the light hit it, however, it seemed to sparkle and change color. She gasped when she realized it was made with Ela. The weaponsmith's wife walked over with a smile.

"It's very beautiful, isn't it?"

Marta nodded slowly. "It's exquisite!"

"Would you like to hold it to test its' weight?"

Marta glanced sheepishly at Jerome, but he was busy talking about metal qualities with the weaponsmith. She nodded slowly and the woman picked it up and handed it to her.

The hilt was fairly heavy, just enough to balance. It fit well enough in her hand, although the leather wrapping did sit uncomfortably.

"Here," the woman took the knife, examined Marta's hand, then rebound the hilt with the leather. After a few minutes, the dagger fit perfectly in her hand.

"Lovely..."

"Ah, that is a fine dagger, Milady, with Ela to boot!" Jerome exclaimed from behind. Marta glanced up to see him smiling at her. He turned to the weaponsmith. "How much for both the sword and the dagger?"

The smith listed off some ridiculous number that made Marta's blood curdle. She began to set the dagger down gently when Jerome simply laughed.

"You're trying to swindle an old man, eh?"

"Well, the lady does seem to like it, so I'll take it down a few hundred."

"Deal."

Marta's cheeks burned with heat as Jerome tossed a bag of coins onto the table. The smith counted them quickly, then handed a couple of coins back.

"You overpaid. Here you go."

Jerome raised a brow before the smith glanced over at Marta who was fondly, albeit guiltily, holding her beautiful dagger. Jerome laughed.

"My Lady, don't worry about it. Your husband expressed that no expense is too much. Although," he cast a sideways glance at the smith, who smiled sheepishly, "some things are more expensive than others. Your honesty has given me confidence in your store, sir, and I will be sure to shop here again." He took the dagger from Marta and showed her how to put it on her belt. One of the Knights who accompanied them held a long bundle wrapped in fabric.

"Is that my sword?" she asked meekly as they stepped out of the store. Jerome grinned wide.

"It is indeed. I would show it to you, however, I want his Majesty to examine it fi—"

A haggard Knight came running up to them and wheezed, "Commander, there has been an attack—"

"How many and where?" Jerome's eyes took on a seriousness that made Marta shudder. But if the camp had been attacked, was Thomas okay?

"Just one, and they have been—" the Knight's gaze flickered between Marta and Jerome, "—taken care of. His Majesty wanted us to escort you back in case there were any more."

Sure enough, a regiment of soldiers rode into town, causing the townspeople to glance at each other nervously. Jerome nodded and turned to Marta.

"My Lady, please, come with me." He held out his arm and Marta took it. She looked at the Knight with a steely pause.

"Is his Majesty safe?"

The Knight nodded. "Yes, milady. No casualties. No injuries, either. A soldier named Wesley took care of the threat."

"Wesley..." Jerome paused. "He is one of my captains. He is an excellent swordsman. I am not surprised he was the one to..." his gaze landed on Marta for a moment. "Hmm. Let's head back, with haste."

He helped her mount Maggie and she adjusted her dress as Jerome mounted his own steed. They rode back at a faster pace than she was used to and it jostled her in spite of the urgency. Her legs and back screamed in protest and Maggie shook her head. *I am sorry...*

"It's alright, Maggie," Marta groaned. "I need to get used to this..." They soon emerged into the camp, and from her spot on the horse, she could see a group of soldiers and Gifteds standing around looking down at something. Jerome helped her dismount and they hurried over. As the soldiers parted, she saw blood splattered on the wall of one of the tents and gasped as Jerome forcefully stepped in front of her.

"Are all of ye mad?!" he cursed thickly as he abruptly turned to Marta. "Your Majesty, this is not a sight befitting of a lady. Let me have Amaryll take you—"

She shook her head. "I want to see it."

Jerome blinked, as did a few of the other soldiers. He stood up straight. "You don't have to, you have already proven you—"

She took in a deep breath. "I may have a Life Gift, but if I don't get used to death sooner or later, how can I help Thomas during battle?" To be honest, she already felt incredibly queasy and weak, and she wasn't even near the body yet.

"My Lady—"

"It is the Queen's choice."

They turned to see Thomas step forward, blood splattered on his face. He wiped it off with a towel and motioned for Marta to step forward.

A grotesque being laid sprawled on the ground, his head completely missing. His skin was mottled and gray, and he had claws for fingers. A young soldier stood there, his tunic still drenched in blood. His fiery red hair was pulled back behind his head in a ponytail and his eyes were closed. He opened them slowly, his green eyes fierce.

"Yer Majesty," he kneeled as Marta stepped forward. His accent was thick, very similar to Geralt's. Thomas put his hand under her elbow in case she fell over as she examined the scene.

"It looks like a demon," was all she could muster. Thomas sighed.

"That's because it mostly is one. Whoever this man was before, there isn't a hint of him left. They're called Pseudonyms, not quite humans anymore but not a demon either. Arailt frequently uses—and re-uses— the empty shells of his deceased subjects to do his bidding. This man's soul died a long time ago."

She shook her head and covered her mouth, feeling queasy.

"Don't worry," Thomas whispered in her ear, "cutting off the head is the only way to stop them from coming back. We will give him a proper burial in memory of his past self. This is just a shell, his soul is long gone."

Marta nodded slowly as tears welled up in her eyes. She looked up at the soldier still kneeling there. "Are you Wesley?"

The young man looked up, one hand over his heart, and he nodded. "Yes, m'lady."

Familiar warmth crept up her spine.

This is your captain.

She paused and blinked in shock. She nodded to the young soldier and leaned up to whisper something in Thomas' ear. His eyes widened and he glanced down at Wesley, examining him.

"I believe that would be a wise choice." Thomas unsheathed his sword and handed it to Marta, who took it with a puzzled look. It was extremely heavy and she nearly dropped it. Thomas held her hands gently until she was able to get a firm grip on it, blushing profusely. Wesley glanced between the two in surprise while Jerome stepped forward with a grin.

"Marta, repeat after me," Thomas said as his gaze rested on Wesley, still kneeling with wide eyes. "I, Marta, Queen of Elyon,"

"I, Marta, Queen of Elyon," she repeated, "Commend your services as a soldier within the ranks of our great army. From this day forward, I dub thee Sir Wesley, and, should you so choose, put my life into your hands as the captain of the Queen's Royal Guard."

A cheer went up as she tapped Wesley's shoulders with the sword. His freckled face burned red, and he looked up at her solemnly.

"'Tis too great an honor t'bestow upon someone th' likes o' me!"

The pair glanced at Jerome as he stepped forward.

"Actually, Wesley, I was about to recommend you to her Majesty for this very purpose. Of anyone here, you are the most capable— and deserving— of this honor. You have my blessing. Guard her Majesty well." He patted Wesley on the back. Marta smiled warmly up at

Thomas, who gave her a slight wink in return.

*****

Thomas grumbled as Marta's sword tumbled across the grass and *plunk*ed in a creek. Marta stood there sheepishly, watching the whole affair as she opened and closed her now-empty hand.

"I, ah…"

"You need a better grip," Thomas conceded with a sigh as he retrieved her sword and dried it off. She stood in a puffy white shirtwaist and brown high-waisted skirt, her face blazing with embarrassment and skin flushed from the exercise. Several days had passed since the incident with the Pseudonym, and Thomas had quickly begun her swordsmanship lessons. Today they had been training for hours and she could tell he was quickly becoming impatient.

"I thought I did…" she mourned. Thomas stepped forward and behind her, positioning her hands.

"Like this. And don't be so stiff." He kicked her feet apart and wrapped his arm around her, holding her right hand and placing her sword in it. "Too loose, and the sword will leave your hand. Too tight, and you run the risk of shattering your wrist."

Thomas didn't even notice Marta's ears turning deeper red as he adjusted her stance. As he leaned over, he caught a whiff of her hair. It smelled like a mixture of soap and rosewater, very lightly scented but enough to break through the smell of sweat and mud.

She smells really nice…

"Th-thank you…" she stammered. He blinked in response.

"What?"

She blushed breathlessly as she turned to look up at him, her face mere inches from his. Her green eyes flickered with golden light. "I washed it this morning…"

Thomas blinked and stepped back. "I… didn't say anything."

Marta blinked as well before her eyes widened. *We're bonding!*

He raised a brow. "Talking without speaking? How strange."

"No, no, Thomas!" she lowered her sword, sheathing it clumsily. "Part of the bond is that… is that you can hear the others' thoughts and sense their emotions. Strongly bonded Gifted-Knight pairs can even communicate up to great distances!"

The King shook his head incredulously and they both glanced over as Amaryll cleared her throat.

"Pardon the intrusion, your Majesties, but I couldn't help but overhear your conversation. Marta is right, if you are hearing each other's thoughts that means you have begun the bonding process. It is reserved for a Gifted One and their Chosen Knight, and it cannot be reversed or revoked. Unless one dies, but... that's an unusual occurrence, since most Gifteds and Knights die the same time their spouse does." Amaryll suddenly had a far-away look in her eyes. "That's the downside of the bond. That, and feeling the other's injuries."

Thomas had a disgusted look on his face. "I don't see any benefit to this."

"It's incredibly useful, since no one else can hear your communication. You will also know if Milady is hurt."

He glanced at her, then turned up his nose. "But what about when she gives birth?"

Amaryll snorted as Marta's cheeks turned a deep crimson again and the grass underneath her feet grew. Thomas had a blank look on his face as he glanced between the two women.

"I'm serious."

"You can—" Amaryll laughed harder, then pulled out a handkerchief to dab at her eyes, "You can purposefully subdue the connection temporarily."

Marta squeaked and held her face, flowers beginning to bloom at her feet. *This is so embarrassing!*

What? came Thomas' incredulous thoughts. *It was a valid question!*

Marta didn't look up as Amaryll walked over to the pair, chuckling under her breath. "Alright, I think that's enough for the poor lady today. Besides," she motioned to the east where a storm was building above the mountains, "the afternoon rain will begin soon."

Wesley stepped forward, one hand on his hilt. Jerome and Finlay were there too, surprisingly. They had waited patiently for their meeting with the king. Thomas nodded at them and turned to Marta.

"I will be in a meeting for most of the evening, please feel free to do whatever you wish." He turned away, a confused expression on his face.

I never thought I'd become so close to— as if something had snapped, his thoughts immediately left her mind. She watched him walk away.

It doesn't go very far, does it? Not yet, anyway. She shook her head and kicked at the flowers underneath her as Wesley stepped forward, handing her a cloak and some water. *If he can hear my thoughts, I'm going to have to be really careful! What if I say something offensive? Oh no, do I want to know what he thinks of me?!* Her mind whirled with questions as they followed Amaryll to her tent to continue her seemingly endless lessons on etiquette.

*****

Peter scowled as he stared at the map, chewing on his finger. The tent flap opened and he glanced up as Thomas, Jerome, and Finlay entered. He nodded to Thomas before returning his gaze to the map.

"What is the status of the military?" Thomas began, going around the room. Jerome gave a good report whilst Finlay exchanged a glance with Peter.

"General Finlay, have you any news on the Pseudonym that infiltrated camp?" Thomas asked in a low voice. Finlay turned his attention to his king and shook his head.

"Nay, m'lord. We cannae tell if he was simply a leftover from a previous attack, or got lost."

"Arailt's creatures do not simply 'get lost'." Jerome scoffed. "He must have been a scout."

"Or an assassin," Peter postulated. The group glanced at him in surprise and he shrugged. "Arailt has eyes everywhere, I wouldn't be surprised if he has heard about your wife by now."

Thomas narrowed his eyes but didn't take the bait. "I want camp patrols to be more frequent and diligent. I don't want anything to happen between here and Elroith, is that understood?"

The generals nodded as Peter returned his focus to the map. The reports went long, the time spent discussing troop movements, lookouts, scouts, and other various pieces of information. As the night wore on, Amaryll joined the group to give her own report. The Gifteds and Knights accompanying the army were doing well and no foreign threats, aside from the Pseudonym, had been observed.

"Why wasn't It seen earlier?" Thomas asked hoarsely. Amaryll sighed and scratched her neck in an uncharacteristic display of stress.

"I am investigating It further, your Excellency, but I can't seem to figure it out. Our Light Gifteds didn't even sense it. I didn't want to say it in front of Milady, but it is alarming that It slipped into camp unnoticed. Before exhuming the body it was determined the Pseudonym had not been within Arailt's ranks for very long. He did, however, have a false eye made of Ela. It has been destroyed, so if it was transmitting anything, the connection has been severed."

Thomas suppressed a groan. "Who knows what has been leaked." He rubbed the bridge of his nose and stared in exhaustion at the map. His mind reeled with what Arailt could possibly know, but one thing was certain; surely he knew about Marta. He lowered his fist and met his generals' gazes with a solemn look. "We will act as if Arailt knows about Marta. Jerome, I want you to work with Wesley to start assembling her Guard. I want at least ten superior soldiers to be in the Guard, two with her at all times. Amaryll, keep the Light Gifteds nearby. If they sense anything off, I want to know about it."

Amaryll and Jerome nodded and left to implement his command. He sighed and rubbed his whole face. *I wanted to get to Elroith before anything was let out... at this rate, the castle will know by the time we get there. I have been trying to avoid thinking about how Sarah is going to handle this...*

Peter spoke to Finlay in a hushed tone. The general nodded and excused himself from the tent. Thomas was lost in his thoughts whilst Peter aggressively sharpened his sword, occasionally sparing Thomas a glare.

"You don't even try to hide your hatred anymore," Thomas finally broke the silence. Peter lifted his gaze to see Thomas examining the map. Thomas shifted and met his brother's stare.

"I don't understand what you mean," Peter shrugged. Thomas lowered his hands but his expression never wavered.

"You spend most of your time glaring at me. Ever since Ropheka you've barely even interacted with me."

Peter scoffed and leaned back in his chair. "What do you want me to say? 'Congratulations on your fake marriage'? You only married her based on a prophecy you barely even remember hearing."

"Last I checked, it was my decision to whom I marry, just as I allowed you to choose yours. Don't tell me you regret your decision already?"

"At least *I* chose strategically to bolster the country. What did you do? You married some peasant in the middle of nowhere. What kind of alliance or benefit can that possibly—"

Thomas held up a finger in warning. "I will not tolerate slander, Peter. I chose whom I chose for a very good reason." *Even though I may not entirely understand it myself, right now.*

Peter held up his hands. "I simply do not understand how anyone in court, or our alliances, will take to this. I think you just fell for a pretty face and couldn't keep it in your trousers."

"Peter," Thomas rumbled low, a vein popping out of his head, his lips tight. "You have gone too far."

"Oh, I'm sorry. That's right," Peter's mouth tipped sardonically. "You haven't actually claimed her yet, have you? Can't do it or don't have the nerve?"

The lanterns flickered dangerously in the tent and the temperature began rising. Balls of light started to form in Thomas' fists before fizzling out as he took a deep calming breath. He turned in one motion and stormed out of the tent. Peter simply laughed.

You're so easy to goad, brother. His grin turned into his characteristic scowl. *And that will be your downfall.*

CHAPTER EIGHT

Seeking Refuge

A lone, bedraggled soldier kneeled before a solid wooden desk outlaid with intricate carvings. His armor was dirty and half-polished as if he had done it in a hurry. There was a large broadsword strapped to his back with several knicks and kinks in the steel. The cloak draped over his shoulder was a deep blue; on the back, two serpents coiled around an apple were emblazoned in silver. The plush rug underneath him was immaculately kept and although he stared at it, he couldn't care less what it looked like. The darkened room was thick with foreboding as he sensed the gaze of the man sitting behind the desk.

"Your Excellency, the Pseudonym was able to confirm that the Life Gifted One Carrick found was indeed amongst Thomas' ranks. It relayed this message."

He held up a shimmering blue ball, and a gust of bone-chillingly cold wind brought it to his Master. An image swam in its depths, revealing King Thomas standing next to a shorter blonde-haired woman. They were watching a pitiful group of soldiers practicing their combat skills. The figure's head tipped to the side as he saw Thomas and the girl blushing at each other.

"And what of the Pseudonym?" the Figures' voice was smooth and silken yet had an undertone that made the man shudder.

"It was..." he swallowed hard, "It was... captured and destroyed... Milord."

The Figure tapped his quill on the wood several times in thought.

"Pity," he purred nonchalantly. The messenger, a general, braced for impact when the figure waved his hand. He felt something zip to his chest and it hung there in the air. It buzzed with energy, but he could not see it. The air smelled metallic and fizzy. The general clenched his eyes shut, expecting pain, but instead the energy moved away and dissipated.

"You're lucky I'm in a good mood, Iris," the Figure sighed and leaned back luxuriously. His silver eyes were the only things Iris could see in the dark as he looked up, sweat beading on his brow. The Figure smiled wide. "It's no fun when things always go your way, is it?"

Iris shook his head slowly, knowing better than to not answer. The Figure chuckled low.

"No, of course it isn't. Which is why I'm not too bothered by this interesting turn of events." He stood and turned around to face a large map on the wall behind him. It outlaid the lands of Hylen and Elyon, and there were several marks everywhere. Notes had been pinned to the map which coordinated with the papers which were sprawled across the desk behind him. The Master twiddled the quill in his fingers. "Bring me the Seekers, as well as General Tullius. Oh, and my scribe." He turned to face Iris with a crooked smile. "I need to pen a letter to our friend."

*****

Marta watched the rain curtain sweeping through the mountain pass and she wrapped her cloak a little closer around her. The army moved ever onward with Thomas riding on the inside to talk to his generals and Wesley on the outside, pensive as ever. Marta continued to feel ill at ease, seemingly in the right place yet far from it. The last few days had grown tense after the Pseudonym attack. No one had told her what truly happened, yet everyone was on edge. She had stopped hearing Thomas' thoughts as well, an indicator they had already started growing apart. *Am I in the right place, God? It seems that I keep running into blocks. Have I been listening to You or something else?* She turned to the side and noticed Wesley staring straight ahead. She cleared her throat as she held Maggie's reigns.

"So, Wesley, have you always been a soldier?"

Wesley cast her a sideways glance and sighed. "Nay ma'am. Me parents are farmers."

"Oh, really! What do they grow?" she asked, innocently intrigued. The twenty-year old chuckled.

"Mostly taters, tho' they do rotate tro' hay and lettuce s'well."

"Potatoes are rough to dig up," she shook her head. "I only ever grew a few of them, and I hated when I would pull them up to find measly little fingerlings on the end."

Wesley laughed at that, his green eyes alight. "Ah thought Life Gifteds could grow anything?"

Marta smiled in embarrassment. "Technically, Life Gifteds can grow whatever they've touched and learned the structure of, but it's fun to let nature do its work too!"

He chuckled. "Ah do suppose 'tis fun to see. Ah hated going out in the fields and uprootin' the plants." He frowned in disdain, his face twisting like he had eaten something sour. "Ah wouldn't wish't on anybody."

She grinned at his remark. "What else do you do? Do you have any other family?"

"Me ma an' pa, an' me siblings. If ye're askin' aboot a wife, Ah don't have one." He glanced forward, heat surging in his cheeks. "...yet."

"Oh?" she asked curiously, tipping her head to the side. Wesley glanced at her, realized she wasn't going to give up, and sighed.

"Well... Brenna's one o' the maids... she's very sweet, an' kind, an' she's always bringing me little extra pieces of food from the kitchen. She's gentle with everyone... she's fierce, though, Ah once saw her take on a boar outside th' gardens. We had boar for dinner that night," he smiled mischievously. "But aboove all else, her smile's so..." he gazed off wistfully. "Heavenly."

She gasped as his ears turned red. "You love her! And by the sound of things, I think she loves you too, right?" she grinned as he glanced at her sheepishly, praying the torment would stop. He nodded and she clasped her hands together excitedly. "So when are you going to ask her to marry you?!"

"Once Ah can afford the ring. Which, now that Ah'm yer capt'n..." he rubbed the back of his neck, his accent getting thicker the more embarrassed he was. Marta bounced giddily on Maggie as something landed on her face.

She felt the rain plopping on her head and skin as everyone started putting up their hoods. The precipitation was swift and powerful, the air chilling immediately. Marta caught Thomas' glance in her direction as he ordered the army to keep moving. The air rumbled with thunder, and Maggie shook her mane.

This is going to be a bad storm.

Marta nodded in acknowledgment. "I think so too, my friend."

She and Wesley fell silent as a town came into view. Everyone sighed in relief. While the small army would not all fit inside, they could seek temporary shelter in the many taverns and inns. The streets were deathly quiet, however, and many of the homes looked empty. Marta felt a chill down her spine as they turned down another empty road. *Where is everyone…?*

I don't know. She jumped in surprise as she sensed Thomas reply. He dismounted in front of the *Dew Drop Inn* and held his hand up to his bride, helping her slide off. Maggie reared back as lightning split the air. Thomas' eyes flickered with light as he gripped Marta close and electricity gathered around them.

"What on—?!" she cried as sparks flew up from the ground. With a wave of his hand they dissipated, and those around stared in wonder. Thomas hissed slightly and held his hand against his chest.

"This is not a regular storm, that was a barrier we just broke through." Thomas glanced at Amaryll, who nodded and relayed instructions to the Gifteds. Several broke off and dispersed through town. Thomas glanced down at his wife with a forced smile, brushing a strand of blonde hair out of her wet face. She blushed and averted her gaze as she pushed herself away from him. The fact she didn't mind how close he was to her bothered her and comforted her at the same time. He, however, frowned in response.

"Search the Inn, I want to get Marta and Wesley inside to safety so we can figure out what is going on."

"I want to go with you!" she tugged on his sleeve. He sighed in exasperation.

"I'm not going to argue with you in front of so many people, Marta. You're not battle-trained yet. I think there might be a Seeker here…"

"I can hold my own in a fight!" she put her hands on her hips, completely glossing over his remark. He simply let go of her. She looked comical standing there, her cheeks puffed out in frustration and her hands on her hips. He chuckled and shook his head.

"Sire, the Inn is clear. We are currently examining the rooms," Peter reported as he emerged from the Inn. Thomas nodded solemnly.

"Thank you. Let's get inside."

The rain was torrential as they stepped through the doors, those in the inn glancing up from their spots. Their eyes widened but they quickly went back to their own drinks, not wanting to interfere. The inn smelled… empty. It took Marta a moment to be able to even catch a whiff of the alcohol around the room. The owner, a pudgy man with a red mustache and thick accent, stepped out from the back room and paused in shock.

"Good, er, afternoon. How canna help?"

"We will need some boarding for the night, please." Thomas smiled warmly. Marta had all but forgotten the quibble outside, enthralled by the tavern. She had only ever been to Geralt's, and his was much different. This tavern had a much larger room and more tables and chairs. There was a small stage on one side, and a large gnarled bar where the innkeeper stood. The men here looked gruffer, but all of them glanced up in curiosity at the wide-eyed young woman gawking at the room. Marta noticed a dark hooded figure in the back corner, keeping to himself. She could sense a darkness about him and she tugged on her husband's arm. Thomas gently put his hand on her shoulder and nodded towards the stairs.

"Our room is upstairs."

Our room. Our room!

Her face flooded with heat, all thoughts about the figure— who had disappeared— gone from mind. Thomas winced slightly as he heard her thoughts. *I can sleep in a different room, if you'd rather—*

She flinched. *No!* She cleared her throat quietly and glanced away. *No, that's fine. I really don't mind.*

He simply nodded and guided her up the stairs. Peter walked back into the tavern, saw them, and stalked off with an indecipherable look on his face. She watched Thomas' expression as his brother left the room, but couldn't hear his thoughts. He glanced down at her, smiled slightly, and continued walking. She watched Amaryll step through the doors and nod at some of the trepidatious patrons.

Soldiers greeted them at the top of the stairs and informed him the rooms were clear. Thomas motioned and Wesley nodded as he took up guard by the door. Another soldier, Seamus, stood at the top of the stairs. He had recently been added to her Guard, and she made it her goal to memorize all of the names of those protecting her. Thomas pushed open the door and stepped inside.

Their room was modestly furnished, with a simple bed, comforters, a pot-bellied stove in one corner, and a small table with chairs. It smelled like burning cedar, so strong Marta covered her mouth to suppress a cough.

Thomas stepped inside cautiously as if looking for something. After a moment he sighed. "Fall is definitely coming on. Storms will be more frequent until we reach Elroith." He walked over to the bed and threw off the covers.

"Are... you alright?" she murmured in surprise.

Thomas examined the mattress and put the sheets back on haphazardly. "Fine." He walked over to the vase on the table and picked it up. She lurched forward when it looked like he was going to throw it, but he frowned and put it back on the table. "Something is off, and I want to make sure you will be okay."

Yes, and it's you! She caught herself thinking. Thomas glanced up at her slowly, then turned to the door.

"I'm going to go downstairs."

"Thomas, I—" she paused as she watched a spark fly from the doorknob to his hand. He stepped back and unsheathed his sword.

Marta, step close to me but stay behind.

She did as she was told. He held his sword at the ready as the door opened and the innkeeper's wife stepped in holding a bucket of water and towels. She yelped in surprise at being met with a sword and the bucket crashed to the floor, spilling water everywhere.

"What on—?!" she reeled back as Thomas stood his ground.

"Amaryll!" he called out the door.

"Busy!" came her reply as there was a horrible crash downstairs. Marta's eyes widened as the woman's expression changed from shock to anger. She jumped up with a growl, but Thomas knocked her backwards with the back of his hilt. Marta jerked as the woman hit hard.

"What's going on?!" Marta cried, shaking in fear. Thomas cursed under his breath as he stood from examining the woman.

"It's a trap. Grab your things, let's go."

She wrenched her still-damp cloak from the wall and clasped it around her neck as they stepped out into the hallway. Wesley met them with wide eyes, sword drawn. Marta stuck close behind as Thomas carefully walked through the hall, examining each room. Downstairs sounded like a full brawl, with glass shattering and people shouting at each other. She saw Seamus at the bottom of the stairs, knocking a man back with his sword. Flashes of light and flame burst from one side of the room as Gifteds flooded the inn.

How did no one see it? Marta caught Thomas' strained thoughts. *This whole place is a trap!* Marta glanced behind as something moved and cried out "Thomas!"

He whirled around and deflected the sword headed straight for her. The innkeeper stood there with a deranged grin on his face. "I'll kill 'er, and end yer cursed line here!"

Thomas deflected another blow, their swords clashing mid-air.

Marta stood back, eyes wide, hand clutched over her chest. *There's got to be something I can do!*

Stay safe! Came Thomas' frantic reply as he kicked the innkeeper in the stomach. The man reeled backwards and cried out as Wesley sliced through his arm. Instead of blood, there was black smoke. Thomas stood up and registered it for but a moment before he turned and deflected a blow from the woman.

Marta stood there frozen in fear. *I have to do something!* She tried to move, but her feet wouldn't budge. *Why... why am I so scared?!* The memory of the attack on Ropheka a few weeks ago hit her full-force, knocking the wind out of her. She stumbled backwards as someone caught her and grabbed her throat.

Thomas dispatched the woman quickly, and she disappeared in a puff of smoke with a screech. The innkeeper howled with laughter, and both Thomas and Wesley turned to see Marta in the grasp of one of the men from downstairs. She struggled as he held a knife to her throat, a hand clamped over her mouth.

"Don't move. Put down your sword, or she dies."

Thomas *tsk'*ed and tossed his sword to the side. Wesley turned as another man appeared from he window behind and he met him with his sword. Marta bit down on the man's hand and he released her. She spilled forward and gasped, "Behind you!"

He turned and dodged just in time for the innkeeper to drive his sword into the spot where the King had just been. He punched the innkeeper square in the nose, sending him reeling into the wall. Marta ducked and turned as the man swiped at her, and she landed a swift kick to his nether regions. The man fell to the ground with a cry, and she kicked him down the stairs. Surprisingly, he did not disappear into smoke, but bled onto the floor. Seamus simply stood out of the way, gave Marta a proud grin, then jerked as someone else engaged him in a fight. She trembled and covered her mouth. *I... I hurt him! I did that!* Adrenaline coursed through her as she laughed in surprise. *I did something useful!*

Thomas grabbed his sword and finished off the innkeeper, who turned to ash. He turned and walked up to Marta, cupping her face gently.

"Are you alright? Are you hurt?"

She shook her head in surprise at his affection, then took his hand. "But you are." Her hand glowed along with the wound on his hand and arm as his skin stitched back together. He smiled and kissed her forehead.

"Thank you. Let's go."

Marta blushed profusely as she hiked up her skirts and followed behind him down the stairs, Wesley right behind her. She grimaced as she stepped around the writhing man at the foot of the stairs before rushing through the fray and out the door. Finlay and Jerome had just finished off a few more attackers as they emerged from the *Dew Drop*, and she noted piles of ash laying everywhere.

"Status?" Thomas panted as he scanned for any danger. The two men shook their heads.

"The whole town was razed. It was a trap," Jerome groaned. Marta stood close to Thomas, one hand on his cloak. A figure moved out of the corner of her eye, and she snapped her fingers as a spark of golden light left her fingertips. Her eyesight shifted and Thomas glowed a golden white. She blinked in alarm. *Colors? They've never turned into different colors before...* Finlay and Jerome were washed in a blue color, yet she registered for a split second the tufts of black inside Finlay's frame. She shook her head. *I was just trying to see what life was around... why do they all look—* her attention snapped to the figure from the tavern, their silhouette as black as a starless night. Clouds of silver swirled around inside him, and as soon as she realized what she was looking at the clouds revealed themselves to be hundreds of ethereal eyes. They all turned in her direction once her Gift revealed to her what he was. She suddenly felt exposed, like the eyes were groping, searching the deepest parts of her soul.

"Thomas, over there!" she pointed as the figure from the tavern dashed behind the barn, her vision returning to normal. Thomas took off and followed him, Jerome and Finlay close behind.

What is that thing?! She cried in alarm, hiking up her skirts as Wesley nodded at her. The pair took off behind the others, and they emerged in a clearing. Soldiers, Gifteds, and Knights had started gathering around a lone figure wearing a thick, dark cloak. He laughed and took off his hood. The creature had jet-black hair and uneven hazel eyes, and everything about him looked haphazard. Yet the darkness that oozed from him made Marta reel back in shock.

"I've got a message for you, Kingie!" he stuck a knobby finger towards Thomas, who stood with sword at the ready. "Master knows about your Queen." He tipped his head to the side as Marta and Wesley stepped up next to Thomas. Thomas didn't break his gaze.

"What about it?"

The hobbled man howled with raspy laughter. "Just another thing to be wrenched from your grasp!" With a flourish, the man disappeared into a plume of black smoke. Gifteds and their Knights lurched forward too late, and a fizzle of someone's Light ability burst in the spot he had been in. Otherwise, he was gone. Marta shuddered. *This feeling... just what was that? It felt like pure evil...!* Thomas noticed her shudder and reached over to ask what was wrong. Screeching from the town snapped both of them out of their thoughts. As they returned, they realized most of the townspeople had turned to ash. Several men were brought forward whilst Amaryll stood there triumphantly.

"Looks like he hired some mercenaries to help with the job. However, it seems they didn't know everyone else was simply an illusion..."

Thomas examined their faces and winced at the man Marta had kicked. *Remind me to never get on your bad side,* he thought as he cast her a glance. She jumped and looked away, her face bursting into color. He chuckled and addressed the men.

"Since this is a spiritual attack, I will turn them over to the Tower and their authority."

Amaryll nodded and waved; several Knights stepped forward and grasped the men to take them away. "I will be sure to mirror the Tower once we are in a safe range."

Thomas turned and held out his hand to Marta. She stepped forward and he held her close against his chest.

—let her get hurt. She heard him think as she listened to his heart beat. He smelled musky, not too unlike the men who would go out to farm and come back in after a long day. It was surprisingly comforting, however, and she hugged him back, wrapping her trembling arms around his torso. Thomas had a stern look on his face as the rain began to let up.

"Peter."

His brother paused in the middle of giving one of his soldiers instructions. He turned around and met Thomas' glare with his own.

"Your Excellency?"

He opened his mouth but hesitated. Marta was still holding onto him.

"See me in the command tent later. We need to discuss the failure of your regiments to properly conduct a search."

Peter winced and turned away indignantly. Marta shuddered as she felt Thomas' anger rising in him. He held her with one arm and motioned with the other as he spoke to Jerome's group.

"Search the town to see if there are any survivors. Afterwards, we will move on. We will send a battalion ahead to set up camp. I don't want to stay here longer than necessary."

The soldiers nodded in agreement and dispersed. Wesley stood nearby, a hand on his sword. Thomas glanced over at him and he stood to attention.

"Captain, I want you nearby in case something else happens."

Wesley nodded. "Yessir."

*****

Marta sighed as she settled onto a fallen tree. The cooks had made their group dinner, using food they found around the town that was still good. No survivors had yet been found, and that weighed heavily on Thomas. He had sent her to get some rest, but had remained with his generals discussing plans.

He stays up so late and wakes up incredibly early. Does he ever get any rest? She sighed as she finished dinner. Whatever they had encountered earlier left her with the uneasy feeling she needed to watch her back at all times. She thanked the cooks and disappeared into her and Thomas' tent. She changed into her nightgown, then settled into the bedroll. She stared at the roof of the tent, clasping her hands on her chest.

Heavenly Father, I felt so confident before that this is where I am supposed to be. And I know it is. But... now that I'm here, I still feel... useless. I'm trying to keep my head up, to see what You are showing me. I never thought I would be that scared... she rolled over and held her arm under her head. *I always wanted to be the one who could rush into battle to help others, to protect those close to me. But I was a coward...* Her eyes pricked with tears as she sniffled. *How am I supposed to be a good Queen if I can't even stand beside my husband when it matters most? Jesus, give me Your strength and Your courage. Help me be strong when my flesh is so very weak. I need You.* She fell asleep quickly, dreaming restlessly about the attacks and battles they had faced. She dreamt about Thomas facing that shadowy figure yet again, then turning to her. She reached out for him and he took her hand. She smiled at him, but in the haze he shoved her towards the figure. The being grasped her close as her chest constricted. She opened her mouth in a scream, but nothing would come out. Thomas' normally stern face twisted into a sneer as he turned away, the figure dragging her deep into mire.

*****

Thomas had started carefully pulling back the covers of his bedroll when Marta shot straight up gasping for air. He nearly jumped out of his skin, instinctively reaching for his sword.

"Marta?!"

She sat there frozen for a moment before sobbing into her hands. Thomas stood there awkwardly, glancing around, then shuffled over and knelt next to her. He gently placed a hand on her shoulder.

"Are you alright?" he whispered softly. She shook violently as she turned and landed in his lap, holding onto him for dear life. His eyes widened and he patted her head slowly. "Did... something happen?" She shook her head. He gently lifted her up off his lap, his face flooding with heat. "Here." He adjusted so she was sitting in his lap with her head on his shoulder. She sat there quietly for so long he thought she had fallen asleep.

"Do you dream a lot?" she whispered. Her question caught him off guard.

Did she have a nightmare? "Not really. I don't usually dream. Sometimes I do, but they're pretty weird." He smiled gently. "One time I had a dream that my brother turned into a pudgy little pig and ran squealing through the castle, Cookie on his heels. I woke up craving bacon."

Marta laughed curtly, wiping her tears with the back of her hand. He frowned despite getting her to laugh.

"I take it you had a nightmare."

She hesitated, then nodded. "I... get them a lot."

He reached up and brushed her hair out of her face as something stirred inside him. "Well, now you have me. You can always wake me up if you're scared." Ah, that was it; *I want to protect her.*

She sniffled and looked up at him seriously. "Do you think I'm a burden?"

A burden?! Is that what she's worried about?? "No, I don't."

She turned away. *He wouldn't understand...*

He chuckled softly although his eyebrow twitched in irritation as he heard her thoughts. "Try me."

She put her face on his shoulder, burying her nose into his neck. Heat flooded his body and he gently pushed her away. "That's... not a good idea right now. I'm sorry." He picked her up by the waist and set her back in her spot on the bedroll. It was still surprising how fragile she was. She looked up at him in confusion, then held herself. He wrapped an arm around her and gave her a chaste side-hug.

What if he wants to get rid of me because I can't be of help? He heard her think. His mouth opened to respond, but he clamped it shut. He felt he didn't know enough about her to be able to explain, so he chose not to say anything. One thing was for sure, though, his feelings for this woman were definitely growing. As she nestled into his shoulder, he wanted nothing more than to protect her from whatever was plaguing her.

And myself. He thought as he swallowed hard, trying desperately to quell the husbandly desire building in him.

CHAPTER NINE

An Unseen Battle

Several days had passed on their journey to Elroith. At night, they would stop and Marta would learn more about her duties as a Queen from Amaryll. They had to stay an extra day at a few stops due to weather, and it was then that Thomas would continue to teach her swordsmanship. She could feel them climbing higher and higher in altitude as they reached the top of a mountain pass. Oddly, though, she couldn't see any trees beyond the ones at the top.

"Are we reaching a valley?" she turned and asked Thomas. He simply smiled at her.

"You'll see."

They crested the hill and her jaw dropped. Tall, gray peaks topped with white stretched all across the horizon. A huge valley lay below them, and she could see rivers and lakes weaving across the valley floor. Trees followed the rivers, but the rest of the valley was blanketed in grass or fields. Several towns could be seen from this height, dotted across the landscape and shining in the early morning sunlight. Already some of the trees on the mountainsides had started exploding in reds, yellows, and oranges. Thomas held up a hand to stop the journey as Marta took it all in.

"I've never seen anything so beautiful!" she exclaimed happily, her breath condensing in front of her. Wesley beamed beside her as Amaryll chuckled.

"Elroith is just beyond that mountain," she pointed to the west, where the largest mountain in the range stood. It was completely covered in snow. "At our pace, we should be there in a little over a week. The castle was actually partially built into that mountain. It's cradled between two large peaks, but words don't do it justice. You'll just have to see it."

The world is so much larger than I thought...

Thomas chuckled at her thoughts. Their mental range had increased significantly; Thomas and Marta could now communicate with each other from across the camp.

It is indeed a much bigger world that you have entered. And this is just our kingdom, you haven't seen any of the others yet.

"Goodness..." she uttered, the cold air stinging her lungs. She wrapped her woolen cloak a little tighter around her as the army continued forward. Thomas pointed out the different towns and told her their names and the history of each one. She listened, enthralled, absorbing everything he said. He gestured to a town nearby.

"That is the town of Rhonwyn, named after a famous Tower elder."

"Oh, she was Light Gifted, wasn't she?"

Thomas nodded with a smile. "You'll see that the Tower has quite a presence in Elyon. Far off in the distance," he pointed, "about a four day's journey away, is Kakorio. This whole valley is a caldera. Many of the towns have natural hot springs running through them, although Kakorio has arguably the best lodgings. It's considered a vacation town."

"He thinks Kakorio is the best because he's *biased*," came Amaryll's retort. Thomas raised a brow as Marta turned to face her.

"What's your favorite, Amaryll?"

She chuckled at Thomas' expression. "His Majesty only likes Kakorio because it's easy to get to. The real fun," she lifted a finger with a gleam in her eye, "is finding the wild springs hidden in the mountains. But you have to hike to get to those ones."

Thomas shook his head. "I'm glad you were able to find the time amidst your duties to wander off." Amaryll snorted playfully and met his challenge, but Marta sensed sorrow in his voice.

Thomas?

He turned and looked at her. At this altitude his face was flushed, but his blue eyes gleamed in the light. *Yes?*

Have you ever had a break to just... spend time by yourself?

He blinked in surprise. Amaryll glanced between the two of them in realization. She chuckled and pulled back a little to talk to one of the Knights riding with her. Thomas turned his gaze forward, but he was pensive.

That isn't really a luxury afforded to a king. I had time when I was younger, but after my mother was killed things just weren't the same. He sighed. She reached over and took his hand in hers with a sad smile.

"I hope we can go to those springs together sometime. I think it would be fun to go on a short adventure with you." She smiled warmly. Thomas grinned back.

He jolted as the sly dark voice in his mind spoke again, the hair on the back of his neck standing on end. *She isn't serious. Who would want to stay by your side? You're a weak, useless king.*

He shook his head. *She seems sincere though—*

Of course she does. Snakes are incredibly convincing. Just look at what happened to Eve.

"Thomas?" Marta asked quietly, her brow furrowed in worry. "You have a strange look on your face, but I can't read your thoughts."

He glanced down at her hand and let go abruptly, turning away with a slight scowl. "Don't assume that just because we are bonding you're always allowed to hear what I think."

She winced as the figurative arrow hit home in her emotions and leaned back on Maggie, his heart hurting at her pained expression. He wanted to reach out to her but she turned away, engaging Wesley in conversation.

See? This only confirms that she's—

Get out of my head! He grumbled as he pulled back on the reigns, falling back to talk to Finlay and Jerome. Amaryll watched the whole affair worriedly.

Sometimes I wonder whose voice he's listening to. She thought as she returned to her conversation.

*****

The King's army camped outside of Rhonwyn that night, but several from their ranks had families there. Thomas allowed them to visit since most of the army remained in camp. Marta didn't have the opportunity to speak to Thomas at all, and he had ordered Wesley to teach her swordsmanship that evening instead of joining her himself. She stood in the training field blankly, lost in her thoughts.

"Milady?" Wesley asked as he lowered his sword and stood up straight. He ran a hand through his red hair. "Y'must be most focused when y'have a weapon in hand."

"Sorry," she shook her head to clear her mind. "Sorry, Wes. I'm ready." She took a defensive stance and lifted her sword as Wesley nodded. He stepped forward and she parried his blow. She turned as he did, but her thoughts snapped back to Thomas. Wesley stopped short, his sword at her neck. She stumbled backwards in shock and landed hard. Wesley immediately dropped the sword and rushed forward.

"Are y'alright?!" he asked quietly in horror, green eyes wide. She nodded, still surprised.

"Yes, I'm sorry. It's my fault. My thoughts are somewhere else right now."

Wesley nodded solemnly. "Let's practice later."

"Yes… good idea."

Wesley reached down a hand to assist her to stand and she collected herself. She sat under a tree nearby as her young captain handed Seamus Marta's sword, the cool fall wind blowing through her braided hair.

Why am I so bothered?

A calm, cool voice invaded her thoughts. *Because you're a burden.*

Her eyes widened slightly.

You're overbearing and controlling. Did you see how Thomas reacted when you tried to read his mind? How selfish of you to assume he'd share anything with you! You knew you were way in over your head with this marriage. You're ill-equipped. You were thrown into a situation and assumed it was—

"I command you to leave in Jesus' name." Marta exhaled slowly. The darkness she didn't realize had fallen on her lifted as a tingling sensation ran up her spine. "Heavenly Father, protect me. Holy Spirit, surround me with Your Presence." She looked up as people walked by, oblivious to the battle she waged. "I put on Your Armor, even as I try to put up my own weak defenses. They crumble and fade, but Yours will last forever." She shook slightly, her hands clasped together in front of her. Peace settled on her soul, and she sighed in relief.

"Your Majesty?"

She opened her teary eyes to see Amaryll standing there. Wesley stood hesitantly nearby, a hand on his hilt and worry etched in his features. Amaryll knelt next to her and took her hand.

"I figured you were in battle. I could sense it." She smiled ruefully. "May I pray for you?"

Marta nodded, tears spilling from her eyes. Amaryll put a hand on Marta's shoulder and closed her eyes.

"Father, where two or more are gathered, You are surely with them. Thank You for the blessing and sacrifice of Your Son. Thank You for my dear friend Marta. You know the battle she faces now as well as the wars in her future. I ask You to be with her now, to protect her and keep her safe from the Evil One. Surround her with Your warrior angels and protect her in all she does." Amaryll hesitated, and Marta was about to speak when her friend continued, "and please bless her marriage with Thomas. Give them the wisdom to rule this kingdom, but also soften their hearts towards one another. May they be warriors in Your Name and for Your Glory. Let love bloom between them and show them a new aspect of Your plan for them. In Jesus' name I pray, amen."

"Amen," Marta added, her cheeks tinged with color. She looked up at her friend and she hugged her close. "Thank you, Amaryll."

"Of course, my friend," the older woman smiled. "Life is too hard to go it alone. That's why we need community, we need each other." She held out her hand and helped her young friend stand. She glanced around and chuckled. "How about we take a break today? There is a beautiful lake nearby, I think you'd like it."

Marta nodded. "Can we?"

"Of course!"

*****

Thomas watched Marta and Amaryll leave the camp, Wesley close behind. With a *humph* he turned his attention back to the map in front of him. Guilt plagued his mind, however, constricting his chest and wrenching the breath from his lungs.

I shouldn't have snapped at her like that. He rubbed the bridge of his nose. *Why was I so irritated by her suddenly? I need to apologize.*

Why? You're the king. If anything, she should apologize to you for her presumptuousness.

He nearly groaned. *Just because I am king doesn't mean I can't be a decent human being.* He turned and abruptly walked out of the tent, leaving Jerome, Finlay, and Peter behind. Peter let out a sound of frustration and waved sarcastically.

"Bye," he sneered. Finlay shared the sentiment, whilst Jerome simply shook his head.

"He's under a lot of stress," he shot a glare at the two men in the tent with him. "It is our privileged responsibility to help his Majesty. He already has enough on his mind. The attacks haven't been helping."

Finlay nodded guiltily but Peter shrugged. "Gives the soldiers more opportunity to practice for—"

"Your highness!" Jerome spat angrily, "Do you not even care for your sister-in-law's safety? She's more of a target now than ever before! It's our *duty* to look out for her!"

Peter's eyes took on a dark look as he stood up with a scowl. "*She* wasn't *my* choice, general. She should have known the risks before agreeing to this sham. I'm still not fully convinced Thomas wasn't charmed or deceived into marrying her." He turned and stormed out of the tent, leaving chaos in his wake. Jerome cursed under his breath and rubbed his face angrily. Finlay stood there quietly, then excused himself saying he needed to go check on his troops. Jerome lifted his hands in exasperation.

"Lord, give me patience."

*****

"Wow!" Marta cried as she gazed across the crystal-clear lake. There was barely a ripple as she dipped her hand in the frigid water. It stung a little as the cold chilled her to the bone. She withdrew her hand and flicked the water off as she examined the rocks on the water's edge. Amaryll chuckled as Wesley stood nearby, as usual with his hand on his sword's hilt.

"Sometimes, when my husband and I were younger, we would jump into a lake like this right after being in a hot spring. It's quite the shock, let me tell you!" Amaryll laughed. Marta glanced up sheepishly.

"You and… your husband?"

Amaryll's smile never faded despite the deep sadness settling in her eyes. "Yes. Michael was my Chosen Knight, at first assigned to me because I didn't want the hassle of finding a Knight I liked." She chuckled wistfully. "But the Lord did a lot of work on me. Michael was my best friend." She turned and gazed out over the lake. "He was struck down during the battle with Garchuk."

Marta stood next to her friend, a lump in her throat. *I had no idea that battle had been so devastating. It's… odd, that's about the same time my parents were—* Amaryll turned and smiled at her friend. "I'm just thankful I was there with him. Several Life Gifteds severed our connection at the last minute so I did not die with him. Some days, when I was really low, I wished I would've died instead of him." She gazed longingly back over the lake. "God has His timing. I realized since I don't know it, it must not be mine to know. But that meant that

I had unfinished business I needed to do here on earth."

Marta had tears streaming down her cheeks by now. Amaryll noticed and cupped her Queen's face in her hands with a mournful smile.

"Oh, Marta, don't cry! He's Home and running free. One day I will see him again, on the glorious day I meet our Maker." She dabbed at Marta's face with a handkerchief. Marta nodded through tears.

"I would have loved to meet him," she whispered hoarsely. Amaryll chuckled.

"He would have loved to meet you, your Majesty."

Wesley jerked and unsheathed his sword. Amaryll and Marta glanced up as a figure approached from the trees. Thomas pushed back his hood and motioned to Wesley.

"I am thankful you are so keen to protect my bride. You are doing well, captain."

Wesley's ears turned red as his hair as he sheathed his sword, bowing low. "My apologies, M'lord."

"No need." Thomas smiled wearily. He glanced up and met Marta's gaze. Her heart skipped a beat.

So handsome… Her face fell as she thought, *did I do something wrong?*

Amaryll smiled at Marta. "I think Wesley and I will take our leave. His Majesty is more than able to protect you." Wesley glanced between king and queen, then followed Amaryll. She put a hand on Thomas' shoulder, nodded solemnly, then went on her way.

"So, Captain, I hear you have a girl…"

Wesley's groan made Marta and Thomas laugh.

"I don't know if he will ever be able to get over that now." Thomas chuckled. Marta nodded as she giggled.

"Maybe I shouldn't have teased him so much about it."

"Sometimes men need a little push." He stepped next to her and gazed out over the lake. They stood there in silence for a while.

"I'm sorry," Thomas finally sighed. He shifted uncomfortably under her gentle gaze as she turned to look at him. "I… did not mean to snap at you."

"And I am sorry I invaded your privacy." She fidgeted with her fingers and glanced away. "I didn't mean to assume I would always be able to read your thoughts. After all, if you heard mine all the time it would probably drive you mad." She laughed sheepishly. "I just noticed that you looked bothered, and… I wanted to help." Thomas reached around her and drew her into a hug, resting his chin on her head.

"I think you are the first person to truly do so." He inhaled slowly, breathing in her scent. It was relaxing and oddly comforting. She nuzzled her face into his neck and kissed him gently.

"I told you I wanted to be your helpmeet."

Warmth coursed through him and he felt his skin tingle. He gently held her back and coughed.

"I, ah, thank you. It's… definitely something I am not used to."

Her eyes flashed with confusion before she turned her attention to the lake. "I was used to being alone, especially on the edge of town. It's strange to think that there is someone I can rely on now." She held herself gently. Thomas followed her gaze and nodded awkwardly.

"Not very many people back at court like me," he confessed with a slight smile. Surprise registered on her face and he nodded. "I'm only twenty-seven. My father did not begin his rule until he was thirty-five, and that was considered young." His mouth tipped in a sardonic grin. "That's one thing he and I had in common, we were both thrust onto the throne with little warning."

Marta nodded and laced her fingers between his, drawing his hand close. "A good friend of mine said that we don't usually understand God's timing, but it is always much better than what we can originally see." Her doubts flooded her mind, but she remembered what Caleb had taught her. She held out her free hand and a rose bloomed in her palm. "I didn't know that His plan would bring me here, or that I would be married to you. In fact, sometimes I wonder if I heard Him right." She held the small flower up and smiled at him. "But I am thankful He brought us together. You're not perfect, and neither am I. I never expected you to be because you're human. So don't expect it of yourself." She leaned up and kissed his cheek. *I have been trying to be perfect in a way, as well. Lord, forgive me for my doubt.*

Conviction settled on his heart as he heard her words. *Have I really been trying to be perfect?* He plucked the rose from her palm and examined it. It was beautiful, meticulously created. The red petals seemed to gleam in the waning sunlight. She smiled faintly and turned it in his hand, revealing a few wilted spots.

"You can spend years learning how to do something and do everything right, yet still fail. The failures can either push you to get better or you can let them drag you down. No one is great at everything, and no one is perfect in any way. Only One Man was, and He gives us the strength we need to keep going."

Thomas held the rose delicately, warmth flowing over his soul. He chuckled under his breath. "There you go, sounding like a Shepherd again."

Marta grinned at that. "We are called to guide each other and to lean on one another. There's a reason the Armor of God does not have a back piece." She turned and stood behind him, back to back.

"I think I understand," he chuckled, turning around then turning his bride to face him. She took his hands in hers. Suddenly there was a cacophony of pots and pans clanging in the distance and he shook his head. "Sounds like dinner is ready. May I escort you?" He held out his arm. Marta took it with a pleased grin.

Oh! I learned about this from Amaryll! She was excited in spite of her apparent decorum.

He chuckled at that. "And you're learning quickly, it seems. What has she taught you so far?"

"Augh, so much! Ah cannae tell all the things—" she paused, mouth agape. She grinned sheepishly as Thomas roared with laughter.

"Wesley and Seamus rubbing off on you, hmm?"

She shrugged with a mischievous smile. "Camilla would always tell me I had either been in the *Dazed Knight* for too long or I was getting excited about something." She held open her arms. "Ah just love talking aboot so much, ya kin?" she drawled dramatically. Thomas had to pause walking as he doubled over in laughter. She stepped back and laughed as well. He finally stood up straight and adjusted his tunic in a useless attempt to regain his composure. One glance at Marta's expression, however, had him in stitches yet again.

I haven't laughed that hard in... God knows how long!

Marta grinned victoriously. "Good! Every decent Healer knows that laughter is the best medicine."

He cast her a bemused glance. "Remind me to laugh at my broken hand next time, then."

"You know what I mean!"

They spent the short journey back to camp talking about the things she had learned, from etiquette to eating properly. They sat down on a log beside a campfire eating the savory stew the cooks had prepared.

"Marta, when we get to Kakorio, would you like to have a proper meal with me?"

She glanced up from her stew and gently set her spoon back in the bowl. "I would be honored to."

He chuckled at her textbook response. "It would just be you and me.

You can practice your etiquette without fear of being in front of anyone."

She nodded. "That sounds wonderful! And that's where the hot springs are, right?"

"Indeed." He returned to his stew. The army was beginning to smell very ripe and although they had been riding past rivers and lakes, the water was too cold and they didn't have enough time to stop to bathe. He glanced at Marta, who continued eating her stew happily.

I think it would be a good idea for the army to bathe before we get to Elroith. Nana would NOT be happy if we all came in smelling like a dead horse.

Marta snorted and held her mouth as she dropped her spoon in the bowl. Thomas raised a brow and laughed. *What?! It's true!*

Marta waved her hand and giggled harder. *I don't know who Nana is, but I could just imagine the hair burning off the proper ladies at court if they are how you say they are.*

Thomas held his hand over his eyes and chuckled. *Nana is the head of the laundry and baths. Do we really smell that bad?*

She wiped off her face with a hankie and gave him a mischievous grin. *Only slightly.*

Slightly!

The pair continued their mental conversation, both erupting in laughter several times. A few of the soldiers, including Finlay, glanced at them in confusion. Amaryll and the other Gifteds and Knights simply chuckled knowingly. Marta paused as she heard music drifting on the breeze. She lowered her spoon and glanced around.

"What's that?"

Thomas tilted his head to the side to listen. "Ah, sounds like some of the soldiers have broken out their instruments."

"Really?! Can we go watch?!"

Thomas chuckled and set both their bowls in the dish bucket. "Certainly, why not."

The pair wandered through the camp to search out the source of the music. As they got closer Marta could hear the familiar notes of a bagpipe and fiddle growing louder. They emerged upon a group of soldiers sitting around a campfire laughing and singing. She smiled wide when she noticed Wesley in the middle with a pair of spoons in his hands. He had a wide reckless grin on his freckled face and tipped his head back as he sang.

"'Twas an evening' by the 'wyn

The hollyhock in bloom
Ah came roun' th' ben'
'Twas she who turned me groom!
"She was standin' there, oh lady fair
Singin' this happy theme
Her eyes alight, Ah knew a'right
'Twas me bonnie, bonnie queen!"

Marta laughed as she clapped along to the tune, joining in with the chorus.

"Hey, Bonnie! Ho, Bonnie!
Me bonnie bonnie queen
Hey, Bonnie! Ho, Bonnie!
Me bonnie bonnie queen!"

The group of soldiers glanced up in surprise as Marta began singing with Wesley, smiling at him as they sang. Wesley nodded with a grin.

"Ne'er a queen o'er land or sea
O'er riches, fields, or men
Nay, but a queen o'er stew 'n tea
Th' flowers n' th' wrens!

Me bonnie queen, s' fair is she
Yet strong and willed too
Think o' me men, n' pray fer me
Fer bein' late's the thing she rues!"

Thomas folded his arms and relaxed as the group of soldiers laughed and sang, his wife leading them in the chorus again. Warmth welled up inside of him. *So beautiful...* The song ended with a flourish and Marta turned towards Thomas in the gleaming firelight with a grin. *Her smile... I think I understand what Wesley felt with Brenna now.* He held out his hand and she took it. He guided her over and held her in a hug. *I want to keep this smile on her face for as long as possible.* Marta sighed and buried her face in his chest happily. His smell brought her comfort, but seeing him smile and feeling him hold her stirred something else in her, something she couldn't quite place.

That night, Marta lay on her bedroll at the edge of the tent and

Thomas came in late per usual. She heard him settle into his roll and she shivered.

It's gotten a lot colder... she bemoaned. Thomas paused and rolled over.

"Do you need another blanket?" he whispered. She shook her head.

"I... already grabbed them all." Sure enough, she had several blankets piled on top of her. He started to sit up.

"I'll go ask if anyone has extra—"

"No!" she shook her head and sat up slightly. Their eyes met and she rolled over, back to him. "I'll be okay. I'm sorry for complaining."

Thomas watched her shiver again, then sighed as an idea crossed his mind. "Marta," he held his arm out, "come here."

She slowly rolled over and looked at him with wide eyes. "Are—are you sure?"

I just have to control myself, he purposefully withheld his thought from her as he nodded. "I don't want you to freeze to death."

"I won't freeze to death..."

He reached over and pulled her bedroll closer to him. He detangled the blankets from on top of her and nestled her right against his chest. He placed the blankets back and wrapped his arm around her.

"Better?"

He could feel the heat rush into her face as she nodded. "Yes. Much."

Marta fell asleep quickly, but it would be several agonizing hours before Thomas could.

CHAPTER TEN

Elves of Kakorio

Kakorio was a beautiful village nestled into the mountains. The air had turned cold and steam wafted from the many pools around town. It had a quaint feel to it. Most of the residents here attended to the many inns that hosted visitors from all over the continent. Thomas had given strict orders that everyone was to bathe and have their clothes cleaned before their arrival in Elroith three days hence. He offered to have Marta ride in a carriage ahead of them now that they were close enough to request one, but she refused, saying she wanted to continue the journey with him. He escorted Marta to the largest inn set right up against the mountain. She was intrigued by the intricate scrollwork and wooden details Kakorio boasted, and the *Token Spring Inn* was the grandest of them all. Wesley and Seamus opened the grand wooden doors to reveal two women busy behind a desk. One stepped out and Marta had to hide her surprise.

Elves?! she cried inwardly as the woman approached and bowed. She had long silky hair colored like the moon pinned up behind her and elegant, smooth features. Her ears were long and pointed, stretching back toward the top of her head. Several earrings dangled from them ranging in all different colors. She wore what looked like an intricate delicate robe, the fabric adorned with lilies. The sleeves hid her hands as she smiled at Marta before respectfully addressing the King in a unique accent.

"Welcome back, your Majesty. It is always a pleasure to see you. Who do we have the honor of meeting?" she nodded politely at Marta. Thomas put his hand on the small of her back and smiled.

"Good to see you, Ria. This is my wife, Queen Marta."

"Your wife!" she covered her mouth in shock. The elf behind the counter dropped something and rushed out of the room. Ria bowed low toward Marta, who took a shocked step back. "My apologies for being so rude, I did not realize you were our Queen! I had heard rumors, but—"

Marta stood there awkwardly and tried not to fidget. "No, no, it's all very… sudden. It's a pleasure to meet you, Miss Ria. Please forgive my impudence, I've simply never met an elf before! You're very beautiful!"

Ria stood with a shocked expression, then chuckled. "Thank you. I get that initial reaction a lot, my Lady. Please, let me show you to your room." She motioned and the pair followed.

Outside in the street, Peter stood scowling as Finlay shifted uncomfortably.

"Whatever you do," Peter whispered menacingly as he leaned in to the general, "make sure nothing happens between them tonight. Got that?"

Finlay gave him him a bewildered glance to which Peter shook his head in warning. Finlay nodded lightly, examined the prince's eyes, and walked away. Amaryll walked up to Peter smiling politely, but turned to enter the inn with a frown. Wesley was right behind, never meeting Peter's glare.

He's up to something, she thought as an elf came rushing over to greet her. "Ah, Selena, you seem to be in the midst of something."

The young elf frowned and flicked her smooth brown hair behind her head. "I won a bet and wanted them to pay up."

Three other elves poked their heads out from around the corner and Amaryll nodded at them. They disappeared as she smiled. "Oh? What was the bet?"

Selena grinned mischievously. "That the king would marry someone whom none of us had ever met."

Amaryll laughed at that. "Well, that's quite the bet! Especially since most visiting royalty stays here on their journeys to Elroith and you all live so long. Tell me," she held Selena's shoulder as her face grew serious, "How can we increase security here at the Inn tonight?"

*****

Marta had her first taste of what it would be like in a castle as Ria guided them to the royal suite. It had a private dining room, a large bedroom with a door to a private enclosed hot spring, a parlor, a separate bathroom with a large tub, and even a simple study. Each room was luxuriously furnished, the curtains and sheets made of silk. Every room had its own fireplace, already burning brightly. Marta could hardly take it all in before tea was delivered and set in the parlor. It was a formal tea, with tiny sandwiches and biscuits on a tiered tray.

"This is so... much more than I deserve!" she walked over to and ran her hand along the incredibly soft couch. She paused and withdrew her hand as though she had been burned.

"Are you alright?" Thomas asked as he noticed. She nodded slowly.

I'm too dirty to touch any of this.

Thomas laughed at that. "Don't worry about it. You're not nearly as bad as some of the others traveling with us. Let's have tea, and then you can take a bath in the spring. I'll take one in here and we can have dinner together later."

Marta nodded and sat slowly as if it pained her. Thomas took off his sword and hung up his jacket, settling on the other couch. Ria knocked and came in with a tray of letters.

"These came for you," she sighed sadly. "I know you normally do not want to work when you are here, but the messenger said they were important..."

Thomas nodded and took the thick stack. Marta shook her head in shock as Ria left.

"There are so many there!"

"Indeed," Thomas groaned as he sorted through the letters. Marta shrank back a little.

"We don't have to have dinner together tonight if it will be too much —"

"It won't," he replied a little too quickly. She blinked in surprise and nodded guiltily.

"Marta." She noticed the stern expression on his face as he lowered the letters. "Do you trust me?"

"I do," she replied instantly. He shook his head.

"Not just as king. As your husband. I know we've only known each other a little over a month, and I don't have much of a leg to stand on. I... haven't had the best marks as far as being a partner is concerned. I promise you, though, dinner will not be a hassle."

Marta paused, then nodded slowly. "I know that you are king, and that you will be busy. I know..." she looked away, a lump forming in her throat. *I know that being around him most of the time will end as soon as we get to the castle. After all, Amaryll told me that as king, he has a lot of responsibilities. But...I honestly wish we could keep traveling... At least out here, I can help him and be with him more.* She winced as Thomas acknowledged her thoughts.

"While I can't be around you as often as I am now, I promise that I will spend some time with you." *You make me feel... calm. At peace. I want to feel that more often.*

She blushed and nodded. "Thank you. I... I feel the same way."

Thomas smiled in reply then returned his focus to the letters. He had her sit beside him to help him go through a couple. He glanced over as she settled in next to him with a pile of letters. The training had bulked her up a little bit, and she didn't look quite so frail. She had a healthy glow and more stamina than she had before. She glanced up at him and he averted his gaze, drawing attention to the stack of letters in his lap.

"I don't know why these ones got through, these would be easy enough for Nick... unless he's slacking," he grumbled under his breath. Marta held a dispatch in her hands with wide eyes. It had a beautiful seal on it and looked very foreign.

"Ah, that's from Ravenswicke. He's an... old friend." He took the letter and opened it. He frowned slightly and tucked the letter in his jacket pocket. *I'll deal with that later.*

"His name is Ravenswicke?" she asked quietly. He glanced up and nodded.

"He's... an odd fellow. Very reclusive. He's powerful enough to be a Tower elder, yet..." he furrowed his nose. "He has chosen to eschew himself from the Tower."

"So he's not a follower?" she blinked in surprise. Thomas laughed and patted his wife's hand.

"You don't have to be a member of the Tower to follow Christ, Marta."

"I—I know that!" she puffed out her cheeks indignantly. He reached up and gently pinched one.

"It's the most common thing to do, yes, yet he is anything *but* common." He chuckled as she playfully swatted him away. They continued through letters, mostly just information on troop movements and things he already knew. Marta spotted a couple of invitations from other countries, notices from the Tower, and so forth. Soon they were done, night had fallen and dinner was fast approaching.

"Well," Thomas looked out the window mournfully, "I'm afraid we won't have much time to enjoy our baths."

"That's fine," Marta smiled. "I can be pretty fast. Although… my hair may be another matter." She held up her limp braid and winced as she noticed the dirt and oil that had collected in it. Thomas reached up and gently tucked a loose strand of hair behind her ear.

"Soon, I will make sure there is a whole team ready to pamper you," he whispered gently.

She blushed at that and turned away. *I don't need a team, I can do it myself… besides, no one has ever seen me—*

A thud outside on the patio made both of them jump. Thomas was up in a flash grabbing his sword, his eyes flickering with light.

"Marta, stay behind me."

She nodded as he edged himself towards the patio door. He did a slow sweep of what he could see, noticed a boot on the ground, then cautiously glanced up.

"What on God's green earth are you doing up there?!"

Marta stepped forward and looked up to see two soldiers clinging onto the peak of the roof. One of them started to slip and his compatriot caught him.

"Sorry yer Majesty! Euh, Majesties! We, ah, were trying to patrol when, uh, we uh… slipped."

"Yessir!" the second one, clinging onto his friend for dear life, added. He was missing a boot, *probably the one that fell,* Marta presumed. There was a horrible creak and a pause before the tile gave way. Thomas stepped inside and gently pushed Marta back as the two men yelled, tumbling off the roof and hitting the ground hard. She gasped as she heard a sickening crunch and rushed forward.

"Are either of you hurt?"

The first man, with brown hair, moaned and sat up. The second one, slightly pudgy with yellow locks, grumbled from underneath him.

"Only slightly… yer… Majesty…"

Thomas stepped forward and helped them stand whilst Marta tended to their wounds. Her hands glowed faintly as she examined each of them.

"Thankee, yer Majesty," the blonde one murmured as Marta finished mending his leg. She smiled warmly and shook her head.

"Thank *you* for keeping us safe. I'm only sorry you got hurt."

He glanced away guiltily before the other one stood at attention.

"Again, our sincere apologies, Milord. It won't happen again."

"See that it doesn't," Thomas snarled. Both men jumped in surprise, then bowed and excused themselves out the front door. Thomas had a stern look on his face, his arms folded.

"Well, I certainly can't have you out here while soldiers are gallivanting about. What has gotten into them? Did they have too much to drink—" he shook his head and pinched the bridge of his nose. "I'll have them draw you a bath in the room and I'll go somewhere else."

Marta started to object but Thomas had already walked off, muttering to himself. Ria and Selena saw to her bath quickly using waters from the hot spring. Thomas excused himself into another room, and Marta sighed pleasantly as she ran her hand through the soothing, healing water.

So warm... She undressed quickly and put a dirt-caked toe in. She hissed slighty and eased herself in. She splashed in the water a little bit before frowning. *He didn't have to leave...* she dunked her head under the water as her cheeks erupted in color, and not from the heat. *I don't think I'd mind...*

*****

Thomas sat bitterly in the warm water grumbling to himself. *They were from Finlay's regiment. Just what the hell was he thinking sending soldiers onto the roof like that?!* He scrubbed himself roughly with a bar of soap. *I guarantee it was under Peter's orders.* He groaned aloud. *He's reckless, totally reckless!* He washed his face and beard and dunked himself into the water. His thoughts drifted to what Marta was doing. *She's probably humming or something. Bathing with birds.* He chuckled at himself. *I wish she would bathe me —*

He sat up and rubbed his face. *Not now. Not now. I don't want to ruin what little standing I have with her already. Although... Peter will probably try and use this against me.* He blinked in realization. *Is that why they were on the roof...?*

He finished his bath and dried off his hair, running a comb through it. *No, I'm overthinking it. But... what if she doesn't want me? And what was with that look she gave me earlier?* He trimmed his beard so he looked more regal and less like a wild man. *Am I reading the situation wrong? What if she ends up hating me because I forced—* he shook his head as he wrapped a robe around himself and stepped out into the hallway. He saw Ria leaving their room and she grinned warmly as she passed.

"Everything is ready for dinner, my Lord. If you require anything else, please ring the bell." She nodded and walked away.

What she means is no one else is coming to the door. Does everyone think we−?! He gently knocked and heard Marta answer "come in!"

He opened the door and shut it quietly, locking it behind him. The parlor was empty but he could see the light on in the dining room. He whispered a thankful prayer that he had learned how to withhold *some* thoughts from Marta as he stepped inside. He pulled up short and blinked in surprise. Marta smiled up at him from her spot at the table, wrapped in a robe that matched his.

"Ria said these are the only two robes like this they have! Isn't it so fluffy?"

Ria, you rogue, he mused as he sat across from his wife. There was an amazing spread laid out before them with roast chicken, salads, potatoes, green beans, rolls, and all sorts of other goodies. It was an extravagant feast and the room was warm with the smell of food. Marta bounced happily and clasped her hands together, her stomach rumbling.

"Will you ask the blessing?"

Thomas paused. He hadn't asked for a blessing over food in years. He cleared his throat and nodded, grabbing his hands and closing his eyes.

"Ah, thank You, Jesus, for this food. And… thank You for my wife, for our safe travels, and for our journey home. Please bless this meal. Amen."

"Amen!" Marta replied happily. She paused as she examined the silverware. She tried picking one but couldn't remember if it was the right one. Her hand hovered over another fork but she withdrew in frustration. Thomas chuckled and pointed.

"When in doubt, outside in. Start with the outermost utensils and work your way in from there."

Marta nodded and picked up a knife and fork. Thomas did the same, serving his wife a piece of the chicken and then cutting some for himself. Marta began to take a bite and suddenly dropped her fork.

"Are you alright?" he asked, gazing at her in confusion. Marta's eyes widened as she picked up the piece of chicken and touched it.

"This chicken has had Psyllium added to it. It…" she began blushing. "It's a natural laxative made from a plantain."

Thomas paused, then roared with laughter. Marta winced slightly, covering her mouth. His amusement made her giggle. He shook his head and covered his face with his hands as he shook.

"That… conniving…son of a—" he sat back and motioned to the

food. "Is all of it laced?"

Marta sheepishly stuck her finger in each food to test to see if there were traces of anything. Her blonde hair, loose for once, fell beside her as she made her way around the table. Thomas tried not to watch.

"No, just the chicken."

"Of course!" he laughed curtly. "Well, someone certainly doesn't want us to enjoy our evening. I'm glad you caught it." He lifted his wine glass and toasted her. "Good job, Marta, for saving us from a... bad situation," he raised a brow as he took a sip. Marta laughed and sat down. They tucked into their meal while avoiding the chicken. Marta wasn't too worried since Thomas didn't seem to be, either.

Thomas was, however, distant during the meal, and as they finished Marta sat back and sighed. "I don't think I've ever had food that tasted so good before. Or so much!" she set her hands on her belly and chuckled. "I'm stuffed. Don't tell the army cooks, but I've been adding spices to their meals when they're not looking. It's nice to have a properly seasoned dish for once."

Thomas simply smiled at her. "I'm glad you enjoyed it... and that we avoided misfortune." They glanced at the whole mostly unscathed chicken sitting on its plate. Marta scratched her neck.

"Yes... that would have been... awful." She stood slowly and set her hands on the table. "Well... I think I'm ready for bed."

Thomas nodded briefly as he stared at his empty plate. Marta waited for him, her mind running at a million miles a minute. This longing that had been quietly building in her threatened to burst from her chest, but how on earth was she supposed to bring it up? When he didn't say anything she sighed quietly and started to walk away, praying she hadn't overstepped.

"Marta?"

She turned to see him leaning back in his chair playing with a fork. He glanced up at her with a surprisingly vulnerable look in his eyes.

"I...know what you're waiting for, but I have to be sure." He stood and walked over to her, putting his hands on her shoulders gently as if she would break if he touched her. "Are you alright with this?"

Marta nodded and smiled. "I know you didn't want to do anything before because of the travel. But..." she put her hand on his chest and smiled at him. Electricity shot across his body and he swallowed hard as he held her hand.

"Are you absolutely certain? I don't want to take advantage of you."

She chuckled and shook her head. "You're not. I promise."

He stepped towards her but jumped in surprise when a thudding came from the door. Marta recoiled as if she had been caught doing something wrong. The pair glanced at each other before Thomas rushed into the other room with a scowl. She could hear hushed voices as he opened the door but it was soon clear Thomas was getting angry. She snuck into the parlor and glanced around the corner.

General Finlay was standing in the doorway, his face a sickly green. Thomas rubbed the bridge of his nose and held up his hands.

"I don't see what I can do about this."

"They want to know if her Majesty can help…" Finlay whimpered. Thomas glanced up as she stepped out from the corner. Finlay looked at her in her robe and his eyes grew wide. His hand shot to his head to cover his eyes, shaking slightly.

"What's happened?" Marta asked disappointedly. Thomas motioned to the general.

"It seems it wasn't just our meal that was laced with… whatever you said it was," he grumbled thickly. "I guess they've opened up an infirmary of sorts—"

She sighed heavily, her shoulders sagging. "Let me get dressed and I'll be right there."

Finlay peeked out from between two fingers and nodded. "I will let them know," he whispered hoarsely before turning and disappearing down the hall. Thomas stood there with a disgusted look before slamming the door shut. Marta jumped as he whisked past her, mumbling something about "my own fault". She watched him go sadly, swallowed hard, and walked into the bedroom to get dressed.

*****

Peter paced in his room with a scowl, nibbling on his thumb. *She is going to be livid if we can't keep them apart. It's one of the only cards we have left to play.* His toe found the table leg and he yelped in pain, grabbing the injured digit and hopping. There was a knock on the door and he stood up straight as he cleared his throat.

"Come in."

Finlay stepped in and bowed, shutting the door behind him.

"Well?" Peter asked simply. Finlay leaned against the door as his face twisted in pain.

"Everything was spiked as you requested, Sire. As you predicted, her Majesty caught it, but the others in the party did not. She is seeing to them as we speak."

Peter heaved a sigh in relief. *Perfect. I'm doing this for your own good, brother.* "Good job. You are dismissed," he waved him off. Finlay hesitated, squirming against the door. Peter cast him a glare and held out his hand. "What is it, Finlay?"

"Sire," he swallowed hard and shifted extremely uncomfortably, "was it really necessary to lace my food as well?"

Peter laughed derisively. "Would you *like* to be accused of treason, General Finlay?"

The cowardly general shook his head emphatically. Peter shrugged. "Then there's your answer."

*****

Marta woke up the next morning with her back against Thomas'. He was breathing quietly, still deep in sleep. The night before brought a tinge of red to her cheeks, her hopes dashed before anything could be done. She had spent all night in the dining-room-turned-infirmary healing numerous Knights and Gifteds, along with Wesley and Seamus and even Finlay from their sorry states. Thomas worked on investigating the cause but even Ria and Selena couldn't figure out what had happened. The drug was nowhere to be found amongst anyone's possessions. Peter had come forward and told him he had been affected as well, but when Marta offered to help, he declined. Both husband and wife collapsed in bed early that morning too exhausted to even speak. She sat up slowly and gazed down at her husband, peaceful only in sleep. She gently ran her hand through his brown hair, amazed at how handsome he was.

I... really wouldn't have minded.

"Hmm?" he mumbled as he stirred. He blinked and turned towards her with bleary eyes. She smiled and kissed his cheek without thinking.

"Good morning," she whispered in embarrassment as he rubbed his face with his free hand. He glanced around and groaned.

"Good morning. Did you—"

A knock at the door interrupted their thoughts and he rolled his eyes. "Nevermind." He stood and shrugged into his robe as Marta stood and dressed quickly. She could hear voices in the next room and she stepped out in a simple skirt and shirtwaist. Peter was in the parlor with Thomas and he glanced over at her before returning his attention to the matter at hand.

"This couldn't wait until we made it home?" Thomas grumbled darkly. Peter shrugged.

"Sarah wanted to know right away."

Sarah? Marta stepped forward and took Thomas' arm. Peter's gaze flickered with frustration.

My sister-in-law. Peter's wife. Thomas replied, sighing and holding his head.

"We don't need to move anyone around. My *wife* will stay with me."

Marta blushed at the way he said that, but Peter stood his ground. "I'm sure she just wants to make things easier for you—"

Thomas shoved the letter against Peter's chest with a growl. "Well, she isn't. Let's get moving, I am eager to be home."

Peter's eyes narrowed as he took the crumpled letter. "Someone woke up on the wrong side of the bed. As you wish, your *Excellency.*" He bowed mockingly and left without sparing Marta a glance. She stood there awkwardly as Thomas characteristically rubbed the bridge of his nose in irritation.

"Watch out for Sarah," he finally sighed. "I asked her to maintain the castle in my absence, since Nick can only do so much. But I fear she lets the power get to her head, and she won't be keen on handing you the reigns. I had hoped she wouldn't find out until we arrived…" he shook his head. "I know you will learn quickly. If she gives you any trouble, will you tell me immediately?" he had a serious look on his face. Marta stepped into his embrace and gazed into his deep blue eyes with a smile, cupping his cheek in her hand.

"I will. I promise."

Outside the door, Peter smirked victoriously.

CHAPTER ELEVEN

Elroith, the Capital of Elyon

Marta couldn't keep her mouth closed as they neared the foreboding iron gate of the main city of Elroith. For the last few days they had traveled past mile after mile of farms and ranches, but now as they approached the fortress walls she was awestruck. The elegant castle could be seen from miles away, built into the imposing chalky cliffs of Mount Elrapha. Hundreds of people lined the main road and cheered as the army entered the city. The main road was wide and long with intricate buildings surrounding them. The city was lined in smooth stone and the horses clopped wearily, ready for a rest. Thousands of citizens streamed into the streets cheering and waving flags.

The flag consisted of two red stripes, one on top and one on bottom, with a white stripe in the middle. The fabric billowed in the wind and hung from nearly every window as far as the eye could see. Thomas and Marta rode beside each other with the army following them.

I didn't think we would get such a warm welcome... Thomas mused as he stared straight ahead. Marta was enamored by the major city, gawking at the numerous shops and markets and businesses. Amaryll rode behind her, a smile plastered on her face as she waved.

The city is massive! I can't even imagine how many businesses are here, how many people are here!

Thomas chuckled at her enthusiasm. Their interactions had been strained the last few days so it was good to see her smiling.

"I'll take you on a tour sometime. The Tower here is magnificent as well. There's the castle," he pointed. She looked up and shook her head at the numerous parapets and bridges stretching from tower to tower. As they got closer she had to lean back to see the top. To her surprise, she saw rooms and windows carved into the mountain beside the castle. *The castle itself is nearly as big as the entirety of Ropheka!*

I… actually think it's bigger.

Marta shot Thomas a bewildered glance and he shrugged with a sheepish grin. The road turned and led up a gradual slope to another stone wall with a thick iron gate. They passed under the gate and Thomas abruptly heaved a sigh of relief.

Are you alright? she asked in concern. Thomas nodded wearily.

It's been ten months since I've been home. It's good to see familiar sights. I can't wait to sleep in my own bed and not on a bedroll.

Marta nodded then turned to examine the courtyard and drive stretching in front of them. She gasped when she spotted an ocean of black uniforms, all the serving men and women standing outside to greet their monarch's return. At the top of the short set of stairs stood numerous well-dressed men and women, but the man in the middle caught her eye. He was a younger man with jet-black hair and a scruffy beard. His brown eyes were soft yet wise, his lips pressed together in a slight grin. She spotted the characteristic blue and white tartan of a Shepherd draped across his shoulders and based on Thomas' description she assumed this must be Nicodemus.

She shivered as a sensation of being stalked, similar to the figure back in the town weeks ago with the hundreds of eyes, settled on her soul. A darkness grew around her and startled her out of her thoughts. She shifted her gaze and met the steely glare of the gorgeous red-headed woman standing beside Nicodemus. The woman's green eyes glinted with hatred, her delicate nose turned up in a sneer. Her beautiful cherry-red lips curled in disdain as she folded her arms. The green silk dress she was wearing was immaculately detailed; it was evident she spared nothing to dress herself in the finest. Jewelry dripped from her ears and neck and Ela stones glittered on her wrists. Marta's jaw dropped at the staggering beauty of this aggressive woman.

"That…would be Sarah," Thomas grumbled under his breath. Marta could barely spare him a glance before returning her gaze to the woman on the stairs.

"She's gorgeous!" she exhaled.

"She's dangerous, is what she is," Amaryll growled softly. "She's up to something, I can see it in her eyes. Your Majesty, may I stay near Marta until the meeting this evening?"

"Permission granted," he sighed heavily. Marta glanced between the two of them in confusion.

Is... is she really that bad?

Worse, he groaned. Fear rose up in her as she met Sarah's gaze once more. Sarah broke her glare as the enterage stopped before the stairs. In perfect sync, the entire group of servants bowed in respect. Nicodemus held out his hands.

"Welcome back, your Majesty!"

Thomas dismounted and helped Marta get down. He nodded in acknowledgement.

"Thank you for your service to the kingdom in my absence, Nicodemus. I reassume the mantle once again."

Marta smiled at the formality. It was strangely appropriate, but she wasn't anticipating Nicodemus stepping down the stairs and placing a glittering crown upon Thomas' head. It was inlaid with beautiful Ela stones, along with other gemstones Marta didn't recognize. It again hit home that he really *was* the king. Thomas clasped his friend's shoulder and smiled wide. Nicodemus grabbed his arm and grinned before turning his soft brown eyes towards Marta.

"Ah, it's nice to finally meet you, your Majesty." Nicodemus bowed low, his hand on his chest. The rest of the servants' corps followed suit. Marta tried not to stagger back as Thomas smiled endearingly. Nicodemus stood tall and beamed with pride before turning to his monarch.

"She's even prettier than you described in your letters, Milord!"

Thomas shook his head in alarm as Marta's cheeks grew hot. *You wrote about me?*

He glanced at her sheepishly as if he had been caught. *Of course...*

Marta composed then introduced herself. "You flatter me, Shepherd. I am Marta, I've been eager to meet you!"

Nicodemus clasped her hand with a smile. He couldn't have been much older than Thomas. "It is my pleasure, your Majesty. I am Nicodemus. But please, call me Nick!"

Marta's attention was drawn back to the stairs where she stifled a gasp. Peter had climbed the steps and taken hold of his wife, dipping her over and kissing her passionately. Marta's cheeks grew rosy as Thomas shook his head in disdain, Nick simply chuckling.

"Things have been... *interesting* in your absence, my Lord. But please, we have a feast prepared for you!"

Thomas took Marta by the arm and nodded. Wesley and Amaryll took up behind the couple as they maneuvered around Peter and Sarah and into the main hall. The darkened room was lined with tapestries, the flag of Elyon draping from the rafters. The chandeliers all flickered dimly as the oil smoked slightly. Numerous hallways branched off from the main hall, and a large staircase dominated the farthest wall. The room smelled musty with age, but the hundreds of flowers sitting on tables that lined the walls lent a sweetness to the air. Marta tried to keep the composure she had been working so hard on the last few weeks, but the castle was too staggering. Thomas chuckled as he turned and led her down a hall.

"I will show you to our room later, and make sure you are escorted around. I will work with Lady Henley to assign you some handmaids. After that, we can have dinner in the north dining room, and..."

Marta's head reeled with the information, and she could feel a pressure around her skull. She touched her temple gently and winced as her fingertip glowed. Amaryll noticed and cleared her throat.

"Your Majesty, we will make sure Queen Marta gets accustomed to the castle. For now, though, you may want to go easy on her!"

Thomas glanced at his wife, who smiled painfully up at him. He winced.

I've overwhelmed her. I knew this would be too much.

Marta could sense him severing his thoughts from her and she grimaced. *It's okay, Thomas. I am definitely feeling way out of my league, but I promise I'll do my best for you.* She smiled sweetly. He sighed and nodded.

"Let's go sit down, first and foremost. I'm sure Cookie has prepared something wonderful."

She could smell the dining hall before they arrived there, her tastebuds watering in excitement. The familiar smell of steamed cabbage, the juicy scent of fresh meat, and the touch of delicate herbs caused her stomach to growl. The small party chuckled as she put her hands on her belly and blushed profusely.

"Ah yes, a fellow food lover!" Nick laughed heartily. "I can't wait to find out what kind of a palate you have."

Wesley and Seamus stood guard by the door as Thomas, Marta, Amaryll, Nick, and Jerome all sat at the ladened table. A fireplace behind Thomas lent a calming warmth to the room. Marta glanced up as a severe looking old man with thin white hair stepped forward and bowed.

"His Highness Prince Peter sends his apologies, he will be unable to attend lunch today," he spoke nasally, his voice terse and just as severe as the rest of him.

"I figured as much. Thank you, Edmond," Thomas sighed. The man straightened and examined Marta from the end of his nose. She nodded and smiled awkwardly. He turned jarringly and removed himself from the room.

"Edmond is the butler," Nick whispered to Marta as food was served with a flourish. "He's a grumpy old man, don't mind him."

Her eyelids flickered as she processed and nodded. The food laid out on the table was exquisite, and her jaw dropped as a whole roast turkey was brought out. Jerome rubbed his hands together in expectation as Amaryll licked her lips.

"Ah, real food!" she exclaimed as she smiled over at Marta. Thomas chuckled and nodded in agreement.

"Nick, would you do us the honors?"

Nick nodded and held out his hands. Marta clasped his in her right hand and Thomas' in her left. Once everyone had joined hands Nick bowed his head.

"Heavenly Father, thank You for Your provisions. Thank You that King Thomas was able to return home safely, and thank You for the blessing he brought in Queen Marta. I ask that You bless this meal, bless the farmers and ranchers who helped provide it, bless the cooks and servants who prepared it, and bless it to our use as we follow Your will. Bless the conversations we have and bless this great country, in Jesus' name."

"Amen," everyone finished. Marta glanced up at Thomas wearily. He nodded and served her a few slices of turkey. She took them gratefully and caught Nick's bewildered glance.

"...everything alright, Nick?" Thomas inquired. Nick shook his head wildly to dispel his thoughts and grinned.

"I had heard that a good woman would change a man, but goodness!" he ran his fingers through his hair and laughed incredulously. "The stern, severe Thomas serving his bride?! Am I dreaming?!" he turned to Amaryll. She shook her head with a grin and took another bite of food, melting in her chair. Thomas rubbed his face in embarrassment as Marta chuckled.

I promise I wasn't... THAT bad... she caught his thoughts. She grinned over at him and picked up her silverware.

I think it's sweet.

She took a bite and touched her cheek in surprise. "This is so good!"

Thomas smiled fondly. "I'm so glad you think so."

She caught a serving woman by the arm and smiled up at her. "May

I please have another two plates, ma'am?"

The woman's eyes grew wide and she glanced at Thomas before nodding. She scurried off as Nick leaned in to her.

"Think nothing of it, Milady. They're not used to royalty being so polite."

Thomas frowned at that. "What do you mean?" he asked darkly. Nick cleared his throat as the woman returned, handing Marta the plates.

"Thank you so much!" she beamed. The woman curtsied and rushed off.

"Sarah, ah..." Nick paused as Thomas held up his hand.

"Say no more."

The men watched as Marta gathered some food on the plates and stood abruptly. Thomas' brow furrowed in confusion as she walked over to Wesley and Seamus, who blinked in surprise. She handed them the plates with a smile.

"M'lady, we will be able t' eat later..." Wesley stammered. She shook her head, her smile never fading.

"You've been traveling just as much as we have. I know I was hungry, and you two young men could out-eat a dwarf!"

Seamus and Wesley exchanged embarrassed glances. Nick chuckled fondly and leaned his chin on his hands as he gazed at the young Queen.

"Ah... Sarah is going to devour her."

Thomas nodded slowly. "I was afraid of that..."

*****

Marta stood on a stone balcony overlooking the glittering city of Elroith, the mountains across the valley draped in pinks and golds. The setting sun was behind the castle, and a chill began to fill the air. A large river wound its lazy way through the valley on its journey to the sea. She could smell the smoke from the thousands of chimneys rising into the sky, but a cool breeze blew through the mountains behind her and brought with it the sweet scent of fall. She inhaled deeply and sighed, shaking her head.

"I feel like I'm dreaming."

Thomas stepped beside her and leaned against the railing, examining their domain.

"It's certainly much different once you see it in person, isn't it?"

Curtains gently wafted in the wind, tugging outside past the beautiful french doors that led into a large parlor. She glanced up at her husband and nodded.

"I… I struggle to feel deserving of any of this." She motioned to her beautiful blue dress. The fabric was the most comfortable she had ever felt, her silk shift soft against her skin. This corset didn't even pinch or tug and her new shoes fit surprisingly perfectly. She reached over and took his hand. "Or of you, for that matter."

His eyes flickered with light as he met his wife's gaze. "What do you mean?" *Have I been too hard on her? Did I show her too much? Have I forced too much on-* his thoughts were interrupted by her deliciously sweet giggle.

"I'm thankful for the time we spent in the wilderness together. I got to know you more, for who you are here," she gently poked his chest, "rather than just *here*," she motioned to the city. He followed her hand and sighed.

"I am not a very interesting person. I… have a lot of darkness that comes with me." He averted his gaze and dropped his head. "I have a lot I struggle with."

She reached up and gently cupped his cheek. The warmth from her hand sent tingles across his body as he held her hand against his face. She smiled comfortingly.

"Do you remember what I said so long ago, on the shore of the lake in Ropheka? I know you're not perfect. I'm not perfect either, so I don't expect you to be. I for one struggle with wondering if I heard God right, but then I look at you and… and I realize I'm supposed to be right where I am. We will both struggle with things, some for the rest of our lives." She shook her head and paused as light danced in her emerald eyes. "The difference now is that we won't struggle alone."

Warmth spilled over his head as he felt his Creator pressing peace into his heart. He smiled and gently held her neck, leaning forward and kissing her. "Thank you," he breathed thickly, leaning back with a soft smile. Her cheeks were flushed with pink. Thomas shook his head as his chest felt like it would burst.

I don't understand what this feeling is! I work so hard to keep my emotions at bay, yet this one has slipped through. It makes me feel irrational and yet I have clarity when I think. Nick was right, I do have more patience than I did before. What is it?

Marta turned and gazed over the city, not hearing his thoughts. The sun set and washed the land in darkness, but not before the fiery reflection off the water set her freshly cleaned hair alight with color. All at once he realized just how beautiful his bride was, how much he cared for her, and he swallowed hard.

"Marta?"

She turned and gazed at him with those dazzling green eyes. "Yes?"

He opened his mouth but nothing would come out. He took a step back and stammered incredulously, "I think I love you."

Her eyes sparked with light despite the darkness washing over the valley. Her lips parted in a smile and she tipped her head to the side, her eyes dancing.

"I think I do, too."

Her words filled him with an inexplicable joy he had never felt before. He reached forward and scooped her up in a hug, cradling her close. He buried his face in her neck and breathed deeply, her sweet scent filling him with comfort. She smelled like the wildflowers that grew in the mountains, like the breeze that carried with it the scent of pine and spruce. He clung to her like his life depended on it.

Marta's heart felt like it would burst as he said those words. The love she had hoped and prayed for was finally realized! Her own heart had been softened gently by the Maker's touch, and she wrapped her arms around her husband. He smelled musky yet his scent was distinctive. It was a mix of rugged mountains and trees, like a river carving through a canyon. Was that even a smell? She laughed under her breath as her mind grew foggy. When he leaned back and kissed her again, she met his affections. They continued their embrace through the evening, waking up in each other's arms.

*****

Iris winced as he heard the sickening *thud* and grunt of a body hitting the ground. He watched out of the corner of his eye as the man trembled and sat up, still reeling.

"My-My Lord, I—"

"Silence."

The man with the silver eyes leveled his gaze and set the edge of his sword on the man's neck. His victim gulped and trembled violently, his voice shaking. His mismatched hazel eyes were alight with fear, his dark hair in mats about his head.

"My king, my god! I swear I only serve you, I only—"

The Master's eyes flashed with venom. "I sent you there to kill the woman, Seeker, not cavort about to show off!" he jerked his arm and sliced through the man's cheek. The Seeker cried out and tumbled backwards. The Figure held out his hand and a dark ball of air swirled around it. He knelt down and slammed his palm onto the Seeker's face, surrounding his head with the ball. The Seeker convulsed and thrashed; Iris had to avert his gaze as an excruciating gulping and sucking sound came from the dying man on the floor. After a few agonizing moments his body fell limp. The ball of air dispersed and the Figure stood slowly, carefully examining the body before him. When he looked up the other Seekers in the room jumped to attention.

"Do I make myself clear?"

"Yes Sir!"

Iris could feel the Figure's silver eyes settle on his head.

"I've given you two chances, Iris. There will not be a third." He kicked the body of the Seeker on the ground as he passed, revealing his puffy purple face. His lips were blue and his eyes stared at Iris lifelessly. Iris swallowed hard.

"Clean this up," the Figure waved to Iris as he walked past the bowing Seekers and into the hall.

CHAPTER TWELVE

The Witch of Ildaile

Marta woke up luxuriously, stretching across the silk sheets. An elaborate canopy greeted her as she slowly sat up.

Their bedroom was *immense*. She could fit one, no, two *Dazed Knight's* across the bedroom alone! Massive windows lined the side she slept on looking out on a sleepy Elroith. She blinked as the sun rose above the far mountains, lending the room a golden glow. Thomas stirred beside her and she glanced down at him with a smile.

"Good morning, my love."

Thomas rolled over blearily rubbing his face. He paused as he caught her smile and glanced around.

"Wait... so it wasn't just a dream?!"

Marta laughed. "No, Thomas, it wasn't!"

He grinned mischievously as he sat up and kissed her deeply, leaning her back against the pillow.

"Well, then, in that case—"

There was a thudding at the door and both of them let out an exasperated sigh. He sat back and rubbed his neck.

"Well, at least we have a whole lifetime, hmm?" she chuckled as she took his hand in hers. He chuckled sheepishly before rolling his eyes as the intruder thumped at the door again.

"Coming, I'm coming!" He made an off-handed comment that made Marta blush as he stepped into the closet to change. He winked at her as he emerged in a tunic and trousers and put on his shoes as he clumsily walked to the door.

Marta slipped out of bed and into the closet to find something to wear. There were numerous dresses here, all in a range of hues and fabrics but all luxurious. She quickly found it difficult to dress herself for once. The blouses and skirts were intricately made but definitely not designed to be put on by herself. She struggled and finally gave up, choosing a simple white button-up blouse hidden in the back of the closet and a pretty blue skirt. She stepped into her shoes and trudged out of the bedroom and into the parlor just as Thomas shut the door.

"Is everything alright?" she asked as he rubbed the bridge of his nose. He sighed heavily and turned to her with a weary look in his eyes.

"There's been another attack."

She steadied herself against the doorframe, the sounds and smells of a burning Ropheka flooding her senses. She nodded slowly.

"Where?"

"On the eastern side of the kingdom, right off the sea."

Marta's eyes grew wide. "Is that where Portsmouth is?"

Thomas nodded, surprised she knew the name of the city. "Yes, that's where it was, in fact."

Marta slowly slid to the ground, her mind reeling. Thomas lunged forward and knelt next to her. Her heart sunk into the depths of her belly and her throat started closing with fear.

"Were the mirror transports re-established?" she croaked. Thomas nodded in confusion.

"Yes, they were cleared a little over a week ago—"

"Oh," Marta let out a groan and covered her face. Thomas shook his head as he felt anger rising up in him. *What's the matter?!*

She shook her head and met his gaze. "That's where Bri and Isaac were going!"

Thomas registered the gravity of her words and nodded. "I'll be sure to make contact with them when I—"

"I want to go too!" she cried, grasping his hands.

"No," he replied sharply. She blinked in surprise as he stood and ran his fingers through his hair. "You're staying here, Marta."

"What!?" she gasped as she stood, walking her hands up the wall to help steady herself. Thomas paced back and forth as he felt his anger rising.

"I said, you're staying here!" he halted and pointed to the floor. Marta shook her head desperately.

"I'm supposed to be with you, to go where you go, remember?!"

"You're supposed to stay *safe!*" he retorted, his voice rising. Caleb's words reverberated through his mind and he clutched at them for his defense against his wife. "Therefore, you will stay here where you will be protected!"

"I am safe with *you!*"

"No, you aren't!" he roared. She flinched as his voice echoed and he immediately regretted his words. He turned to the side and took a deep breath, calming his tone. "Marta… I don't know what's going on yet. Arailt has deliberately sent Pseudonyms and Seekers after you. Here you will have more protection than out there."

Marta struggled to fight back tears. Her voice quivered as she stammered "What is a Seeker?"

Thomas shook his head. "Not good, is what they are. I… I need to go meet the generals. Wesley and your Guard will be here and I know you will find friends. Besides, Nick is here." He stepped over to cup her cheek but she recoiled. He held his hand in the air and closed it slowly, clearing his throat. "We will be using the mirror transport, I believe. So… I won't be gone for as long this time. A few weeks, maybe?"

Marta wrapped her arms around herself as her heart threatened to break. *Once again, I am relegated to the sidelines. I am kept hidden away 'for my own good'. I'm useless.*

Thomas didn't hear her thoughts, nor did he want to. His heart tore at the seams as he watched his wife struggle. Rather than meet her to comfort her, he turned away.

"I have to go to the meeting. I'll make sure breakfast is sent up for you." He walked out, shutting the door behind him. He leaned against it and sighed heavily.

I'm a fool. He rubbed his face bitterly and stood up straight. *She's seen me for how I can be. A selfish, weak man.* Amaryll rushed around the bend in the hallway, followed closely by Nick. The two nodded and Thomas set his jaw. *I should never have let her see that side of me in the first place. No one should…*

Marta stared at the empty doorway her husband had just stormed through and stifled a sob. After all their time spent together, their intimacy last night, how could things fall apart so quickly?! She turned and examined the luxurious parlor, decorated with tapestries and elegant paintings. The carpet was soft under her feet and the chairs looked like she could melt right into them. The extravagance of her new home felt like a beautiful cloth slapped on a dirty wound.

Is this where I am supposed to be? She stepped forward towards the balcony, holding her hand up to protect her eyes from the rising sun.

Am I where You want me to be, Lord?
For the first time, she didn't hear an answer.

*****

"Portsmouth suffered an attack on their north side, most of the fields and ranches razed and burned. We haven't had a significant amount of casualties yet but the battle remains ongoing. There was a massive regiment of Hylen forces stationed in the mountains north of Portsmouth, along the border of Rodenheim," William, a general in his mid-fifties, reported with a sigh. His hair was a dirty blonde cut short for ease. His hardened expression never wavered as he turned with the others to a large mirror set at the end of the table. A dwarf sat on the other side, a glittering crown upon his own bright blonde hair. It was braided about his head, his beard billowing down his chest. The dwarven king nodded with a groan.

"Ve haf dizpashed a group of varriors to ze borders," he grumbled with a heavy accent, "und are verking on figuring out vhat happened."

Thomas nodded slowly, taking in all the information. "Based on what I can see, perhaps we can send a regiment of soldiers and Gifteds through the mirror to—"

There was a frantic knock on the door that jolted everyone at the table. Thomas met Jerome's gaze and nodded. The general bowed and stepped to the door. Everyone watched quietly as Jerome received a letter from a Knight and brought it to the King.

Thomas took it and read it quickly. He held it out and it burst into flames in his palm.

"There are enough Death Wizards there that they are turning our people into Pseudonyms," his voice was remarkably calm. Amaryll covered her mouth in horror as Peter and Finlay shook their heads. Thomas slammed his fist on the table and glared at the map.

"I want every able-bodied Knight, Gifted, and any soldiers we can spare out there *tonight*." Thomas met the gazes of those around the table as they nodded in agreement. "Bolster the castle guard and secure the borders. I don't want any of them getting away."

Amaryll nodded and turned to relay orders to a Knight standing behind her. Finlay and Jerome bowed to leave, heading out to their regiments. William patted Thomas on the back as the king of Rodenheim cleared his throat.

"Lerd Thomas, ve vill meet you there."

Thomas nodded and the mirror connection was cut, the image of the dwarf swirling into the reflection of Thomas' own weary face.

William stood up straight with a sigh. "My Lord, we will succeed."

Thomas caught Nicodemus' glance and nodded thoughtfully. *I hope for everyone's sake you're right, general.*

*****

Lady Henley, a delicate older woman with white streaked chestnut brown hair, chuckled ruefully. Marta stood in the parlor with a bewildered expression at the two young women bowing politely in front of her.

"Yer Majesty, Ah have handpicked these two t'help ye. Should ye allow, they will be yer handmaidens. This is Kate," she motioned to the older one, a blonde woman maybe only two years younger than Marta. She had soft features, shoulder-length hair, and a small nose, but her hazel eyes gleamed with adventure. Marta smiled and nodded politely.

"This is Brenna," Henley motioned to the other girl, who looked to be about nineteen. Her raven hair was pulled back behind her head and she dipped in respect. Her uncharacteristically blue eyes gleamed softly. Marta glanced towards the door, where Seamus and another one of her Guardsmen, Breton, a dark man with short black hair, stood at the ready.

"You don't happen to be Wesley's Brenna, do you?"

Kate nudged Brenna with a coy smile. Brenna rubbed her neck sheepishly.

"Well, when ye say 't like that, M'lady…"

Marta smiled wide and stepped forward, taking Brenna's hands in hers. "It's so good to finally meet you! Wesley has told me so much about you. And as my handmaiden, you'll be able to see him more often! It's perfect!"

Brenna's face grew red as she stared at the ground in embarrassment. "Th-thankee, M'lady…!"

Marta grinned and turned to Kate. "It's a pleasure to meet you both. I must confess, I don't know how things work around here, so I may need a bit of help for a while."

The two women grinned and curtsied. "Of course!"

Lady Henley nodded with respect. "Well, then, ladies. You know your roles. Treat her Majesty well."

The pair nodded as Henley excused herself from the room. Marta glanced about, spotted the tea on the table, and motioned for them to sit. They glanced at each other and chuckled.

"Milady, ye don't invite the help to sit."

"Why not?" Marta tipped her head to the side as she sat across from them. Brenna squirmed in her black skirt and blouse, adjusting the white apron around her waist and shoulders.

"Well, we aren't of the same caliber as ye."

"Says who?" Marta seemed genuinely confused. Brenna exhaled slowly before turning as Kate shrugged and stepped around the couch.

"She's the Queen, she makes the rules." Kate sat down and smoothed out her own black skirt with a thoughtful expression. Brenna examined the empty seat beside her, grimaced, then sat daintily. Seamus and Breton had to stifle a laugh at the women's nervous expressions. Marta clasped her hands together excitedly before motioning to the teapot.

"Tea?"

Brenna had to restrain herself as Kate swooped in and poured tea for everyone. Marta's brow raised.

"I thought you weren't supposed to pour tea for yourself? I would've poured for you."

Kate grinned sheepishly as she handed her a cup. "You're right, Milady. I got ahead of myself. To be honest, we've never been served by a royal before, nor have we shared tea with them."

"'Tis frowned upon!" Brenna added exasperatingly. Marta took the cup and inhaled deeply. It was a fruity, floral tea, a light pink color and tantalizingly sweet. It was very different from her normal cup of spicy black tea shared with Amaryll.

"Well… I think it's ridiculous. God doesn't see status," Marta shrugged after taking a sip, "so why should I?"

Brenna's jaw dropped as Kate snorted her tea. She scrambled for a handkerchief before laughing at herself.

"I like her already!" Kate howled.

Brenna gave her compatriot a nervous glance as Marta simply smiled. There was a knock at the door and the men jumped. Seamus started to open it before stepping back in surprise as the door opened. Marta's heart plummeted as the fiery red-headed princess stood in her doorway, taking in the unusual scene. Her green eyes blazed as she rested her gaze on the handmaids. Brenna and Kate leapt to their feet and stood up straight as Sarah waltzed inside. Marta began to stand and recoiled as a *slap* echoed through the room. Her mouth dropped as

Brenna's cheek turned red where she was struck, the young woman doing her best to retain her composure.

"Excuse me?!" Marta exclaimed in shock as Sarah quietly put her glove back on.

"You're excused," Sarah sighed luxuriously, adjusting her fingers. She glared as Marta pushed past her and put her glowing hands on Brenna's cheeks. Sarah's brow lifted for a moment as she watched Brenna's cheek return to it's pale normal. Marta turned to face Sarah with an indignant glare.

"I don't know who you are, but you can't go around treating others like—"

"Why ever not?" she replied lazily, standing her ground. "They're the servants. You'll need to learn their status under you lest they take advantage of your… kindness," she sneered, her eyes perusing Marta from head to toe. The feeling like her very soul was being examined welled up in her and she tried not to wilt. Sarah humphed and feigned a short bow.

"I am Princess Sarah of Ildaile, Prince Peter's wife. It is a pleasure to meet you, your *Majesty*."

Marta couldn't help but hear Peter's venom laced in his wife's voice. It took everything within her to remain calm.

"I didn't realize it was within your *status* to barge into the King and Queen's private room," Marta inhaled, "your Highness."

Seamus and Breton exchanged wide-eyed glances as Kate suppressed a snicker. Sarah's eye twitched as hatred burned in her irises. She opened her red lips to speak before a sound startled both of them out of their thoughts. Amaryll stood in the open doorway, her eyes flickering between the two women.

"Your Majesty, King Thomas has requested your presence."

Marta nodded and sighed silently in relief. She motioned for Kate and Brenna to follow as she walked towards the door. She turned at the last moment and nodded at Sarah.

"Next time, wait for an answer." With that, she stepped into the hall. She could feel Sarah's glare drilling a hole through her back as Wesley met them in the hallway.

Marta's heart was thundering in her ears and as soon as they rounded the corner she exhaled sharply and leaned against the wall, clutching at her chest. Amaryll turned with wide eyes as Kate covered her mouth and tried not to laugh.

"Did you— did you see Lady Sarah's face?!" Kate doubled over and laughed silently into her hand. Brenna stepped over to Marta and gently reached out her hand, but then withdrew.

"Are y'alright, M'lady?"

Marta stood up and turned around with wide eyes, a mortified grin tugging at her lips. "I can't believe I said that..." she finally mustered. Wesley glanced between the two women before Amaryll spoke up.

"She gave you the face not many have dared to see again, Milady. What did you do?!"

Marta frantically explained the situation. She caught Wesley's eyes flickering dangerously when she got to the part about Sarah slapping Brenna. Brenna shuffled uncomfortably as she finished the story and shrugged. Amaryll whistled in awe.

"I wasn't expecting you to get on her bad side *that* quickly... oh, this isn't good."

Marta's eyelids flickered as regret spiked in her chest. "I... should I not have done that..."

Amaryll rubbed the back of her neck and shrugged. "Too late now, I suppose. I only worry about..." a groan escaped her lips as she continued, "—let's get going, his Majesty's waiting."

The four of them followed behind Amaryll as they silently traversed the elaborate wooden hallways lined with thick rugs. They walked down a staircase and into a large hall. At the end, two massive doors stood wide open, revealing an enormous ballroom. Her jaw dropped as the small entourage was led inside and down a short set of stairs. Floor-to-ceiling windows lined the walls, the ones on the left looking out over the city and the ones on the right opening up onto a balcony overlooking the castle gardens. Thomas stood on the other side of the room speaking with Nick. She grimaced as she noticed his armor already strapped on and freshly polished, his familiar sword affixed to his side.

Thomas glanced up as he spotted his wife enter the room and paused mid-conversation. Nick followed his gaze and chuckled under his breath.

Look at him. This morning he was angry, but as soon as he sees her it all melts away.

She looks scared. Thomas blinked in alarm. *Why is she scared?*

Marta winced as she caught the tail end of his thoughts. *I, erm, had a run-in with Sarah...*

He stepped back in surprise as the group bowed in respect. Amaryll glanced between the two and rubbed her neck.

"Well, Marta, why don't you explain the situation."

She did so and Thomas had to fight himself not to snicker. *You really said all that?!*

I really did... she replied mournfully. *She's not going to hurt Brenna or Kate because of me, will she?*

Thomas sighed and shook his head. *I'm more worried about her hurting you...* He groaned and rubbed the bridge of his nose.

"This complicates things greatly. I wanted you here to protect you, Marta, not stir up trouble!"

"Does this mean I get to go with you?!" she replied eagerly. The rest of the group glanced at each other awkwardly as Thomas' eyes narrowed.

"What? Of course not-!" he hesitated and clamped his mouth shut, his anger welling up inside him again. He threw up his hands bitterly. "If anything, this just worries me more! Do you have any idea what you've done?!"

Marta stepped back as her wounds began to resurface. "If you think she's going to kill me, then take me with you!"

"She isn't going to kill you, Marta! Why would she be a part of the family if she would do such a thing?!"

His words gave her pause and she clamped her mouth shut. She fidgeted sheepishly and stared at the ground. *Family... she's part of my family, now. And... even though I may not like her or agree with her, I... should at least be kind.* Warmth flooded her spine and she shuddered. Thomas pinched the bridge of his nose and grumbled under his breath.

"Your Majesty," Nick spoke quietly and intentionally, "I will be sure to keep an eye on the situation. Besides, I'll be teaching Queen Marta how to run things while—"

"You have so much on your plate already, Nick. I don't want to add more."

"Perhaps," came a familiar voice, "I could help with that."

The group turned to see Peter and Finlay step forward. Peter bowed low, much to Marta's surprise.

"My wife sends her apologies, your Majesty. She has been under a great deal of stress and wasn't anticipating losing her place in the castle."

Nick scoffed and turned away as Peter stood. Marta couldn't sense the intent behind his words, so she simply shook her head.

"I appreciate the thought, Lord Peter, but I would rather it if she apologized in person. I want to apologize as well, I should have treated her with more kindness than I did."

Nick and Amaryll's jaws dropped as Marta dipped in respect. Thomas felt a touch of pride for his wife as Peter cleared his throat.

"Yes, indeed. Anyway, I know my dear Sarah can be abrasive. She has assured me she won't cause any problems while we are gone."

Thomas' eyes narrowed at that. "I hope so, Peter. If you truly care for my wife you will be able to keep yours in check."

Nick coughed in an attempt to hide his laugh. Amaryll whistled again as Peter chuckled blandly, his lips curving into a sneer.

"Of course, your Excellency."

Thomas returned his attention to Marta, who stood there with wide eyes. He gently held her shoulders as she turned to look at him.

"Marta, we will be gone only for a few weeks, Lord willing. Nick will be here for you during that, and you can talk to your friends back in Ropheka as well. I'll send letters as time allows." He chastely kissed the top of her head as she sighed heavily.

"Be safe. Please…" she grasped his hands in hers, "come back in one piece."

Thomas chuckled under his breath. "I will try."

*****

Marta returned to a destroyed suite that evening— broken vases with scattered flowers were shattered on the floor. The bed was in shambles and furniture had been angrily tipped over.

Message received… she mourned.

CHAPTER THIRTEEN

A Raven and a Rose

Thomas grunted as he parried a blow, his opponent skilled and quick. He swiftly dodged out of the way as another dark soldier careened towards him. A quick cut and the soldier was dispatched. The other one lunged and Thomas barely had a moment to step out of the way as the sharp steel grazed his arm. He recoiled and staggered backwards, the soldier before him cackling.

His enemy's reverie was cut short as Jerome's sword pierced his chest. The soldier slumped to the ground as Jerome stepped forward, panting heavily.

"Are you alright, Milord?"

Thomas nodded between breaths and turned. Two weeks of brutal warfare had turned these idyllic hills and fields into a bloodbath. Once yellowed with grain and harvest, the hills were streaked with the black blood of Hylen's army. The salty sea air brought with it the sounds of clanging and crashing of soldiers, Gifteds, and Knights fighting for their lives. Jerome held up his shield and deflected a blackened arrow headed for Thomas, and a bright light burst on the hillside. Another Light Gifted eliminated the enemy archer in one fell swoop. He glanced over at the Gifted-Knight duo, Brianna and Isaac, locked in battle. It seemed that after Ropheka they had learned more combat skills which proved invaluable on the battlefield.

Marta will be pleased to know they're alive.

The thought of his wife and their last interaction made him wince. *I'm a horrible husband, how could I leave her like that?*

"Thomas!"

He lunged out of the way as a hissing Pseudonym threw itself at him. He jerked and sliced through the creature's neck sending it gurgling and sinking to the ground. He heaved in breaths, shaking his head to clear his thoughts. He and Jerome turned as King Wilhelm of Rodenheim barreled towards them, battle axe in hand. The blond dwarf pulled up short and nodded towards the sea.

"Ze Death Vizards haf been dealt vith. Zis is ze last of zem."

Thomas nodded and lifted his sword, wincing as his arm stung in protest. He raised his sword high and yelled "For Elyon!"

Wilhelm lifted his own weapon high, invigorating his dwarven warriors in their native tongue. "Zum Ruhm von Rodenheim!"

The armies cascaded down the hill for the final push as the dark warriors of Hylen crashed into them head-on.

*****

Marta flinched as she heard the echo of a door slam down the hall. She quickly shut her book and glanced at Kate and Brenna sitting with their sewing. They met her startled gaze with their own. Wesley and Seamus stepped in front of the door as the sound of Sarah screaming at her maids reverberated through the walls. Marta felt like she was going to be sick.

No wonder everyone was so relieved when Thomas came home. She was so much better behaved then, even if only for a day. Two weeks had passed since her husband left and familiar tears of regret sprang to her eyes. *I wish I hadn't gotten so mad at him.*

The tempest stilled and everyone let out a sigh of relief. She leaned back and ran her fingers through her hair.

"Is she always like this?" she mumbled quietly as if Sarah could hear. Brenna sighed as Kate nodded.

"Yes ma'am. Ever since she got dumped here three years ago."

"Ah doon' know why she's like this, she's treated well!" Brenna threw her hands up in the air. Marta shook her head and sighed.

"What a horrible way to live. I truly pity her," she sighed and set her book to the side. "Well, now that I've thoroughly lost my focus, how about we go down to the castle gardens?"

"Ah'd love to, yer Majesty."

Wesley and Seamus followed behind the ladies, hands on their swords. The castle was not nearly as lively as it had been when Thomas was there. Servants avoided Marta, but she soon realized they were hiding from any royalty. Sarah was a cruel taskmistress frequently physically punishing her maids and those who served her.

Marta winced as she remembered how Sarah had left her room the night Thomas left. Nick helped her piece it back together, but unfortunately, petty destruction was not a cause for serious reprimand. Marta swiftly realized just how afraid of Sarah everyone was and where there was fear, there was power. She had gone to apologize for her own attitude, but Sarah laughed her out the door. She rarely saw the princess at all after that, blessedly.

They stepped outside and into the expansive castle gardens. Mountains loomed on either side of them as she walked along her now well-worn path through the flowers, bushes, and trees. While more accustomed to healing, she enjoyed cultivating the gardens, reaching out a golden hand and touching a rose. It bloomed with gorgeous white and pink petals, its' sweet fragrance filling the air. Marta tugged her cloak closer around her as a chill blew over them, reminding them of the impending winter. Fall was firmly in place, and the nights got so cold the flowers and shrubs had begun to hibernate. It was a hauntingly beautiful reminder of life. She could smell the fallen aspen leaves from the mountains carried on the cold afternoon breeze. A hawk cried overhead on its way to its' nest, taking dinner with it.

Marta quietly sat on a stone bench in the middle of the aging garden and Kate and Brenna sat next to her. From here she could hear the distant roar of a waterfall cascading down the mountain. A small stream gurgled as it passed through the garden on its journey to the sea. Massive oak trees loomed above them and maples had already started to lose their leaves. She sighed again, feeling at peace in the outdoors like she always had.

I want to bring Thomas here, although I'm sure he's familiar with it. I miss him greatly.

The young Queen had learned a lot in the past few weeks, even taking on some of a queen's regular duties. Nick was pleased with her progress and had started to become a confidant for her. While she wasn't comfortable opening up as much to him as she was Caleb and Camilla, they had had several enlightening conversations over tea. She opened up her book again, a Bible, and began reading where she had left off.

Let all bitterness and wrath and anger and clamor and slander be put away
from you, along with all malice.

Marta scoffed. *If only Sarah could do the same. She treats everyone with disrespect, she's cantankerous and crude. She's ungrateful and—!* Her thoughts screeched to a halt as she read the next verse. She winced as conviction settled on her soul.

Be kind to one another, tenderhearted, forgiving one another, as God in Christ forgave you.

She swallowed hard. *Forgive her? HER? I—* she closed the Good Book and rubbed her face.

"Ah, Ephesians is one of my favorite letters ever written."

Marta glanced up at Nick standing before her with a bemused smile on his face. Kate and Brenna jumped and dropped their sewing projects in alarm, Brenna hissing as she stabbed her finger with her needle.

"Where—where did you come from?!" Kate exclaimed as Brenna stuck a finger in her mouth. Marta shook her head and blinked slowly, not even having heard him approach.

"Ah, sorry about that," Nick chuckled and rubbed the back of his neck. "I was walking around the gardens whilst hiding myself... sometimes it's the only thing that allows me a moment to my own thoughts."

Marta chuckled and leaned back. "It's amazing all the abilities being Light Gifted can mean. One can have the defensive abilities like Caleb, the offensive like Thomas, and then the just plain strange."

Nick grinned. "Like me?"

"Perhaps!" she laughed. He chuckled and knelt in front of her, his expression turning serious.

"May I ask what is bothering you? And no, I don't have discernment — it's just written all over your face," he smiled warmly. "I ask as your Shepherd and... as a friend."

Marta sighed wearily, running her hand over the leather-bound tome. *I want to talk to someone about it. I do.* She glanced up at him, his gentle smile never wavering.

"Yes... you may ask. I... I struggle with... *her,*" she grumbled, unable to even say her name. "I had heard a little bit about her before I came here, but— ugh, look at her! How selfish can one woman be?!" she held up her hands. Now that the gates in her heart had creaked open everything she had held onto for weeks came flooding out along with her tears. "I—I am *livid* at her behavior towards the maids, the soldiers, even you!" she motioned to him. He nodded once in acknowledgement. She held out her hands to the book on her lap. "How can I possibly forgive *her*?!"

"My Lady... may I ask you a question?"

She swallowed at that ever familiar look, the one Caleb would give her when he was about to teach her something important. A large part of her didn't want to know what he had to say, but something deep inside her pleaded to let him speak. She wiped her tears away and nodded as her voice quivered.

"Of course, Nick."

"How does God forgive you?"

She blinked. She glanced to the side, at her hands, then back up at him. "Through Jesus, of course. His death on the cross and His resurrection."

"You could say we are forgiven by His Grace, right?"

Familiar conviction punched her in the gut. She turned away as her anger rose up in her again. "And Sarah can seek out His Grace too…" she mumbled miserably.

Nick simply chuckled and stood, his knees cracking as he stretched them out. Marta stifled a laugh as he leaned over with a wince.

"Ah… I'm really fitting the role of an old Shepherd, aren't I?"

"You're not even that much older than Thomas! Don't say such ridiculous things," she leaned forward and touched his outstretched palm with a glowing hand. He sighed in relief and smiled at her as she withdrew back onto the bench. *I have a salve that might be able to help with that, maybe that can help me pass the time.*

"Thank you, my Lady. As for her Highness Sarah… it's hard to deal with those who hurt us, especially when they are supposed to be family. While she has access to forgiveness, it's up to her to grasp it. All we can do is extend forgiveness and grace," he held out a hand and she took it, standing slowly. He held out his arm and escorted her through the garden as her entourage followed behind. "Forgiveness does not mean that what others do is right, or even okay." He glanced down at his monarch as she shook her head.

"I try to forgive her. She's just so… infuriating! And she never changes!" she cried in exasperation. "God may be able to forgive her, but… I don't know if I have the strength to…"

Nick nodded thoughtfully. "There are a lot of things we can't do with our own strength. 'We can love because Christ first loved us.' Think of it like… like a cup." He stopped by the creek and bent down to scoop up water in his hand. It dribbled through his fingers and disappeared quickly. "We are cups, and God's love and grace is the water. If you don't have any water in your cup," he made a pouring motion from one hand to the other, "you can't give it out. But if you continually let God pour into you…" he scooped up water and poured it into his other hand, scooping up over and over again until his other hand and sleeve were drenched. He grinned up at her. "You can saturate them with His love."

Marta stared forlornly at the little creek, averting her gaze from Nick. She rubbed her arm in guilt. *I've tried that, Nick. I have. Why do you think I'm out here? I can't stand to be around her. I don't have anything left to give...* A sudden realization struck her and nearly wrenched the breath from her lungs. "Nick... have you ever..." she swallowed hard and chose her words carefully. "Have you ever... stopped hearing His Voice?"

Nick tipped his head to the side in concern. "Stopped hearing—?"

"Nicodemus Aurelius! There y'are!"

Nick flinched as Lady Henley and Edmond strode forward on the stone path. Nick winced and smiled sheepishly.

"Ah, Lady Henley, what a surprise! I was just finishing up and—" he let out a cry as she grasped him by the ear and pulled him down to her level.

"Doon play wit' me, Nico! Ye've reports t' finish!"

"Ack— yes, ma'am!"

Henley spotted Marta, gasped, and bowed, bringing Nick down with her.

"Hey hey hey hey, go easy on—ah!"

Marta watched with a mixture of regret and bemusement as Henley stood.

"Milady, forgive me. Ah've been lookin' fer 'im fer some time now."

Marta waved nervously. "No no, it's okay. I understand. Good luck, Nick."

He waved before Henley tugged on his ear again and trudged back towards the castle while ignoring his protests. Edmond stepped forward and bowed curtly.

"My Lady, the noble Ladies from court are assembling in the tea room. As Queen, it is your responsibility to meet with them and entertain them."

Marta's eyes grew wide as she nodded. *Oh no, I completely forgot that was today!* She glanced down at her plain green dress and brushed it off.

"Ah, do I look alright?"

Edmond took a brief glance and sighed, closing his eyes. "Ladies?"

Brenna and Kate stepped forward and bowed in respect. "We will get Milady taken care of, sir."

He nodded and left without so much as a goodbye. Marta glanced down at her dress then at her handmaids with a confused look. "What? Do I look bad?"

Kate and Brenna smiled knowingly and directed her inside.

"Ye look great, Milady, but ye're goon to war."

War?! She thought in alarm as they walked inside as thunder rumbled overhead, Wesley and Seamus following behind.

*****

Why did I agree to this, Marta's eyes widened at the group of immaculately dressed women bowing in respect. She stood in the doorway to the arboretum fidgeting uncomfortably in an elegant blue blouse and skirt. The bustle at her lower back felt awkwardly large and the blue-tinted Ela earrings hanging off her ears felt too flashy. Her normally simply braided blonde hair was instead pulled up behind her head, cascading freely down her back with decorative braids draping from an opal hairpiece. The four women before her stood with varying expressions. The building smelled fresh and woodsy with tall oak trees and colorful aspens lining the stone walkway. The gardeners had recently swept everything out but already a few yellow leaves had fallen onto the path. The sound of rain pelting the roof lent a soothing atmosphere to the otherwise nerve-wracking moment.

Marta inhaled deeply and nodded in respect. "Good afternoon, everyone. Thank you for coming. It is my pleasure to make your acquaintance. I am Mar— Queen Marta," she corrected with a wince, remembering Edmond's scolding earlier to address herself properly.

The woman on the left, slightly larger with brown hair, stepped forward and dipped in respect. Her accent wasn't as thick as some but Marta could catch it. "Good afternoon, Milady. I am Duchess Lorna. I am honored to meet yeh!"

Marta smiled at the young woman's bright countenance. "The honor is mine, Duchess Lorna."

The second woman stepped forward and curtsied, her eyes flickering between Marta and the door. Her blonde hair was pulled back into a taut bun. "I—I am Duchess Fiona, my Lady."

Marta nodded in respect, smiling wide. "Hello, Duchess Fiona."

The third woman, a brunette, barely curtsied. She examined Marta with a glare. "Your Majesty. I am Countess Fenella."

Marta shuddered at her glare but continued with a smile. "Lady

Fenella, thank you for coming."

Fenella scoffed and stepped back as the final woman stepped forward. The strawberry-blonde woman had a blank look on her face, one Marta couldn't decipher as good or bad. She curtsied low.

"Yer Majesty, Ah'm Lady Ravina. 'Tis me honor t'make yer acquaintance."

Marta felt hesitant as the woman's bright green eyes met hers, her accent thick and her voice deeper than the others. She dipped her head in respect and murmured, "Thank you, Lady Ravina. Shall we?" she motioned to a table where tea had been set out. Lorna and Fiona turned to sit when Fenella spoke, folding her arms.

"Where is her Grace, Princess Sarah? Shouldn't she be here too as a Lady of the House?"

Marta froze. *Oh, no! I completely forgot to invite her!* She turned and motioned to Edmond, who stepped forward solemnly.

"Edmond, would you please go retrieve Princess Sarah?"

He cast her a glare before bowing low. "As you wish, my Lady."

She grimaced as he walked out. *Sorry, Edmond...* She turned back and forced a smile. "Let's sit while we wait."

Fenella smirked as she turned away. Ravina watched her with a not-so-dainty shrug then settled her gaze back onto Marta. Marta squirmed under her perusement and motioned. "After you?"

Ravina turned, ever expressionless, and sat at the table. Marta took her seat and tried desperately not to fidget. "Well, I am excited to be able to share this—"

The door to the arboretum burst open and Marta flinched at the familiar *clack, clack, clack* of high heels on stone. She shifted as Sarah stormed towards the table with a fire in her eyes. She dipped with a mocking smile at Marta before taking an empty chair next to Fenella. Marta cleared her throat and nodded.

"N—now that we're all here, shall we begin?"

Several serving women stepped forward and served tea, setting out tiered tray after tray with scones, pastries, sandwiches, and more layered on them. She reached out to take a cookie but she met Sarah's angry glance and withdrew.

"So, Lady Ravina!" Lorna began with a nervous chuckle as she grasped her tea cup, "Y' said your husband just recently became a Lord?"

Ravina set down her cup and nodded solemnly. She raised it again and took a big gulp, much to the amusement—and horror— of the ladies around the table.

"Ye, he did." She wiped her mouth with her sleeve and motioned for a maid, who stepped forward and bowed. "Ye got anything stronger, like whiskey, ye kin?"

The maid glanced at Marta in alarm and shook her head. "M-my Lady, I don't—"

Ravina waved her off. "A'right. Thought Ah'd ask."

Marta had to stifle a bewildered laugh. *She's fun, I wonder if she's always like this.*

"So, your Majesty," Sarah drawled as she ran her finger along the glass of the table with a disgusted look, "how are your lessons coming along? It must be so *difficult* to be thrust into nobility, what, with growing up impoverished and all."

Lorna and Fiona exchanged nervous glances as Marta forced a smile. *She's trying to goad me.*

"It has been a huge change, Lady Sarah. I appreciate the patience of my mentors." She took a small sip of her tea. "I'm afraid you must have heard a rumor, however, for I was never impoverished. I simply lived at my means."

"Oh?" Sarah bolstered her attack as she leaned forward with a glint in her eyes, "I didn't realize the Tower paid their Gifteds so well. Or did you have a lot of families pay you to stay in town being the only Life Gifted there? Perhaps you weren't very good at it seeing as though they kept you stuck in one place for so long. Did you use..." her mouth tipped insinuatingly, "*other* ways of earning your keep?"

Marta's brow twitched as she remembered the faces and voices of those she had healed, of the toothy grin of Markus McKay and the brokenness of Duncan's brother as he wailed for his wife. Angry tears pricked at her eyes and she struggled to remain calm.

"Lady—"

"Lady Sarah," Lorna growled, "surely you are not accusing our Lady of having..." she struggled to find the word, "...frequented less than honorable establishments?"

Sarah shrugged and leaned back. "I heard she spent most of her time at a tavern and you are only all-too-familiar with the type of *lady* that acquaints herself with people there, aren't you, Lorna?"

Lorna's eyes widened and she stared at her cup bitterly, humiliated into silence. Sarah chuckled victoriously.

"It's true that I visited the *Dazed Knight* occasionally, but that's because—"

"Oh, so you were a regular? Interesting."

Marta gripped her cup and tried to still her breathing. "The owner is a good friend of mine and he—"

"Oh, he *is*? Do you still *visit* him on little secretive mirror trips back home?" Sarah tipped her head to the side. Marta's lips pressed together as her anger threatened to blow her reserve. The trees around them shuddered with only Lorna and Fiona seeming to notice.

"The only *business* I conducted there was to sell salves and tinctures as well as get dinner. That's *all*," Marta growled. "Geralt would never allow the type of debauchery you are insinuating. Unlike *some* women, I can fend for myself, in more ways than one."

Ravina snickered as Sarah's grin slid into a frown. Sarah cast the older woman a glare before leaning back. Ravina delicately dabbed at her mouth with a napkin and averted her gaze, watching the leaves cascading to the floor. Fenella glanced at Sarah in alarm as the Princess stood abruptly.

"Thank you for tea, your *Majesty*." She turned and knocked over Marta's teacup, spilling the hot liquid into Marta's lap. Marta hissed in pain as maids lunged forward to help. Sarah's eyes gleamed.

"Whoops," she motioned to Fenella, who stood with a grin. "Lady Fenella, I require your assistance."

"Yes, my Lady."

Marta watched the two women leave through tears as maids handed her napkins. She could see a gentle golden light emanating from her thighs but it disappeared quickly. Lorna, Fiona, and Ravina gazed at their queen forlornly as she tried to quell the tears threatening to spill over.

"I... apologize you had to see that," Marta croaked through a tightening throat, dabbing at her eyes with Geralt's handkerchief. She glanced at the monogram and held the fabric against her nose. The smell of home was almost gone now, Geralt's stew and mead a distant memory.

"Nay, Milady..." Lorna mourned, "I'm sorry. Lady Sarah can be... difficult."

Fiona squeaked in alarm and slapped her friends' arm. "Don't say that! She'll crucify you in court if she hears you—"

"She already has!" Lorna threw up her hands. "It canna get much worse for me now."

Marta's eyes flickered with light as she reached forward and set a comforting hand onto Lorna's. "May I ask what happened?"

Lorna's eyes filled with sorrow and she sighed. "There… there's gossip going around that my husband visited a tavern of ill-repute." Her eyes welled up with tears and she glanced away, withdrawing her hand as she held herself. "He says he only went for a meeting, but… several of the… *women* there say otherwise…"

Marta's heart tore into two. *I can't even imagine having your partner do something like that.* Fear bubbled up inside her as a dark thought slipped into her mind. *What if Thomas…* Lorna dabbed at her eyes with a handkerchief as Fiona patted her shoulder tenderly.

"Ah doon know what to do," Lorna's accent got thick as her voice flooded with emotion, "what, with a bairn on th' way an' all—"

Marta's eyes widened. "You're pregnant?"

Lorna nodded slowly. "Five months, now. What am Ah supposed to do if—" she stifled a sob and stood abruptly. "I—I apologize, Milady. If you'll excuse me—"

Marta watched sadly as Lorna rushed out of the room weeping. Fiona curtsied to Marta and flashed her a concerned smile before following behind.

Marta felt Ravina's eyes settle on her as she stared at the table. *I was only trying to help… should I not have said anything? Poor girl… I can't even imagine being pregnant and rumors spreading about my husbands supposed unfaithfulness… I don't—*

"Yer husband won't do that to ye, as cowardly as he is."

Marta blinked as tears fell from her eyes, slowly meeting Ravina's gaze. "I… he… what?"

Ravina leaned forward on her arm and gazed at Marta with dazzling green eyes. She held out her hand.

"Ah haven't properly introduced meself yet." With a snap a bright light burst from Ravina and Marta recoiled in shock. She rubbed her eyes and blinked as an old man with silvery hair and bright green eyes sat where Ravina had been. Wesley and Breton lunged forward unsheathing their swords, but the man lifted a glowing golden finger. They halted as golden ethereal butterflies appeared from thin air and flew up into their faces. The man cackled in amusement as the Guardsmen tried to swat them away.

"Ye needn't worry, lads!" he laughed again and rested his gaze on a bewildered Marta. He held out his hand.

"Pleased t'meet ye, yer Majesty. Ah'm Ravenswicke."

Marta's eyes widened further as she trepidatiously took his hand. He yanked her over and kissed the back of her hand.

"Ah, apologies, M'lady. I ferget me own strength pretending t'be a lady," he winced as he released her arm. She sat back into her chair and blinked.

THIS is Ravenswicke?!

He cackled again at Marta's look. The older man wore a brown tunic and green-blue plaid kilt with a faded brown leather belt tied around his waist. He carried numerous bags filled with all sorts of pungent odors and Marta coughed as she covered her mouth and nose. *These are some strong-smelling herbs!* Wesley and Breton shook their heads as the butterflies disappeared. Edmond bent forward and held out a tray, a cup of foul-smelling liquid sitting on it.

"Ah, Edmond, good ol' Edmond! Thankee, friend!" Ravenswicke took the cup and downed it in one gulp. Edmond stood slowly and for the first time Marta caught a hint of a smile tugging at the old man's lips.

"Always a pleasure to see you, Lord Ravenswicke. When the maids said someone requested a strong drink, I knew it was you."

The grizzled old man waved at him as he finished the glass with a pleased sigh. "Leave off the titles, ye cantankerous ol' fool."

Edmond bowed smartly and left. Marta watched him go with wide eyes then noticed the maids were also gone. She turned round and round but couldn't see them at all.

"Ah sent them back inside," Ravenswicke smiled as he lifted his glass. "Doon worry, they'll come to. Eventually." He turned his glass upside down with a frown. She shook her head.

"Why did you pretend to be someone you're not?" was all she could muster. He paused, head back and tongue stuck out as he tried to get a drop out of the glass. He lurched forward with a wild grin.

"'Tis no fun walkin' troo th' gates wit'out a bit o' surprise!" he scratched at his scruffy reddish-gray beard. "...'Sides, yer *husband* doon like't when Ah come a-callin'."

She stifled a laugh. *I can only imagine how Thomas reacts around him. He's very... surprising!*

The ancient man stared pitifully at his empty glass like a puppy who finished dinner too quickly. He shook his head and met Marta's gaze with glittering eyes.

"Ah heard tha' stubborn King Thomas went an' foun' his bride, so Ah had t'see fer mehself! He sure picked a lovely lady," he grinned wide. She chuckled in embarrassment.

"Thank you, Ravenswicke."

"Thas' meh name, doon call me late fer supper."

Marta laughed, overwhelmed by everything that had happened. The old man grinned as she wiped her eyes then grew solemn.

"Ye've finally met the 'witch of Ildaile', eh?"

Marta's expression fell. "I... who..."

Ravenswicke shook his head and leaned back, waving his hand. "Ah told Thomas, 'ye gotta get rid a' her', but did he listen? Naaaaaay!" he cried, imitating a horse. She giggled as he winked at her. "If only he saw wha' Ah see when Ah look't 'er..."

Dread filled Marta's chest. "What... what *do* you see when you look at her...?"

His eyes grew dull. "Ah see a lot o' darkness, Milady."

She blinked at that. "Wait... what Gift do you have?"

His laugh bellowed around the room. "Ah doon like th' terms o' th' Tower, too many old codgers stuck in their ways," he turned up his nose and waved as if smelling something foul. "But..." he lifted a finger as his eyes twinkled, "ye kin think o' me as Light Gifted, like th' sneaky Shepherd over there." He snapped and Nick appeared on the other side of the table, arms folded. He raised a brow at the older man who never broke his gaze off of Marta as she looked at her friend in surprise.

"You couldn't let me stay invisible, could you?"

"'Tis untrustworthy t' sneak 'round the castle like that, Nicky. 'Specially 'round a lady." Ravenswicke grinned at Marta as she returned her gaze to him. Nick sighed heavily and took a seat.

"*You're* the one pretending to be a lady, not me."

"Ye never would've let me in."

Nick opened his mouth to retort, found nothing, and shrugged. "I suppose."

The two men shared a smile as Marta shook her head.

"Does she look like a dark green with black swirling around inside her?"

Ravenswicke jerked his head towards her as Nick simply raised a brow.

"Nay... but very similar. Ah thought ye was Life Gifted?"

She nodded slowly. "I am... but sometimes, I can reach out with my abilities to..." she furrowed her brow as she tried to put to words what she experienced. "One time I could see... I don't know, people's colors? Normally I can just tell how many living things are nearby, like animals and people, but in ...this... case they changed colors."

Ravenswicke leaned forward and rested his head on his hands. "Int'restin'... can y'explain?"

"When we were ambushed in one of the towns on our way home a lot of the people in the inn turned to ash when they were 'killed'. When we were outside, I saw a figure move out of the corner of my eye. I couldn't be sure if I actually saw something so I used my ability to reach out. The... creature... was pitch-black and silver swirled around inside him." She shuddered violently. "Once I started actually looking at it, the silver turned out to be hundreds—*thousands*— of eyes."

Ravenswicke whistled and leaned back as Nick's jaw dropped.

"My Lady..." Nick gasped, "You actually *saw* a Seeker?!"

She glanced nervously between the two men as Ravenswicke stroked his beard. "I get the feeling there's more to what you're saying than just 'seeing' something..."

"Normally," Ravenswicke interrupted, "ye jus' get the *feelin'* a Seeker's nearby. 'Tis a specific kinna Lightseer trait to discern th' soul."

"Lightseer?"

Nick shook his head. "A Light Gifted with unique abilities. Queen Rosa was one."

"Ah," Ravenswicke sighed heavily, as if a familiar weight had settled onto his chest. "Rosa was a masterful Lightseer. She knew jus' the right words t' help someone. Like she could see th' things plaguin' ye."

At the mens' mournful looks, Marta raised her hand. "You... seem to have known Queen Rosa really well."

Ravenswicke's eyes flashed with anger and he turned to Nick, who held up his hands in defense.

"Don't look at me, *I'm* not her husband."

"Did th'ungrateful coward not even *mention* me?!" he rumbled dangerously. Marta's eyes widened.

"He, uhm, he got your letter—"

"Oh, did he?!" his eyes gleamed as he pounded his fist on the table. "An' he didn't even reply?! The—"

"He's been at another battle, Wicke," Nick groaned in warning. "Cut the man some slack. He got married only a month and a half ago, he's had other things on his mind."

Marta blushed as Ravenswicke grumbled and rubbed his face. He paused, lowered his hands, and sighed heavily as his shoulders sagged with grief.

"Ye could say Ah knew Rosa well. She was me sister."

Her eyes widened in shock. "Your *sister*?!"

He chuckled at her surprise. "Ye, 'twas me sister. King Martin fell in love wit' her onna trip t' Theocia. Great man, he was." He held up a shriveled finger towards Nick. "Doon think he did the deed 'imself, Nicky, 'twas murder, ya kin?"

"Th…ee…?" Marta stammered.

"The-osh-ia. 'Tis where we're from," he smiled proudly.

Marta glanced at Nick in confusion. *I haven't seen that kingdom on the map…*

Nick sighed heavily. "It was a very small kingdom, Arailt captured it ages ago."

"Ye didn't even bring up Theocia?!"

"Peace, Ravenswicke. A lady can only learn so much at one time."

Marta rubbed her temples. "So much to know…"

Ravenswicke closed his mouth then chuckled ruefully at the young exhausted queen. "Ye're a lot like her, Lady Marta. If only yer husband were…" his face twisted as if he had eaten something sour.

"Actually, Wicke, you bring up a good point. Marta, where was Thomas when this happened?"

"Right next to me…"

Nick glanced at the older man, a smile tugging at his lips. "Do you think…?"

Ravenswicke shook his head and reached into his pouch to pull out a pipe. He stuffed foul-smelling herbs into the end and flicked his thumb. A small flame lit on the end of his finger and he lit the pipe, sucking on it and exhaling a puff of smoke. He finally shook his head as he leaned back, folding his arms.

"'Tis rarely heard of—"

"But it *is* possible, isn't it? Especially being Rosa's son?"

Marta glanced between the two men trying to take everything in. *Did I do something wrong?*

Ravenswicke puffed. "Ah need t'think on this. Fer now, doon mention this t'anyone," he leveled a serious gaze onto Marta, who nodded emphatically. He nodded once with a grunt. "Good. Now, aboot tha' Seeker, ye—"

"RAVEEEEEEEENSWIIIIIIICKE!"

Marta and Nick jumped as the pipe fell out of Ravenswicke's mouth at the shrill scream. He caught it before it hit the ground with wide eyes.

"Ah, le's finish this later. Ah gotta go."

"Wait, what about—!"

Ravenswicke winked at her with the pipe in his mouth and snapped, bursting into a cloud of golden butterflies. They flew out an open window as Nana, an older woman with gray hair, barreled into the room wielding a wooden laundry spoon. She glanced about angrily, spotted Marta, and gasped. She bowed low.

"Me goodness, Ah didn't see y' there, Milady! Me apologies!"

Marta shook her head slowly, still reeling from what just happened. "Ah… it's… alright…"

Nana straightened, searched around, then nodded. "Pardon me." She turned with a dark glare and stormed out of the room, muttering "Where is he?!"

Nick covered his face with his hands, sobbing with laughter. Marta slowly looked over at him.

"Don't tell me he was… married to Nana!"

Nick leaned back and howled, nodding. "Is," he stammered through tears, "is married."

"And he just left her here?!"

Nick pulled out a handkerchief from his pocket and wiped off his face, struggling to compose himself. "Ah… he's a nomad, and Nana knew that when they got married. He travels around a lot. They moved here when Rosa married Martin, but he took off after a particularly bad argument about a year ago. He still hasn't apologized." He shook his head. "It was absolutely his fault and he knows it, but I guess he still can't find the courage to face his wife."

Marta shook her head incredulously. *What a strange man…* She fidgeted for a moment before looking up at Nick.

"Nick… what is a Seeker?"

He met her nervous gaze and sighed. "A Seeker is one of Arailt's elite, someone who gave themselves so completely over to him that they're possessed, fueled by rage and a lust for power. They specialize at hunting down Gifteds. They can sense when an Ability is used and can sniff them out, very much like a hunting dog. They're extremely powerful, stronger than most Death Wizards even. Not many Gifteds have faced a Seeker and lived."

Marta shook her head and toyed with a teaspoon. "So why didn't…"

"Why didn't you die?"

She met his concerned gaze and nodded.

"Seekers are excellent assassins but very poor soldiers. When faced against numerous Gifteds they lose their advantage. That's why they're usually only sent out to search for and kill a specific person."

And that person was me, she gulped. Nick reached forward and held her hand tenderly.

"Don't worry, you're very well protected here. You don't have to worry about Thomas, either; he's surrounded by good people." He nodded at Wesley and Breton standing to the side, and they nodded in reply. She shook her head incredulously. *So that's why Thomas didn't want me out there…*

"My Lady!"

Nick leaned back as Marta glanced up. Brenna and Kate rushed over to the table wheezing.

"M'lady… we… heard… ye had a run-in wit'…"

Marta held Brenna's hand carefully. "Catch your breath. Yes, I met the infamous Ravenswicke. Are you two okay?"

The ladies nodded breathlessly. "Yes ma'am. We wanted to make sure you were okay after tea with Lady Sarah."

"I appreciate it," she smiled sadly as she glanced at the empty table. A thought struck her and she stood. "I'd like to go to the study, please. I need to pen a letter."

The ladies nodded as Nick stood with a smile. "Let me know if you need anything, Milady. We will continue your lessons this evening."

Marta gazed at her tutor with trepidation. "I… look forward to it."

"No more peculiar Light Gifted abilities, I promise."

"You'd better keep it!" her frown grew into a bemused grin. He chuckled.

"At least for tonight!"

"Augh!"

CHAPTER FOURTEEN

Anger, the Weapon of Fools

Two Weeks Later

Marta set another letter down on the desk with a sigh. Nick glanced up at her from over his tiny gold framed glasses in his spot at Thomas' desk. He examined the stack of finished letters with a nod.

"Great job, my Lady. You're getting faster."

She rubbed her chin and stared vacantly at the papers.

"Yes... I suppose I am... Is being royalty always this boring?"

Nick chuckled ruefully. "In times of peace, there is less paperwork but it is quite boring nevertheless. King Martin had done a lot of work on putting more responsibility on the people, appointing judges and leaders of good repute. Some towns and cities need help but... usually this only takes an hour or two to do."

She leaned on her desk with a sigh, rubbing her aching wrist and arm. "I hope we can get to that point sooner rather than later... for a number of reasons."

He chuckled and set down his glasses. The study was beautifully furnished with a fireplace across from the desk and a large window on the side filling the room with light. An expansive window seat was surrounded by bookshelves stretching back behind the desk. They had brought in a simple writing desk for Marta and placed it in front of the window. Seamus and Breton stood guard at the door.

"Say, is Wesley finally...?"

Marta's eyes gleamed, her mood instantly rising. "Yes, he is! That's why I haven't been able to focus. I'm so excited to hear how it goes!"

Nick chuckled. "They will be a good match for each other." He stood and stretched with a groan, then lowered his arms and adjusted his waistcoat. He held up a letter and searched around for something. Marta spotted Ravenswicke's crest on the seal.

"That's odd, I thought I had grabbed..."

Marta walked over with an inquisitive look on her face. "What are you looking for?"

"A book... I thought I had grabbed it... perhaps not. Will you join me in going to the library?"

"Absolutely!" Marta exclaimed with excitement. Nick held out his arm and escorted her down the ornate hallway to the library, Seamus and Breton following dutifully behind.

The library was a massive three-story room with numerous balconies and swirling stairs. Soaring windows stretched the full height of the room and several fireplaces were placed strategically in between. Marta had found that the chairs here were the comfiest in the castle, although that could just be because she found herself curling up here nearly every night with a good book. Several groups of couches and tables were strategically placed about the room, with a few off-duty guards and maids reading to their heart's content. Nick went straight to the third level and walked over to an elegantly carved bookshelf with glass doors. Marta peered over the railing and down at the wooden floor.

Such a wonderful room... this is definitely my favorite spot. Well, I do like the gardens... and the bedroom is very comfortable... and...

"Ah-ha!" Nick shut the glass case and locked it, producing a small red leather-bound tome. Although he tried to hide the cover Marta spotted the faded letters; *Lightseers.* "Found it. Let's head back."

Marta picked up her skirts and followed him down the spiral staircase. A set of doors burst open and they heard frantic footsteps downstairs. She glanced over the edge and spotted Kate searching wildly.

"I think he finally did it," Marta chuckled. Nick nodded and they met Kate on the bottom floor. She grasped Marta's hands, elated, a wide grin on her face.

"Milady! Milady! Brenna's gonna be a lady! Sir Wesley asked her to marry him in the gardens, it sounded so romantic!"

Marta smiled sheepishly at that. Wesley had actually approached her asking for help on how he should ask the woman he loved to marry him. She had suggested the gardens, noticing that Brenna always had a smile on her face when they were there.

"I take it she said yes?" Marta laughed.

"Of course!!!" Kate squealed. Nick laughed heartily at that.

"Alright, I need to head back. You can take the rest of the day off, Marta, you've done enough for today."

"Are you sure?" she asked quietly as he turned to leave. He noticed her forlorn look and tipped his head to the side.

"Of course," he murmured as he turned back towards her. "Is something wrong?"

Marta fidgeted nervously. "I... I feel like I'm not doing enough. I can't be out on the battlefield, so I want to help more here."

"My lady, you do help. Just look around you, the serving men and women have been happier because of the way you treat them, the—"

"M'lady!"

The group glanced up as Brenna rushed into the library, skirts in hand. Wesley strode in behind her with a sheepish grin on his face. Marta smiled wide as Brenna ran up to her, her face tinged with pink.

"M'lady, he-! We-!"

"It's about time!" Marta laughed as she scooped her friend up in a hug. Seamus patted Wesley on the back and Breton gripped his shoulder and shook his hand. Marta held out her arm and Kate joined the hug.

"I will leave you be, my friends," Nick mused as he began walking out. He nodded in respect to Wesley, who nodded in return. "Congratulations, captain."

"Thankee, Shepherd. Ah'll be comin' t'ye shortly regarding this."

Nick raised a brow. "Oh? Actual Shepherd duties? Preposterous!"

Everyone laughed as Nick tipped a figurative hat and strode out the doors. Marta looked down at her two dear friends with a wide grin. "How about we celebrate with some cake, hmm?"

There was a terrible scream that echoed down the corridor, jolting everyone in the library. Lady Henley came rushing into the room grasping her skirts.

"Yer Majesty! Yer-ah!" she tripped over the threshold and stumbled forward, catching herself at the last second. Wesley and Seamus stepped forward as Marta turned.

"Lady Henley, what—?"

"She's gone too far!" Henley exclaimed breathlessly, her eyes alight with panic. "'Tis Jenna, she's bleedin' awful bad, Ah canna stop 't!"

Marta hiked up her skirts and ran out of the room, her ankle boots stomping with every step, Kate and Brenna right behind. Panic thundered through her as she rushed down the hall.

"Where is she?!" Marta cried. Henley opened her mouth to speak when Sarah's shrill voice screeched down the hall.

"You weak, useless, boorish imbecile!"

Marta took off running towards the cursing and stopped short in the corridor. Two maids cowered in the corner as soldiers stood around a body on the floor. Sarah's back was to Marta but she could see the blood on her hands.

"Get out of my way! These stupid brats need to learn some *respect!*" she lunged at the soldier with a bloodied shoe. She screamed in surprise as a vine wrapped itself around her chest and hoisted her into the air. It wrapped around her hands and slammed her on the ground as Marta rushed forward. The soldiers parted as she knelt to the ground beside the unconscious maid on the floor.

"*You!*" Sarah shrieked as she fought against the vines containing her. "How dare you lay a hand on me!"

She clamped her mouth shut at Marta's dangerous glare. She continued thrashing and screaming about the maid as Marta set golden glowing hands on the woman's body. Marta trembled violently as she pulled the girl away from death, the wounds in her skull and chest healing rapidly. The hallway fell silent aside from Sarah's berating as Marta focused all her energy on healing the poor girl. When the servant finally opened her eyes and gasped for air the small crowd heaved a collective sigh of relief. The young maid blinked in confusion as Marta helped her stand.

"Please take her to the infirmary right way and make sure she's seen to quickly." She passed the young woman's hand to two of the castle guardsmen. They nodded and gently guided her down the hall.

"The little brat deserved it! Do you know how many of my petticoats she's ruined? I bet she's stealing my jewels too, the little—"

A sharp *slap* resounded through the hall and echoed ominously down the corridor. Marta stood there with wide-eyes, her hand raised. Sarah's head was turned to the side, her normally perfect red curls strewn about her face. Marta inhaled sharply and stepped back as she held her throbbing wrist.

I, I didn't mean to, I shouldn't have, I-!

Sarah's head turned slowly as she faced her, her green eyes bright with hatred. She spit to the side and sneered.

"Oh? Is that all you got, my perfect, *benevolent* Queen?"

Guilt threatened to swallow her whole as she shook with rage. "If you *ever* lay a hand on one of your maids again, I will be sure that you receive the same punishment you give them." With a snap of her fingers the vines unraveled around Sarah and disappeared. Sarah gasped and worked her hands, numb from how tight the bonds had been. She rubbed her wrist and stood elegantly, smoothing off her dress. She met Marta's glare before turning away with a huff, *clack*ing down the hallway as if nothing had happened.

"My... Lady?"

Marta sank to her knees and stared at her hands. The back of her right hand stung as the skin turned bright red. She covered her face as tears rolled down her cheeks.

"I... I was so... so *angry*...!" she hiccuped as she trembled. Brenna and Kate knelt on either side of her with terse expressions.

"Milady, it—"

"Your Majesty!"

Marta looked up slowly from her spot on the floor as Nick rounded the corner. He hesitated when he saw her tears but she patted them away quickly with Geralt's handkerchief.

"Yes, Nick?"

Nick examined the situation before kneeling down to help her stand. Once on her feet he sighed wearily but smiled.

"We just received a mirror communication from King Thomas. They're returning home."

*****

Thomas traced the edge of his tankard with his finger idly. The roar of the party around him made his head throb in pain. He rolled his eyes and leaned forward onto the table swirling his half-filled flagon of mead. Portsmouth, along with all the soldiers and armies who had responded, were celebrating the victory over Hylen's forces. He sat at a table with King Wilhelm, Jerome, Peter, Finlay, Amaryll, and other generals from Rodenheim. Amaryll was trying to drink the dwarves under the table but they were putting up a fight. Wilhelm faced off against the gleeful Gifted commander with a scowl.

"Ze beer here iz veak!"

"Then you shouldn't have a problem with it, should you?" Amaryll grinned wickedly as she downed another mug to the cheers of Knights and Gifteds around her. Wilhelm grinned in amusement as he waved. The smells of bread, ale, and victory smiled around the group.

"Another round! I have never lost to a human, never mind a voman!

I vill not start now!"

The dwarves cheered for their king. Thomas rubbed his face and groaned.

"This is insufferable."

Jerome glanced over at him with a gleam in his eye. "What, that Amaryll might actually lose?"

"Not on yer—*hic*— life, Jerome!" she yelled. Jerome shook his head and laughed. Thomas stood up abruptly and walked to the edge of the patio they were on. Portsmouth stretched before them, the city lit up with festivities. Lights were strewn from house to house all the way to the sea. On a quiet night one could hear the ocean lapping against the shore. A frigid arctic sea wind blew in his face, bringing with it the stench of fish and salt. He reached into his pocket and pulled out the worn letter he had read over and over again every night.

My love,

I pray all is well on the battlefront. I miss you dearly, the nights grow cold with your absence. I have had... a few... altercations with Sarah, but I promise you I'm trying to be better! We mostly avoid each other which is probably for the best.

I wanted to pen this letter to you for a specific reason, however. Nick explained to me what a Seeker is and what they do. Realizing now the kind of foe we are up against... I'm sorry for trying to come with you. I'm sorry I disrespected you in front of everyone. In my desire to be by your side I neglected to think about how dangerous things can be. While I still want to be there with you... I must learn to trust you as my husband. Trust you to make the right decisions, and... trust you to come back. I am not sleeping well, but, I'm sure you're not either. I don't want to make this about me but... After reading it multiple times, he finally deciphered the next sentence, which she had crossed out as though she had second thoughts about penning it; *'I dream nearly every night that you die on the battlefield.' I am praying for you.*

My studies are going well. Nick is a very diligent teacher. I love my handmaidens, Brenna and Kate. They are becoming my dearest friends here. I have not reached out to Camilla recently except by letter, since Nick said mirror communications are still finicky.

I hope you come home soon. I am eager to see you again. Be safe.

All my love,

Marta

He sighed and folded the letter back up and placed it in his vest pocket. He leaned on the railing and rubbed his face.

I can't believe she apologized to me when it should be me *apologizing to* her. *I was too stern with her, I let too many of my emotions show. This battle has reminded me of the harsh reality of living. I grow weary of this fighting. Elyon still isn't prepared enough for this fight, despite all these years.*

The familiar voice roared at him again. *Just like you.*

He groaned and turned to walk away but froze in place. Peter walked up to him with a sneer.

"Is the party not to your liking?"

Thomas rubbed his face in exasperation. "I don't have the energy to deal with you tonight, Peter. For once would you just leave me alone?"

The desperation in Thomas' eyes drew a sneer from Peter's lips, but Peter hesitated a moment. Something in him shifted ever so slightly.

"Perhaps I was asking in true concern."

"When have you ever been concerned about me?" Thomas retorted angrily. Immediately the walls launched back up into place and Peter turned to look out towards the sea.

"Suit yourself, Sire. This is the best place with a view either way."

Thomas glanced out over the city and saw nothing but the lives of those in his care. *If I fail, no one will be safe anymore. Arailt would kill everyone here, young and old.* He rotated his injured shoulder and winced as he held it with his other arm. *He would especially ravage Marta* — he shook his head to dispel the frightening thoughts he constantly ruminated on. *How did I become so infatuated with a woman like this? Someone who I happened to cross paths with? Or, if I truly did hear Him right, someone I was supposed to meet at that time and place.* He gazed back out over the ocean as a cheer went up behind him. *I wish I could bring Marta here, or at least talk to her. She would have the answer.*

A howling noise jerked the brother's attentions back to the table. Wilhelm and Amaryll had both slumped onto the ground. The crowd gathered around them and a few of them exchanged bags of coins.

"So who won?" Thomas asked with a bemused smile. Jerome looked up and shrugged with a grin.

"Neither, they both passed out at the same moment. Guess it's a draw."

Peter and Thomas exchanged glances before laughing at the whole affair. Thomas stepped forward and helped Jerome get Amaryll to her swaying feet as Peter tried to hide his smile.

"Let's get her back to the inn. I want to leave at first light; I am eager to be home."

*****

Marta winced as she desperately tried to put on her shoe. Kate rushed over and motioned for her to sit.

"My Lady, we are here to help!"

Marta shook her head with a sad look, her ruby earrings swaying back and forth.

"I don't want to be a burden!"

"Ye're not, Milady!" Brenna exclaimed as she knelt and put the tiny burgundy shoe onto Marta's foot. As Brenna stood Marta turned and glanced at herself in the mirror. Her white shoulders were a stark contrast to the deep red dress she wore, beautifully embroidered with swirls and beads. She turned before the mirror and noted that the A-line style complimented her perfectly. Although it was considered an older style, Marta preferred it to the large back bustles she had worn previously.

"I just want to see Thomas..." she sighed mournfully, feeling suddenly young and foolish.

"His Majesty is getting prepared for the ball too. He's going to escort you, so don't worry!"

She held out her hands as Brenna helped her into white gloves. *I don't care about pomp and circumstance, I just want to see my husband!*

That eager to see me, hmm?

Her cheeks flooded with color as she glanced towards the door at the sound of her husband's thoughts.

Thomas! You're home!

Indeed. We just walked through the mirror. Believe me, I... want to see you too. Jerome and Finlay had to hold me back from running through the mirror this morning.

Marta chuckled, drawing confused glances from the other two women.

"Oh, Thomas is back. I'm... ah..."

Kate held up her hand with a smile. "Say no more. Gifted-Knight bond, righto." The two women continued preparing the young queen as she sighed again.

I've missed you, she fought to control her tears. *Did you get my letter?*

I did, and I'm sorry I didn't respond. Things got a little out of hand but I'll tell you about that later. For now...

The three women jumped as they heard a knock at the door.

"Jus' a minute!" Brenna called as Kate finished up a few last-minute details. She tucked a loose strand behind Marta's head and smiled.

"He's going to be so happy to see you. Alright, Brenna, we're ready!"

Marta turned as Brenna opened the door and bowed. Her jaw dropped as Thomas strode inside wearing a matching red waistcoat and white pants. His golden crown sat atop his head and he rested his hand on his elegant sword hilt when his eyes met hers. He smiled wide as light flickered through his blue eyes.

"Marta!"

She rushed forward and he scooped her up in an embrace. She buried her face in his neck and tried not to sob.

"Thank God you're okay. I've missed you so!"

Thomas reached behind her head and drew her in for a kiss, trying to hide his wince. "I love you too," he grinned mischievously. She laughed and hugged him tightly again. She felt him jerk slightly and leaned back in concern.

"Are you hurt somewhere?"

Thomas sighed and pointed to his shoulder. "No use hiding it from you. Just don't over-exert yourself, okay?"

Her hands were already glowing as he spoke. She smiled and placed her hand on his shoulder. He grimaced as the bone and muscle moved slightly and righted themselves. His skin patched itself back together and he rotated his arm.

"I'm still amazed you can do things like that."

She beamed widely. "Our God can do wondrous things, I'm simply a vessel."

He chuckled. "Yes. He is, isn't He? Oh!" he motioned to Kate. "Was it brought up?"

Kate grinned wide. "Yes, my Lord. Let me get it."

Marta cast Thomas a confused glance as Kate emerged from the bedroom with a beautifully engraved wooden box. The King opened it to reveal a dainty golden crown inlaid with Ela and Opal. He lifted it gently and placed it on her head. It fit perfectly and she blushed as the two girls and her husband stepped back to admire her.

"Milady, ye're stunning!"

"Simply gorgeous!"

"Beautiful," was all Thomas could stammer. Marta glanced in the mirror and blushed a deep red. Thomas chuckled and held out his arm to her with a smile. "Ready?"

She turned and smiled wide. "As I'll ever be!"

He nodded and escorted her down the hallway towards the dining room. She nodded at her Guardsmen as they left. Wesley chuckled under his breath as Seamus elbowed him.

"Did y'see how fast his Majesty ran down the hall? I'm surprised he caught his breath in time!"

Wesley grinned as the door opened again. "Ah did, Seamus. Th' girl y'love kin make ye do strange things." He turned as Brenna stepped out in her own elegant dress. Marta insisted she borrow one of hers, and Brenna looked like a princess in the demure emerald green gown. Wesley wore a tunic and waistcoat denoting him as an officer, and his red hair was slicked back. His eyes widened as Seamus laughed.

"Easy on yer feet, captain!"

He held out his arm to Brenna and flashed Seamus a smile. "Aye aye sir."

CHAPTER FIFTEEN

Two Truths and a Lie

Marta could smell Cookie's feast wafting through the halls as the young king and queen greeted their guests. Most had emerged through the mirror room not an hour prior, dressed and ready for the formal event. Thomas introduced her to numerous soldiers and their families as well as a few visiting nobility. She greeted Lorna and her husband Robert, a rather severe looking man. Marta couldn't tell if it was a front against the recent gossip or how he actually was. The pair bowed and stood as the monarchs greeted them. Lorna's eyes grew wide as Marta took her hands in hers.

"How are you feeling, my friend? How's the baby?"

Lorna blushed sheepishly as Robert cracked a faint smile. "Ah'm—" she cleared her throat, "I'm doing well, Milady. Thank you for asking. This is my husband Robert," she motioned. Marta turned and smiled at the blond man.

"Pleased to meet you, Lord Robert. I was told you were instrumental in implementing a new policy to reconstruct the roads in rural areas. Ropheka, where I am from, was one such town that benefited from your efforts. Thank you so much!" she curtsied politely. Robert and Lorna's eyes widened as she stood up straight.

"My Lady, how did you know...?" Lorna asked quietly.

"I've been doing some studying," she held up a finger and winked. Robert chuckled.

"It is indeed a relief to know our queen is familiar with our rural communities. They are just as important as the cities. I would be honored to get your thoughts on this subject sometime."

"I would be pleased to help however I can!" she grinned. Thomas placed his hand at the small of her back and nodded.

"Oh," Thomas turned and smiled to the pair, "congratulations on the baby. I'm sure you're very excited!"

The couple exchanged a glance. Robert sighed heavily.

"I am, indeed. It has been... rough lately," he lowered his voice as a few people walked past them, "but God has blessed my wife and I throughout it."

Thomas raised a brow as Marta coughed a chuckle into her handkerchief.

"Ah, sorry, I'm a little nervous."

"No, I completely understand!" Lorna held Marta's free hand with a smile. "We will see you at the ball after dinner!"

"Wonderful! Please enjoy your meal!"

Thomas and Marta watched them go sadly.

What's going on with them?

Sarah is spreading a rumor that Robert slept with women at a tavern. Based on what I see, he wouldn't—

Thomas growled under his breath, "This woman is becoming a headache more and more. I should never have let her into the castle—"

Marta gently touched his shoulder and he glanced down at his bride. She smiled softly.

"Let's worry about that later. I'm so excited for Lorna and Robert, especially when they meet their son!"

"Son?" he blinked in confusion. "You can tell?"

She nodded excitedly. "Yes! Ah can tell aboot this time in her pregnancy, it's a Life Gifted trait." She chuckled at herself and cleared her throat. "Sorry. Many women would come to me to see if they actually were carrying or to find out what the baby was so they could name them before they were born. I had one woman with twins whose husband fainted when I told them—" she laughed and covered her mouth as Thomas chuckled.

"That sounds like an interesting Gift."

"Your Gift confuses me! There are so many aspects to being a Light Gifted. There's the defensive type, the fighting type like you have, and then the just plan peculiar like Nicodemus and Ravenswicke—"

Thomas halted in the hallway as his eyes grew cold. "You met Ravenswicke?"

She clamped her mouth shut. *Oh no, I promised Nick I wouldn't mention—*

"And you willfully promised to withhold something from me?!"

She winced and shrunk back. "It— I was going to tell you no matter what, but I wanted to wait until after the ball… nothing happened, I promise! He just introduced himself to me and told me that you wouldn't cheat on me and that Rosa was his sister and—"

Thomas characteristically rubbed the bridge of his nose and fought to restrain his anger. He paused as her words sunk in, breaking his walls a little.

"He had to tell you I wouldn't cheat on you?"

She started waffling as she got more and more nervous. "I—it— it was after Lady Lorna left the tea in tears because Sarah brought up the rumor about Robert and I was just, I wanted, I, ah, it was just a stray thought, and—"

He sighed heavily and shook his head. "Alright, tell me later. I want you to know," he turned so he was facing her, "that I would never do that to you."

"I would never, either! No matter what. Sorry, but when you married me you signed up for *everything*!" she chuckled. Now that her smile was back Thomas could breathe easier.

Her stomach growled in protest suddenly as she caught a whiff of the large roast wafting from the dining room. Several guests walked by and introduced themselves, as it appeared Thomas and Marta had finished their conversation.

Oh, I'm so hungry… I can't wait, I can already taste it!

Did you not eat today? Thomas cast her a quick glance as the guests in front of them turned to leave. She shook her head sadly.

I was told no one is allowed to eat before a feast… so nothing was made except for the serving men and women.

Says who?

Sarah—

He groaned and rubbed his aching forehead. He was about to say something when someone cleared their throat behind them.

"King Thomas, iz thees your queen?"

Marta nearly jumped in surprise as she glanced down at the imposing dwarf standing before them. His blond hair was braided and beaded magnificently and his beard had intricate designs. He wore a bright blue and white tunic with a formidable battle-ax strapped elegantly on his back.

Isn't that heavy?!

Thomas chuckled. "Yes, King Wilhelm, this is my wife Marta. Marta, this is King Wilhelm of Rodenheim."

The two nodded politely at each other. Marta smiled wide.

"It's a pleasure to meet you! I've never had the honor of meeting a dwarf before, so I am especially blessed to meet a king first!"

Wilhelm's hearty laugh bellowed down the hall. "Ah, ze pleasure eez mine. Zees eez my vife, Matylda." A beautiful female dwarf stepped forward, her brown locks cascading down her back with numerous braids and jewels studded in her hair. She nodded respectfully, the golden crown upon her head glittering in the light. Marta was struck by her beauty and poise and tried not to gawk.

"Queen Matylda, you're absolutely stunning!"

The older woman chuckled. "Zank you, Queen Marta. You are as vell. It is nice to finally meet you."

There was a gentle *gong* echoing down the hall calling everyone in for dinner. Thomas examined his pocket watch and nodded.

"Right on time. See you soon!" he waved as the dwarven monarchs strode away together. Marta couldn't stop smiling.

So many new people! This is fun! Will there be any elves here too?

He sighed heavily. *Unfortunately, no. The elves who live here haven't had a kingdom in years. It's... another thing Arailt destroyed. Hopefully we can restore their homeland to them soon. Their warriors used to serve with us, but they've been protecting their settlements recently.*

She held Thomas' arm gently as they walked into the glittering banquet hall. Four tables had been set up with a fifth one on the far side of the room. The monarchs all sat at that table and she spotted Peter sitting next to where she would sit with Sarah by his side. She was talking to Fenella and her husband sitting nearby. King Wilhelm and Queen Matylda took their places by Thomas' seat. She caught a glance of Brenna and Wesley sitting at a table with other high-ranking officers from the battle at Portsmouth. She nearly tripped when she spotted Bri and Isaac waving at her from the table. She waved back enthusiastically.

I am so glad they're okay! And they're here!

Thomas winced as he realized he forgot to let her know they survived the battle. With the preparations for the military strategies and the ball, it completely slipped his mind. He guided her over to their seats and nodded to Edmond. The white haired steward hit the gong one last time as everyone found their seats and quieted down.

"Good evening, everyone. Thank you for joining us. Today, we celebrate the triumph over Hylen's forces and gather to remember the lives that were lost during this brutal war. May God bring peace to their families. Please, enjoy your meals, and as soon as you are finished feasting you may head to the ballroom for the rest of the evening's festivities."

Doors opened on either side of the room and scores of serving men and women, including the dwarves Wilhelm brought, emerged with trays of food. Thomas helped Marta sit and she nodded politely at Peter. He had a blank look on his face and paid no attention to her.

Is... Peter alright?

Thomas glanced over at his brother. *He's been a little off the last week or so, but this is...*

Peter blinked and shook his head. For a moment Marta thought she saw his blue eyes clear. His face contorted in his usual scowl and he leaned back.

"What?"

She shook her head slowly. "You just looked... ill..."

"I'm fine," he waved her off and turned his attention to Sarah. Her hackles raised as she sat back.

Something is definitely off here... her thoughts were interrupted as a large plate and bowl of soup were placed in front of her. She thanked the serving man and smiled at Thomas, holding out her hand.

"Would you ask the blessing for us?"

He took her hand and relaxed faintly. "Of course." After the prayer they set into their meals. Marta had to pace herself with how hungry she was. Thomas was engaged in conversation with Wilhelm as she perused the room. She recognized many of the officers there, including her own few Guardsmen. They each took turns on rotation behind her although she requested that Wesley spend as much time with Brenna as possible. Two more men had been added to her Guard, now a measly five men compared to the ten Thomas originally wanted. There was Wesley, Seamus, and Breton, along with the two newcomers, Dougal and Lyle.

Dougal was a tall and thin young man with brown hair and hazel eyes. Sometimes he would turn his head a certain way and she swore she saw a younger Caleb standing there. He had a charming gangliness about him, yet his finesse on the battlefield was anything but charming. Wesley chose him for his keen eye and excellent archery skills. Lyle was older than the rest of the guards, with broad shoulders and a grey-flecked beard. His red hair was dark and streaked with silver, pulled back behind his head. While he looked imposing, Marta soon discovered that Lyle was actually very calm and gentle when he needed to be. He was wise and cunning, and while slow, his broadsword crushed anything in his path. Lyle's wife was one of the serving women in the castle and their sons were in the army as well. She was thrilled to hear he would be a grandfather soon.

The sound of cutlery tapping on glass wrenched her from her thoughts. Thomas turned as the hall hushed and gazed at the red-haired princess standing with a champagne flute in her hand.

"Hello everyone, thank you for joining us here today, and thank you for your service to Elyon," her voice was like silk, pleasant and refined. It was completely different from her normal tone. Seamus and Breton rolled their eyes as she continued. "I have an announcement to make."

Marta felt Thomas lean back in his chair and cross his arms. *What could possibly warrant an interruption like this,* he groaned.

Sarah cast a sideways glance at a confused Marta and lifted her glass. "Peter and I are expecting."

Marta's jaw dropped as Thomas' eyes widened. Peter smiled sheepishly as Sarah sat back down to a smattering of applause. Numerous people mumbled their congratulations as Fenella shrieked in excitement. Thomas reached over and patted Peter on the back. He responded by half-smiling with a panicked expression.

No they're not...

Thomas sat back and looked at Marta. She stared at the food in front of her and rubbed her arm absentmindedly before meeting his gaze.

You can tell, can't you. I can tell she's lying too. Thomas' eyes flickered with light. Marta nodded slowly.

I can't be completely sure because I wasn't looking for it, but when I touched her the other day... well... slapped her... she winced as his eyes widened, *I could really only sense one life there.*

I wonder what would make her lie about—

"Ah, better get on it, Lord Thomas," Wilhelm joked as he nudged the king. Thomas smiled sheepishly as Marta rubbed her head.

Why would *she lie? Does Nick—?* She glanced over to see their faithful Shepherd at the end of the row, his face pale. He caught her gaze and discreetly shook his head.

He knows it, too. But if any of us bring it up, she'll respond by accusing me of jealousy.

I don't know what their plan is, Thomas finished his plate, *but I don't like it. Let's play along for now and we can figure it out later.*

Marta nodded and could barely finish her own meal. Sarah and Peter had left the table as the center of attention to be congratulated by other guests. Thomas escorted his bride out of the emptying room and caught Sarah's sardonic smirk in their direction. She lifted her glass of champagne towards them and took a dainty sip. Thomas turned as he scoffed and pulled Marta down the hall.

Thomas, wait, you're going too fast!

He pulled up short and glanced at his smaller wife, panting as she tried to catch her breath.

"Sorry, I haven't been able to get outside to practice combat recently. I've been too busy learning about the castle..."

"No, I..." *I haven't had a lot of patience recently,* he thought to himself. Marta took his arm, not hearing his thoughts, and sucked in a slow breath.

"I'm excited to be able to dance with you, though."

Thomas chuckled. "I am, too. Were you able to take time for some lessons?"

Marta shook her head as they entered the large ballroom, the party already in full swing. An orchestra made up of fiddlers, bassists, violinists, a bagpiper, a pianist and a tall floor harpist were all playing to their heart's content.

"I knew how to dance already. Geralt would frequently host dances, he and Camilla were always so elegant when they danced together!" she chuckled fondly. "They really just need to see eachother. I kept telling them, but neither wanted to listen," she huffed indignantly. Thomas raised a brow as a smile played at his lips.

"You seem to be quite the matchmaker, my wife."

She grinned as light flickered through her eyes. "I just like seeing my friends happy."

"Well, I'm glad to hear that. For now," he bowed politely and offered his hand, "would you give me the honor of joining me for a dance?"

She took his hand and curtsied in reply. "I'd be honored to, your Majesty."

*****

Wesley beamed as his fiancee twirled under his hand, spinning and clasping his free hand with hers. Brenna was radiant as he tipped her and gently kissed her nose. The pair paused then continued their dance.

"Wes, Ah'm so excited," Brenna whispered quietly. "Things have been so much better since Milady came."

He nodded and smiled. "'Tis been great. Ah worry aboot Lady Sarah, but cannae do much. Hopefully Lord Thomas can help more." He twirled her again. She nodded and sighed happily.

"Ah canna wait t' start our lives together!"

"Me either."

They glanced up as they heard a snort. Sarah stood there with Fenella, holding an open fan against her lips.

"I can't tell what makes me want to be ill more, listening to you babble on with your disgusting accents or seeing you so enamored with each other that neither of you can see straight! It's a wonder you ever actually protect her Majesty, captain."

Brenna glanced towards the middle of the ballroom. Marta and Thomas were in the midst of a dance, both oblivious to anything except the other. She sighed and turned as Wesley wrapped his arm around her.

"Le's go, Bren. Ah could use some fresh air." He turned around and guided her away.

"Oh, so you do actually pay attention, Lord Wesley? Interesting—"

"Needless mockery is unbecoming of a woman of your stature, my *Lady*," came an imposing voice.

Brenna and Wesley turned around briefly to catch Nicodemus standing between them and Sarah. Her eyes narrowed at the stalwart Shepherd.

"I would suggest you mind your place, Shepherd. Now that Thomas is back you aren't—"

"You're absolutely correct. Now that his *Majesty* is back I can resume my normal duties. Maintaining the peace is one of the duties of a Shepherd, is it not? Insulting someone for how they speak may be common in Ildaile but I assure you it is very much frowned upon here."

Sarah huffed in shock and waved her fan in her face. "I am in too precarious a condition to be able to withstand this insolence. Fenella, let's go outside."

Nick watched them disappear into the gardens. He turned and met Wesley's grateful look. The two men nodded quietly to each other and Wesley guided Brenna to the other side of the room near an open window. He rubbed his face and put his hand on his neck. "Precarious my—"

"Ah, Shepherd. Why the long face?" Jerome stepped forward, a hand on the hilt of his sword. Nick sighed in relief.

"Jerome. You know… trying to put out fires."

"It's hard to do when someone in particular is constantly blazing," Jerome snorted. Nick made a sound of agreement.

*****

Thomas bowed and Marta curtsied with flushed grins. He led her to the side of the room and offered her a drink.

"I'm impressed by how well you dance."

She chuckled and lifted her glass. "I've read enough novels to know that it's unusual for someone of a lower class to know how to dance. Maybe I wanted to be the exception?" she winked and took a sip, then coughed as it got caught in her throat. Thomas fought back his laughter as he handed her a handkerchief. She took it gratefully as her cheeks bloomed in color. "Or maybe I'm just surprised I didn't trip all over everyone with how clumsy I am," she laughed sheepishly.

"I'm impressed by that, too."

The pair chuckled as they watched the other couples swishing across the dance floor. Thomas wrapped his arm around Marta's shoulder and kissed the top of her head. She caught a glimpse of Amaryll walking out into the gardens, apparently in a hurry.

"Hey, there's Amaryll. I was wondering where she was."

He chuckled under his breath as he lifted his glass. "She tried to out drink the dwarf king."

"What!!" she cried, eyes wide. He nodded.

"Miraculously, neither won. However, speaking in terms of hangovers…" he motioned to the gleeful king dancing with his queen, then over where Amaryll had disappeared. Marta gasped.

"Oh, dear. I'm going to go see if she's okay."

"Alright, I'll be in here if you need me."

Marta smiled and excused herself. Thomas watched his beautiful bride float across the ballroom and head outside. He heard a chuckle beside him and turned to see Nick.

"She truly is happy to see you. It's been so depressing to see her moping around the castle."

Thomas sighed. "Under normal circumstances, I would have let her tour the city."

Nick stood up straight and nodded. "I know you would." He set down his glass and folded his arms. "I was able to hear a little more about your travels from her, and I do have a few questions."

"She already told me about Wicke."

Nick's eyes widened and he glanced to the side. "Uh... I didn't let him in, I swear—"

He held up a hand. "I'm sure there's a story there, I'm not too worried about it. Although, I'm sure he was upset about my not telling Marta about my mother."

Nick tilted his head sheepishly. "Right in one, as always, my Lord. Your uncle certainly has some... interesting aggravators."

He chuckled ruefully. "Go ahead and grill me, Nick."

Nick's demeanor changed as he grew serious. Thomas shifted, uncomfortable all of a sudden.

"My Lord, what do you know about Lightseers?"

*****

Marta emerged in the gardens, the evening cold and snow once again threatening in the air. She stopped herself and rubbed her arms. *I should've brought a cloak...* She spotted Amaryll's silhouette leaning on the wall of the terrace below. Marta picked up her skirts and walked over.

"You could've called for me."

Amaryll winced and glanced up at her, holding a small chunk of icy stone against her head. She chuckled ruefully and lowered it. "You were having too much fun dancing with your husband."

Marta set a glowing hand on Amaryll's head. The fire Gifted winced then sighed in relief as Marta alleviated her pain. She shook her head as Amaryll stood straighter and stretched.

"Ugh, I'm never drinking with a dwarf ever again... thank you, Milady." Amaryll smiled and put her hand on Marta's shoulder. "I—"

"What are you two doing here?! How dare you spy on me!"

The women turned to see Sarah shrieking up at Seamus and Dougal, who had followed Marta outside. Seamus bowed politely.

"Lady Sarah, we are here for—"

"That's your *highness* to you!"

Marta could feel Seamus' eye twitching. She stepped forward and waved.

"My apologies, Lady Sarah. I came out here to check on—"

Sarah whirled around and pointed her finger at Marta. "You're here because you think I'm lying, don't you?! You're just jealous because your husband hasn't even touched you! You just had to confirm for yourself to get a leg up on me! Well get your grubby hands away from me!" Sarah shoved Marta backwards. She stepped on the back of her dress and tumbled to the ground as a horrible ripping noise gained the attention of those nearby. Amaryll knelt and caught Marta before her head could hit the stone and Seamus and Dougal rushed to her side. Sarah waved her fan back and forth slowly, a wicked grin plastered on her face.

"Whoops, guess you won't be able to—"

"Don't you *ever* speak of my husband that way again, do you hear?!" Marta growled dangerously. The bush nearby burst as thorns sprouted from inside. Sarah glanced over and returned to glaring at Marta. Amaryll helped her stand and she shook her head.

"Thomas has given you a roof and a home and you spit in his face! I will not tolerate your slander, don't you *ever* accuse my husband of unfaithfulness you ungrateful—!"

"Marta!"

The group looked up to see Thomas and Peter standing on the balcony above them. Thomas's worried gaze flickered between Marta and Sarah as he turned and rushed down the stairs. Angry beyond belief and humiliated, Marta burst into tears as Thomas wrapped his arms around her. He glared at Sarah, who took a step back.

"She threatened me! I'm in a very delicate position, I can't just—"

"Sarah, that's enough." Everyone glanced at Peter in surprise as he stepped forward from the shadows at the bottom of the stairs and held out his hand. "Let's go inside."

Sarah narrowed her steely eyes at her husband and mumbled something under her breath. She turned and smacked Peter's hand with her fan as she trudged up the stairs and into the hall. Thomas rubbed Marta's back in an effort to comfort her. She tried desperately to quell her angry tears but found it hard to do so. She felt Amaryll wrap a cloak around her shoulders and Thomas helped wrap her in it. She didn't know if her dress had ripped beyond repair. Despite the thoughts swirling through her mind, one thing was certain;

Sarah most definitely was not with child.

CHAPTER SIXTEEN

Ambushed

Marta rubbed her face wearily. The last few days since the victory ball had been spent diving headfirst into her duties as Queen. The footman in front of her bowed and made his leave. The throne room was much smaller than one would expect, much more cozy than she had imagined. Once a week Thomas would host audiences with the citizens of Elyon. It was actually quite rare to have very many people arrive, a testament to the hierarchy in place to help citizens of all stages in life. Today a few curious citizens came to visit, mostly with curiosity to meet the new Queen. Thomas stepped away a few hours prior to work with Nick on something. Marta was pleased to meet new people but felt exhausted and out of her element.

The large engraved door opened and she straightened as another citizen entered. He was an older man with thin white hair who stooped over slightly. He shuffled forward with his tam o'shanter in his hands. Marta stood and grabbed a chair from the side of the small hall, much to the surprise of everyone in the room. She placed it down before anyone could stop her and motioned for the elderly man to sit. His eyes widened and he shook his head.

"Ah, me Lady! Ah'm a pure stoter, Ah dinnae deserve this!"

Marta smiled gently and took his arm. "You're very deserving, sir. I can tell you have worked hard for many years. I am honored to meet a gentleman such as yourself."

The man chuckled and sat, easing himself back into the plush chair with a sigh of contentment. "Bless me, ye're really woot they say."

Marta tipped her head to the side as she handed him a cup of tea from the tray nearby. He sat up and took it gratefully.

"Tea served by an angel! Ah've died an' goon t'heaven. Thankee

Milady!"

She laughed and stepped back as Amaryll brought her over a chair. She sat beside the grandfather and set her hands on her lap.

"I'm no angel, sir, but I do appreciate the compliment. I am Marta."

"Me name's Tobias, yer Majesty. Ah'm honored t'meet ye."

"Likewise. What can I do for you, Tobias?"

The old man chuckled, the deep laugh lines in his face creasing ever more. "Ah wonted t'see th' Queen, an' Ah'm surprised Ah got an audience wit' ye. Ah was hopin' t'see his Excellency as well, but... I dinna see 'im."

"He's currently with our Shepherd, would you like someone to call for him?"

"Nay, Milady... Ah've a feelin' this needs t'end up in yer hands." He reached a knobby hand forward and deposited something secretly in her palm. The minute the item touched her skin she felt something tingle. She opened her fingers to reveal a dark blue and purple crystal shard, no larger than a bronzer. Her eyes widened for a moment before the old man picked it up and placed it in a worn piece of leather, wrapping it up and putting it back in her hand. He leaned over so only she could hear.

"Ah'm a retired Knight, t'was a part of King Martin's regiment. Me son was, too. He was one o' the ones in the room when our King died. This," he motioned as he closed her hand around the fabric, "was found on his body. Me son found't on his uniform later. Said t'was a lot o' these crystals in th' King's wounds."

"I'm assuming something happened to keep him quiet?"

Tobias nodded. "Soon as he found 't, he went t'report it. T'was told no crystals were found on th' King's body."

"Someone got rid of the evidence," her eyes widened as she whispered.

"Ah cannac say who, for Ah din' know. But one thing is certain," he shook his head, "'tis a Mordiern shard in yer hand."

She shuddered as the realization swept over her. *It wasn't suicide. It was murder. Amaryll was right!* She glanced around nervously, Wesley and Lyle stepping closer in trying to read her expression. She shook her head and they retreated.

"Can you tell me who your son is? I can try to find him discreetly and ask—"

Tobias heaved a mournful sigh. "Ah wish Ah could, Milady. My sweet Henrik was killed in the battle at Mulligen."

Her heart plummeted into her stomach. She reached forward and took his hand with a grieved expression. "My condolences for your loss, Sir Tobias. I thank him and you for your service to the kingdom. While I may not have known him, I know his presence is sorely missed."

"Thankee, Milady," he painfully reached into his pocket to pull out a yellowed handkerchief to dab away his tears. The fabric was thin and fuzzy with several holes in it. He sighed and put it back into his pocket. "Ah think the thing tha' did *that*," he pointed to her hand, "is still in Elroith. Ah can feel't."

She nodded solemnly. "Thank you, Sir Tobias. Truly. I promise I will help King Thomas get to the bottom of this." She helped him stand and kissed his soft white cheek gently. The old man blushed and smiled sheepishly.

"Gawan, Milady, ye're too kind. Lang may yer lum reek!" he bowed and picked up his squashed tam. He nodded with a smile and shuffled to the door. She watched him go and glanced down at her hand.

Whoever did this not only snuck it past the guards, they... wait, it was found in *his wounds? How strange...* She pocketed the bundle as Thomas and Nick walked into the throne room with severe expressions.

"That's ridiculous, Nick. I don't see how I—"

"It's entirely possible, my Lord. Even her Majesty could—" they paused as Marta smiled guiltily. Thomas noticed the chairs and chuckled under his breath.

"Marta... it's dangerous to be so close to people we don't know."

"He wasn't going to hurt me, I swear!" she winced slightly as her leg felt numb where the crystal sat. *Even a shard is this powerful?*

Thomas raised a brow as he caught her thoughts and began to speak when one of the guards caught their attention.

"You can't just rush in here, you need to—"

"Please, my baby, I need help! Please!"

Marta and Thomas exchanged glances at the frantic woman's voice and he nodded to the guards by the door.

"Let her in."

The door opened and a dark-haired woman in a gray dress rushed in holding a tightly wrapped bundle.

"Please, please let me see my Lady! My baby, he needs help, he's sick, I need-"

Marta started forward but stopped herself to turn and glance at Thomas. He nodded and she rushed over. The woman collapsed to the ground and Marta landed on her knees in front of her.

"What's going on? What happened?"

Thomas' eyes suddenly flickered with light and he lunged forward as he unsheathed his sword, yelling "Marta, wait—!"

The woman lifted the fabric around the baby to reveal a bundle of hay. Marta met the woman's darkened empty eyes and panicked as a deranged grin crossed the intruder's lips. She jerked backwards as the woman launched onto her, grabbing her throat and strangling her. Guards and Knights lunged forward but a blast of air threw them backwards.

Marta squirmed for breath as the memory of Carrick's grip flooded her with terror. She reached up to push her off using vines, but the creature cackled and grasped Marta's hand with her own, slamming it to the ground.

"MARTA!" Thomas screamed as he fought against the air swirling around her.

"You're dead, Life Queen," the woman smiled wide. Marta wheezed as she fought for air.

Death Wizard! She's a Death Wizard!

The woman's grip started piercing Marta's neck and she could feel warm liquid flowing behind her head. The valiant guards fighting against the wind watched with horror as black tendrils started growing across Marta's neck and up her face.

There was a bright flash of light and a cracking *whoosh*. Marta watched as the woman's black eyes widened and she turned her head. It was gone in a second as Thomas' blade found true, spewing black blood and smoke everywhere. Marta scrambled back as the woman's headless body fell onto her and dissolved into ash. She could feel her Gift stirring within her and beginning to heal her wounds. She collapsed onto her back and croaked as she tried to catch her breath. Wesley and Lyle gently yet forcefully dragged her away from the pile of ash. Thomas knelt next to her and cradled her head. His blue eyes were filled with tears and his face strained with worry.

"Marta, are you alright?!"

She coughed hoarsely and nodded as she looked around with wild eyes. He held her to his chest, breathing out praise. "Thank You God, thank You, thank You..."

Her eyes welled up with tears as she swallowed painfully, her throat dry and cracked. He released his grip as Nick and Amaryll rushed over. The black tendrils had receded off her face but nearly encircled her neck. Thomas shook his head.

"How do we help her?"

Nick knelt on the other side of her and gently touched her neck. She hissed in pain as he drew his finger across her throat, boosting her energy with his own. The tendrils disappeared under his touch and were soon gone. Her vision blurred and she felt woozy.

"She's lost a lot of energy, we—"

"So how do I give it to her?!" Thomas cried with worry. Nick glanced at him and looked back at Marta.

"Pocket," she whispered hoarsely, "take... out..."

Thomas paused as he registered her words then reached into her pocket and pulled out the bundle of fabric. He nearly dropped the crystal shard and caught it with his bare hand. His eyes widened and he quickly wrapped it up again but not before Nick could see it.

"Where did you get a Mordiern crystal—?!"

"Quiet," she croaked and shook her head. "I'll... explain... don't let... see..."

Thomas nodded and put the shard in his pocket. "Alright. Let's get you to the room." He scooped her up in his arms and walked out the door, Nick and her Guardsmen following behind.

*****

"Aside from figuring out how a Death Wizard got in here, I'm very intrigued that Sir Tobias felt the need to come here with this evidence," Nick sighed from the doorway as Thomas sat next to Marta who was resting on their bed. He brushed a loose blonde strand out of her face, yet she never stirred from sleep. He shook his head.

"From what Marta has been able to communicate to me, he seems to think the... killer is still in Elroith. Possibly in the castle."

"That would certainly warrant discretion. I knew King' Martin's body was examined thoroughly but... I saw the report, there weren't any crystals on him." He held up a small glass jar containing the sinister bluish-purple crystal. "This is pure Mordiern, too..."

Thomas shook his head as his emotions raged within him. "I don't have time to think about that right now. I want every Gifted and Knight available to search the castle— no, the whole city! I need to find —" he clamped his mouth shut as Nick's firm hand landed on his shoulder. The Shepherd's eyes were gentle and understanding.

"Take a breath, Thomas. Amaryll is already working on it. You did an excellent job breaking through the wizard's shield."

Thomas glanced down at his pale wife, breathing hard in sleep. Anger began to rise in him.

This is my fault. I wasn't there for her. I let her go to help thinking it was safe. I was a fool, and now she's been hurt because of me. I'm a worthless husband.

"Thomas, whose voice are you listening to?"

He glanced up at the Shepherd with a desperate look in his eyes.

"My own, Nick. Don't preach to me right now."

"I was simply asking to—"

"Well don't," he snarled. Nick sighed heavily.

He won't talk to anyone about the demons plaguing his mind. If he doesn't go to God with them, they'll only continue to ravage his heart. He can't keep going to Marta for answers, but I don't think she's realized that's what he's doing yet. You will never find God in someone else, my friend, he mourned as Thomas stood and regained his composure.

"I want all of her Guards on duty, understand? And post several Light Gifteds outside and at least one inside."

"Yes, Sir."

Thomas glared as Nick simply shrugged.

"I will make sure it is done, your Excellency."

"Good. Be sure of it."

Nick watched Thomas storm out of the room and sighed. *Oh, good Lord, please help us.*

*****

The two maids recoiled in shock as the vase exploded beside their heads, shattering into hundreds of pieces on the floor. Sarah stormed back and forth in her parlor pulling at her fiery red hair. She muttered under her breath and paused.

"Get out of my sight!" she screamed. The maids didn't have to be told twice, Peter flinching as the door slammed. Sarah continued pacing and muttering, chewing on her finger and drawing blood.

"I don't get it," she spluttered, "I don't get it. It was all so well-planned. I did everything I could to drive her out. She stayed. I humiliated her. She didn't take it. I one-upped her. She said nothing." She tore off her cuticle with her teeth and spit to the side, blood landing on the pristine floor. Peter watched with folded arms.

"Perhaps she—"

"And then!" she continued with a screech, "I go through all that work, all those hours of preparation to bring in the Death Wizard and they *failed?!*"

"Shut up! Do you want someone to hear your mad raving?!" Peter growled, glancing at the door nervously. She pulled at another handful of hair and groaned.

"I don't know what else to do. I don't know. I'm going to get rid of her one way or another, but that stupid king is always—" she paused mid-rant, her hair frazzled around her head and a crazed look in her eye. Her mouth tipped in a sardonic grin as she stood and smoothed her hair back. "That's it."

Peter shuddered though he couldn't say why. "Oh?"

Sarah's deranged green eyes met Peter's weary blue ones. "I just have to separate her from the group. A lone sheep is easy to pluck away when the sheepdog isn't nearby."

*****

Three Days Later

Marta sighed wearily as she settled into the couch in the parlor. Brenna and Kate winced as she groaned slightly in pain, rubbing her neck.

"Can Ah get y'anything, Milady? More tea?"

"More tea with licorice and marshmallow root would be wonderful, thank you."

Brenna nodded and bowed before leaving the room. Kate stood nearby as Marta pulled out her small sewing project. She had barely seen Thomas at all since the incident; he was constantly searching the city for answers. That morning, he had received word that a possible Seeker had been spotted in a town two days' travel away, so he, Nick, Jerome, and Amaryll had left to investigate. Her Guards were left with her at the castle along with several Light Gifteds and Finlay's regiments.

I wish I could just talk to him… he's been so frantic lately. I'm doing better, just sore now… I just want to spend time with him, she sighed again. Kate sat next to her and put her hand on her knee.

"Don't worry, Milady, King Thomas will be back soon. I'm sure of it! Maybe he will get to the bottom of this, too."

Marta smiled softly at her young friend. "I feel something looming on the horizon, but I can't quite place it. I feel so much better when he's nearby, but…"

Kate nodded slowly. "You've been through a lot in the last few days. And after the stories you told us about the battle in Ropheka, I'm sure you're exhausted mentally too."

"You could say that again," she chuckled ruefully. They glanced up as there was a gentle knock on the door. Wesley and Breton glanced at the door.

"Come in."

Brenna stepped inside and nodded at the Guardsmen before walking over with a bewildered expression.

"What's happened?" Marta asked in alarm as Brenna set down a teapot and teacup. She handed Marta a sealed letter. She recognized Sarah's sigil immediately.

"What does *she* want?" she grumbled under her breath as Kate handed her a letter opener. She read the letter quickly as a range of emotions displayed on her face.

"Milady?"

Marta folded up the letter and stared at it blankly. "She's invited me to tea in two days' time. She… she says she wants to apologize."

"Hah! Apologize my—" Brenna smacked Kate before she could say anything else. "Ow! Sorry… But really, *that* witch? *Apologize?!* No way!"

Marta shook her head listlessly. "That's what I thought too, but… what if she's sincere? She's even gone so far as to provide guards to make sure I'm protected."

"My Lady, pardon my intrusion," Wesley stepped forward. She nodded.

"You may speak, friend."

"I am not comfortable with you going to Lady Sarah's alone. I would request to accompany you."

"Me too!" Kate exclaimed. Breton nodded and stepped forward. "I would, as well."

Marta nodded slowly, then winced at the memory of Sarah's tantrum in the gardens. "If I bring everyone, she may think I'm ganging up on her or that I don't trust her."

"But y'doon't," Brenna quipped. She blushed as everyone glanced at her in surprise. "What? 'Tis true!"

Marta chucked softly. "You may be right, Brenna, but… I'd like to give her the chance. Isn't that what God calls us to do? Forgive our enemies? As far as protection… Maybe we can keep you two outside, hmm? Although I know I'll be in good hands with my Captain. She wants me to join her in the south wing… I've never been there before."

"Oh, that's where the late Queen's garden is!" Kate grinned.

"She had a garden?"

"Indeed! It's not accessed very often, but there's a trail that leads up into the mountains behind the castle from there. It's patrolled fairly frequently. I've heard you can even find a hidden hot spring up there!" she caught the exasperated glances from Wesley and Brenna and smiled sheepishly. "Sorry, I got ahead of myself. There is a beautiful lanai hewn from the mountainside, it is perfectly safe."

Wesley sighed. "I will be sure to patrol it myself, my Lady, to be sure there is nothing off. If you would like to go, please take me with you."

She nodded. "I wouldn't have it any other way."

*****

Two Days Later

Sarah's smile faded slightly as Marta and her blasted Captain emerged in the secluded garden. She glanced between the two as they stepped forward.

"Ah, your Majesty. I had hoped this would be a *private* meeting. I have enough guards here, as you can see," she motioned to three burly men standing by the tea table. Marta nodded solemnly.

"I appreciate the thought, Lady Sarah, but I will keep my captain with me."

"Yes…" Sarah suppressed a sneer. "Of course. Please, come sit. I'm thankful you could join me."

Marta followed behind Sarah trepidatiously, Wesley right behind them both. She motioned for Marta to sit and followed suit, a mocking grin plastered all over her face.

"Now, then, Milady," she began after pouring tea, "as I said in my letter, I wanted to invite you out here to smooth things over."

She really wants to apologize?! Marta choked on her tea and set it down, holding her chest.

"Oh—oh?"

Sarah's eyes flickered to the lanai as she nodded slowly. "Yes. In fact, I've brought you a present. Here," she stood and motioned her towards another table resting between the guards. Wesley stood behind his queen with a hand on his sword, eyes wary.

I've never seen these guards before. I don't like this... he grumbled to himself as Marta stepped up next to the table. Sarah reached forward and pulled over a box, holding it gingerly.

"I had some jewelry made for you. I think it will look lovely with your skin tone. May I?"

Marta tried to quell the alarm rising in her chest as she held out her arm. *It's fine, it's just a bracelet,* she mused as she watched Sarah take something out of the box. *What's the worst that—?*

As soon as the bracelet *clicked* around her wrist she immediately felt a significant drain of energy. She audibly gasped and doubled over before a hand clamped around her mouth. She heard Wesley unsheath his sword but there was a sickening *crunch* and he collapsed. She struggled at the hands grasping her mouth and tried to grow something to protect herself; nothing could be produced, however, and the attempt to use her Gift sucked away her strength even more. Sarah's eyes were alight with flame as she grabbed Marta's left hand and wrenched off her wedding ring.

"Oh no," Sarah feigned mock surprise as she clamped another bracelet onto Marta's empty wrist. "You lost your ring."

Marta bit down on the man's hand but that just resulted in a rush of air to her face. The third man stood with hand outstretched, a ball of air in his hand. He held it over her face and the breath rushed from her lungs. She gulped and gasped, her vision tunneling and turning to black. Before the world faded, the last thing she heard was Sarah's smooth voice.

"Good luck, Marta."

The queen slumped into the men's arms and Sarah's eyes narrowed in madness. She motioned and two more men appeared from the shadows.

"Find the Guards she posted around here to watch and kill them."

"Yes, ma'am."

*****

Kate held her hand over Brenna's mouth as they watched the men toss Marta and Wesley's bodies into two chests with holes drilled into them. Sarah turned suddenly and the two women jerked behind the corner. Sarah examined the lanai slowly, then turned back to the men. Kate and Brenna watched as she was handed a sack of coins by the cloaked man. Kate caught a glimpse of a serpent pinned to his cloak before they turned and disappeared.

Once Sarah was out of sight the two women stumbled over each other in an effort to run out.

"We need to tell someone!" Kate cried as she panicked. "Who knows where they could be taking them!"

Brenna's eyes were full of tears as she twirled the engagement ring on her own finger. "Ah, Ah cannae-"

A man rounded the corner and they crashed into him. They stumbled backwards and stood mouths agape as Finlay rubbed his head.

"Oi, watch where ye're goon!"

"General!" Kate exclaimed breathlessly. "You have to help us! Queen Marta, she's been kidnapped!"

Finlay's face paled as his gaze flickered between the two desperate women.

"What d'ye mean, 'kidnapped'??"

"She an' Wes were taken by soldiers!" Brenna cried. "T'was Lady Sarah who—"

Finlay held up a hand. The women paused as he rubbed his face.

"Ah…. Ah'll take care of 't. Fer now, though, DOON say a word t' anyone!" he held up a finger in warning. "If ye go 'round tellin' aboot this, Sarah may catch wind of 't and off ye, if ye know what Ah mean. Fer right now, lemme handle this."

The two women nodded their heads slowly. Kate grasped his hand desperately and he recoiled in response.

"Please, general, *please* save our Lady!"

Finlay swallowed hard. "Ah will… try."

CHAPTER SEVENTEEN

Darkness Falls

Marta woke bleary-eyed to a rhythmic shifting motion. She could hear the *clop, clop, clop* of numerous horses' hooves on a rocky road. She blinked several times and winced as her arms ached in protest, her numb hands chained to a ring on the wall above her head. Her mouth was dry and her throat parched from the gag tied tight around her head. She turned to examine her surroundings in the dim light.

Wesley was slumped against the wall across from her, bound and gagged the same way. His head lolled from side to side as what must be a carriage lurched on its' unknown journey. She tried desperately to clear her thoughts and focus but a deep exhaustion had taken hold of her. She glanced upwards to see two purple-and-blue crystal embedded metal cuffs on her wrists, her eyes widening as the early morning light revealed the Mordiern.

I can't use my Gift. I can barely think straight! God, please, please save us! She hiccuped as tears began to fill her eyes and fear welled up within her, grasping her chest in its claws. She shook her head and shuddered in a breath. *Think, think. Easy, Kate and Brenna would've seen it, as long as they got out they can tell —*

Her heart plummeted. *What if Sarah saw them?* She shook her head violently. *No, I can't think about that. I can't. Thomas is going to find us. I know it. He...* the dimness that surrounded them seemed to pierce her soul as her mind reeled with a sudden realization. *...what if he doesn't?*

She grasped at her last vestiges of strength as the carriage continued ever onward.

*****

Thomas examined the town of Girden from atop his horse, his eyes flickering with light. Townspeople had retreated to their homes once the news broke that a Seeker might be there. The streets were empty and the whole town seemed to hold their breath. Amaryll's eyes were ever searching and Jerome sat quietly. Nick glanced around from on top of Maggie with a strained look.

There's nothing here, he glanced at his king sadly. *He knows it, too.*

Thomas rubbed his face angrily and broke the tense silence. "Either they're gone or it was a red herring."

Amaryll nodded solemnly. "I agree."

He grumbled under his breath and turned his horse. The small company that had joined them glanced at each other wearily, having ridden overnight. Amaryll waved and a contingent of Knights and Gifteds dispersed through town to do a final check and to disseminate information to the townspeople. Thomas turned to Nick but hesitated as fear overwhelmed him. His face twisted in shock as he held his chest.

What on earth...?

Nick's eyes flashed with light and he glanced behind them. "I sense it too, my Lord. Something's happened."

"Where?" Thomas asked shakily, not knowing if he wanted the answer. Nick shook his head.

"I'm not sure. Can you focus on it? Perhaps you'll be able to tell."

Thomas closed his eyes a moment and a flash of an image came to mind. He could see Marta standing with her Shepherds Caleb and Camilla. He immediately reached into his pocket and pulled out his watch.

"My Lord, be careful what you say, the mirrors still could be—"

Thomas held up a hand as he turned the delicate tool around and opened up the back compartment. He caught a glimpse of his worried expression in the mirror before tapping the glass. The Ela rimming the mirror glowed blue for a moment and the mirror's surface swam like the ripples on a lake. The image cleared and he saw his reflection once more.

Marta didn't answer... he thought in alarm. He tried one more time but to no avail. He shook his head and tried to quiet his anxious thoughts as he tapped the mirror again, the surface swimming dizzyingly. The image cleared and he could see Caleb sitting at his desk in the Tower. The Shepherd glanced up at the mirror on the wall and his eyes grew wide.

"Yer Majesty! It's good t'see ye. What kin—"

"You're a Lightseer, right?" Thomas blurted. Caleb sat up and shifted.

"Ah… Ah've been compared to one, yes. Has—"

"Something's happened and I don't know what, all I know is that I needed to contact you or Marta, and Marta didn't answer her mirror."

"Marta has been on our minds today, more than usual. Have you—"

The image suddenly fizzled and crackled and the mirror went dark. Thomas' eyes widened as the glass cleared to reveal his surprised face.

"What…?!"

Nick closed the mirror quickly. "Someone interfered. That's exactly what's happened when Arailt interrupts the connection."

Thomas cursed and pocketed the watch. If there had been a transport mirror in Girden they would be able to be home by now. "We need to get home, I don't care what it takes."

"Yes, Sire."

*****

Kate and Brenna snuck down the hallway after Finlay left, keeping an eye out for Sarah or any of her guards.

"Ah doon like't. Ah doon trust 'im." Brenna shook her head as she trembled with fear. Kate nodded slowly.

"Who else can we tell?"

"Th' Guardsmen! They're waitin' outside!"

The women nodded and rushed down the hall. They opened the door and Dougal fell backwards. Lyle and Seamus helped him stand as Breton nodded at the women.

"Is everything alright—"

"Shhh! Out, we need to get out of here. The parlor, let's go there, *now!*"

The men glanced at each other and nodded solemnly. They rushed up to Marta and Thomas' room and shut the door behind them quickly. Brenna finally started sobbing and collapsed to the floor. Seamus kneeled beside her with wide eyes.

"Lady Brenna—"

"Kidnapped, she's been kidnapped! Along with Captain Wesley!" Kate blurted. "We told General Finlay but he told us not to tell anyone lest Sarah kill us. I don't know where they're taking them, but they left up the trail—"

Dougal lunged for the door with a hand on his sword. Lyle stopped him with a firm hand.

"Wait, lad. Finish yer story, my Lady."

Kate nodded and explained the whole situation to them. The Guardsmen glanced at each other nervously.

"Yer sure ye saw an orb of air?"

Kate nodded frantically. Lyle and Seamus exchanged a nod.

"'Twas a Dark Wizard, then. Even if we took off after them now, King Thomas took most of the Light Gifteds. There are only two here an Ah doon' know if we'd walk away alive. 'Twas part of a campaign years ago tha' befell a single Death Wizard... nearly lost me life then, over fifty soldiers did," Lyle grumbled through his beard. "Ah want t'go after them, too, but we need t' stay alive t' tell his Majesty."

Seamus helped an inconsolable Brenna sit up and handed her a handkerchief. Dougal scowled as he leaned against the door and Lyle put a comforting hand on Kate's shoulder.

"Two o' us will ride out t' meet his Majesty. We'll let 'im know—"

There was a pounding on the door that shook the room. Dougal lurched forward and opened the door. Two soldiers stood there with wide eyes.

"Lady Sarah has requested that all serving men and women, as well as the castle guards, assemble in the main hall."

The group glanced at each other nervously. Lyle nodded.

"A'right. We'll be right there."

*****

Marta's eyes widened as Wesley jerked and suddenly opened his own. He winced as his head throbbed in pain. He examined the situation quickly, looking at Marta and then examining his own bonds. He met her gaze and shook his head. She nodded slowly.

He looked up at the chains around his wrists and hopped in an attempt to break it. They were solidly made, however, and didn't even budge. She could hear him groan through his gag.

Snow blew through the grates at the top of the square wooden carriage and both of them shivered in response. By her measure, it was early afternoon. She could feel them climbing higher in altitude and soon both of them could see their breath condensing in front of their chilled noses.

We're traveling through the mountains. I can't tell what direction... if the weather turns bad, no one will be able to see our tracks. Her heart desperately clung to the fleeting hope slipping from her grasp.

The carriage slowed and came to a stop. They could hear footsteps crunching on snow and a rattling of chains. The back door opened and snow burst into the small prison. A large man with dark hair reached forward and grabbed her wrists, unlocked the ring, and dragged her out. Another man did the same to Wesley, who didn't fight back.

If I fight now, they'll only incapacitate me and I won't be able to take an opportunity if one comes.

"Ah, you're both being very obedient. We were hoping for a fight."

The man tossed Marta into a snowbank. She shook her head and wiped off her face as she sat up, the snow clinging to her eyebrows and eyelashes. The man grabbed the back of her neck and dragged her towards a dilapidated wooden building. She could smell the smoke rising from the chimney and she shivered as the melted snow seeped through her clothes and melted into her eyes, chilling her to the bone. The man shoved her and Wesley into the building and they landed hard. It was lightly furnished and looked more like a hunting cabin than an actual home. Several cots lay around the room and a stove was freshly stoked. Two more burly men turned and nodded as the five men entered. The man with the serpent pin took off his hood and grinned at Marta.

"Lord Arailt will be pleased to finally meet you. I'll be rewarded well for this." He knelt beside her and grabbed her jaw, pulling her face closer to his. His breath made her toes curl and his dark eyes felt hollow as he laughed. She caught a glimpse of the men behind him exchanging glances. He threw her backwards and she hit her head on the wall, her back scraping against the logs making up the walls. Her vision swam as her head pounded; tears welled up in her eyes at the throbbing. It had been over a decade since she felt pain like this, normally her Gift would start healing her without her needing to do anything. Without that ability she moaned as she felt like she'd throw up.

"Hah! Used to getting pampered now, are you? And you," his gaze settled on Wesley, "I wonder how you feel knowing you," he kicked Marta, "can't," he wrenched her to her feet by her hair, "do," he finally tossed her to the men, "anything about it!" He cackled as Wesley's eyes blazed. The men attached Marta to another ring on the wall, this time making her stand. Her injuries throbbed and she suppressed a moan as her body weight sat on her wrists. She quickly lost feeling in her hands and had to stand on tiptoes to get any relief. The wizard continued smirking at Wesley.

"It's going to be a long trip for both of you. As soon as we are across the border we have ways of transporting you directly to Sorengard. Unfortunately it won't be comfortable for you!"

"Hey, you said we'd be paid. Where's the money."

The wizard whirled around to the men with a scowl. "I told you, I paid you a quarter before this and once we meet my partners in Hylen you'll get the rest! Do you take me for a liar?!" A wind picked up in the room, whipping up the blankets and cloaks and stoking the fire. The head brute, the dark-haired man who stood a head taller than the rest, folded his arms.

"No, this wasn't the deal."

"Well, I'm altering the deal. Don't make me alter it further," the wizard growled. One of the henchmen nudged the tall one and shook his head. The head thug paused before glaring at the wizard.

"Fine."

Marta grimaced as she opened her eyes. Wesley was watching the whole affair with a blank look. He caught her gaze and winked reassuringly.

God, please… please save us soon…

*****

The four Guardsmen and two handmaidens stood towards the back of the large group assembled in the main hall, everyone whispering and wondering what was going on. Sarah stood midway up the stairs with Peter on one side of her and Finlay standing at the bottom. Kate and Brenna exchanged nervous glances as Sarah held up her hand.

"Hello everyone," she smiled wickedly, "I have some very grave news to share with you." She lifted an envelope with Marta's seal on it. Kate gasped in surprise.

"Why that—!"

Lyle put a hand on her shoulder and a finger to his lips. Kate clenched her fists and returned her attention to the stairs.

"It seems that Lady Marta, although one can hardly call her one now, has been having second thoughts about being queen for some time now. She confided in me that she did not love our dear king and has chosen to elope with her captain."

Several maids glanced towards Brenna as the room erupted in

shock. She wanted to blurt out *she would never do that!* She wanted to run up there, to throw something, to do *anything*, but her feet stuck to the ground. *Ah know Ah canna do anything, but how dare she slander our Lady and m'dear Wesley so!*

Sarah waited for the cacophony to die down. "I hear some of you saying that Marta would never do such a thing to our strong, benevolent king, yet here is the proof; her wedding ring, which she entrusted to me as proof of her adultery. Although, that wasn't how she phrased it." She held up Marta's mothers' wedding ring, glinting in the dim lamplight. Dougal looked like he would explode at any second and the rest of the Guardsmen wore serious expressions.

"As such, I will alert his Majesty upon his return. Please be patient with him and anticipate his anger. Queen's Guard," she directed her attention to the four men standing there, "since your services are no longer needed, you are disbanded. Please report to the barracks for your new assignments immediately."

When none of them budged, Sarah narrowed her eyes. "What insolence! Do you not realize I out-rank you?"

Peter sighed heavily. "It is as she says, gentlemen. Please report to the barracks."

Lyle stepped forward with a hand on his chest. "We were formed by his Excellency th' King, therefore by law, only he can disband th' Guard. We are neither doing this outta negligence nor impudence. We are simply following th' law."

Sarah looked like she would burst with each word Lyle spoke. "How dare you!" she growled as her face grew red. "Guards, arrest this man for resisting orders!"

The castle guards in the room glanced at each other nervously. When no one moved, Sarah roared again. "Must I hang you all for treason?!"

"My Lady, it is as the Guardsman says. We cannot arrest him for following the law."

She threw her hands up in the air. "Whatever! Expect your due, Guardsman. I will be sure you pay for this. The rest of you, make no mention of Marta lest you want to be thrown in the dungeon!" she turned and stormed up the stairs, muttering under her breath. The serving men and women spoke together in hushed voices as they wandered back to their duties. It was evident no one believed her, but there were enough guards loyal to Sarah to prod them out of saying anything. Several glared at the Guardsmen as they passed. Lyle stood, arms folded, and shook his head.

"Lady Brenna, Lady Kate, Ah request tha' ye stay wit' me family 'til this blows over an' we can figure out wha's goon on. Ah've the feelin' Sarah's set her sights upon us, an' who knows wha' she'll do."

The ladies nodded solemnly. Seamus, Dougal, and Breton nodded as well.

"We will remain with you, too, and I suggest none of us travels without a partner."

Lyle nodded. "Good point, Breton."

"How will we tell his Majesty?" Kate asked quietly as several of Sarah's guards neared them. Lyle glanced up at the men with a glare.

"We'll have t' do't secretly, it seems." He turned suddenly, his eyes searching.

"What is it?" Seamus asked as he stepped closer, a hand on his sword.

"Th' Light Gifteds. They're not here."

*****

Sarah stood on the balcony overlooking the kingdom with an ugly scowl on her normally-perfect face. She watched in the distance as the contingent bearing the King and the Shepherd barreled towards the castle. It seemed word had gotten out somehow... but how much? She chomped down on her thumb and thought quickly.

"M'Lady...?"

She turned as General Finlay bowed and stepped forward. She glanced at the group in the distance and turned back to him.

"Excellent. I have orders from the king to arrest those handmaids and Guardsmen for treason. Do it quickly, before he gets here!" she handed him a sheet of paper and he took it. He examined it quickly and his eyes widened as he saw the king's seal.

"How did ye get ahold o' the—?!"

"Nevermind that! Go now you stupid oaf!" she shoved him out of the room and shut the door behind him, leaning against it as she continued to bite on her fingers.

I have a plan. I have a plan. As long as everything goes according to plan... she stood and took a deep breath. *I have to get into character.*

*****

Lyle shook his head as Dougal slammed his fist into the wall, Brenna jumping in surprise. The four Guardsmen and two maids stood outside in the gardens talking about their next moves.

"It's been three days, and we *still* can't find the Light Gifteds!" Dougal growled.

"She probably sent them away," Breton sighed heavily. Lyle nodded solemnly.

"Ah hope tha's all she did, Ah wouldn't wanna get on th' bad side o' the Tower—"

The men unsheathed their swords as soldiers burst into the gardens, their own weapons drawn. They pressed in and surrounded the men, who kept the ladies behind them.

"Wha's goon on?!"

General Finlay stepped forward with a solemn expression and held out a piece of paper with the king's seal on it.

"Under orders of His Majesty, King Thomas, ye're under arrest fer treason."

The group's hearts fell as they all spotted the seal. Lyle scanned the document quickly and raised a brow.

"Ah'd believe ye, general, yet the order dinnae bear a signature. King Thomas always signs his official documents."

Finlay instinctively turned it over and glanced at it, winced, and shook his head.

"He's very upset aboot his wife. Now stand doon!"

When they made no effort to move or put down their weapons, Finlay nodded to the soldiers around.

"Ye've left me no choice. Soldiers, seize them!"

Lyle was the first attacked and he tossed three soldiers away like they were stale pieces of bread. Dougal got caught by the brunt end of a pommel and stumbled backwards. Brenna and Kate gasped and jumped out of the way as Seamus and Breton exchanged blows with soldiers as well.

"Stay behind us!" Lyle roared as he took on another two soldiers. Metal rang through the air and the gardens echoed with the sounds of grunting and cursing. Dougal blinked as his head throbbed in pain and noticed the soldiers had diverted their attention to the rest of the group. Seeing his chance, he crawled behind the bushed and took off at a sprint towards the ballroom doors. Finlay noticed him as he climbed the steps and shook with fear.

"Soldiers, he's getting away! GET HIM!"

Several men broke off behind as Lyle nodded at the young man. "Godspeed, lad. Ye're our hope now."

*****

Thomas entered the promenade at breakneck speed, jumping off and landing as his horse galloped on. Nick and Amaryll were close behind as Thomas rushed into the castle. There was an eerie silence about the place with no guards, Knights, nor maids wandering the halls.

"Marta?!" he called, his echo the only answer. Nick and Amaryll rushed inside next to him, huffing and puffing out of breath.

"My Lord, there—"

Thomas rushed towards the stairs and paused as he felt eyes settle on him. He stood up straight and turned around to see Sarah standing on the mezzanine above him with a terse look.

"My Lord…"

"Where is my wife?" Thomas asked desperately. Sarah walked over to the stairs and took each step slowly. Her eyes were dim and apparently puffy with tears. Each step she took was like thunder in his ears. She stopped on the step above him and solemnly handed over a letter with Marta's sigil. He took it and opened it quickly.

My King,

I apologize that this must be the way we part. I do not think I am fit to be your queen, nor have I ever truly felt that way. I am too low-born for this role. I am moving on, and you should, too. Wesley is my companion now and he and I will truly be happy together. I pray you will be happy with whatever mate you find, and hope—

He crumpled the letter before he could read anymore. "This is horse —"

Sarah held out the glittering ring in her palm. Her eyes were sad as tears began rolling down her cheeks. "She wanted me to give this to you."

Thomas took the ring quietly. Nick and Amaryll lurched forward and grasped the letter from his hands, reading it quickly.

"You can't be serious, this isn't even her handwriting!" Nick exclaimed breathlessly.

"What have you done to her, you witch?!" Amaryll growled as fire burst around her. Sarah took a step back and nearly fell onto the stairs.

"I didn't do anything! She left of her own accord, you can ask

Peter!"

Thomas lifted his gaze to see his brother standing at the top of the stairs. Peter's expression was unreadable, and he glanced away.

"It's true, Thomas. I bore witness to this."

Nick caught Amaryll as she lunged forward with a growl. Thomas could hear a dull cacophony around him but couldn't make out the words. He returned his gaze to the delicate ring in his hand as his stomach lurched and his chest felt hollow.

She left me.

Those words knocked the breath out of his lungs. An odd sense of relief, painful and empty, whirled around inside him. *Good. She deserved better anyway. I don't blame her.*

His heart wrenched and threatened to tear. *No, no she couldn't have left! She said she loved me, she wouldn't leave me, she—*

Dark, twisted thoughts began to drown out the quiet voice stirring him into action. His shoulders slumped and he took a step back. Sarah noticed and her eyes lit with joy as her mouth remained crumpled in a frown. He turned the ring over and had a realization.

"I'm sorry, your Majesty. I didn't intend for you to find out this way." Sarah wiped away a tear.

"Sarah, where are her Guardsmen?"

"H-her Guardsmen? They— they were—"

A door slammed open down the hall and frantic stomping echoed through the castle. Dougal nearly tripped over himself as he turned the corner, puffing to catch his breath. Thomas' eyes widened when he noticed the blood trickling down his forehead and the young man pulled up short when he spotted Thomas.

"Your Majesty!" he immediately went down to one knee. Soldiers appeared around the corner— ones Thomas recognized from Finlay's regiment— and started to swipe at him with their swords before they too realized who stood before them.

"M-my Lord!"

"What is going on here?!" Thomas roared. The soldiers fell to their knees as he stormed over to them. "Dougal, what's going on?"

"We are being arrested, my Lord."

"For what?!"

"False suspicions of treason, your Majesty. The handmaids Brenna and Kate know what happened to her Majesty and—"

"Those lying, scheming women!" Sarah yelled, glancing around as her voice broke. "They were part of it and are coming up with baseless accusations—"

"Under whose orders are you being arrested?"

"Supposedly yours, your Excellency. But Lyle knew better."

Thomas cursed. "Where is the arrest taking place?"

"In the gardens."

"Take me there immediately. Peter, Sarah, you will join us. Jerome and Amaryll, make sure they follow."

The group nodded as Thomas took off running behind Dougal, who had given Sarah a satisfied smirk. She growled and started screeching about how Kate and Brenna were liars and thieves. Thomas paid her no mind as they emerged in the garden to the sounds of metal-on-metal ringing through the air. Across the yellowing grass he saw three Guardsmen going up against twenty or so men, the women standing together behind them.

"ENOUGH OF THIS!"

The garden grew quiet immediately. The gurgling of the stream was the only thing any outsiders could hear, but the soldiers all heard the thundering in their own ears. Everyone turned and Lyle, Seamus, and Breton were the first ones on their knees. Kate and Brenna, both exhausted and terrified, curtsied politely. Finlay jerked as he saw Peter and Thomas and bowed low.

"Y-yer Excellency, Ah—"

"Where are these so-called orders?"

Finlay exchanged a mournful glance with Peter, who averted his gaze as Finlay produced the parchment from his waistcoat pocket. Thomas ripped it from his hands and examined it.

"Forgery and illegal use of the King's seal. This is high treason, General Finlay, the punishment of which is death. Who gave you these orders?"

Finlay swallowed hard at the dangerous look in Thomas' eyes. "Ah... Ah did. Ah... made them... m'self..."

The soveriegn tipped his head to the side as a sardonic grin twisted his lips. "Come, now, Finlay, you're not nearly clever enough nor gutsy enough to come up with this on your own. Tell me," he lunged and grasped the collar of Finlay's uniform coat, "who gave you these orders?!"

Finlay worked his mouth but wouldn't say anything. Thomas tossed him forward and turned to the soldiers.

"Jerome, send in the castle knights." After a moment several stepped forward, having entered into the ballroom at the sound of the fray. He motioned to Sarah and his brother. "I am placing Sarah and Peter under house arrest until we can figure out what happened. Finlay will be placed in the dungeon immediately."

"What!" Sarah and Peter exclaimed as Finlay averted his gaze. She squealed as two men grasped her arms. Peter didn't fight as the men stepped towards him and Sarah cried.

"I told you, I didn't do anything! There—!"

Thomas' eyes flashed with light as he growled, "Only someone who has access to my study could have gotten my seal, and so far you have done nothing but lie to me. In addition," he pulled out the small gold ring that once sat on his wife's finger, "this is Marta's mother's ring. She wouldn't part with it even if her life depended on it."

Sarah's eyes widened and she screeched as the guards pulled her up the stairs and into the ballroom. "No! No! I speak the truth, you can ask— no, NO!"

Nick and Amaryll stared at Thomas as Sarah screamed through the halls, silenced only by the sound of a slamming door. Thomas turned the ring over and over in his hands.

Where are you, God?

"Thomas, we need to act fast if we want to find her. Who knows how long she's been gone!" Nick put his hands on his head as Amaryll cursed under her breath.

"I should've known better than to leave her alone!"

Thomas turned lethargically. First his father, now his wife? *You really hate me, don't You, God? You think I'm a fool. You've created me to amuse yourself.* Nick and Amaryll blinked at the darkness filling Thomas' eyes.

"Thomas, don't listen to Sarah. We can find her, she didn't leave you! There's no way!" Nick grasped Thomas' shoulders and shook him. As he did, something inside Thomas broke into a million pieces.

"And if she did?" he whispered thickly, the darkness seeping into his chest. The pair shook their heads.

"What are you saying?" Nick asked in disgust. Thomas shrugged slowly.

"I'm saying, what if she did leave? Could I blame her? I kept her trapped here like a bird in a cage. You said so yourself, she was miserable here."

"She wanted to be with *you*, that's why she was sad! Not because—"

"Maybe it's for the best," he scoffed sardonically.

"Snap out of it!" Amaryll cried. "You can't be serious?!"

"What if she's hurt, Thomas?! Huh?" Nick grabbed the king's shoulders and gave him a shake. His voice lowered dangerously. "What if she's injured or— what if she's pregnant?"

Thomas shook his head in disgust. "What? There's no way she—"

"Is there? Because you know Life Gifteds can be—"

He shoved Nick away and held his head, his face paling. *I... hadn't thought of that. She didn't say anything, I didn't hear her say anything, but—* "N-no, she couldn't be, she would've—"

Nick's eyes flashed with light as Lyle stood and cleared his throat.

"Pardon the interruption, my Lord, but these ladies know what happened."

I knew there was something more going on here, Nick bemoaned.

"There ain't a lotta time. 'Twas kidnapped, she was. These two witnessed it," he motioned to Brenna and Kate, who nodded. Nick rubbed his face as Thomas paled.

"How long has Lady Marta been gone?"

"Three days," Breton whispered, "we would've gone after her but there was a Death Wizard with them."

"I saw a serpent pinned to his cloak," Kate added quietly.

Their eyes widened and both Thomas and Nick cursed. "This has gotten so much worse. If you are correct, then she has been taken by Arailt."

Kate and Brenna gasped and covered their mouths as the Guardsmen all put a hand on their swords. Nick began pacing back and forth, stroking his beard in thought. Amaryll stood with shocked expression as Thomas stared into the distance.

"This is not the place to discuss this," Nick groaned. "Let's get to the King's study. And... get you all patched up."

The weary Guards nodded and sighed in relief, turning to the ladies. Brenna and Kate exchanged glances and nodded. Thomas could feel despair creeping up into his throat.

God... what have I done?

CHAPTER EIGHTEEN

God of the Valleys

Based on the scratches she had made into the wall of the carriage, Marta and Wesley had been traveling for a little over a week and a half. Any hope of rescue was nearly gone, most of her days spent sleeping when the carriage wasn't lurching too badly. Blizzards had slowed their progress through the mountains and lent scant hope that someone would find them. Meals were served once a day, with poorly made soup shoveled into their faces before either could say a word. Their gags were quickly replaced and they continued on their journey. Marta felt lethargic and weak and Wesley looked gaunt and thin. She could feel her cheekbones as she rested her head against her weary arms, her wrists bruised and constantly numb. Her feet ached and felt half-frozen, her delicate boots not suited for being worn this long. Her toes constantly itched and burned when they weren't freezing.

The carriage had been traveling on steady ground for a few hours now and both of them knew the border between Hylen and Elyon was growing near; so, too, was their dread at what they would find there. The carriage rocked as men yelled outside. The pair jerked around as the carriage tipped, Marta's feet leaving the ground as she hung in the air. She sucked in a breath and prayed with all her might that the carriage wouldn't topple over. With a *crunch* the carriage landed upright then lurched as the wheels broke. The carriage shifted and this time Wesley slid across the floor and put his feet on the wall beside her to steady himself. There was a tense silence before the back door was wrenched open and the head man stood there covered in blood.

"Good. Yer still alive." He motioned and the other henchmen rushed in and unhooked them from the walls. Marta's eyes filled with tears. *Have they come to their senses? Are we free? Are they taking us back—* as soon as she stepped outside her heart plummeted. They stood in a large flat forest surrounded by evergreens and the ground clothed in white. Large tufts of snow fell lazily from the gray sky. The Death Wizard's cloak lay in the cold covered in black blood. A pile of ash lay beside it with several bags and various articles of clothing. The snow around looked like it had been blown back by a fierce wind. One of the thugs shoved her forward and the head man gripped her face to take off her gag.

"Ah doon know who ye really are, but y'ain't no queen. That dress will fetch a handsome price though. Git," he shoved her behind a tree and she fell to her knees, her mouth dry as a bone. Her heart thundered in her ears as he tossed a plain green woolen dress on her head. Wesley growled and tried to throw off one of the men holding onto him. The man in charge folded his arms as the others laughed.

"Goon. Git the dress off."

In front of them?! Her face paled as fear crept up into her throat. The head thug waved to the others and they picked her up and threw her back into the carriage.

"Ye've five minutes. After that's fair game."

She didn't have to be told twice. They unhooked her chains but left the Mordiern bracelets on. It was difficult and slow going but she was able to shrug out of her dirty dress and into the much warmer green woolen one. They had even provided a thin linen shift, a welcome sight as she peeled off her soiled clothes. It was itchy and not well made but felt like the clothes she used to wear before being sent to the castle. She stepped out just as the thugs rounded the corner and she held up her hands. The black bracelets *thunked* on her wrists as she shook her head.

"Thank… you," she crackled, her voice breaking and her throat parched. The leader of the dark group raised a brow as he turned with Wesley.

"Hmph. Yer turn, officer. Ye make a fuss and Ah'll slit her throat." Marta jerked as one of the thugs grabbed her and held a knife to her neck. They took him into the carriage and watched him change. Marta closed her eyes until he was shoved back out onto the road. He wore a plain brown tunic and trousers, with simple shoes on his feet. The thug picked Marta up and she squealed as they peeled off her boots.

"Lord above!" the man stumbled backwards and covered his nose. She could smell it, too, but her feet felt much better after being released from their prison. She didn't dare look as the head thug stepped over.

"Aye, tha's a bad case o' digger foot. Ye canna work with that. Le's git to town, maybe we kin find someone ta help." He quickly wrapped her feet in linen to give them some protection and tossed her boots into the broken carriage.

Marta stumbled forward and hissed as her feet sunk painfully into the frigid soggy snow. The large man hefted her onto his shoulder and carried her like a sack of potatoes to the horses nearby. He set her in front of him and the group started off. Wesley was bound and still gagged, but Marta was as quiet as a mouse.

If I don't put up a fuss, maybe they won't gag me.

It wasn't long before they emerged in a small mining town. It looked like the wooden buildings were hastily made, with gaps stopped up with mud and slats covering the windows. There were several saloons and an inn as well as a general store and a couple of barrack-like buildings. A broken sign with scrawled paint denoting the name of the town hung sideways as they entered; *Winfield.* The group stopped at the *Last Chance Inn* and went around back. They pounded on the door and a man yelled from inside.

"Hoi, doon git yer knickers in a twist! Ah'm comin'!"

Marta shivered as night began to fall and the cold seeped into her bones. The door swung open and an older, severe looking gentleman stood in the doorway. The scent of fresh stew wafted out the door and the starving prisoners' stomachs growled. The man's left eye was closed and he had bandages around his head. He glanced down at Marta and Wesley and nodded.

"Two new workers, eh Braum?"

"This one's gootta bad case o' digger foot. Goot anything fer it?"

The man narrowed his eyes. "What'll ye pay fer it?"

"Ye owe me yer life, Greg."

The older man heaved a sigh. "Fine, fine. Bring 'em in. Ye know where the cages be."

They were brought inside and Marta breathed a sigh of relief. The warmth permeated her being and her shivering stopped. *Thank You, Lord...*

The thugs brought them into a room off the kitchen with several cages in it. There were a few prisoners inside, most looking even more gaunt than they. Marta and Wesley were put into the cage closest to the door with the biggest lock and attached to chains on the floor. Braum removed Wesley's gag and he coughed violently. He took out a flask of some kind, swigged a huge sip, then tipped Wesley's head back and shoved it in his mouth. He had to grip Wesley's face and nose to get him to drink.

"There. Finest Hylen whiskey that is. That'll keep ye calm."

Marta shook her head as he turned towards her, Wesley spluttering in surprise. He laughed.

"Ah, too strong fer the likes a ye. Ah'll git Greg in here t'look at yer feet."

The door slammed shut and plunged the room into darkness. It reeked of mold and human feces mixed with blood. After dealing with their own travels the last few weeks, it didn't affect her as much as she thought it would have. She watched Wesley hold his chest and curse between coughs.

"Ah... tha's strong whiskey..." he grumbled. Marta brushed a dirty lock of blonde hair out of her face and caught the eyes of a group of children in another cell. They quickly averted their gazes and returned to huddling together for warmth.

They're trafficking through here... how disgusting. I don't know how far over the border we are, but... this does not bode well.

The door opened again and a thin young woman poked her head inside. Braum shoved her in and opened the cage Marta was in.

"Doon look too hard, Millie. Jus' do what yer supposed tuh."

The raven haired woman stepped inside timidly and jumped as the cell door shut behind her. She tucked a loose strand of hair behind her ear and turned her attention to Marta with wide brown eyes. She knelt in front of her and slowly took off the linens.

"Ah...!" Marta hissed as her skin peeled with it. Millie's eyes widened further and she spoke to Greg in a language Marta didn't understand and he answered her angrily. Millie winced and pulled out a small bag. She recognized the smell of poultices and tinctures immediately. Greg brought in a bucket of warm soapy water and a rag and she began the laborious process of thoroughly cleaning Marta's feet. After gently cleansing her skin and cleaning out the blisters she applied a thick paste onto her feet. Marta gripped the bars and clenched her teeth in pain as her skin felt like it was on fire. Millie finished quickly and started wrapping up her feet in fresh bandages.

"Thank you so much..." Marta wheezed gratefully. She paused and met her gaze.

"You should not be thanking me. I am only enabling a life of pain. It would have been better if you had died out there." She stood abruptly and walked out with Greg close behind. Marta sighed and leaned forward to hold her ankles, the chains around her wrists clinking with every move she made.

"Yer... feet look... better," Wesley hiccuped. Marta gazed at her friend painfully.

"They really did give you something strong, didn't they?"

"'Cause they... be... 'fraid." His eyes were dull as he leaned back against the stone. "Ah'm... goon... nap."

She nodded solemnly. *I think their greed got the better of them and that's why they killed the wizard. Perhaps this will buy us some time before Arailt finds us.* She shuddered at the thought of this unrecognizable enemy finding them and gazed up at the barred window in the corner of the room.

God... I don't know why this is happening. I've prayed every day for rescue and yet... it seems so far away. You seem so far away. I will cling to my hope in You, but... it's so hard. Her eyes welled up with tears. Did God hear her prayers anymore? At one time, she would have said He always hears someone's prayers; yet being in the land of her enemy, far away from those who could help and in the midst of a dark valley... He felt anything but near.

*****

Several days had passed in the cramped cell with more prisoners added every day. Marta sat next to Wesley and rubbed her aching feet. He had fallen asleep hours ago, quickly tired out. He would try to exercise in the cell by walking back and forth. Marta would try to, too, but the bracelets sucked every ounce of strength she had and her feet were still recovering. Based on what they had heard they would be traveling shortly, and neither wanted to lose an opportunity to escape. The room's inhabitants jolted as the door slammed open and a large man waddled inside followed by Greg and Braum. Wesley sat up and rubbed his weary eyes as they watched the group enter. The pudgy man had thin red hair and a well-kept mustache, his teeth gripping a putrid-smelling cigar. He wore a blue-and-silver officer's uniform with ashen gray pants. They could hear the *clink, clink, clink* of the numerous medals pinned to his chest as he strode in and perused the cells. His gray eyes settled on Marta and Wesley as he puffed.

"Those two."

They jerked as Braum swung the cell door open and grabbed their chains. He hauled them out of the cell and held the back of their necks as the man examined them.

"Hmm… I don't know if this one can work," he stomped on Marta's foot. She yelped in pain and grabbed her foot as Wesley fought to get between her and the man. Greg took over and pinned Wesley to the wall by his throat.

"Strong one, ain't he?"

"Ah know she doon' look't," Braum cooed, "but she's in good shape an' well worth the price, Angus."

His beady eyes ran up and down her frame as she squirmed under his gaze. He chuckled low.

"Awful pretty, ain't she? I'll take 'em both. She'll be of some use to me if she can't work." She shuddered and prayed she would have the strength to do whatever work there was, aside from *that*. Angus gripped her wrist and turned her arm over, examining the bracelet.

"Why the Mordiern?" he growled low, blowing smoke into her face. "She a Gifted?"

"Doon' know doon' care. Here's the key, ye kin fin' out fer yerself." Braum tossed a black key to Angus and he caught it deftly. He glanced at it and pocketed it carefully.

"Fine." He jerked his head and a man out in the kitchen set down a heavy trunk. The thugs accompanying Braum whooped and hollered as they opened it. Braum grinned and shook Angus' hand.

"Good workin' wit ye again, Angus."

"Don't mention it," he wiped his hand off on his jacket and returned his attention to Marta and Wesley. Wes growled at Greg, who still had him pinned. Angus stepped over and met him eye-to-eye.

"Easy there, boy. I can see you're fond of the girl." He turned and examined Marta out of the corner of his eye, speaking in the foreign tongue they had heard several times now. He laughed and turned to Wes. "Y'look similar too. I'm assuming she's your sister?"

"Yes," he coughed. He caught Marta's grateful glance as Angus chuckled low.

"Well, now, if you two behave, you can stay together. I run a strict business, you see, and any deviation is not tolerated well. Let's go."

Braum and Greg led Marta and Wesley out the door, through the kitchen, and out the back. The sky was a bright, clear blue and water dripped off the icicles hanging on the roof. It smelled crisp and fresh and the cold air stung her lungs. She stumbled towards a horse-drawn carriage with an open cage, several people already chained inside. They didn't look her way as Angus laughed, more men in similar uniforms stepping forward to take them.

"Get a good whiff, lady. This'll be the last time y'ever see the daylight."

*****

A Few Weeks Earlier

Thomas rubbed his face in agony as he sat on the edge of his desk. Already the room felt suffocating with all four of the Queen's Guard, her handmaids, Nick, Jerome, and Amaryll standing about the room. The implications of their words wrenched the breath from his lungs.

"You're certain you saw a serpent pin on the man's cloak, Kate?" Nick asked quietly.

She nodded. "Yes sir, I'd put my life on it."

"You don't have to do that," Amaryll chuckled softly. Thomas stared at the fire roaring in the fireplace. Although no one said it, they all knew Marta and Wesley had been taken by one of Arailt's right-hand-men, a death wizard notable enough to be adorned with the serpent's seal. The fear that he would lose her rose like the fire before him and it nearly consumed him. His thoughts swirled and berated him incessantly, accusing him of killing his wife. He shook his head and held his temples.

"We need to find out where Sarah sold her and where they were going. Begin a search party just in case we don't get anything out of her."

Jerome nodded and excused himself out of the room to begin the process. The older gentleman in Marta's Guard—Lyle, was it?—stepped forward and bowed.

"Yer Excellency, if ye'd allow, we wish t' join th' search since th' ladies will be safe now."

"Yes… yes, of course," Thomas waved absentmindedly. Lyle paused and stood up straight.

"Ah promise ye… we'll find 'er, Milord."

He watched as the four men and the two maids left, nodding at Nick as they went. He leaned up off the desk and wandered over to the bookshelf in an effort to quell his raging thoughts. Nick watched him sadly and turned.

"Amaryll, would you give us a few minutes please?"

"Of course. I need to go lock down the mirrors anyway." Her eyes rested on her monarch for but a second before she turned and left the room. Nick paused and watched Thomas finger a chess piece on the board in the corner. The men stood in tense silence.

"What is it, Nicodemus," Thomas finally exhaled. Nick shook his head slowly.

"May I have leave to speak freely, Milord? As a friend?"

He sighed and waved his hand. "If you're going to tell me I'm a coward—"

"I'm not."

Thomas met his gaze. "You'd be right."

Nick blinked in surprise as Thomas walked behind his desk and sat. "I'm sorry?"

"I said, you'd be right. I'm a coward and I always have been," his voice got lower and lower as he spoke and a darkness settled into his eyes. He fingered his quill listlessly. "I am doomed to live a life of those closest to me being taken away just when I get comfortable. My mother. My father. Peter, even, and now my wife. I'm just a joke," he scoffed. The voices in his head told him he was saying too much but another part of him truly didn't care any more. When he met Nick's eyes he expected repulsion or fear, but instead he saw a deep sadness.

"I could stand here and tell you otherwise, but it seems you're so deep in this pit you've fallen into that mere words won't help." Nick stepped forward and put his hands on the desk. "Do you remember what the Scriptures say? God has a purpose for you, He—"

"Perhaps to take out His wrath on someone! I never asked for *this*!" he motioned around the room spitefully. Nick shook his head.

"He already took His wrath out on one person to atone for everything. God is not mad at you, Thomas."

"Then why," he growled through his teeth, "would such misfortune befall me? My wife is *gone*, Nick. She's gone! I have no idea where she went and who knows what we will be able to get out of Sarah! Wicke was right, I never should have let her here in the first place!"

Nick opened his mouth to speak but his eyes widened instead. He shook his head and Thomas jolted as a hand landed on his shoulder.

"Me boy, yer askin' questions only God Hisself kin answer."

Thomas stood and reeled around, nearly toppling over the desk. A dusty, weary Ravenswicke stood before him with a pained expression.

"Uncle?!"

"Ye rang?" he chuckled ruefully. "Ah came as fast as Ah could when Ah heard the news. A good friend a mine was worried about yeh, said the mirror connection got cut when yeh were trying to talk to 'im."

Caleb! Thomas and Nick thought as Wicke laughed at their expressions.

"Now now, doon look so surprised! Ah heard everythin' so no need t' essplain," he wandered over to the window seat and groaned as he sat, flipping up the fly hanging from his shoulder and down the back of his green kilt. "God has His plans an' we has ours. They doon' always align like we want."

Thomas's blue eyes narrowed as the old man's green ones gleamed. "Look at you, arriving only when you want to be a part of the action. You want to be a hero, uncle? Why didn't you stop this then, huh?!"

Wicke held up a wrinkled hand. "Thomas, Ah know ye're mad aboot it. Ah'm not here t'argue, but Ah'm not goon sit on the sidelines any longer an watch ye destroy yerself. Ye've got a wicked temper and yer wife needs ye despite it."

"He's right," Nick sighed heavily. Thomas turned and gripped his desk.

"You too, now?! Is everyone against me?"

"We ain't against ye, Thomas. We're doon' this fer yer own good! Y'ask so many questions but din'ave any faith! Ye kin ask an' ask an' ask an' nary get an answer 'til y'see our Maker. Some things take *faith*."

"Faith," Thomas retorted with a scoff. "Faith, is that the answer to everything? Just sprinkle some *faith* dust on it and everything will get better, will it? I've had faith, Ravenswicke! I trusted Him with everything and He took everything away from me!"

"We don't know what His purposes are," Nick replied calmly as Wicke stood and walked over to the bookshelf, "And He does not promise us an easy life. He promises us a great eternity. Despite the things going wrong on earth, we can have faith and we can trust in Him because He has experienced everything before."

"Is that so? Then tell me, oh wise Shepherd," he spat, "how would He know what it feels like to put your trust in your God and be abandoned by Him?!"

"'*My God, my God, why have you forsaken me?*'" Wicke glanced up as the two men slowly turned towards him and noticed the Scriptures in his hands. "Sound familiar? Tha's Jesus cryin' out t'God. He, unlike ye, knew true abandonment. He felt the Darkness. '*His name shall be called Wonderful Counselor,*' fer He experienced every human emotion, temptation, and woe. He suffered, Thomas. He knows ye better than ye know yerself. An' while yer Queen will learn more about ye," he put his hand on Thomas' shoulder, "only God knows ye inside an' out.

He has answers fer those who'll listen."

"'Ask, and it will be given,'" Nick recited, "'Seek, and you will find; knock, and the door will be opened.' You'll hear Him if you have ears to hear and a heart that listens. He won't give you all the answers but He will stay by your side through it all and give you peace."

Thomas gazed miserably at the two important men in his life. The war inside him continued raging on, a thousand voices screaming at him from all directions.

They're wrong! He'll never answer you! He's left you!

Your wife is dead, why bother anymore?

You deserve this, all of this!

What if she's alive? She'll never trust you again!

You'll never have enough faith to be good enough for God!

"Thomas, for once would you let us in?! We care about you, we aren't going to hurt you!" Nick cried angrily. Thomas shook his head to dispel his thoughts but the voices grew louder and louder. Wicke put his hand on Nick's shoulder and flicked his head towards the door. Nick grumbled and rubbed his face before storming out. Thomas flinched as he slammed the door shut behind him.

"Thomas, ye—"

"Please, Wicke. Give me a few minutes."

He paused and stood up straight. He nodded at his nephew solemnly. "Of course. Ah woon't be too far. An... Thomas, Ah do respect ye, lad. Ye're a good man." He patted Thomas' shoulder and left quietly.

Thomas stood there staring at the ground for an excruciating amount of time. He grabbed the inkwell off his desk and launched it at the fireplace. He grasped his disheveled brown hair as the black ink exploded everywhere and stalked around the room.

Faith, he says, I just need faith. What do I do when I have none to spare?! He glanced down at the book sitting on his desk and caught Marta's wedding ring sitting on it. Her words, her laughter, and her smile flooded his thoughts and he groaned aloud. He picked up the ring and turned to throw it into the fire when a verse in the Book caught his attention.

'If you had faith like a grain of mustard seed, you could say to this tree, 'Be uprooted and planted in the sea', and it would obey you.' Faith as small as a speck of dust? But I've had large amounts of faith before, I have a Gift to prove He's there! Yet when I pray... why can't I hear Him? He set the ring down and stared at it. *I want... I want to pretend this never happened. I want this*

hurt to go away, to ignore it and just go on with my life. Yet… Marta means so much to me. Does that make me weak? The voices shouted an overwhelming *YES!*

He turned and gazed at the fire. *If I don't do anything about it… what will become of her? She'll die. Horribly, too…* Caleb's prophecy rang in his ears and he finally realized what it meant. His head spun and he felt like his feet would give out underneath him. *I was the one who left her. I ran off on a wild goose chase because I was angry and desperate and now Marta is God-knows-where fighting for her life. All while I'm here moping and feeling sorry for myself!* He growled and shoved everything off his desk in a fit of rage. He heaved in breaths and clenched his chest as it threatened to burst. *It's my fault. It's all my fault.*

It's always your fault.

It always will be.

You'll never live up to your father's expectations.

You'll never be a good king.

He clenched his fists and fell to his knees before the fire, his heart threatening to explode. *I don't want this pain, I ran away from this pain so many times and yet I can't get rid of it now! I have to be strong, I can't show any weakness. I'm the king! What do I do to be rid of this?!*

Ravenswicke and Nicodemus' voices echoed through his mind. *Ask and it will be given.* He swallowed hard and stared at the flames licking at the hearth.

"Hey… God?"

Seek, and you will find.

"I… I've really messed up this time, haven't I?"

Knock, and the door will be opened.

"I…uhm… really need Your help," he choked through the lump in his throat. He lifted a hand to his head as he trembled. It had been years since he had prayed like this and he felt foolish doing so now. He scoffed at himself and shook his head. "Not that I've asked for help before… and never got an answer. Why is that? Show me why You didn't answer me, show me where You were in all of this!"

A memory came to mind. It was so soft, so quiet, he barely noticed it behind the raging voices in his ears. He blinked and focused. It was his wedding day. "So… what, my marriage? That's the answer?" He gasped in surprise as he remembered praying desperately for the battle to end, and then won a decisive victory at Ropheka. In doing so, he also met Marta. The relief sweeping over him was replaced by anger. "Then what about my father?" As the words left his mouth long-pent-up tears spilled over his eyelids. A sob wrenched from his throat, "why would you take him away so soon? I was unprepared…"

Another set of memories shuffled through his mind. All of them were moments in time where King Martin had sat Thomas and Peter down and taught them about running the country. Those countless hours of studying, research, visiting nobles and regular folks alike, learning what they had to say and how to be a wise ruler. He recalled the day he met Nicodemus as a young boy and how they grew up together, learning how to help one another in their duties. He shook his head as the tears continued to flow.

"You… You knew this would happen."

A new set of memories went by, these ones of the numerous townspeople and citizens of Elyon thanking him for his efforts. How Marta and Geralt stood up for him despite the injured man being right, how so many people looked to him for guidance. The kingdom hadn't fallen apart yet. Despite their losses on the battlefield, the people of Elyon remained free.

"You… it was all You. It had to be. I couldn't have done any of that. Why on earth would You put me here? Yet You seem to be doing so much despite my shortcomings…" he watched the fire flicker as a gentle conviction settled on his soul and the voices quieted for a moment.

"I'm sorry." He choked on a sob. "I'm sorry I didn't see it before. I'm sorry I don't have faith, that I looked to my wife to fulfill that for me. I'm sorry I have not been a good steward of what You've given me." Like a cork coming out of a bottle emotions coursed through his body, wrenching his heart to and fro. He winced in agony yet felt a rush of relief. With no one around, no one watching or waiting or calculating… he could finally release the weight. He slumped forward and held his face as he bent over towards the ground.

"I believe, God. I believe You. I believe in You. I believe in Your Son and Your Spirit. I'm sorry I quenched it. I'm sorry I didn't trust you. You have shown that You are faithful even when I am not," he groaned as he shook. These tears were like a healing stream of fresh water soaking into his soul. He never dared cry in front of people but now all that was out the window. Alone in his study his sobs echoed throughout the room. A familiar intense heat, like oil pouring onto his head, quieted his mourning.

So you're finally ready to listen.

He sat up slowly, leaning his weary head back against the desk.

"Yes… yes, I am."

CHAPTER NINETEEN

Into the Mines

Iris flinched as the figure before him howled with laughter. The Seekers in the room winced from their positions kneeling on the floor. The silver-eyed figure stood from his desk slowly, chuckling to himself.

"Ah… What a fool. First Carrick, then Shoya, and now Tullius. Are all of my generals and Seekers this incompetent?" he motioned to the group in the room with a growl. They shook their heads but didn't dare speak. He stood there for a moment and then launched a delicate chessboard across the room, sending the pieces sprawling across the carpet.

"*I said, is everyone this —?!*"

"No your Excellency!"

"No Sir!"

"We apologize for our impudence!"

The figure rubbed his face angrily. "Then why, pray tell, is it impossible for you to find *one woman?!*" he roared as a wind picked up in the room. "You know where Tullius fell, so why haven't you tracked down the mercenaries yet?!"

Iris stood quickly. "Your Majesty, we have begun the process of tracing her. We have not found her yet due to interference—"

"What *interference*, Iris?"

He gulped. "Th-the king of Elyon has—"

Another gust of wind picked up and rocketed papers and pens around the room. Books began falling from shelves and the map behind him fluttered. Iris continued after taking a trepidatious step backwards.

"—has been searching for her as well. It seems the plan with the informant has gone awry, but I assure you we are using as many forces as possible to find and locate the queen."

"She is within *my* borders and yet still out of my grasp. You have failed me for the last time, Iris."

Iris took another step backwards with wide eyes as the figure stepped towards him. He shook his head and caught the glances of the Seekers in the room; they averted their gaze. Iris fell to the floor prone with his face on the carpet.

"My king, my god, please spare me! I swear to you I will not fail. I have numerous Seekers under my command, we will be sure to find her before Thomas does! I swear on my life that I—"

"You dare grovel at my feet?"

Iris' heart caught in his throat. "I—"

"I get what I want, Iris, and you have denied me that. What makes you think you have any right to live?"

He shuddered in a breath. Nothing, really. He was as good as dead but everything in him begged him to try anyway.

"I... have no right..."

"Exactly." He could hear the pleasure in his king's voice. It seemed he had said the right thing to earn his favor, at least somewhat. He tried to still his raging heart as the figure knelt and tipped up his head.

"However... this will not go without punishment. You took something precious away from me, so I will take something precious to you. How about a hand?"

Iris could hear the blood thundering in his ears as adrenaline coursed through him.

"Or your tongue, perhaps? Then I wouldn't have to listen to you begging for your pitiful life. Oh!" A sardonic grin crossed his twisted lips, "I know. Let's take something befitting your name, hmm?"

Screams echoed through the palace until late that evening.

*****

Wesley winced as the wagon jerked, slamming his backside onto the hard wooden seat. He rubbed his back and looked across from him to check on Marta, who sat with a blank look. She caught his gaze and smiled wearily before turning to look forward. He sighed heavily and rubbed his neck.

Ah cannae tell what's goon through her mind. Ah've nary had a chance to catch me breath, never mind find a way outta here. How long's 't been? Three weeks? Jus' whot's takin' em so long t'get here? The realization that Sarah

222

may have actually succeeded stole the breath out of his lungs. *Bren…* *Ah really hope ye're okay. Ah'm goon get her Majesty home, jus' yeh wait!*

Marta groaned as the wagon turned through the mountain pass and out into a large quarry. The side of the mountain had been carved out and there was a large flat place lined with gravel. To the side, she could see the sun setting over snowy peaks with rolling meadows before it. She turned back to see two large iron doors awaiting them with minecart rails coming out beneath them. Numerous soldiers stood on either side laughing and lazing around. They shot to attention as soon as the wagon stopped and Angus stepped out. He motioned to the few remaining slaves in the cage and laughed.

"Welcome to yer new home! Take a deep breath and look around now, this is the last you'll ever see of the sunset!"

Marta and Wesley were tied to a rope behind the other pitiful slaves and dragged towards the doors. She winced as she stepped onto jagged chunks of gravel with her bare feet. The 5-stories-tall iron doors began creaking open as they neared them. Several large minecarts emerged from the darkness and she reeled back as a putrid smell wafted from their interior. Angus held a handkerchief over his nose as they passed.

"The honey wagons are just one aspect of life yeh pathetic creatures will learn to live with."

There was another set of iron doors, identical to the last, closed tight before them. The doors behind them began creaking again and Marta watched as the last beams of amber sunlight peeked through the cracks and disappeared with a *thud*. The tall room was plunged into darkness and she could smell the cool damp earth. After a moment the doors in front of them began to open. Lamplight flickered through the cracks and warmer earthy wind rushed into the room. The air smelled stale and sweaty but the warmth was welcome from the frigid temperatures outside.

The first thing she saw was a large cavern lit by amber-colored gas lamps. The second thing were the bodies strung by their necks from the rafters, their limp forms swaying back and forth slightly. She covered her mouth and looked away, afraid she'd lose what little lunch she had had. The small group jerked forward as Angus bellowed.

"A'right everyone, got some new faces for yah! Be sure to treat 'em nicely, you hear?"

Marta watched Wesley stiffen and she poked her head around the group. A hundred weary souls were scattered about the room sitting on dirty worn-through mats. Their eyes were dark and lifeless, their faces thin and gaunt. There were very few children here, although Marta could see a few clinging to their mothers. They were even smaller than the children she knew in Ropheka and their torn tunics hung off their emaciated bodies. She instinctively wanted to rush over to them, but the moment she took a step to help the Mordiern bracelets sucked any resolve she had completely out of her. As the lanterns flickered she caught a glimpse of several mineshafts leading outwards from the main room.

"Meals are served twice a day," a very unenthused soldier grumbled as he dismantled the ropes tying them together, "use the honey pots when you need to go. You'll be assigned your duties by a foreman tomorrow. Don't worry, you'll get used to the new routine soon."

One of them men in line bolted for the door as soon as his hands were freed. He landed one solid punch on an officer before an arrow whizzed through the air, finding its mark in his back. He hit the ground hard and Marta took a horrified step back into Wesley as the man breathed his last.

"Don't even think about escaping this place unless you want to end up like him," Angus mused as he kicked the man's body. "We have rules here, of which you'll learn as you go. You break the rules, well..." he pointed upwards at the bodies. Marta put her head against Wesley's chest as she felt like she would throw up again. He patted her head gently and glared at Angus in disgust.

Thomas, where are you?! Have you truly forgotten about me? And... where are You, God? How could You let this happen? All those times she had said "have faith" or "it's His timing" or "only He knows why" grated on her soul. At one time she believed those words wholeheartedly, but now...?

Marta yelped as strong hands gripped her arms and ripped her away from Wesley. Angus stepped over and waved the soldiers down.

"Easy, men. Not a bruise on her, you hear? She has uses if she can't mine."

The man behind her laughed and tossed her forward. She scrambled to catch her footing as Wesley caught her.

"Seems she's already taken."

"That's her brother, you dimwit. Can't you see the resemblance?"

"I *do* have a—!" she muffled as Wesley's hand clamped down on her mouth and whispered in her ear.

"Shh, until we can figure out what's going on, you are not the

Queen and I am not your Captain. It will be safer that way."

Marta shook him off and stepped back. He could see agony and terror in her glistening green eyes. In his, she could see his anguish. She diverted her gaze and rubbed her arm slowly.

"Now, then, there are some empty mats around here somewhere..." Angus chuckled.

Marta and Wesley quietly shuffled over as they were led inbetween rows and rows of quiet slaves to two bedrolls. Wesley was assigned the one on one side of the aisle, whereas Marta was assigned the one across. Marta turned and noticed an older woman smiling gently at her, sitting on the bedroll next to her own. Her long silver hair was braided down her back and her wise blue eyes gleamed despite the darkness enveloping the room.

"Well Ah'll be, a new fren! Sit, sit, dearie."

Marta's eyes widened at the woman's all-too-familiar accent. "Are you from El-?!"

"Gonnae no' dae that," the woman murmured as she put a finger to her mouth and winked. "Better t'not sae everythin' inna pig pen, ya kin?" she gently nodded towards the soldiers milling about the room. One of them was watching them closely and turned away with a huff. Marta started to sit and caught a glimpse of a figure standing in the corner. He was one of the silver-and-blue clad officers but he stared at the ground with a mournful expression. She shook her head and sat down. The older woman held out her hand with a toothy smile.

"Pleased t'meet yah, Ah'm Jeannie."

"I'm... Marta."

"Marta! What ah beautiful name. Ah'm glad ye gave me yer real one, since Ah know how dangerous 'tis. Dinnae worry, Ah woon't let anyone know. If'n yeh wanna know, Ah'm from Elyon, yes. Specifically Laochailan, 'tis a small town a wee bit South-West ah Rhonwyn, if'n yeh know where that is."

Her spirits began to lift for a moment as she nodded, "Yes, I do! I'm from Ropheka, we would route our letters from Laochailan."

Jeannie laughed under her breath. "Ah, a Rophekan eh? Yer accent is light but Ah can see't. Good Lord above, look at those poor toes!" she shook her head and covered her mouth. Marta glanced at her feet and instinctively tucked them under her.

"Ah... sorry, I—"

"Those brutes! Ah cannae believe— here, Ah've got a spare tha' might fit ye." She turned and rustled through a small bag near her and produced two thin leather sandals. She motioned and Marta put her feet out. She put the sandals next to them and grunted in acceptance. "It'll do, that."

Marta blinked as she noticed the dark purple crystal embedded bracelets on Jeannie's own wrists. She stared for a moment before whispering, "You're a Gifted One?"

Jeannie examined her wrists and then motioned to Marta's. "Tha's a story fer another time, but Ah do see ye're one too. 'Tis a shame they're putting the Mordiern to use so quickly... mmm mmm mmm," she shook her head disdainfully. Marta caught Wesley's curious look and nodded slowly.

"Hello sir, Ah'm Jeannie."

Wesley blinked in surprise as the older woman Marta had been talking with leaned across the aisle and held out her hand. He took it gently and she clasped his hand warmly.

"Ah'm Wesley, ma'am."

"Ma'am! Ye've got a true gentleman on yer hands, Miss Marta. Ye sound like yer from Elroith, sir. Farmers laddie, by the look a ye?"

His eyes widened as he nodded. "How did ye—?"

"Ah've been roun' this ol' world a time or two. Ye were smart to pretend t' be related, 'tis not safe fer a lass here. Ah, but Ah've said too much. 'Tis time fer bed, ye'd best rest up 'fore the mornin'. They work us hard here."

Wesley sighed heavily, watching Marta as she curled up on her mat. She was soon asleep despite the hard ground, something he figured was a result of her travels with the army. However, the fact no one had come for them yet bothered him greatly. It had been three weeks since they had been taken! Even worse was his worry for Brenna.

Lord, please keep 'er safe. Keep us safe. Give Milord strength and th' wisdom t'find us. An', if Ye could... please let 't be soon.

He rolled onto his mat and stared at the ceiling before his own heavy eyelids closed.

*****

"It's been three weeks since Marta and Wesley were kidnapped and we *still* haven't gotten anything out of Sarah!"

Thomas glanced up at Amaryll as she shook her head angrily and continued. "I'm about ready to go in there myself and—"

"I understand, Commander. I want the truth too but we can't just torture her!" Nick groaned.

"Why not? After all, who knows how her Majesty is being—!"

A cacophony of *shush*es filled the air as Nick, Jerome, and Amaryll turned to Thomas. Wicke sat on the window seat and chuckled to himself. Thomas absentmindedly pinched the bridge of his nose in thought as he stared at the map laid out on his desk. They had plotted out different routes the group could have taken through the mountains to reach Hylen, but the passes were heavy with snow and despite Elyon's training in winter travel it was still difficult to navigate. The new group of soldiers had been trained and were dispatched, greatly aiding Elyon's forces. Still, though, worry tugged at the edges of his mind.

"We need more information... something that can lead us in the right direction," he mumbled under his breath, ambivalent to the conversation that had just occurred before him. Nick sighed with a slight smile.

Before, something like this would have set Thomas off on the war path. He's really letting the Lord work on his heart.

"Have we heard back from the scout units?" Thomas continued as he turned towards the group. Jerome shook his head.

"No sir. After the Tower shut down the mirror communications we haven't heard anything."

"Nick, have you received any word on when we will regain the use of our mirrors?"

The Light Gifted shook his head. "No... mirror transports are still available in emergency situations but Arailt was able to intercept communication again. The elders think he's started... sacrificing people to get the energy needed to do so, since most of his wizards were killed in battle. He's particularly focused on our communications."

"Ours?" Amaryll interjected. "Why would he be interested in us if he's already gotten—"

The room deafened and Thomas blinked in surprise. He could see people talking but couldn't hear them. His vision tipped and everything had a warm amber hue to it. He blinked in confusion and felt a gentle hand on his shoulder.

"He's tryin' t' tell ye somethin', lad. Let Him."

He nodded at Ravenswicke solemnly and closed his eyes, not knowing what else to do. He jumped when he felt a cold breeze blast in his face. He opened his eyes and turned around and around on a snowy road in the middle of the forest. He could smell the wet snow and feel the cold piercing his skin. *Where... am I?*He shivered and glanced down the road. As if it was highlighted by amber light, he saw a broken wagon almost completely obscured by a white blanket of snow. He walked over as his boots *crunched* on the ground and examined the wreckage. He brushed the heavy wet snow off the door and yanked on it. It opened with a jerk and got caught several times. He wedged his torso inside and searched the dilapidated, snow-dusted interior.

He spotted a familiar pair of boots discarded in the corner. His eyes widened as he reached in and grasped the worn blue pair of boots he had given Marta. They dropped through his hand unexpectedly and he jerked around as he felt something coming down the road. He scrambled out the door and fell backwards into the snow. As he struggled to stand he saw darkness, like smoky black tendrils, crawling out of the forest behind him. He struggled to his feet and caught a glimpse of something under his boot. He picked up a thick black cloak and turned it over to reveal a silver pin.

"The death wizard... was killed? Then what happened to—?!"

A screech brought him to his knees as his eardrums felt like they would rupture. His heart pounded in his chest as he saw a figure rushing through the forest towards him. It was human-shaped but all he saw were the hundreds of eyes locked on him.

Seeker!

Just as he lunged out of the way, the scene instantly changed and he fell forward onto the floor of his study. He could feel the snow he had picked up in his hands as he jumped land around him and the group jerked backwards.

"Thomas?!"

He coughed and sat up, wiping off his face. The warmth from the fire began seeping through his clothes and he glanced down, noticing the snow surrounding him.

"Wh... what?!"

"Your Majesty...?"

Thomas met the gazes of the stupefied group of friends before him, but a new pair of hazel eyes made him shake his head in surprise.

"Caleb?!"

The older Shepherd stepped forward, a terse grin playing at his lips behind his graying beard.

"Ah knew't. Ah knew Ah had t'come here. Lord above, who knew ye'd be a Light Seer like yer dear Mam! S'good t'see yeh, King Thomas." He held out his hand and Thomas took it, standing shakily. Snow fell off his shoulders and he flicked the moisture off his hands.

"What are you doing here?? How—?!"

Caleb tipped his head back and gave his usual bellowing laugh. "Ah used the mirror, though that was a struggle in an' of isself. Speaking of!" He nodded at Wicke and addressed the rest of the group. "The elder's were able to intercept one of Arailt's communications from his general, Iris. They've lost Marta, they doon know where she is."

"What!" the group gasped as the news hit them. Thomas nodded solemnly, still feeling the cold and the eyes from the Seeker.

"That makes sense," the young king replied calmly. Caleb's eyes widened as he examined him.

"Is this really King Thomas?" he asked Nick, who laughed and nodded.

"Yes, it is. I think it's his story to tell, though. But back to the task at hand, you said they… *lost* her?"

Caleb nodded. "Yes, they did. From our understanding, somethin' went wrong as they were transportin' her and Sir Wesley. They seem t'be alive, though, at last knowledge."

"Oh thank God," Amaryll stammered as tears filled her eyes. Relief swept over Thomas as he stared at his hands, still wet with snow.

"I don't know entirely what happened, but… I saw a prison carriage with Marta's boots in it."

Caleb laughed and motioned to the puddle at his feet. "Seems ye did more than jus' see it, Milord. I'm interested t'hear what happened, but m'curiosity kin wait. What else did yeh see?"

"I saw the cloak Brenna and Kate mentioned, with the serpents pin on it. I think the death wizard with them was killed though I don't know how. I was…" he shuddered suddenly as the reality of what had been hunting him struck him. The Shepherds and Wicke nodded as Amaryll and Jerome exchanged confused glances. "I saw a Seeker."

Wicke clicked his tongue. "Aboot time."

He turned to his uncle and raised a brow. "Excuse me?"

Wicke shrugged and smiled as he stuffed his pipe. "Yer wife saw one too, yet it took yeh long 'nuff t'see it yerself." He flicked his thumb to light it but Thomas pinched the flame out.

"How could she see one?"

Wicke pouted as Nick stepped forward. "From you, your Majesty. We can explain that later."

Caleb's eyes were alight. "She saw one? Oh, dear me… yer Gift may just rival that of yer mam, yer Majesty. To share yer Gift like that… hmm…"

"Let's go ahead and discuss this further after dinner, now that we have Caleb here. I am very interested to hear how—"

There was a frantic pounding on the door. Jerome answered it and he stepped back after a moment, his eyes wide.

"Your Majesty… Lady Sarah is gone!"

CHAPTER TWENTY

The Lost Sheep

A clang of wooden spoons on pots rattling through the cavern startled Marta awake from her nightmares. She had tossed and turned all night on her small mat as evidenced by the thin crumpled-up blanket at her feet. She sat up wearily and rubbed her tired eyes.

"Everyone up! Breakfast!"

She yawned as Wesley sat up and rubbed his own bloodshot eyes.

"At least we get some grub…" he grumbled blearily.

"A wee bit," came Jeannie's voice. The pair turned and were greeted by the older woman's smiling face. "Good mornin', Miss Marta and Sir Wesley. Ye sure did have a hard night there, Marta, ye were tossin' all over th' place!"

Marta avoided Wesley's concerned look as he helped her stand and followed behind the line of weary slaves. "I… get nightmares a lot."

Jeannie's expression fell as she nodded. "Ah do understand. Sometimes the Enemy uses even our wee bit o' respite against us."

Not knowing what to say, she simply nodded. The line continued past several officers leering at the slaves in line, occasionally hurling insults and the like as people passed. A few of their comments brought red to her cheeks and she turned away. She could feel Wesley bristle and simply put a hand on his shoulder.

"They're not worth it, Wes."

"Ah… Ah know…" he grumbled angrily. Breakfast was a stale piece of bread and a small palm-sized piece of some kind of dried meat. The slaves went back to their bunks and ate quickly as the soldiers began pestering them to finish. Marta and Wesley sat and she started to eat her bread when she heard Jeannie beside her.

"-an' bless me new frens, Marta an' Wesley. Amen."

Marta blinked slowly and stared at her bread. *When was the last time I thanked God for a meal? Back at the inn? Or even longer? ...does it even matter?* She chomped bitterly into her rock-hard bread and swallowed painfully, her throat closing up as her eyes pricked with angry tears. Her chest felt heavy and hollow all at the same time.

"So what's going on in the world?"

Marta and Wesley glanced up as several people stood around one of the men who had been brought in with them. He shrugged.

"What do ye all know?"

"Last we heard, Hylen had breached Elyon's border and a war was starting."

They choked on their pieces of bread. Jeannie glanced up and listened as the man's eyes grew wide.

"A war very much *has* started. And almost been won, though at a great cost. King Thomas has—"

"Wait wait, King *Thomas?!*"

The man winced. "Ah... yeah. King Martin was assassinated, he—"

Another one of the new slaves scoffed. "Are yeh kidding me? 'Twas his own doing, that cowardly good-for-nothing—"

"He *was* assassinated." Wesley grumbled loud enough for the group to hear. The men turned their attention to him.

"How was it done?"

"Was it Hylen's doing?"

Wesley sighed and rubbed his bruised cheekbone. "Ah'm not entirely sure *how*," he lied, "but Ah do know our king wouldn't—"

The men groaned and turned away, seemingly uninterested in someone who didn't have clear information. Marta smiled wearily and mouthed *thank you*, to which Wesley nodded solemnly.

"Oh, but King Thomas has really shown Arailt what-for! He's pushed back the wizards an—"

"Wait, are you saying the king is winning?"

"Elyon is turning the tide?!"

"As if he would come here."

The new voice caught their attention. A man who looked to be in his mid-forties with graying blond hair stepped forward, his lips contorted in a sneer. Marta could see loathing in his dim blue eyes.

"Aaron, you never think anything will—"

"It won't," he grumbled as he stepped forward. "Continue, though, I'm interested to hear what else is going on."

The man nodded. "There's been great battles! King Thomas and his generals have fought bravely, and their Gifteds have really lent a hand! I heard one story that King Thomas faced off against Arailt himself and sent the man sprawling across the battlefield!"

That... certainly didn't happen. Marta chuckled under her breath. *Although they have fought bravely—*

"He found his queen, too."

Marta and Wesley froze. They glanced at each other before turning to the group again. More people had joined and several soldiers were getting ancy because of it.

"He did?"

The man nodded. "Supposedly, she's a Life Gifted. I heard a rumor that Queen Rosa—"

"Impossible, they don't exist anymore."

Marta bristled at the tone in Aaron's voice. He folded his arms and scowled at the man as he continued. "Life Gifteds don't exist."

"What do you mean, they don't exist? They—"

"There hasn't been any use for them after the disciples passed. That Gift simply doesn't manifest anymore."

Marta couldn't believe what she was hearing. She started to open her mouth to speak when Jeannie gently touched her shoulder. She turned and the older woman shook her head sadly, holding a finger to her lips.

"That's ridiculous, the Scriptures even say that the Gift of Healing is for—"

Aaron scoffed. "You're simply taking it out of context. When have you ever seen a Life Gifted?"

"Well... I haven't, but—"

"Exactly my point. There's no need for them the same way there was back then, therefore they do not exist."

Marta stared at her empty hands, the Mordiern glistening ominously in the lamplight. *People actually... believe that? But that's my Gift! If only I didn't have these stupid cuffs on I could—*

Her heart plummeted. *I could what? Prove him wrong? He'd probably say it was witchcraft of some kind. If I didn't have these cuffs, I wouldn't even be here! I could have fought back, I could have rescued Wesley, I could be back home— but these stupid cuffs!* In a fit of anger she slammed her wrist on a rock at her feet, the Mordiern glancing off unscathed. Her wrist hurt from the impact, however, and she stifled a cry. Jeannie turned her towards her and wiped away Marta's tears off her cheeks.

"Ye've had a long season, dearie. Doon' give up now, ye hear? Yer needed an very much loved. He's gotta plan fer yeh tha' will be better than ye ever dreamed of."

She scoffed bitterly. "Plan? Is this the plan He has for me? If so, I don't want any part in it." She regretted her words immediately as Wesley's shoulders sank and Jeannie's expression twisted in pain.

"Ah knoo 'tis hard t'think o' right now, sweet Marta, but Ah kin promise ye He has ye no matter what."

Marta brushed Jeannies hand away and averted her gaze. "Let's get to work, I guess." Without waiting for their response, she turned and joined the rest of the group of slaves meandering into the tunnels. Wes and Jeannie exchanged a glance before joining the fray themselves.

*****

Marta slowly sipped on a ladle of lukewarm water and leaned against the tunnel wall. They had been tasked with mining out Mordiern crystals and Ela ore, which were supposedly abundant in this mine. It felt more like a wild goose chase than anything. Still, the soldiers would use any means at their disposal to keep the slaves working as diligently as possible. The "honey wagons" as they were called were portable bathrooms situated on the rails. They stunk to high heaven and there was no privacy when one had to be used. She was thankful she had a long enough dress; others did not have that luxury. Her palms were blistered and calloused from the pickaxes and hoes and shovels they had to use. As long as a solider wasn't leering or shouting commands or whipping at you, mining actually was a little cathartic. She laughed at herself and shook her head.

What's become of me, that I think mining is relaxing? Sometimes they let us talk... it's strange how many folk from Elyon are here. Their accents are all so thick I'm having a hard time not emulating them.

A silky voice interrupted her thoughts. Was that... singing? She turned and strained her ear towards the sound. Sure enough, she could just barely make out a voice echoing through the mineshafts.

"Me Lord 's near t'the broken hearted, near t'the poor in Spir't. He leads me by still wooter, He pours grace upon me soul."

The sweet, gentle voice brought back long-forgotten memories of her mother and father sitting by the fire. She stood and wandered through the mineshaft looking for the source of the sound. It didn't take her long to find Jeannie, ever-smiling, singing to a group of children as they sorted through crude ore in large mine carts. To her surprise, the children were smiling and singing along with her.

"*Me Lord's me strength an' shield, an ever-present help in trouble. Me knight an' me defender, me Lord t'will ever be wit' me.*"

Marta turned away as tears filled her eyes. *Will He? How could He be here, in this dark place? Why would He bring so many people here just to suffer?*

Jeannie glanced up and smiled at her. "Ah, Miss Marta. Come, come. Ah've been tellin' the bairns a story."

Several children smiled up at her as she shuffled over and began helping them sort through ore. Out of the corner of her eye she spotted the same officer from last night, the one who stood against the wall with a sad look on his face. He once again looked like he had something on his mind yet never spared her a glance. Jeannie cleared her throat.

"Now, where was Ah…. Yes! Ah remember!" She smiled as she continued to sing. "*Listen to me words, lassies, take this to yer hearts oh lads, for Ah tell of a wonderful man. Let me tell ye aboot mah Jesus. He makes a way when there be no way, when all seem dark He shines His light. He left th' grave behind and rose into glorious day, fer He died fer ye an' me. He hears all prayers, He hears yer cries, He knoos yer heart 'fore yeh speak. He will wipe away yer tears an' pain, for He loves ye, yes He do!*"

Marta lowered the ore in her hand as a familiar feeling pressed ever so slightly into her chest. *I used to believe everythin' she's sayin', yet…* Jeannie turned and patted the head of one of the children, and Marta caught a glimpse of Jeannie's necklace under her dress. It was a small clear-blue stone set into a silver clasp of a lion and a lamb. Her eyes widened as Jeannie returned her attention to the cart.

"You're a Shepherd?"

Jeannie hesitated as she held a rock but didn't meet her gaze. There was… mourning in her eyes.

"All who follow th' Lord be Shepherds, in a way."

"But I mean an actual Shepherd Shepherd."

The young officer glanced up as Jeannie sighed. "Ah used to be. Le's finish this up, dinner will be ready soon."

"Marta!"

The group turned as Wesley entered the room. The young officer immediately looked away and put a hand on his sword. Her captain rushed over to her out of breath.

"Ah was worried aboot ye. Ye cain't go off like that, please."

Marta felt the guilt settle firmly onto her shoulders, dragging her further to the ground.

"… Ah'm sorry, Wes."

He paused and chuckled softly, his usual demeanor returning. "Look't yeh, ye're starting' t'sound like a *real* Elyonian!"

Marta stared at him for a moment before laughing curtly. She gently pushed him away as he grinned.

"Yer accent is gettin' thicker, though, Miss Marta." Jeannie chuckled. Marta glanced at her sheepishly and sighed.

"Ah suppose." She winced as she said it again, to which Jeannie and Wes chuckled warmly. A bell attached to a string began ringing. The young officer stood up and motioned to the mineshaft.

"Time to go."

*****

Thomas watched Amaryll as she examined the strangely colored glass on the floor. Peter's face was as white as a sheet as he stood in the corner with his arms behind his back. He winced at Seamus' grip on his arms. Purple glass littered the floor of his room with Nick standing by an empty mirror frame.

"It's a one-way mirror," Amaryll finally sighed. "These are illegal, although it's just another thing she didn't care about."

"Any idea where she went?" Thomas asked, noticing Peter averting his eyes. Nick and Amaryll shook their heads.

"Far away from here, probably," the Shepherd groaned.

Thomas turned his attention to his younger brother, who stared out the window with a hardened gaze. Three weeks of house arrest had done a number on him… his clothes were disheveled and his blond hair a mess. The thing that alarmed Thomas, however, was the broken look in Peter's eyes.

Can I blame him? His wife abandoned him to die. I can't just look away knowing he's complicit here.

"Lord Thomas," Peter finally croaked, "may I speak to you privately?"

The occupants of the room were floored. Peter hadn't eaten or spoken to anyone in days, aside from his wife, as far as they knew. All eyes were on Thomas as he pondered his request.

"Amaryll, Jerome, guards, please leave us. Nick and Seamus, you stay."

Peter could feel his brother's gaze boring a hole into his skull as the room emptied. He stared at the floor and grimaced as his arms screamed in protest tied tightly behind his back. Thomas stepped forward with a new, indecipherable look on his face. Peter nearly scoffed when he sensed… pity.

"You really think so low of me, Thomas?"

His eyes flickered with light. "I am worried about you."

He turned away and pursed his lips. "You never were before. Why would that change now?"

After an excruciatingly long silence Peter glanced up. Where he expected rage, all he saw was sympathy in Thomas' blue eyes.

"You're right, Peter. And I am sorry."

He scoffed. "Are you serious? You think a mere apology will fix everything? Forget it, I don't have anything to say to you."

Thomas inhaled sharply. "Peter, I need your help."

"Well, you're not getting it. I don't know where she is, your wife nor mine. Just kill me already and get it over with."

Thomas gripped his fists as rage welled up in him, his old habits refusing to die. He grit his teeth. "You really just want to die? You don't even want to think I would spare my own brother?"

Peter pursed his lips and didn't respond. Thomas opened his mouth to speak but had the wherewithal to hold his tongue. He turned away and struggled to fight his emotions.

"I'm ready to listen when you want to talk."

Peter watched his brother leave the room quietly. He didn't even slam the door. He turned and gazed back out the window.

Nothing I could do would ever fix the mess I've gotten myself into. He stared bitterly at the floor. *I have done too much damage to be redeemed, Thomas, no matter how good your intentions are.*

*****

One Week Later

Marta gnawed on her stale bread quietly. After just a week, both her and Wesley were able to learn what they needed to in order to work effectively and escape the gazes of the soldiers and officers constantly watching them. Marta and Wesley were joined with Jeannie, who would sing throughout the day to the children and anyone who would listen. As Jeannie would start singing, Marta's raging thoughts would still. Surprisingly, her nightmares had stopped as well. The older woman returned to her mat, having just given some of the children who worked with them part of her ration of bread.

"Jeannie?"

The older woman turned and smiled. "Yes, lass?"

"Has God ever… stopped talkin' t'ye?" Marta whispered thickly.

"Ah… there have been times Ah thought He wasn't speakin', yes. But," she held up a finger and smiled in the same way she would when she was about to tell a story, "Ah've found 'twas me own faulty hearing and not His voice that wasn't workin'. He is always speakin' t'us, but 'tis up t'us t'listen."

Marta gazed off into the distance as the darkness stirred up in her heart. "Ah think He stopped talkin' to me…"

"He's never given up on ye, dear, though ye may have given up on Him."

Her wise words cut through her like a sharpened knife. Her defenses rose as she shook her head and tears spilled over her cheeks.

"Ah didn' give up on 'im! He gave up on me! He put me in this place! This 's HIS fault!"

Jeannie's face fell and she opened her mouth to speak when she was interrupted.

"You jus' haven't prayed hard enough, obviously."

The pair turned to see Aaron standing behind them shaking his head. "That's all you have to do. It's all about faith, and if bad things happen to you it's because you're not faithful."

"Wha' kind o' nonsense is—?!" Jeannie began before Aaron held up his hand.

"He's near to the faithful and pure in heart, is He not? Therefore, if He's not near to you then something's wrong with what you're doing and you'd better repent."

His faulty theology grated on Marta's nerves, but no small part of her was starting to agree with him. *Have I done something wrong? Was I not being a good queen? Should I have gone with Thomas instead of staying behind?* Her shoulders drooped as despair settled into her soul. Jeannie rubbed her face angrily.

"Well, Aaron, if'n ye're right, then why are ye here, too?"

He shrugged. "I trusted the wrong people. That mistake cost me my life."

Jeannie shook her head disdainfully as Wesley stepped over.

"Ah 'gree with Jeannie. God doon give up on ye, He pursues us. T'was His Son who died t'give us freedom, He wants t'be near t'us. Ah'm livin' proof He doon' give up."

Marta glanced up at her friend in surprise. She had never really heard him talk about God, but it seemed his proximity to the Shepherd had bolstered his faith. *If only I could say the same about mine…*

Aaron scoffed at the young man and shook his head. "It seems you have a lot to learn. Whatever." He turned and walked off, grumbling about "new" religion. Wesley laughed under his breath and turned to Marta.

"Y'know he's wrong, right Mila— M-Marta?"

Jeannie pretended not to notice his error as Marta sighed.

"Ah do know that, Wes. Ah'm glad t'see ye've grown more." A dark pit in her heart seemed to swallow her joy and she turned away with a grunt. *I'm too far gone, I think… not that I want to have anything to do with God anymore.*

"Yet ye're still fightin' yerself," Jeannie murmured as she looked up from her mat. Marta met her gaze and something inside her shifted. Her eyes welled up with tears and despair filled her chest.

"Ah doon know Him anymore. Ah thought Ah did, but… Ah… Ah cannae…" the words caught in her throat and she swallowed hard. "Ah want to… believe He's here, that He is my refuge and strength." She held up her trembling hands. "But… where is He in this?" she motioned around bitterly as her accent thinned for a moment. "I survived the attack on Ropheka and Thomas had these same questions but—" her face paled as she realized her blunder. Wesley held his breath as his eyes widened. Jeannie simply chuckled.

"Ah know who y'are, yer Majesty."

Marta turned slowly and blinked in surprise. "You… y'do?!"

The older woman nodded slowly. "Yer a Life Gifted. Like me."

"You— ye're a! A!"

She chuckled at their bewilderment. "Y'were astute enough to notice the bands, but Ah could see't in ye the minute ye walked through those doors. Ye're a Life Gifted and have been for a long time, ain't yeh?"

Marta could hardly believe what she heard as she nodded frantically. "My mother was, too!"

Jeannie tipped her head to the side as golden light passed through her blue eyes. "Wait, doon' tell me. Hmm… blonde-almost-red hair… green eyes… that chin…" she held Marta's face and examined her features. Marta couldn't help but think of Ravenswicke as Jeannie perused her.

"Lemme guess… was Kylah yer mam? An' Ah believe Alistaire was her Knight?"

Tears filled Marta's eyes. Unable to speak she simply nodded. "You... y'knew my parents?"

Jeannie's smile nearly lit up the room. "Ah was her instructor ages ago. My, what a sight!" She cupped Marta's cheek as her own eyes filled with tears. "Kylah was one a the best students Ah had. Ah loved her like she was me own daughter. Oh, th' stories Ah could tell! One time yer parents had t'go to another Tower to help returning Knights and Gifteds, an she delivered a wee bairn with one hand and healed the father with the other, it was a strange sight t'see! After wakin' up from his wounds the da spotted his daughter and passed right back out!"

Marta laughed and wiped away tears as Jeannie chuckled at the memory. "What other stories do y'have of my mom?"

"Plenty, dear, plenty. Yer mam was a strong woman... put me in my place a time 'r two, Ah'll say! She had a mighty fine temper. Mmm mmm. An ye've joined a long an' noble line, too! Have ye ever heard of Marieke and Joshua? They're the ones who founded Elyon, they did. Th' loch behind th' castle in Elroith's named after her."

Wesley smiled at the two women as Jeannie recounted tale after tale of her mother and father's adventures, some Marta had never heard before. He sighed and stared at his hands in the darkness.

Lord... Marta is hurtin' awful bad. But Ah kin see Y'brought Miss Jeannie t'help her. However this ends... Ah ask that Ye bring her back to You. Protect m'dear Bren, an mold me into the man Y'want me t'be. Ah want t'glorify You here, even when it's so dark.

A comforting warmth filled his chest and lent strength to his body and mind. He inhaled deeply and exhaled slow. *Thank Ye Lord. Ah need You now an' every day. Give Lord Thomas wisdom an' clarity an' bring 'im people t'help 'im become the man Ye want, too.*

*****

Caleb rubbed his bleary eyes and wrapped his cloak closer around him. The dark stone hallways of the castle were illuminated by the falling snow outside, casting shadows on the decorations and tables and suits of armor. Several castle guards on their late-night patrols nodded at him as he walked by. He waved in response and smiled, adjusting the blue-and-white tartan wool about his shoulders. The castle was cold at night despite the numerous fires lit and dutiful serving women stoking them. He sighed once the guards were out of earshot.

"Ah've been here a week, Lord… An' no sign of Marta. Please protect her. Ah've a feelin' she's in her own valley."

He turned a corner and saw light seeping out from under a door. *Who's awake at this hour? Though, Ah could ask myself the same question. Wait…* He paused before the door. *Ain't this Thomas' study?* He felt the gentle nudge and knocked quietly. He could hear startled movement.

"Who's there?"

"It's me, Caleb, Milord. Y'alright?"

There was a tense silence before he heard Thomas sigh. "Come in, Shepherd."

He pushed open the door and stepped inside to a dimly-lit study. It was warm and cozy and a pile of firewood had been placed beside the hearth. Thomas sat at his desk with a quill in his hand. Caleb recognized the Word sitting in front of him and closed the door slowly. Thomas motioned to the Book.

"This was my father's. I didn't realize how often he used it, the leather is worn thin. He's tucked a lot of notes in here, too…"

Caleb chuckled through a soft groan as he sat in one of the armchairs next to the fire. "Ah've made plenty of notes of my own, it drives Camilla crazy." He smiled fondly. Thomas smiled wearily.

"Thank you for taking such good care of us in Ropheka, we really are indebted to you and the others."

Caleb held up a hand. "Doon' worry aboot it, yer Majesty. God calls us t' care for everyone, an' that's what we do."

"I appreciate it." He returned his gaze to the scriptures before him with hesitation. Caleb folded his hands in his lap and gazed around the office. Thomas poured him a cup of tea from the still steaming pot on the tray beside him and handed it to him.

What a beautiful room. Ah'm sure Marta loved it here.

"Caleb… I'm sorry I didn't listen to you."

The Shepherd blinked as his blue eyes sparkled. "What d'ye mean?"

Thomas groaned and rubbed his face. "In my effort to try and protect Marta I left her. If I was here, I could have been able to protect her. She wouldn't be in pain or in trouble. And what if she's…" he swallowed hard and shook his head to dispel his thoughts. Caleb chuckled softly.

"If ye live yer life based on the 'what ifs' ye'll never truly live. This isn't the *worst* misinterpretation of a prophecy I've seen…" he lifted his cup and took a sip. Thomas blinked and wanted to ask, but thought better of it. Caleb chuckled as he set his cup down. "Nicodemus has been telling' me ye've spent a lot of time in fellowship with the Lord. Ah'm pleased t'see the man o' God ye're becoming."

He slowly lifted his gaze and gestured to the Book. "I've been searching for a while now but I'm having trouble wrapping my head around this... what exactly does it mean to be a man of God?"

Caleb paused and turned to Thomas slowly, golden light passing through his eyes. He chuckled low.

"Many a man before you has struggled with that question, Lord Thomas. Let's start with the first part. What does't mean t'be a man? He has designed yeh with a wildness in yer heart, a desire fer adventure. He has made ye a fighter an' a lover. He made ye after a part of Hisself, in His image. He made women in His image too, but they reflect different aspects of our Creator than we do. God is a warrior jus' as much as a poet. He has instilled specific traits in us as men. Let me ask ye... how did God create Adam?"

Thomas pondered his words for a few moments. "From dust?"

"Indeed. An' where did He make Adam?"

Thomas thought and thought but couldn't find an answer. He pointed to the Book and Caleb nodded with a smile.

"Go ahead."

He thumbed through its pages but it didn't take him long to find what he was looking for.

"He was made... outside the Garden?"

Caleb nodded. "'Twas made in the wilderness our father Adam was. That's why it's so ingrained in us, that cry for the wild and untamed parts of life. The Enemy comes in and tries to scare us or take that away."

"That makes sense..." Thomas leaned back in thought. "Please, go on."

He chuckled slowly. "It's goon be a long night."

"I haven't been able to sleep... if you're alright with it."

"T' be honest, Ah haven't been able to either."

The men chuckled in shared misery. The morning light would illuminate the room long before their conversation would wane.

CHAPTER TWENTY-ONE

A Light in the Darkness

"Goon. Try it."

Marta sighed heavily as she lifted her pickaxe. Jeannie smiled reassuringly from her spot by a mine cart.

"God isn't bound t'those cuffs, dear one. Remember what the Good Shepherd Hisself said? *Seek an' ye will find?*"

She chiseled into the rock for several moments before groaning. *I feel ridiculous.* Jeannie was hard at work and humming away, Wesley was shoveling dirt and rocks into the mine carts nearby. Marta watched them work and hissed as a whip cracked across her back.

"Get to work!"

Her friends glanced up as she groaned aloud but held up a hand to them. She winced and started chiseling again despite her back screaming in protest. It had been several days—or was it more?—since she discovered Jeannie was a Life Gifted as well, and she had learned many new techniques from the older woman. She couldn't practice any of them… but she hoped they would all get out soon so she could learn from her new tutor. Her eyes stung with tears as she continued.

God…? It… it's me. There was no familiar warmth, no comforting presence. She shuddered in a breath and moved down the wall a bit to get to another spot. *I… haven't really heard You or felt You in a long time. I feel foolish trying to talk to You now…* Tears carved through the dirt and grime on her face and she wiped them away with the back of her hand. *I want to believe You're here in this. I want to put my faith in You.* Her words gave her pause. *…do I really? A part of me does, but another part of me is so tired and weary… I don't want to go on anymore. This darkness seeps into my chest and I want it all to end. I don't want to be in pain anymore!* She stifled a sob as her pickaxe landed hard into the stone. She sniffled and wiped the tears off onto her dress. She gritted her teeth and took another swing. The pickaxe stuck and she struggled to get it out. With one good yank it came free and the rock fractured. She watched with wide eyes as the crack ran up and down the wall.

Fearsome, guttural words growled behind her. She jumped and turned to see a haggard-looking dark-haired dwarf standing there. She blinked a few times before stepping out of the way.

"Y'all are just rootin' for a way to die, ain't ya? Bless me!"

She watched as two more dirt-laden dwarves emerged with wood beams and other materials. "—Ah, Ah'm sorry, but… Ah didn' realize there were dwarves here!"

The older dwarf huffed at her. "Well, there certainly are! Name's Clyde, by the way, not that y'asked er nuttin'. Been here a long time we have. Don't come out near too often, those Hylen monsters keep us locked up. Yeah, you heard me!" he grinned at the angry soldier standing behind them. He glanced at Marta and walked away with a huff, his whip trailing behind. Clyde turned to Marta and she saw several gaps in his teeth, some replaced by nuggets of minerals of some kind. The other two dwarves had started measuring the crack in the wall and setting up supports.

"They cain't touch us cause we a rare breed, we are. Our brothers and sisters hide themselves real well in the mountains now, but that horrid king needs us." He patted the wall. "Y'darn split the thing, hoowee! We could sense it 'fore ya even got here, though I thought it would be much father down the mineshaft… Y'all gotta be careful else the whole thing will collapse on ya. These fractures ain't—"

A cracking noise was replaced by fearsome rumbling. Marta took a step back as the dwarves turned back to look down the shaft.

"That ain't good…"

"CAVE-IN!"

The bells started ringing up and down the shafts as a blast of air swept through, bringing with it dust and chunks of rock. Jeannie and Wesley grabbed the four children standing nearby and began to run as a roar echoed through the chambers.

"Marta, come on!"

Marta turned and ran with Clyde and the other two dwarves as the shaft started collapsing, dirt and rock and rubble bursting around them. She narrowly avoided a falling beam and turned back to make sure the dwarves made it through.

"Ya crazy girl?! Get going!"

She huffed and the four continued their run. Other slaves and soldiers ran in front of them and out into the main cavern. The beam in front of them cracked and split as the roof was brought down. Marta jumped through in time but Clyde got caught. He screamed as a rock fell onto his legs. She turned as rubble continued to fall and she grasped his arms.

"Get going, lady, leave me! It's too late!"

"No!" Marta screeched as she kept tugging. Wesley dropped the children and ran over to help. As the tunnel collapsed they pulled Clyde out just in time. The dust puffed into the chamber as they dragged the groaning dwarf to the side. She wiped the blood off her brow and knelt beside him to see to his injuries. The chamber was deathly quiet as soldiers poured in from a locked anteroom. Angus waddled in and glared around.

"Take inventory, get a count of who's missing!"

Clyde groaned as Marta rolled him over. His ankle was shattered but the rest of his body seemed to be intact. She glanced towards the doorway and ran over. Wesley stood and grasped her arm.

"What d'ye think ye're doin'?!"

"We have t'save 'em!" she cried miserably as she fought him off. He maintained his grip and shook his head sadly.

"Marta, they were too far back!"

"No, no no Ah have t'save them, we can! Ah've got to!" She struggled and then sank to her knees as a sob wrenched from her throat. "What good am Ah if Ah cannae…"

Jeannie rushed over and tended to Clyde's broken ankle, using a pickaxe handle to stabilize the broken bone. Wesley knelt beside his friend and she clutched at his tunic.

"Ah've failed, Wes. Ah've failed as a wife, as a Gifted, as a follower… Ah've failed everything. Wha's th'point anymore? What am Ah supposed t'do if Ah cannae use my Gift?" She continued sobbing into his chest as he glanced around wearily.

Oh, Lord, help her.

*****

Thomas fidgeted with the sword strapped to his hip and leaned back on the arm of the throne in the ballroom. The darkened room had several knights standing guard. Lyle and the other three Guardsmen knelt before their king with grave expressions.

"We were able t'find the wagon ye mentioned, yer Majesty. We lost th'trail from there. They were near the Hylen border in the North-west."

He nodded slowly. Nick groaned and rubbed the back of his neck before turning to Caleb, who simply nodded.

"We didn't find the Seeker either, Milord," Seamus added. Thomas nodded as Caleb interjected.

"Yeh probably saw't because y'were using your Gift. Seekers can tell when a Gift is utilized and use't as a beacon of sorts."

Lyle nodded solemnly. "Everythin' was as ye described it, though. Even down t'the door bein' ajar."

Thomas sighed in relief. *So it is as Caleb and Nick said... it appears I am a Light Seer. I wonder how mother would see things... would she 'experience' them too?*

"Thank you. You're dismissed for the evening."

A frantic soldier burst into the hall and ran down the entire length of the ballroom in seconds. He pulled up short just to bow.

"Your Majesty, Prince Peter has requested an audience with you."

Thomas froze. *Its been over a week...* He nodded to the Guardsmen. "Please bring him here."

The Guards saluted and took off quickly. Caleb and Nick stepped forward.

"Do you think he's finally ready to talk?" Nick asked quietly.

"I'm not sure," he sighed heavily with a shrug, "but I've taken your advice, Caleb, and I've been praying for him. Perhaps.... Perhaps this is an answer to prayer." Thomas got a far-away look in his eyes as the wizened Shepherd chuckled. Nick glanced between the two and turned to Caleb with a sheepish grin.

"At least *someone* talked some sense into him!"

"I heard that," Thomas grinned at his friend. Nick laughed nervously and shrugged. The doors burst open once more and Thomas saw the gaunt shape of his brother. Seamus and Breton dragged him into the room and deposited him on the floor before the king. Peter's blond hair was tattered around his head and he smelled like he hadn't bathed in days. He didn't meet Thomas' gaze.

"Your... Majesty..." he finally croaked. He jerked as Thomas enveloped him in a hug on the floor. "Wh-what?!"

Thomas held his brother tight. "What have you done to yourself, Peter?! You look inches away from death!" He sat back and held his brother's shoulders. Peter's face was drawn and dark circles had etched themselves under his eyes. He shook his head incredulously.

"Why would you treat me this way? Don't you remember what I did? You should have executed me! Why haven't you?"

Thomas shook his head and laughed curtly. "You think I could kill my own brother? I wouldn't kill your wife, either, Peter, much as the thought tempts me sometimes."

He shook his head again as a thousand angry voices screamed *guilty* at him. Thomas' expression drew serious.

"Peter... what made you this way? Please, tell me. I'm begging you. I don't want to fight you anymore." He held his arms out wide. "I don't want to fight you."

Peter examined his brother's eyes for an excruciating amount of time. Thomas lowered his arms and shook his head.

"Why—"

"You."

Thomas blinked. "What do you mean—?"

"Everything was for you," he scoffed.

"I don't understand—"

"Of course you don't!" Peter laughed bitterly and looked away. "*You* were always going to be king. *You* were the one prophesied over. *You* were the one 'destined for greatness' and I—" emotions that had been bottled for years started slipping past the barricades in his heart. His throat closed up as tears filled his bloodshot eyes. "Me? I was just... the second-best in everything. Sure, father gave me attention. But *you?* You were special. I was the back-up plan. You excelled in your studies, I failed them. You were the golden child and I was the failure. Everything I have ever done has been for *you!*" he spat bitterly.

Thomas felt a lone tear roll down his cheek. "Peter, I—"

"Yes, you. It was always about you, everything was for *you! You you you you—*" the dam burst and Peter slumped over sobbing. Thomas sat baffled, struggling to find the right words to say. A familiar Voice spoke to his soul;

What he needs is Me.

Peter flinched as he felt Thomas touch his shoulder. "What are you —?!"

Thomas held his brother close in a hug, putting one hand on his head. He inhaled shakily. "Heavenly Father... thank You for my brother. Thank You for blessing our family with him."

"What are you doing?!"

"I ask You to examine my own heart, God, and show me how I have hurt my brother. In my effort to protect him, I hurt him. And I am so, so sorry." Tears streamed down Thomas' cheeks as he pulled his brother in tight. Peter's eyes were wide. "I ask for Your forgiveness. Teach me how to be a better brother… a better brother, husband, and man. Lead me and lead our family. Please," he swallowed hard, "please bring my brother to You. Show him Your strength and grace. Show him Your love and peace."

Peter squirmed as a war raged within him, a deep longing he tried to quell with anything *but* God bursting in his soul. *God? God has no use for me. He has no purpose for me. He doesn't even want to think about me, just like father didn't—*

A quiet Voice, like a soft breeze over a still lake, whispered,

I see you, and I love you more than you will ever know.

A chill erupted through Peter's body, shaking him to his very core. Where did this new Voice come from? It felt… calming, yet more powerful than anything he had ever heard. He shook his head and groaned as a million familiar shouts screamed at him all at once in desperation.

You're a failure!

You will never amount to anything your brother has ever done!

Useless, worthless rat!

You're weak!

You're not good enough. You never will be!

Nothing you do will ever save you, you've done too much!

No god can save you now!

"Stop, stop, please!" Peter cried as he shook his head violently. Thomas relaxed his grip as his brother curled up on the floor in agony. He glanced at Nick and Caleb for help, but their eyes were closed and hands stretched out in prayer. Thomas heard Nick say something under his breath and Peter stilled. Peter heaved in breath and his eyes were wild.

"Peter. Peter!" Thomas grabbed his brothers' face and made him look up. Peter's face was wet with tears and Thomas shook his head.

"Peter… I'm sorry. I'm sorry. I was so caught up in my own head I didn't spare you a thought and I am so sorry."

Peter shook his head wearily. "I—"

"No, please, let me finish. Father loved you. He did. He was always bragging about how proud he was of you to the other kingdoms. He could never figure out how to tell you. And I love you too! I am so proud of you. You are a brilliant tactician and I value your input. You are a crucial addition to the kingdom of Elyon and I need you. You may not be book-smart," he smiled awkwardly as Peter met his gaze, "but you're a genius when it comes to actual application."

Peter blinked and shuddered in a breath. "I don't deserve love. Not after what I've done."

"I can't convince you and I can't save you, Peter. Only God can. But for now… can we start over?"

"There's no way we can just start over—!"

"Then let's start here. Come with me. Help me find Marta. Once we find her, we can figure everything else out."

Peter's eyes narrowed, but not in the sarcastic way Thomas was used to receiving. They were narrowed in disbelief. "You mean you're not going to hang me for treason?"

He sighed. "There… there will be repercussions, but for now, I'm worried about my wife."

Peter turned his head to the side and sighed. "I was worried about mine, too, but she's gone. She left me." He shook his head and laughed, spewing a list of curse words that made the Shepherds' toes curl. "She left me without so much as a—"

"Peter," Thomas' eyes were sharp, "I need your help now. Focus. Please, tell me. Where was Marta taken?"

Peter averted his gaze. "…to Arailt."

The Guardsmen glanced at each other as Thomas sighed and helped Peter stand. "What happened after that? Arailt has lost her. Where is she?"

"That… that I don't know. I don't!" he panicked as he saw Lyle's eyes darken. "There was a problem. The mercenaries the Death Wizard hired realized they were being swindled so they killed him. Last I heard, there was speculation that the mercenaries had sold them to another group but no one has been able to find them since—"

"Where did they kill him?"

"Ten miles east of the Hylen border."

Lyle and the Guards nodded. "That was where we found the wagon."

"Where were they headed?"

"They were originally headed to Runesberg where a contingent was waiting to transport them directly to the capital, but due to heavy snow they had to take a different route. There are only a few towns near there, they think they went to one of the mining towns."

Thomas nodded and turned to Nick. He nodded back.

"I'll examine the maps right away."

"Excellent. Call Jerome, I want to start preparing the army. It sounds like they got too close to the border and who knows what we will find if we have to cross over. This information does not leave this room, as of right now we might have an upper hand if Arailt still hasn't found her. We need to locate those mercenaries before he does."

The group nodded and began to disband. He turned to his brother with concern etched in his features.

"Peter. Come with us. Now, more than ever, I need your help."

Peter warred with himself. On the one hand, this could prove to be his redemption. If he could be seen as useful, maybe Thomas would spare him. On the other hand, he knew his sins far outweighed what good he could do. Still, though... maybe he could try?

"...alright."

Thomas paused and smiled wide before patting his brother's shoulder awkwardly. "Thank you, Peter. For now, though... you'd better go get cleaned up."

The younger brother nodded sullenly and turned as Seamus escorted him out of the room. Thomas glanced out the window overlooking the snowy city of Elroith and sighed.

Heavenly Father, please, protect my wife. Protect her captain and keep them safe. Hang in there, Marta. We will find you.

*****

Fifteen people had gone missing in the collapse, along with the two dwarves. Clyde looked like he would make a full recovery, though they didn't see much of him. Part of the shafts were being dug out and new supports put in place so time was spent back on their bedrolls. Numerous people were thankful for the respite, but the soldiers and officers grew uneasy with the slaves' complacency.

Marta had remained quiet for a few days after the accident, sleeping most of the time. Jeannie gently ran her fingers through Marta's disheveled hair and hummed a song under her breath.

"He's near t' th' broken hearted, close t'the poor in spirit. He binds us up an' lays us down t' rest in green pastures. He restores my soul. Though Ah walk through valleys of death an' trial, He is surely with me."

Marta listened attentively, her eyes still closed. Despite the death and the depravity, Jeannie would always sing. It was comforting and unnerving all at once. Jeannie started singing again and Marta's heart caught in her throat when she recognized the tune her mother would always sing.

"Death's lost it's sting, th' grave 's empty. Come t'the tomb all ye who seek, an' find that it lays empty. Our Goodly Fere hast triumphed o'er sin."

She sat up slowly as she joined in with her own crackly voice, *"where can Ah go where He is not? Where can Ah hide where He can't find? He searches th' hills an' valleys, He finds m'soul. Like a Good Shepherd He wraps me in His arms an' returns me t'safety an' hope."*

Jeannie cupped Marta's cheek and smiled. "Y'learn't well, m'dear. You can run, but nary will there be a day where He won't run after ye. He loves ye too much."

A gentle plucking, like that of a string on a mournful harp, tugged at her heart. She wiped away her tears and nodded. *I can't outrun Ye... but do Y'still want me after all this? After my anger and my lack of faith?*

A Voice too quiet for her to hear but one that resonated in her heart murmured **Faith as small as a mustard seed can move mountains. I am your portion and strength.**

"Alright everyone, guess what day it is today?" Angus laughed. The group glanced up to see him standing at the head of the chamber, hands on his hips. Several officers stood around him laughing. Marta recognized the somber-looking officer standing off to the side awkwardly. Something about him always drew her attention to the dark-haired youth. He seemed too young to be an officer of his status, yet here he was. Had something happened to bring him here? He didn't seem to enjoy it, but Marta never heard a word of complaint cross his lips.

"No one wants to answer, hmm? Well, it's Christmas! You know what that means?"

Marta's eyes widened. *Christmas?! It's already been over two months since...?* She caught the gaze of a little girl down the row from her gumming on her day's ration of bread.

"That's right, time to give us gifts!"

The soldiers broke off and wandered around, taking chunks of bread from everyone. If they didn't give as much as the soldiers' wanted them to or if they had eaten their portions already, the soldiers would only give one warning.

"...come on, miss."

Marta blinked and noticed the young officer standing in front of her holding out a basket. His brown eyes were dim and his face terse as he wiggled the basket.

"Please, just give up a small bit and—"

Marta's stomach growled but she felt a gentle familiar chill reach out to her heart. Hesitating, she put in her entire loaf. The man blinked in surprise.

"You're... you're giving the whole thing? Why?"

"Christmas is aboot giving," she murmured quietly as she settled into her spot. "'Tis aboot th'Greatest Gift given t'us."

"What could that possibly be?"

She tilted her head to the side. "Not what, but Who. That Who is Jesus."

The young man laughed disdainfully but his eyes gleamed. "Jesus isn't bread."

"On the contrary, He is the Bread of Life."

He opened his mouth to speak when Angus bellowed his name.

"Ewan, what are you lollygagging for?! On to the next one, hurry it up!"

Ewan nodded and took one more curious look at Marta before continuing down the line. She noticed out of the corner of her eye as Ewan discreetly dumped a couple of loaves into the little girls' lap and quickly moved on. Marta smiled slightly and turned back to Jeannie.

"Ah... think Ah heard Him."

"Did ye, now?" Jeannie smiled knowingly. Marta glanced at her hands and nodded slowly.

"It... it didn't sound th' same as before... Ah remembered the Scriptures instead."

"Marta, that is His Word. He speaks through't."

She nodded slowly. *My refuge and strength... okay, God. I'm going to trust You to get us out of here.* Foreboding nearly swallowed her whole but she resisted it, shuddering instead. *...please get us out of here alive.*

CHAPTER TWENTY-TWO

Power of the Air

Marta watched a young-looking dwarf scuttle around the outside of the chamber and disappear through a small doorway. An imposing iron door slammed shut behind her but no one seemed to notice. She returned her attention to breaking open the chunk of rock in her hands.

Why are *there dwarves here? They don't sound anything like the ones from Rodenheim. I wonder where they're from...* She shook her head at the rapid influx of memories, from meeting King Wilhelm for the first time to the wonderful evening of dancing with her husband. Her heart ached and tears once again sprang to her eyes.

God... does Thomas still love me? I... I feel like I've been abandoned here by him and by You. I know I heard Your Voice when You told me to marry him, but... she clutched her chest to try and ease the sharp pain blistering through her. She struggled to still her trembling lip. *... I love You, God. I do. I'm sorry I doubt so much. And... I do still love him, too. I pray he still loves me by the end of this, but that may be too much to ask...*

She jumped when she felt Jeannie's gentle hand on her back. She looked up at the older woman as she smiled down at her young charge.

"Ye've been thinkin' an awful lot again, sweet Marta, Ah kin see the smoke billowin' out yer ears!"

Marta chuckled and turned back to the cart to say something when Jeannie gently turned her cheek back towards her.

"Ye've a beautiful smile, Milady. Ah've never seen't."

She paused as her smile faded a moment. She glanced up at Wesley standing on the other side of the cart and he nodded in affirmation.

"'Tis been a long time since ye've smiled like that."

Marta's cheeks filled with color as she scratched the back of her neck. "Ah... Ah guess Ah haven't. Thanks t'ye, Jeannie an' Wes, Ah think Ah can again."

The small group chuckled to themselves and continued going through ores. Jeannie would hum and the other two would join her in song.

*****

Ewan watched the strange group in quiet longing. What could make them so happy? He was still stuck on the young woman who had given him all her bread some days ago. What kind of thing could possess her to do that? Watching their camaraderie day in and day out made him want to be a part of it. He sighed and turned away, adjusting his blue-and-silver jacket. *I have been sold into this service, and not by my choice. My fate has been chosen and there is nothing I can do to change it...* He glanced back over at the group as they laughed, drawing the attention of those around. *Still, though...*

*****

"Jeannie? What exactly are th'dwarves dooin' here?" Marta asked quietly. Jeannie paused her humming for a moment to think.

"Ah believe Ah heard one o' 'em say they were workin' on refinin' the ore we find. Ah'm sure, since they're brilliant engineers, they're forced into researchin' other stuff, too."

Marta nodded and returned to her task when a thought struck her. *Refining the ore...* "Do they work with Mordiern, too?"

Jeannie winked at her and continued humming. Her eyes widened and she glanced at Wesley. *They do! What if... what if they know about the Mordiern on the King's body?! What if they're the ones who—!*

The iron door opened again and the young dwarf came back out. Marta watched her scurry away.

I need to find out what's behind that door... She cracked open another rock to find... nothing. Jeannie chuckled.

"Whoops," she dumped a dim blue chunk in Marta's hands. "Oh look't, ye've found some Ela ore. Ye'd best go take't over to th'door."

"You're sly." Marta chuckled. Jeannie shrugged and continued humming as Wesley shook his head and laughed. Marta turned and walked past the rows of bedrolls and under the watchful gaze of officers around. She came to the iron door and knocked quietly. There was a clattering behind the door as a small rectangular slit at dwarf-height slid open.

"Y'all find somethin'?"

Marta knelt to meet the dwarf's line of sight. Clyde grinned at her from behind the door.

"Ah, miss Marta! Pleased to see yah, ma'am! Thanking you for saving me again!" He shut the window and opened the door. She stepped back and smiled at her friend as he hobbled forward, his leg encased in a strange metal contraption. She blinked and noticed the many gears and thin metal pieces stuck together around his limb. He glanced down and chuckled.

"A beauty, ain't she? Alan whipped her up for me. What can I do for yah?"

She handed him the chunk of ore. He pulled down his visor and adjusted a magnifying glass on it to examine the stone. He whistled after a moment.

"Y'all found a good, pure chunk o' Ela, ya sure did. Where was it?"

"Came from rock excavated from th' far left tunnel."

Clyde lifted the visor and wiped his face before nodding solemnly. "Aight. We'll take this back and process it right away." He started to turn but she took a measly step forward to stop him. He turned and glanced her up and down. "Did you need somethin' else, miss?"

"Ah... Ah'm... curious, do ye... do y'refine Mordiern, as well?" her voice dropped low. Clyde got a knowing look in his eye and nodded.

"I cain't do nothin' 'bout your cuffs—"

"Oh, no no, tha's—tha's not wha' Ah'm askin' fer." She glanced up nervously as a few soldiers took note of how long she was lingering and began making their way over. "Can ye refine Ela to... t'augment an' mask Mordiern?"

Clyde's golden eyes widened in disbelief. "Ain't no one's told— how did you—?!"

"Hoi, what're ye holdin' him up fer? Get back to work." A soldier yanked Marta's hair and pulled her away from the dwarf. Clyde had a far off-look in his eyes as he shook his head.

"Thanking you for the ore, miss, and for explaining where it is. Sorry boys, I kept asking questions."

The soldiers huffed as Marta collected herself and returned to the mine cart. She tried desperately to quell the panic rising inside of her.

I knew it! They do know! What if they were the ones who made it? Amaryll said Arailt was enslaving dwarves and forcing them to make new machines and discoveries... they must have figured something out with the Ela!

Jeannie glanced up and handed her another rock as she came by. Wesley watched her out of the corner of his eye with a curious look.

"Find what ye were lookin' fer?"

"More... questions than answers, but answers nonetheless."

Wes turned his head to the side and raised a brow. Marta met his gaze and sighed.

"Remember me theory aboot... King Martin?"

He nodded. "Ah do."

"...Ah was right, though Ah doon' know the extent."

His eyes widened and he returned to his work quickly as a soldier passed by behind them.

"Ye think 'twas them, then?"

"Ah doon' think 'twas their intent, but... Ah cannae deny they know somethin'."

He nodded as Jeannie chuckled.

"Thomas's lucky to have ye as his wife. Ye're sharp and fearless when it comes down t'it."

Marta flushed and turned away. "Ah'm more of a coward than y'think, Jeannie. Ah wouldn' move me feet or act when Ah coulda."

"Doon' we all? Bravery ain't the absence o'fear, 'tis the act of doin' the right thing despite bein' 'fraid."

She rubbed her neck and sighed. *I hope I can be brave. I hope Thomas is doing okay... I miss talking to him. I wish I could go back and tell him not to leave, or to have gone with him. But...* she glanced up at Jeannie singing under her breath and Wesley singing along with her, and she smiled. *...I'm glad I got to meet Jeannie.*

*****

Thomas' heart skipped a beat as the horses crested a familiar hill. Despite the snowpack and the cold, the wagon in the distance was as familiar as his own hand holding the reigns in front of him. He spurred hs steed on a little faster, pulling ahead of the small group. He slid off the horse and stopped beside the broken-down carriage. It had finally collapsed under the weight of the snow and the Death Wizard's remains were long gone. Lyle and Nick rushed up beside him.

"'Tis the same as we found it, Milord."

"Thank you, Lyle." He glanced up and down the road and turned around towards the forest. Snow shattered off of pine needles as a cool breeze blew in his face. The memory of the darkness seeping out from this same forest lent a chill to the air and he shuddered.

"My Lord, there's a—"

He turned as Amaryll addressed him and he nodded. "There's a Seeker nearby. I can sense it too."

"Then it's already found us." Nick groaned. The group nodded.

"Assemble the Gifteds, prepare for a fight."

No sooner had he spoken than a horrid screech filled the air. Everyone clamped their hands over their ears as the sound shook them to their cores. A black figure flashed by out of the corner of his eye and one of the Gifteds reeled backwards as her Knight took the full brunt of the blow. The Knight's body slumped to the side and the Gifted took one step before she, too, collapsed. The small regiment sprang into action as the screeching figure flew by for another round. Hissing was heard in the distance as a group of Pseudonyms charged up the road.

Thomas unsheathed his sword and blocked the dark figure as it lunged at him. The deranged Seeker had dark eyes that flickered as he grinned in the King's face.

"There you are!"

He knocked the Seeker back and took a defensive stance. The Seeker combed his fingers through his jet-black hair and laughed as the rest of the group intercepted the Pseudonyms.

"I've been looking for you! Imagine my surprise when the King himself shows up in the middle of nowhere, all alone? I don't know how you evaded me last time but I assure you!" Black tendrils erupted from his body and their sharp points poised themselves at Thomas, "I will not let it happen again!"

God, give me strength! Thomas gritted his teeth and parried the attack. As his sword made contact with the black tendrils he felt a pull on his energy. His sword instantly glowed a brilliant golden color and *zapped* the Seeker backwards. He reeled back and watched as the Seeker stood, eyes wide in amazement.

"What—?!"

Thomas smiled. "You were saying?" He lunged forward with a roar as lightning sparked around him.

*****

Marta took a step back as Wesley shoveled the rock at her feet into the mine cart. After clearing the debris and rebuilding parts of the tunnel the slaves were once again put back to work. He hefted his large shovelful into the full cart and wiped his brow.

"Aight, Ah'm goon' take this back."

Marta nodded and waved as Wesley and three other men began pulling on the heavy cart. Jeannie and several others were down the shaft in another chamber. Marta could hear her singing again, and she hummed along as she swung her pickaxe to the tune.

"Ah woon' fear fer the Lord's with me, His rod and His staff comfort me —
" she jerked backwards as her pickaxe sunk into the wall. She started trembling as the memory of the cave-in resurfaced and she turned to run. Instead of the whole shaft crumbling, she was met with silence. She paused a few moments before going back to the pickaxe. She tried pulling it out and the wall gave way to reveal a passageway into the mountain. She blinked as a cool breeze blew in her face.

Is this a way out?! Surely it isn't? Without thinking she grabbed a lantern and stepped over the rubble, wandering into the darkened tunnel.

The sound of the other miners and Jeannie's singing faded abruptly and she turned around. A dirt wall met her. She stepped back, startled. *What?! Where's the —?!* A soft, distant hum wafted through the air. She turned around slowly and blinked at light spilling from around the corner of the tunnel. She stepped forward and peered around the edge despite the alarms going off inside her head. She was met with an ornately decorated study. Windows to the right let in soft early-morning light, whilst the lanterns and candles around the room illuminated the numerous maps and quills littered about. The carpet was immaculate and the wood carvings around the room intricately weaved back and forth along the walls. A large wooden desk, also inlaid with gorgeous carvings, dominated the room.

She realized the humming was coming from the man across the room, his back turned to her. A large map of Elyon and her surrounding countries was tacked to the wall and he seemed to be marking something. His blond hair was tied back behind his head and his demeanor exuded regality. His waistcoat was a dark blue and his shirt was a brilliant white. Something *cracked* under her foot and she glanced down to see a broken chess piece on the floor. She knelt and picked up the broken black queen.

"Ah."

She nearly jumped out of her skin as the man addressed her and she dropped the broken pieces. His silver eyes sparkled in the dim light and he twiddled a quill between his fingers. His face was youthful despite several wrinkles forming on his cheeks and eyes. By her guess, she had to say he was in his early forties. She squirmed under his gaze as he perused her across the room, ragged and dirty as she was.

"I was wondering where you'd be," he turned and made a few marks on the map. His accent was different than anything she had ever heard. She leaned to the side to try and see around him but the map was obscured by the dim light and the man's frame. He lifted the quill and turned back to her with a flourish.

"Where... am I?" she stammered as she glanced about the room, which seemed to groan in response.

The man's smile never left his face. "I think I should be asking you the same thing, my lady, seeing as though *you* were the one to stumble into *my* study."

She turned towards the window and saw a sleepy city stretching out before her. The mountains in the distance were growing brighter as the sun began its ascent behind them. The sky was a hazy early morning blue and she could see stars sparkling in its expanse. *Strange... we woke up a few hours ago.*

Without thinking, she mumbled as a thought struck her, "how are there windows in th'mine...?"

"The—?" his silvery eyes began to sparkle again and he muttered something under his breath, turning and hurriedly marking the map behind him. Nervousness flooded her senses and she started to turn, thinking she must be hallucinating.

"You won't be able to go back that way," the man cooed as he finished his notes. Marta shook her head as he slowly turned towards her.

"What d'yeh mean, it's right—" the tunnel was replaced by a beautiful wooden door. She glanced around in surprise as dread sucked the air from her lungs. "...there."

"As I said, you can't go back unless I want you to... your Majesty."

She turned quickly as he stepped out from behind his desk and mockingly bowed low, his silvery eyes never moving from her.

"How did y'know—?!"

"I know a lot of things, my dear. Things your pretty little head wouldn't understand. But now that I have you here and know where you are..." she recoiled as he lunged forward and pinned her against the door. She squirmed as he gripped her face and tried to shake him off to no avail. His eyes glittered in the dim light as he grinned, "it makes things a lot easier for me!"

She struggled and pushed him back. He stepped back willingly and held up his hand, his mouth tipped in a rueful grin. "You'll find that help will not be coming for you this time."

She glanced around the room desperately, swallowing hard. Everything felt so real, from the plush rug under her tired feet to the soft, clean breeze flowing through the windows. She held her aching jaw as her gaze leveled on the man in front of her, his lips turned up in a sneer.

"Who are you?"

"I ask the questions here, and you will provide the answers."

She barely withheld a scoff. *Something about him is really unsettling. Who is he, and where am I? Am I really in a different place? What about Jeannie and Wesley?!*

The man lifted his hand. "You're certainly ruminating about something."

She glared at him. "Wouldn' ye like t'know? Y'seem aggravated enough without me needin' t'say anything."

His head tipped to the side, his grin never wavering. "Oh, your mere *existence* aggravates me, Marta."

Her eyes widened. The room suddenly felt stuffy, the air heavy. The lanterns flickered ominously.

"I—!"

"Marta!"

The man's grin dissolved into a scowl as Marta turned around. In a blink, the door was the dirt tunnel, and Jeannie came careening around the corner with a rope tied around her waist trailing behind her. She pulled up short as she saw Marta, and her expression shifted as soon as she and the man made eye contact.

"Shepherd," he spat, his gleeful expression all but gone. Jeannie stood up straight and held out her hand.

"Marta. Le's go."

She rushed over and took her hand. The man scoffed.

"I knew I should have killed you when I had the chance all those years ago."

Jeannie narrowed her eyes. "Whether Ah live er die, 'tis be of no consequence t'me, only that Ah guided people t'the true Light."

The man rolled his eyes. "Spare me the sermon, Jeannette. Your days are numbered." He lazily glanced at Marta trembling next to Jeannie. His lips parted in a vicious grin. "I look forward to meeting you again soon, Queen Marta."

The room began to dissolve as if her vision was blurring. The last things she saw were the man's silver eyes gleaming in the darkness. She shuddered as Jeannie held her close.

"Ye're lucky yer alive," Jeannie sighed as she held her friend close. Marta shook her head.

"I doon' understand, tha' wasn't a dream?! Who was that?!" she whispered hoarsely. Jeannie stepped back in surprise, her eyes wide.

"Marta…" her expression fell, "you've just met the ruler of Hylen. That was Arailt."

She blinked. Then blinked again. She motioned to the dirt wall. *"That… was the Arailt?!"*

Jeannie nodded solemnly. "An' now he knows where y'are. We doon' have much time, we need t'get ye out of here."

"Hold on, wait! What aboot—?!"

The room shifted suddenly and the lantern Marta had brought with her *thunked* beside her feet. She held it up and blinked in surprise as brilliant blues glittered around them. The pair turned as the walls revealed a rich Ela vein, pulsing and illuminating a faint blue light. Sharp jagged purple crystals grew in small geodes around the room and seemed to be pulling the light into them. Jeannie shook her head.

"Ye found an Ela pocket. A rather large one, too. No wonder ye…" she shook her head. Marta's pulse fired rapidly as she struggled to grasp the situation. She turned to a somber Jeannie with wild eyes.

"How'm Ah supposed t'leave without ye, er Wes, er Clyde, er anyone else? Ah can't jus' leave ye here!"

Jeannie's soft features were drawn back into a frown and the dim lamplight made her seem even older. She sighed heavily.

"In order fer any o' us t'be free… yeh need t'stay alive, yer Majesty."

"Then le's all come here an' use the Ela t'get out!"

The older woman shook her head sadly. "Marta, 'twasn't you who made that Ela connection."

Marta heaved in a breath as the implications of what Jeannie was saying settled on her. *Oh, please, God, please help Thomas find us in time. Please Thomas… please come find us!*

*****

Thomas watched the Seeker's empty clothes collapse into a pile of ash. The forest quieted once again as the battle came to an end. He

261

heaved a sigh of relief and turned to see a blood-splattered Amaryll nod at him.

"Five casualties, two of which were Gifteds, one Knight. Two soldiers went down as well."

He lifted his sword and wiped it off in the snow. "Send a messenger to the army to move forward. He knows we are here already. We must be swift."

"Your Majesty," Nick grimaced as he stepped over a dead Pseudonym, not accustomed to battle. "I just received word from Caleb back at the castle, Wicke was able to intercept another mirror transmission from one of Arailt's generals. They have pulled back their search for the mercenaries."

His heart plummeted. "Have they found her?"

"Not yet, but we don't know why they would pull back the search unless they had received intel."

Thomas turned and met Peter's gaze. His brother had fought valiantly in the battle beside him, but any joy or loathing he would have had was completely gone. Thomas desperately wanted to reach out to his brother to rescue him from his thoughts, but he had to focus on the task at hand.

Lord, please reach out to Peter even though I can't. He wiped his face and sighed.

"There's one more thing, Milord. They had narrowed their search to three nearby towns."

"Did they say which one held the most promise?"

"No."

He nodded and thought quickly as Nick pulled out a map. Amaryll, Peter, and Jerome stepped forward as well. Thomas chewed on his finger for a moment.

"Amaryll and Nick, you two go to Biltmore in the south. Jerome, take a regiment to Viktor in the West. Peter, you come with me to Winfield. Lyle, with me. Breton, you're with Jerome, Seamus and Dougal, you're with Amaryll and Nick. Be careful and limit your use of Gifts, we are walking into enemy territory here and I don't want to lose anyone else. Godspeed, everyone."

The group nodded and disbanded quickly. Nick rolled up the map and grasped Thomas' shoulder.

"We'll find her."

He nodded solemnly. "We will all be within a day's travel of each other. If anything happens, summon the army."

Thomas turned to Peter with a slight grin on his face.

"Ready to go?"

Peter hesitated but nodded. *He trusts me to go with him? I don't deserve this...* He watched his brother effortlessly hand command over to his general and commander, then worked with the Gifteds and Knights who would be accompanying them to gather supplies. Thomas was fluid and focused, a natural leader in Peter's mind. He shook his head and scoffed under his breath. *And I thought I could do better than he can? I was a fool. He was born for this, I... wasn't. I'm not sure what I'm here for.* A snowflake landed on his nose and he flinched slightly in surprise. He held out his hand as more snow began falling from the sky.

I suppose at least for now I can help find Marta. I... do actually hope she's okay. She... was always really nice to me.

*****

Jeannie sat somberly on her mat, a distant look in her weary eyes. Marta watched her carefully, having been unable to sleep, then crawled over to her mentor. She could see in the dim lamplight that tears were pouring down the old woman's cheeks.

"Jeannie?!" she exclaimed in alarm, lowering her voice. This stirred Wesley from his slumber and he sat up, groggily rubbing his eyes.

Jeannie's blue eyes cleared as she looked down at her friend and slowly patted her cheek, smiling ruefully.

"Ah, Marta... m'dear, dear Marta..." she enveloped the young woman in a hug, pulling her close to her chest and kissing the top of her head. Marta shook her head worriedly.

"Can... can Ah ask?"

Jeannie groaned, her shoulders sagging like the weight of the world had settled on them. Wesley shuffled closer and the older woman reached over and cupped the young man's cheek fondly.

"Y'two are like true brother an' sister. Ah feel like ye're me own bairns. Ah want ye both t'know that Ah love ye dearly, Ah know God's got a plan for ye both."

Marta sat up with a panicked expression, tears threatening to spill over her own eyelids. "Why does't feel like ye're sayin' goodbye?"

Jeannie met her worried gaze with her own. "Ah'm not long fer this world, Marta. Ah can feel't."

The younger woman leaned back in despair. "No, no doon' say—

" she jolted as she felt Jeannie's shriveled hands grasp hers, her palms rough yet her grip gentle.

"Marta, Ah want ye t'have this." She closed Marta's hands around a warm object. Marta's eyes widened as she recognized the necklace Jeannie always wore. Tears streaked down her face and she shook her head as Jeannie smiled.

"Here, lemme help ye," she motioned Marta to turn. She turned slowly as sobs wrenched themselves from her throat. Jeannie lifted her dirty hair out of the way and clasped the necklace around her neck. She put her hands on Marta's shoulder as she turned to look at her dear friend.

"What y'say is true… innit?" Marta lunged forward and hugged Jeannie's waist, folding over into her lap. Jeannie ran her fingers comfortingly through Marta's unwashed hair and smiled sadly at Wesley as he wiped away his own tears.

"The Good Lord has His plans. When Ah do go, ye'll know where Ah am. Take heart, m'dears. He has overcome this world. He will always find ye, even now help is on th' way. Ye'll be the best Queen Elyon has ever seen, Ah know't. Keep her safe, Wesley, an' give yer beloved Brenna me blessing as well."

Marta and Wesley hugged Jeannie close. She laughed softly and shook her head.

"Ye're makin' me cry, sweet ones!"

"Ah love ye, Jeannie," Marta gurgled through tears. Wesley nodded his head.

"Ah do too. Thank y'fer everythin'."

"An thank ye both. Ah love ye too."

When Marta and Wesley woke up the next morning, Jeannie was nowhere to be found.

CHAPTER TWENTY-THREE

Den of Lions

The hood pulled tight around his head obscured Thomas' vision as he stepped into the dark *Last Chance Inn*. The saloons had turned up useless and he prayed they could at least get a clue while they were here. The few patrons glanced up at the three hooded figures in the doorway as a chubby man with a dull left eye stepped out from the back.

"Sit anywhere ye like, I'll be with yeh in a moment."

Thomas nodded and picked a table off to the side. A larger man nodded at him from the table beside him as they sat. Peter glanced around nervously as Lyle leaned onto the table. It shifted under his weight as he tried to act inconspicuous. The chubby man waddled over and nodded.

"Name's Greg. Anything Ah can get for yah?"

"Whiskey," Lyle grumbled. Peter and Thomas glanced at him in surprise but turned to Greg as the man chuckled.

"Ah, ye've been to Hylen before it seems. Only those who know how good our whiskey is will order't."

Thomas felt the nervous room heave a collective sigh of relief and return to their drinks. Thomas ordered one as well while Peter passed. Lyle leaned back and nodded at Thomas.

Wesley chose a good man to be a part of his team. I'm thankful Lyle was with us, the people here might have been too nervous otherwise.

Greg returned with the drinks and disappeared once more. Lyle took a small sip and exhaled loudly.

"Good whiskey, that is."

Thomas took a small sip and suppressed a cough as he felt his toes curl. *Good Lord, that's strong!*

"Not t'yer likin', Ah take it?"

Thomas glanced at the large man sitting at the table beside them and chuckled, though he didn't know why. "Can't say I'm as experienced as my friend here."

The man chuckled in response and uncorked a steel flask. He leaned back and took a large swig before slamming it down on the table. "Y'all fer hire?"

Unseen to the man, light flashed through Thomas' eyes. "Perhaps."

Peter glanced at his brother in surprise as a dark smile crossed Lyle's lips. The man chuckled.

"Ye seem to be worth yer spit. What kin' work ye do?"

"Depends on the job." Thomas swirled his cup around. "What's on the table?"

"Transportation of goods."

Thomas' eye twitched. "The living kind?"

The man laughed as one of his partners shook his head nervously.

"Boss, y'can't jus—"

"Oh, shut it. Ah kin do what Ah want. We have all the money in the world now, we kin take on bigger jobs." He turned back to Thomas with a drunken grin. "Aye, the livin' kind."

Thomas hesitated as he went to take a sip. "I don't go into Elyon, don't have a good reputation there."

The man laughed. "Neither do we. There's a mine on the other side o'the mountain that pays real well for those who kin work. Most a' th' time we just nab 'em as they try and get across the border into Elyon." He leaned back and sighed contentedly. "Wonder how that small blonde lass is faring after—"

The room jerked in surprise as Thomas stood abruptly and held his sword to the man's throat. Peter jumped up and Lyle chuckled darkly as the other patrons unsheathed their own weapons.

"Describe her." Thomas rumbled low, his eyes alight with flame. The man swallowed hard as he instantly sobered, his hands in the air.

"N-now hold on just—"

"Describe her and tell me where the mine is."

*****

Marta heaved another rock into the mine cart and wiped her brow. She leaned against the side and let out a sigh, her worry for Jeannie ever present in her thoughts. They had been sent to work in the Ela pocket Marta had discovered earlier along with several other workers. Wesley cursed under his breath as he lunged to catch a broken piece of Ela. Their faces were covered in dust and grime from the excavation and dark blue dust had settled onto their skin. She sighed wearily and rubbed her cuffs, the Mordiern pulsing and resonating with the Mordiern around them and sucking her strength away. She winced as she struggled to lift a small rock.

I feel pathetic…

They glanced up in alarm as frantic shouts echoed down the mineshaft.

"Is it another cave-in?" one of the workers beside them cried. Another worker rounded the corner and stuck their head into the pocket, stopping up short when she spotted them and panting heavily.

"Marta! Oh, God, Marta!"

Marta dropped the rock she had been holding and rushed forward, Wesley right behind. She clasped the woman's hands and shook her head.

"Wha' 'tis it?" she whispered thickly. The woman's eyes were puffy with tears and she opened her mouth, but nothing would come out. She finally shook her head and gasped, "Jeannie!" before covering her mouth with a sob. Marta's eyes flickered for a moment before she took off running down the corridor. Wesley paused with the woman, who steeled herself against the wall. She waved him off and he had to sprint to catch up to Marta.

A large crowd had gathered in the main cavern and they could hear the wailing as they approached. Fear swelled to a crescendo in her chest as she burst into the room. The crowd parted as she skidded to a stop, staring at her with wide eyes. She searched around frantically.

"Wha's happened?!"

She felt the darkness seeping up into her feet and rising through her body as she followed everyone's gazes to the ceiling. Wesley clamped his hands over her eyes but it was too late. She stumbled backwards as a cry ripped from her throat. Jeannie's lifeless blue eyes stared at the ground as her body gently rotated back and forth from where she hung. A few people reeled back as Marta turned to the side and retched. Wesley held her desperately as she wailed, a devastated pain in his eyes.

"No! Noo!" she tipped her head back and screamed in despair, her heart torn open and her whole body numb. She could feel the darkness and the mire sinking into her faster and faster as hopelessness surrounded her. Wesley's own face was streaked with tears as his mouth curved into a snarl.

"Those pigs!" He spat bitterly and averted his gaze. He helped Marta to the ground as she wailed and grasped at his tunic. She heaved in sobs and shuddered as her mind and body threatened to break.

A hush fell over the crowd as the familiar *clink, clink, clink* of medals grew closer. Marta wrenched her eyes open, still in Wesley's arms, as Angus stepped forward with a deranged grin. He motioned to the room as his lips parted in a sneer.

"*This* is what happens when you defy our lord! *This* is what befalls those who spread falsehoods and lies, who dare defy our great god Arailt!" His eyes settled on Marta, piercing her to the core. "Let this be a reminder to you all who really owns you." He turned with a flourish and stomped out of the cavern. Marta shook her head and gulped for air.

No, no she didn't deserve this! God, why?! Why would... she clung to the hope she had quietly fostered, guarding the small flame against the buffeting winds of despair that threatened to snuff it out. She gasped when Wesley recoiled as a soldier yanked him backwards.

"Get back to work!" he barked, cracking his whip across Marta's back. She let out a garbled cry as she collapsed to the dirt. A deep dark heaviness settled in her chest as her eyes grew dim.

This... this pain, it's too much for me to handle! It's too much! The whip cracked again and tore open her skin. She cried out as she struggled to her knees. A dark thought seeped its way into her mind; *this physical pain is so much more bearable than the pain in your heart. It's much easier to bleed... in fact, it feels better. It will help you cope with the loss. Why don't you just—*

"Get out of the way!" the soldier growled. Marta glanced up to see Wesley standing over her, arms outstretched.

"Wes...?" she gurgled.

"Don' hit her. Hit me."

Marta blinked as the soldier gripped his whip angrily. "Whatever. Both of you, get back to work!" he cracked his whip in warning but stormed off with a scowl. Marta trembled violently as Wesley turned and stared at her solemnly.

"Doon' let it tell ye ye'll be better off dead. Marta... Milady, we need ye. Thomas needs ye. I need ye," his eyes welled up with tears. "Remember wha' the Shepherd said? '*In this world ye'll have trouble*'?"

"'*Take heart,*'" she cried as she slowly sat up on her knees, inhaling sharply, "'*Ah've overcome th'world.*'". Comfort, like a small refreshing spring, dripped slowly into her heart. Despite the darkness and the helplessness, the despair and fear, warmth seeped ever so softly into her soul. Wesley reached down and helped her stagger to her feet. She inhaled slowly and nodded, grasping at the necklace Jeannie had given her.

"Thankee."

Wesley smiled faintly and walked her back into the mineshaft. The children wept as they chiseled into the rock lifelessly. Marta watched them and paused.

"*Come t'me, little children, an' rest in me arms.*" They glanced up at her as she sang a familiar song, a gentle smile on her lips. "*Ah'm yer refuge, yer hidin' place. Ah love ye more than ye'll ever know.*"

"How can you be so calm?!"

Marta and Wesley turned to see a miserable Ewan standing behind them, his uniform jacket open. Tears streamed down his face as he shook his head.

"She's dead! How can you sing? How can you praise your God when He let this happen to her?!"

Marta heard her own voice through Ewan's as the events of the last few months replayed themselves in her mind. She glanced at the children, who had wide eyes, before returning back to Ewan.

"Ah doon' know myself." She laughed curtly as his eyes widened in disbelief. "Ah wantae cry an'never get up again. Ah wantae go be wit' her." She smiled at Wesley as he placed a concerned hand on her shoulder. She shook her head. "Ah'm not meant to be where she is yet. Ah only know that the darkness may try to hide th' light, but," she lifted a finger, "it will never truly snuff Him out. Ah can only say that this peace is from Him."

"Your God can give you peace like this? I think you're mad!"

"Ah may be," she smiled sadly, "but Ah kin tell ye, she's runnin' free now."

Ewan watched Marta and Wesley turn and walk away. What she said didn't make sense yet something in him longed to believe her. The odds were increasingly stacking up against them, however, and the officers were beginning to notice their attitudes. Nothing infuriated them more than happy slaves.

I hope that whatever God you serve will save you soon.

*****

Thomas wiped his sword with a clean rag one of his soldiers had given him, his back turned to the five men kneeling behind him with swords at their throats. They shivered in the street as snow fell in large tufts, the sky growing dark as night fell.

"Are you sure you have given me all the information you know?" He growled as he turned and leveled his gaze on the largest man. He shook his head frantically.

"N-no sir- AH AH mean y-yes, Ah have! Ah promise!"

Thomas sighed as he sheathed his sword. Nick and Amaryll rushed up to him and nodded.

"The army has crossed the border. So far no threat has been mobilized against us, although the Gifteds are sensing a large movement of dark forces."

Thomas nodded. "He's found her. We need to hurry." He glanced around and spotted a tall hill just outside of town, the trees cleared out for miles for use in the mines. He turned back to the mercenaries and nodded at the Guardsmen holding them there. "Free the slaves in the inn and lock everyone inside into the cells. I will leave a regiment here to watch them." He leaned over into the men's faces. "Once I retrieve my *Queen*, I will let *her* decide your fate."

The men gulped and jerked as the Guards forced them to their feet and took them away. Peter stepped beside Thomas quietly.

"Thomas… Arailt would be going to get her himself. He's going to bring a lot of wizards and Seekers with him."

Thomas nodded solemnly. "Then let's address the troops. It's going to be a long night."

Peter's heart thundered in his chest as they climbed the hill and looked out upon the thousands of men in Elyon's army, most new soldiers who had never seen battle. To the side were a hundred or so men and women, Knights and Gifteds alike, ready for battle. Thomas lifted his hand and silence fell over the meadow.

"Defenders of Elyon and Guardians of the Tower, thank you for your service to our people and our country. We stand in the midst of the lions den and march onwards into its depths. Our God goes before us and will sustain us through this battle! He has already secured a victory against the dark powers of this world. No longer will we wait for war to find us. We bring the war to them!"

The mountains shook with the sound of a thousand voices roaring in expectation. Thomas turned to Peter, who nodded solemnly.

"On your command, your Majesty."

Thomas nodded and turned towards the mountain pass. *We are coming, Marta. Hold on.*

*****

Marta heard Wesley shifting on his mat across from her, ill at ease in sleep. She sighed and turned her head to the side. Exhaustion had taken hold of her as her body began to break down. Too many sleepless nights, little food, and the constant pull of energy had left her numb and lethargic. She gazed at the ceiling as tears pricked in her eyes. *Will I be joining you soon, Jeannie?*

The room jolted awake as the cavern echoed with Angus' angry bellows, "Out of my way!"

One by one the slaves around the room sat up as they were wrenched from sleep. Wesley sat up quickly, highly alert. He crawled over to Marta as two cloaked men entered the room beside Angus, their faces hidden by the dim lamplight and their hoods pulled tight around their heads. Angus stopped in the middle of the room with a desperate look on his face.

"Where is the Queen of Elyon?!"

The room erupted into hushed whispers as Marta's heart plummeted into her stomach. She and Wesley shared a terrified glance as Angus stomped his foot.

"I said, where is she?!"

People averted their gazes as soldiers and officers flooded the room. Marta's fear thundered in her ears, her body glued to the floor. Angus lunged forward and grabbed one of the young girls by the hair, yanking her to her feet and holding a knife to her throat. Her mother cried out and rushed forward but one of the figures' reached out a hand and a gust of wind blew the woman back several feet in warning.

"Tell me now before this girl loses her head! Where is—!"

"I am she."

A heavy pause fell over the room as Marta staggered to her feet and held her head up high.

"I am the Queen of Elyon."

Angus stammered in surprise as Wesley stood as well, taking his place next to his liege with a warriors demeanor.

"I knew there was something strange about you two but—?! Prove it!"

Marta held out her wrists, the Mordiern laced cuffs glinting ominously in the lamplight. She smiled ruefully as her accent thinned for a moment.

"The Queen of Elyon is Life Gifted, no? Take off the cuffs, even for a moment, and I'll prove it."

Angus glared at her menacingly as the figures shifted uncomfortably. "If this is a trick, I will separate this girl's head from her shoulders in an instant!"

Marta simply held out her hands. "No trick. Ah promise."

Angus glanced around before his gaze fell on a shocked Ewan. He jerked his head to the side and Ewan swallowed hard.

"Ewan... go on."

He took the key from Angus and slowly approached. Every step sounded like thunder in his ears, but Marta smiled faintly at him as he stopped in front of her.

"Ah woon' hurt ye, Ewan. Ah promise."

The young officer shook his head forlornly. "I know you won't."

"Get on with it!"

Ewan reached down and unlocked the cuffs. They fell off with a *clang* and Marta rubbed her bruised wrists. Deep purple lines had etched themselves across her skin where the Mordiern had sat. She gasped in pain as a sickly golden light swirled around her, her old wounds and scars bubbling in their attempt to heal. She leaned forward as the breath wrenched from her lungs. Her eyes widened at the sudden realization she could die as the last drop of her energy trickled away. The world spun into darkness and she felt Wesley and Ewan grab her on either side.

I'm... I'm not ready, God!

A light burst forth into the darkness. She sucked in a breath of fresh air and trembled as her vision cleared. The necklace was burning brightly and she could feel immediate reinvigoration. Numerous thoughts and feelings sucker-punched her all at once; the necklace was made with high-caliber Ela expertly crafted to provide a significant amount of energy, the Ela in the mines seemed to reverberate as her Gift pulled energy towards her, and Angus stood there trembling like a mouse. He dropped the girl and she rushed over to her mother.

Marta glanced at her hands and blinked in surprise as golden light swirled around her. She held out her palm and a beautiful rose grew on it. She laughed and looked at Wesley, who smiled wearily and nodded.

The slaves stood slowly as the light swelled to a climax. The soldiers and officers screamed in pain as the light blinded them yet didn't affect the prisoners. Ewan stared in surprise as his vision was unaffected. Marta dropped to her knees as a familiar Voice thundered in her ears.

You are my daughter, one whom I love, My friend. I have never left you even though You didn't hear My Voice.

Ewan and Wesley held her arms as she bent over in a sob, regretful tears pouring from her heart and soul. "I'm so sorry, God. I'm so sorry. I forgot who You are, I let the Enemy tell me who I am. I forgot my identity in You. Please, please forgive me!"

I love you, Marta. Trust in Me and I will guide you through every hill and every valley.

She let out a sob as the darkness fled her soul, a brilliant golden light bursting from her chest. Wesley and Ewan held on tight as the darkness in the room screeched and disappeared. All fell silent for a moment and the light dissipated, leaving nothing but the groans of soldiers echoing around the cavern.

The silence was split by a sickly *thud*. The trio gasped in surprise as Angus' lifeless body tumbled to the floor, a pickaxe in his skull. Aaron stood there heaving in breaths and trembling violently. He stared at his hands and looked up at Marta before glancing awkwardly about the room.

"Well? What are we waiting for?"

Wesley steeled Marta as she smiled wide and nodded. She glanced up at Ewan and he blinked in surprise.

"Ah... y-your Majesty!"

"Ewan, come wit' us."

The young man's eyes widened. "What?! But, but I—!"

Wesley clamped his hand on his shoulder. "Ah could really use talent like yers in the Guard. But le's get outta here first!"

The group turned as slaves all over the room wielded their tools and quickly put an end to the officers and soldiers in the room. Wesley helped Ewan out of his uniform jacket as Marta rushed across the room and knelt beside a lifeless Angus. She rifled through his pockets and found a ring of keys. Someone slung rope around her neck and she gurgled as they pulled her back. One of the Death Wizards, his eyes red and vision blurred, grumbled as he held her close.

"No, no he's so close, we can earn his favor still! We must—!"

A sharp vine grew in her hand and she twisted. The rope dropped as the wizard dissolved into ash. She struggled for air as Wes and Ewan rushed over to her and helped her stand. She assessed the situation quickly and nodded to the door where several curious dwarves stood. She ran over and flung it open wide.

"Come on, le's go!"

Several dwarves stood awkwardly about the workshop while others scrambled for the door. Clyde limped forward with a sullen look on his face.

"We ain't lived this long just to die out thar, miss."

Her heart fell at his words. "Ye're not leavin'? Y'want t'stay imprisoned?!"

Clyde shrugged as a few dwarves nodded in agreement. "We're kept useful here. Ain't no-one messes with us. We can do whatever we want as long as we find new—"

"Clyde, tha's the stupidest thing Ah've ever heard."

The dwarf blinked at her bluntness. "I—?!"

"Ye'd rather stay here in the clutches of a madman who does nothin' but use ye instead o' riskin' somethin' out there?! Where is that dwarven tenacity and stubbornness Ah hear aboot?! Certainly not here!"

The dwarves glanced at each other shamefully. Clyde turned his face away and rubbed his arm.

"We ain't fighters, lady. We're only good at engineering."

"So fight that way!"

Aaron ran over to them out of breath. "The inner doors won't open, the soldiers on the other side are keeping it shut!"

She shook her head and thought quickly. "Is there any other way out?"

"No, that's the only way in or out."

Her eyes flickered with light as her gaze rested on Clyde. "Y'know a way out, doon' ye."

Clyde sighed heavily. "Doors can only withstand so much force before they give, even iron doors like that."

Marta knelt and held his hand. "Clyde, please. Ah need yer help. We need yer help. All of ye," she motioned to the other dwarves. Clyde sighed heavily and rubbed his neck.

"Well, if'n you put it that way…"

Marta smiled wide and stood as Clyde strode through the doorway, cracking his knuckles.

"Alright everyone, let's saddle up! Grab all the mine carts you can, dump 'em if you have to! Bring them out here!"

Marta and Wesley nodded at each other as they rushed into action. Soon the cavern was full of heavy mine carts aligned with the doors. Clyde and the other dwarves had disconnected the mechanisms and stood to the side.

"On my mark. One, two, *three!*" The slaves worked together to use the carts as a battering ram. The door thudded and rock spilled from the ceiling as the carts hit, but it didn't budge. They repositioned and prepared again.

"One, two, three!"

Another *thud*. This time more rock and rubble cascaded down from the ceiling and people had to lunge out of the way lest they get crushed. Clyde examined the roof and shook his head.

"We got one more good push, but the ceiling's gonna come down with the darn thing. Ladies, grab yer kiddos and everyone prepare to rush through!"

The slaves held their breath. Marta lifted a hand and vines grew along the ceiling, acting as a sort of net. Clyde whistled and shook his head.

"Hoowee Miss Marta, you might just buy us some time. Alright, one more time! One!"

The room prepared. Wesley and Ewan stood on either side of Marta as they gripped the cart.

"Two!"

There was rumbling from outside. Marta hesitated as Clyde's arm came down.

"THREE!"

The slaves roared as the mine carts careened into the doors. They landed with a *thud* and the iron barriers tilted back. They heard screams of the soldiers and officers trapped in the mid-room as the iron doors landed against the other ones. They, too, cracked and gave way. Marta struggled to keep the room from collapsing as the slaves rushed into the cold air. The sounds of metal scraping and roars of battle met their weary ears. The slaves's eyes widened as the dust settled and revealed a battle outside their doors. Marta turned and gasped in surprise when she spotted familiar red armor.

"It's Thomas! It's Elyon! They're here!"

Aaron turned and lifted his pickaxe. "Let's finish this!"

The slaves roared and entered the fray. Marta nodded to Clyde as the dwarves escaped the collapsing mine. Once everyone was out she released her vines and the mine shuddered as it collapsed. Wesley and Ewan pulled her out of the way as rock and debris burst from the mountain, claiming several people as it caved in. The battle continued to wage onward and she felt a sudden foreboding. She turned and saw the full force of the Hylen army bearing down on Elyon's forces. She had little time to scan the crowd as her heart leapt into her throat.

Where's Thomas?!

CHAPTER TWENTY-FOUR

The Road Less Traveled By

Thomas reeled backwards as he blocked another Dark Wizard's blow. Amaryll quickly finished the being off with a burst of flame. The weary king jumped as the iron doors of the mine cracked open.

"The mine's opened… from the inside?!" Amaryll cried breathlessly. Thomas nodded and quickly scanned the slaves pouring out, but he couldn't spot his wife.

Where—?

He turned and deflected a blow as lightning streaked off his sword. Arailt laughed maniacally as he pressed his dark sword against the young king's blade. Thomas steeled himself as the metal blades scraped against each other and Arailt leapt back. He held out his hands as his silver eyes sparkled.

"What a coincidence. Not only do I get to kill your wife, but I can finally take care of you as well!"

Thomas grit his teeth as Arailt's sword burst with dark energy. The lightning on his own sword continued to crackle and buzz as Arailt tipped his head to the side.

"Just like I took care of your father."

Thomas roared and met his blow, slinging his sword to the side. Lightning arched through the air as their swords met, the two men swinging and parrying their way across the battlefield. Unlike Thomas, Arailt was fresh to the field and had plenty of energy. He puffed as Arailt stalked back and forth in front of him, big fluffs of snow lilting around them.

God, give me strength!

A shout behind him caught him off guard and he stumbled forward as a dark dagger pierced his chest. The cloaked figure behind him withdrew their blade and he sank to his knees. Arailt waltzed forward and tipped Thomas' head up with the end of his blade.

"How the mighty Elyon has fallen."

Thomas winced in pain and prepared for the blow.

*****

A cry drew Marta's attention and she gasped as two of the slaves pulled a bloodied Aaron out from under a pile of rubble. She rushed over and landed on her knees next to him. He clutched at his stomach and blood streamed down his face. She shook her head as the battle raged around them, snow swirling from the sky.

"Stay still!" she whispered as her hands began to glow. She croaked out a groan when she realized the extent of his injuries. Tears welled up in her eyes as he grasped her arm, leaving a handprint of blood.

"Marta…" he spluttered, "I'm sorry."

"For what?!" she began crying. He smiled wearily, his teeth stained red.

"For discouraging you. For letting the darkness in my own heart seep into yours. I… hope you can…" he turned and his eyes widened as he stared at something in the distance. Warmth spilled over her spine as she shook her head and held his hand.

"Ah forgive ye, Aaron."

She let out a sob as the light faded from his eyes and his body settled. She covered her mouth as tears began pouring down her face. The battle waged ever onward as Wesley and Ewan stood beside her, brandishing swords they had collected off the ground. She gently reached forward and closed his eyes.

A roar grabbed her attention and she stood and turned around. Her eyes widened as she spotted Thomas stagger forwards and fall to his knees before a cloaked figure in the middle of the battle. She gasped as her chest erupted in pain, like a fire singing her torso. The figured moved and revealed Arailt stepping towards Thomas, a sword at his throat and his mouth tipped in a sardonic grin.

The nightmares that had plagued her for months, the image of a silver-eyed figure standing over her husband hit her full-force. The memories brought the sound of battle to a still as fear gripped her chest.

"THOMAS!" she screamed as she lunged forward.

Arailt swung.

Silence.

Marta heaved in breaths and trembled violently, a dark sword firmly stuck into the wood she grew over her arm. The cloaked figure stumbled backwards as Peter engaged them with a roar. Arailt's eyes grew dark as Thomas blinked and blearily looked up at his wife.

"M...Marta?"

Arailt narrowed his eyes and recoiled as Marta pushed her palm forward, a sharp vine shooting out and piercing his neck. He yanked the sword out and swiped at her. She jumped backwards as the sword grazed her face. She held a glowing hand and yelled as she threw her hand up again, this time piercing Arailt's shoulder. He stumbled backwards and cursed. As she lunged again a gust of air lifted him into the air and backwards. The wind picked up and the cloaked figure escaped Peter's clutches, along with the other officers in his ranks. Peter's breath caught in his throat as he thought he saw a strand of red hair spill out of the figure's cloak before they landed, but he quickly shook the notion off as darkness obscured their face. The sound of glass shattering echoed around the field as the enemy army disappeared, purple glass left in their wake.

Marta turned and caught Thomas as he fell sideways, blood spilling down his chest. His face was deathly pale.

"No no no, Thomas! Thomas, look't me!" she cupped his cheek in her own bloodied hands and held his chest. Golden light seeped from her hand and into his torso. Her own felt like it was on fire as she used all the energy she could to heal him. "Please, please Jesus please save m'husband! Oh, Thomas, stay wit' me!"

His eyes fluttered slightly as he registered what was going on.

"Marta..." he gurgled weakly, his voice raspy. Marta nodded and smiled through tears.

"Yes, 'tis me, 'tis me Thomas. Look't me, jus' keep lookin' at me." She panicked as his gaze shifted. "No, Thomas, look at me!" she enunciated as his head lolled to the side. Her hand glowed ever brighter as his blue eyes began to dim.

"Thomas, ye're goon t'live alright? You and I are goon' t'get out of this. We are goon have numerous children together, we are going t'grow old together, we will go on lots of adventures— jus' stay with me!" she let out a guttural cry.

"What an accent..." Thomas wheezed with a laugh. Marta sniffled and met his gaze. "And... children..." His face twisted suddenly. "Are you pregnant?!"

"What?!" she exclaimed breathlessly. She shook her head with a pained smile and a relived laugh. "Nay, but Ah need ye t'stick 'round t'fix that."

Thomas chuckled and held his wife's hand to his chest. "Always... so positive..."

The battle stilled as Hylen's grunt forces realized they had been abandoned by their superiors. With a cry they turned and ran towards the hills, pursued by angry slaves and Elyon's army. Wesley and Ewan stood near Marta and pushed away any enemy who dared come close. She glanced up as several Gifteds rushed forward and began lending their strength to her and Thomas' wounds. She looked back into his eyes and cupped his cheek.

"Thomas, please. I need you," she gurgled through tears. He smiled wide.

"Don't—ugh!— worry. I'm not going down that... easily."

She hesitated before crying in relief. She bent down and brought his face to hers, kissing him deeply. He returned it as best he could before sinking into her arms. Had she not been a Life Gifted, she would have thought him dead, but his mind just couldn't handle the exhaustion anymore. She and the other Gifteds continued bringing him to a stable condition as Amaryll and Peter rushed forward. They examined the scene and Marta glanced up with a pained expression. Her green eyes rested on Peter for a moment, and where he expected hatred, he only saw deep sorrow. He fell to his knees and put his hand over his heart as her eyes widened.

"Your Majesty, I know words cannot fix what I have done and what I allowed to happen. I was blinded by my own greed and pride." His eyes welled up with tears and his voice was thick with emotion. "Whatever punishment you see fit to bestow I will gladly accept. I am so, so sorry. I was wrong about you, about my brother, about all of this!" he struggled to keep himself together. Marta glanced down at Thomas, asleep in her arms, and leveled her gaze on her brother-in-law as light flickered through her eyes.

"I forgive you."

The weight of her words nearly knocked him over, wrenching the breath from his lungs. He shook his head incredulously when she didn't say any more. "Surely," he whispered hoarsely, "it isn't that easy!"

Marta smiled wearily. "With God 'tis. Seek His forgiveness, Peter. He's th' only one who can save you."

He felt a *drip, drip, drip* of warmth cascading down his head, back, legs, and feet. It cut to his soul. He grasped his chest as it felt like it would explode and bent over in a cry. "No, no, it can't be. It can't be that easy. Surely, I, I—" he felt Marta's hand on his head.

"Trust in the Lord with all your heart," she sang quietly with a weary smile, *"and lean not on yer own understandin'.* It doon take ye doing anythin', Peter, 'cept havin' faith." She glanced up at Ewan, who had an understanding look on his face. He nodded as she continued. "He will forgive you if you ask, and 'tis because of Him that Ah can."

Peter sobbed, his chest feeling like it had wrenched open and everything spilled out for all to see. "I don't deserve to be forgiven."

"Do any o'us?" Marta asked quietly. "An yet, He sent His own Son t'die in our place, despite our unwillingness an' despite our unworthiness. He rescued us in spite of our failures, our sins. What He offers is grace, an' 'tis a gift freely given." She smiled faintly as warmth swelled in her soul, "He gives us a new identity through Jesus."

"How...?" he croaked as he looked up through tears. "How can I get this grace? What do I have to do?"

Her own tears spilled down her face as she smiled at the man who once loathed her. "You just ask Him. *'If ye declare with yer mouth 'Jesus is Lord' an' believe in yer heart that God raised Him from the dead, ye will be saved.'"* She took his hand gently in hers, reaching up to hold Ewan's as well. *"'Fer 'tis with yer hearts that ye believe and are justified, and 'tis with yer mouth ye profess yer faith an' are saved.'* He died fer ye, for ye both. But He didn' stay that way! He rose again in glorious victory. Death holds no sting fer Him. He came so that we may have life."

"I... I think I understand."

She and Peter glanced up at Ewan, tears streaming down his face as he nodded. "I think I get it. He died despite everything I've done. How could a God love someone that much?"

She smiled warmly as Wesley put his hand on his shoulder. "Cause He is love, Ewan. An' He madly loves ye. Both a' ye." He turned towards Peter, who nodded slowly. Wesley reached down and gently held Peter's shoulder.

"Do ye both believe God sent His only Son t'save ye?"

The men shuddered in a breath at his question. "Yes."

"An' do ye believe He died fer ye an' rose again?"

"Yes," Ewan blurted. Peter hesitated before meeting Marta's soft gaze.

"Yes. I do."

"Then ask Him fer forgiveness," Marta whispered with a smile. The two men bowed their heads. Peter spoke shakily as he asked for forgiveness from the One who Saves. Warmth streamed down his head and back and he lurched forward as his chest constricted. It felt like something had come in and was seeking out the darkness in his heart, scraping it out and cleaning every nook and cranny. He sobbed nearly to the point of retching as the darkness in his heart fled, the thousands of voices silenced in an instant. For the first time in a very, very long time, he felt a weight lift off of his shoulders.

*****

Braum grimaced as Marta and Wesley stood with arms folded before them in the empty street. After a warm bath and a change of clothes, Marta looked every bit as regal as she had the day they took her, albeit much more thin. She turned with a huff and motioned to Wesley.

"Captain, Ah leave their punishment in yer capable hands."

Wesley's eyes gleamed as he leaned over to Lyle, his gaze never breaking from Braum's.

"Lyle... would ye kindly bring me a barrel o' the finest Hylan whiskey?"

Lyle laughed and saluted. "Right away, sir."

Marta chuckled as the men on the ground groaned. She caught a familiar face at the end of the row staring downwards, and she walked over and knelt before a pensive Millie. Millie glanced up and looked back down at the ground.

"Your Majesty, I—"

Marta held up a hand and smiled gently. "Y'showed me kindness in a dark place, so Ah will show ye the same. Ye're more than welcome to join us in Elyon, but what y'choose t'do from there is yer choice."

She stood and walked away with a sad smile as Millie burst into tears as Seamus released her bonds. Thomas stood talking to Amaryll and Nick and they glanced up as Marta approached. Thomas turned and smiled wide as he wrapped his arms around his wife.

"It's so good to see you, my love."

"Good t'see ye up an' aboot."

He kissed her deeply and leaned back. "I don't mind the accent, but... is it going to stick around?"

"Perhaps!"

The group laughed together as Nick excused himself. He opened up his pocket watch and tapped the small mirror. It swam and revealed a worried Ravenswicke and Caleb. They waited with bated breath as he laughed.

"We made it!"

The men cheered and hugged each other as Nick chuckled to himself. He turned and watched Thomas gently cup his wife's cheek and smiled warmly.

I hope this happiness can last… at least a while longer.

Snow continued to fall on the small town as weary soldiers and Gifteds continued to tear down camp, eager to return home.

*****

The cloaked figure from the battle knelt before the solid wood desk in the dark study, the blade they had used to stab Thomas in their skillful hands. The purple blade pulsed and dimmed as they gazed up at their master. Arailt stared at the map bitterly, his arms on either side of the desk. His blond hair was in bloody mats around his face and a tight bandage weaved its way around his neck. He stood up slowly with a scowl, wincing as he put pressure on his injured shoulder.

"I severely underestimated them. I will not make that mistake again." His eyes rested on the figure before him and he walked around the desk. He gently pulled back the hood of the fiery red-head and smiled warmly.

"You did well. Your training has progressed quickly."

"I'm sorry I failed you, Master," they whispered hoarsely. Arailt shook his head and smiled.

"We will defeat them together, and when they are gone, you shall rule beside me as queen."

Sarah's red lips curled into a smile. "I look forward to it."

Continued in Book Two, *Elyon's Covenant*

Acknowledgements

Thank you, reader, for picking up this book and taking a chance. I hope this story brought you hope and encouraged you as much as it did for me, if not more! If you are an aspiring author, I want to encourage you to keep going. It is a hard process, but God has great plans for you and your story. Don't give up! Trust Him and Glorify Him and He will guide you through.

This book and series would not be possible without a LOT of people. If you don't see your name here, please don't fret! I have so many people to thank that it would take forever to read about.

Firstly, the partner of my heart, Matthew. You and I created this story and world together, and you have let me take it and run with it. The numerous hours of listening to my crazy rantings, my plot twists, getting your thoughts and ideas for the world— this book is in your hands because of you. Thank you so much my love. Here's to many more adventures, written on paper and in our lives!

Mom, Dad, you are my dear family. You have always believed in me even when I didn't believe in myself. You equipped me with my faith and have helped me live it out. I can glorify Him because you first instilled it in me. Thank you!

Doug, my own Wes, I know you have struggled a lot, but you have a knack for encouraging me. You have stayed my hand on things and have lifted my spirits. I love you so much.

My Spoon Family! Paula, Tom, Corinna and Calvin— gosh, you guys literally made this book happen. Thank you for editing and giving me your honest thoughts, thank you for the hours of conversation whenever we would come visit, and most of all— THANK YOU FOR YOUR SPOONS! I'm sorry I left you hanging on chapter 16 for so long… but I so appreciate your enthusiasm. On days I didn't want to write or I thought this was worthless, you would text me and give me the spoons I needed to keep going. Thank you thank you thank you!

My wonderful Mama and sweet Aunt Martha; thank you for your love, encouragement, and support. It means the world to me!

Finally, my amazing Beta readers, Kelley, Jordan, David, and Izzy. I am thankful for all your feedback and your help in this project.